J.G. BALLARD was born in 1930 in Shanghai, where his father was a businessman. After wartime internment in a civilian prison camp, he and his family returned to England in 1946. After reading medicine at Cambridge for two years, he worked as a copywriter and Covent Garden porter before going to Canada with the RAF. He published his first major novel, *The Drowned World*, in 1962. His acclaimed novels include *The Crystal World*, *The Atrocity Exhibition*, *Crash* (filmed by David Cronenberg), *High-Rise*, *The Unlimited Dream Company*, *Empire of the Sun* (filmed by Steven Spielberg), *The Kindness of Women*, *Cocaine Nights*, *Super-Cannes* and *Millennium People*. Ballard's autobiography, *Miracles of Life*, was published in 2008. J. G. Ballard died in 2009.

From the reviews of *Kingdom Come*:

'A singular combination of the eerily familiar, the faintly preposterous and the utterly compelling, all leavened with Ballard's characteristic deadpan humour'   *Telegraph* magazine

'Ballard's vision is scary and utterly real … Compelling'
DAVID FLUSFEDER, *FT* magazine

'J.G. Ballard's *Kingdom Come* is a dyspeptic vision of a dystopian Britain that has already arrived. He is a close observer of our national malaise: indiscriminate consumerism combined with a sense of entitlement, and therefore of resentment'
ANTHONY DANIELS, *Spectator* Books of the Year

'A futurist whodunit, whose topsy-turvy logic unsettles … [Ballard] is on tip-top form. No one else writes with such enchanted clarity or strange power'   *Scotsman*

'[An] important, ch...   ...pendent

'*Kingdom Come* is a worthy addition to an extraordinary body of work. It is impossible to read one of J.G. Ballard's books and not to marvel at his style and ability to capture the times in which we live. His writing has been a source of excitement and inspiration to me since I was reading library books under the covers by the light of a battery torch'

LOUISE WELSH, author of *The Cutting Room*

'Ballard is the supreme literary outlaw, a maverick whose strange imagination combines surrealist lunacy with a prophet's vision … [*Kingdom Come* is] a subversive and highly political book, Ballard exposing not only his society but his time … As he has throughout his career, J.G. Ballard has written another prophetic tale of our sickly epoch, for us to ponder'   *Irish Times*

'Ballard has a wonderfully honed sardonic tone and a great sense of irony which works brilliantly with this subject'

Irish Independent

'A chilling dystopian thriller … [Ballard's] portrayal of London is mesmeric. You read this novel for his prescient vision, his acute insights and his shards of wit'   *Tatler*

By the same author

J.G. BALLARD

Kingdom Come

FOURTH ESTATE • *London*

Fourth Estate
An imprint of HarperCollins*Publishers*
77–85 Fulham Palace Road
Hammersmith
London W6 8JB

This edition published by Fourth Estate 2012
6

First published in Great Britain by Fourth Estate 2006
and in paperback by Harper Perennial 2007

Copyright © J.G. Ballard 2006

PS Section copyright © Sarah O'Reilly 2007,
except 'Remaking the World' copyright © J. G. Ballard 2007

PS™ is a trademark of HarperCollins*Publishers* Ltd

J.G. Ballard asserts the moral right to be identified as the author of this work

A catalogue record for this book is available from the British Library

ISBN 978-0-00-723247-5

Set in Bembo by
Palimpset Book Production Limited,
Grangemouth, Stirlingshire

Printed and bound in Great Britain by Clays Ltd, St Ives plc

MIX
Paper from
responsible sources
FSC™ C007454

FSC™ is a non-profit international organisation established to promote
the responsible management of the world's forests. Products carrying the
FSC label are independently certified to assure consumers that they come
from forests that are managed to meet the social, economic and
ecological needs of present and future generations,
and other controlled sources.

Find out more about HarperCollins and the environment at
www.harpercollins.co.uk/green

PART I

1

The St George's Cross

THE SUBURBS DREAM of violence. Asleep in their drowsy villas, sheltered by benevolent shopping malls, they wait patiently for the nightmares that will wake them into a more passionate world . . .

Wishful thinking, I told myself as Heathrow airport shrank into the rear-view mirror, and more than a little foolish, an advertising man's ingrained habit of tasting the wrapper rather than the biscuit. But they were thoughts that were difficult to push aside. I steered the Jensen into the slow lane of the M4, and began to read the route signs welcoming me to the outer London suburbs. Ashford, Staines, Hillingdon – impossible destinations that featured only on the mental maps of desperate marketing men. Beyond Heathrow lay the empires of consumerism, and the mystery that obsessed me until the day I walked out of my agency for the last time. How to rouse a dormant people who had everything, who had bought the dreams that money can buy and knew they had found a bargain?

The indicator ticked at the dashboard, a nagging arrow that I was certain I had never selected. But a hundred yards ahead was a slip road that I had somehow known was waiting for me. I slowed and left the motorway, entering a green-banked culvert that curved in on itself, past a sign urging me to visit a new business park and conference centre. I braked sharply, thought of reversing back to the motorway, then gave up. Always let the road decide . . .

Like many central Londoners, I felt vaguely uneasy whenever I left the inner city and approached the suburban outlands. But in fact I had spent my advertising career in an eager courtship of the suburbs. Far from the jittery, synapse-testing metropolis, the perimeter towns dozing against the protective shoulder of the M25 were virtually an invention of the advertising industry, or so account executives like myself liked to think. The suburbs, we would all believe to our last gasp, were defined by the products we sold them, by the brands and trademarks and logos that alone defined their lives.

Yet somehow they resisted us, growing sleek and confident, the real centre of the nation, forever holding us at arm's length. Gazing out at the placid sea of bricky gables, at the pleasant parks and school playgrounds, I felt a pang of resentment, the same pain I remembered when my wife kissed me fondly, waved a little shyly from the door of our Chelsea apartment, and walked out on me for good. Affection could reveal itself in the most heartless moments.

But I had a special reason for feeling uneasy – only a few weeks earlier, these amiable suburbs had sat up and snarled, then sprung forward to kill my father.

At nine that morning, a fortnight after my father's funeral, I set off from London towards Brooklands, the town between Weybridge and Woking that had grown up around the motor-racing circuit of the 1930s. My father had spent his childhood in Brooklands and, after a lifetime of flying, the old airline pilot had returned there to pass his retirement. I was going to call on his solicitors, see that the probate of his will was under way, and put his flat up for sale, formally closing down a life that I had never shared. According to the solicitor, Geoffrey Fairfax, the flat was within sight of the disused racetrack, a dream of speed that must have reminded the old man of all the runways that still fled through his mind. When I packed away his uniforms and locked the door behind me, a last line would draw itself under the former British Airways pilot, an absentee parent I once hero-worshipped but rarely met.

He had left my strong-willed but highly strung mother when I was five, flown millions of miles to the most dangerous airports in the world, survived two attempted hijackings and then died in a bizarre shooting incident in a suburban shopping mall. A mental patient on day release smuggled a weapon into the atrium of the Brooklands Metro-Centre and fired at random into the lunch-hour crowd. Three people died, and fifteen were injured. A single bullet killed my father, a death that belonged in Manila or Bogotá or East Los Angeles, rather than in a bosky English suburb. Sadly, my father had outlived his relatives and most of his friends, but at least I had arranged the funeral service and seen him off to the other side.

As I left the motorway behind me, the prospect of actually turning the key in my father's front door began to loom in the windscreen like a faintly threatening head-up display. A large part of him would still be there – the scent of his body on the towels and clothes, the contents of his laundry basket, the odd smell of old bestsellers on his bookshelves. But his presence would be matched by my absence, the gaps that would be everywhere like empty cells in a honeycomb, human voids that his own son had never been able to fill when he abandoned his family for a universe of skies.

The spaces were as much inside me. Instead of dragging around Harvey Nichols with my mother, or sitting through an eternity of Fortnum's teas, I should have been with my father, building our first kite, playing French cricket in the garden, learning how to light a bonfire and sail a dinghy. At least I went on to a career in advertising, successful until I made the mistake of marrying a colleague and providing myself with a rival I could never hope to beat.

I reached the exit of the slip road, trailing a huge transporter loaded with micro-cars, each shiny enough to eat, or at least lick, toffee-apple cellulose brightening the day. The transporter paused at the traffic lights, an iron bull ready to rush the corrida of the open road, then thundered towards a nearby industrial estate.

Already I was lost. I had entered what the AA map represented as an area of ancient Thames Valley towns – Chertsey, Weybridge, Walton – but no towns were visible around me, and there were few signs of permanent human settlement. I was moving through a terrain of inter-urban sprawl, a geography of sensory deprivation, a zone of dual carriageways and petrol stations, business parks and signposts to Heathrow, disused farmland filled with butane tanks, warehouses clad in exotic metal sheeting. I drove past a brownfield site dominated by a massive sign announcing the Heathrow South extension with its unlimited freight capacity, though this was an empty land, where everything had already been sent on ahead. Nothing now made sense except in terms of a transient airport culture. Warning displays alerted each other, and the entire land-scape was coded for danger. CCTV cameras crouched over ware-house gates, and filter-left signs pulsed tirelessly, pointing to the sanctuaries of high-security science parks.

A terrace of small houses appeared, hiding in the shadow of a reservoir embankment, linked to any sense of community only by the used-car lots that surrounded it. Moving towards a notional south, I passed a Chinese takeaway, a discount furniture warehouse, an attack-dog kennels and a grim housing estate like a partly rehabilitated prison camp. There were no cinemas, churches or civic centres, and the endless billboards advertising a glossy consumerism sustained the only cultural life.

On my left, traffic moved down a side street, family saloons hunting for somewhere to park. Three hundred yards away, a line of shopfronts caught the sun. A suburban town had conjured itself from the nexus of access roads and dual carriageways. Rescue was offering itself to a lost traveller in the form of neon signs outside a chain store selling garden equipment and a travel agent advertising 'executive leisure'.

I waited for the lights to change, an eternity compressed into a few seconds. The traffic signals presided like small-minded deities over their deserted crossroads. I lowered my foot onto the accelerator, ready to jump the red, and noticed that a police car was waiting behind me. Like the nearby town, it had materialized out of the empty air, alerted by the wayward imagination of an impatient driver in a powerful sports car. The entire defensive landscape was waiting for a crime to be committed.

Ten minutes later I eased myself onto a banquette in an empty Indian restaurant, somewhere in the centre of the off-motorway town that had come to my aid. Spreading my map over the elderly menu, a book of laminated pages unchanged for years, I tried to work out where I was. Vaguely south-west of Heathrow, I guessed, in one of the motorway towns that had grown unchecked since the 1960s, home to a population that only felt fully at ease within the catchment area of an international airport.

Here, a filling station beside a dual carriageway enshrined a deeper sense of community than any church or chapel, a greater awareness of a shared culture than a library or municipal gallery could offer. I had left the Jensen in the multi-storey car park that dominated the town, a massive concrete edifice of ten canted floors more mysterious in its way than the Minotaur's labyrinth at Knossos – where, a little perversely, my wife suggested we should spend our honeymoon. But the presence of this vast structure reflected the truism that parking was well on the way to becoming the British population's greatest spiritual need.

I asked the manager where we were, offering him the map, but he was too distracted to answer. A nervous Bengali in his fifties, he watched the traffic moving down the high street. Someone had thrown a brick at the plate-glass window, and the scimitar of a giant crack veered from ceiling to floor. The manager had tried to steer me into the rear of the empty restaurant, saying that the window table was reserved, but I ignored him and sat beside the fractured glass, curious to observe the town and its daily round.

The passers-by were too busy with their shopping to notice me. They seemed prosperous and content, confidently strolling around a town that was entirely composed of shops and small department stores. Even the health centre had redesigned itself as a retail space, its window filled with blood-pressure kits and fitness DVDs. The streets were brightly lit, cheerful and cleanly swept, so unlike the inner London I knew. Whatever the name of this town, there were no drifting newspapers and chewing-gum pavements, no citizenry of the cardboard box. This was a place where it was impossible to borrow a book, attend a concert, say a prayer, consult a parish record or give to charity. In short, the town was an end state of consumerism. I liked it, and felt a certain pride that I had helped to set its values. History and tradition, the slow death by suffocation of an older Britain, played no part in its people's lives. They lived in an eternal retail present, where the deepest moral decisions concerned the purchase of a refrigerator or washing machine. But at least these Thames Valley natives with their airport culture would never start a war.

A pleasant middle-aged couple paused by the window, leaning against each other in a show of affection. Happy for them, I tapped the broken glass and gave a vigorous thumbs up. Startled by the apparition smiling a few inches from him, the husband stepped forward to protect his wife and touched the metal flag in the lapel of his jacket.

I had seen the flag as I drove into the town, the cross of St George on its white field, flying above the housing estates and business parks. The red crusader's cross was everywhere, unfurling from flagstaffs in front gardens, giving the anonymous town a festive air. Whatever else, the people here were proud of their Englishness, a core belief no army of copywriters would ever take from them.

Sipping my flavour-free lager – another agency triumph – I studied the map as the manager hovered around my table. But I was in no hurry to order, and not merely because I had a shrewd idea of the sort of food on offer. The one fixed point on the map was my father's flat in Brooklands, only a few miles to the south of where I sat. I could almost believe that he was waiting behind his desk, ready to interview me for a new post, the job of being his son.

What would he see, in those make-or-break thirty seconds when the interviewee entered his room? Applicant: Richard Pearson, forty-two years old, unemployed account executive. Likeable, but can seem slightly shifty. One-time secret smoker and former junior Wimbledon player with right elbow spur. Failed husband completely outwitted by his former wife. Good-humoured and optimistic, but privately a little desperate. He thinks of himself as a kind of terrorist, but all he is good at is warming the slippers of late capitalism. Applying for the post of son and heir, though very hazy about duties and entitlements . . .

I was very hazy, and not only about my father.

A week before his death I drove a close friend to Gatwick airport, at the end of my happiest months in many years. A Canadian academic on a year's sabbatical, she was flying back to her job in the modern history department at Vancouver University. I liked her confidence and humour, and her frank concern for me. 'Come on, Dick! Jump! Bale out!' She talked of my joining her, perhaps finding work in the media studies department. 'It's an academic dustbin, but you can rattle the lid.' She knew I had been eased out of the agency – my last campaign had been an expensive fiasco – and urged me to look hard at myself, never an inviting proposition. I started to miss her keenly a month before she left, and was more than tempted to pull the ripcord and join her.

Then, at the Gatwick departure gate, she discovered my passport in her handbag, zipped away in a side pocket since our return from a Rome weekend. Baffled, she stared at the war-criminal photo. 'Richard . . . ? Who? Dick, my God! That's you!' She shrieked loudly enough to alert a security guard. I took this as a powerful unconscious signal. Vancouver and an escape into academia would have to wait. If someone who liked me and shared my bed could forget my name at the first glimpse of a departure lounge I needed urgently to reinvent myself. Perhaps my father would help me.

I finished my lager, watched by the manager, who had come to the window and was staring uneasily at the sky above the multistorey garage. I was about to ask him about the St George's badges worn by many of the passers-by, but he turned the 'Closed' sign to the street and retreated quickly to the rear of the restaurant.

Sirens sounded, and groups of shoppers gazed up at the clouds of smoke floating across the precinct. Two police cars sped by, roof lights flashing.

Something had happened to disturb the deep consumerist peace. The manager disappeared into his kitchen, and a woman's voice cried in alarm. Leaving enough cash to settle the bill, I folded the map, unlatched the door and let myself out of the restaurant. A fire engine bullied its way through the crowd, siren turning the air into a headache. I followed on foot, pushing past the pedestrians who stared at the darkening sky.

A few hundred yards from the town centre, near the road I had taken from the motorway, a car was burning on the perimeter of a modest council estate. Residents stood in their front gardens, arms folded as they watched the flames rise from a battered Volvo. A policeman discharged his fire extinguisher into the passenger cabin, while a fellow officer held back the crowd. They were staring at the shabby house of one of their neighbours, where a policewoman stood by the front door, gazing in a resigned way at the untended garden. Splashes of white paint traced a gaudy slogan over the masonry, and I assumed that an unpopular arrival had sullied the atmosphere of the estate, perhaps a released murderer or a paedophile exposed by the local vigilantes who had torched the car.

I eased my way through the onlookers, many still carrying their shopping bags, viewing the scene like an unexpected publicity display in a dull department store. Their expressions were hostile but wary, and they ignored the fire engine that pulled up behind them. They took their lead from three men in St George's shirts who stood beside the gate, employees of a local hardware chain whose logo was stamped on their breast pockets. Their muscular, slightly paranoid presence reminded me of stewards at a football match, but there was no stadium anywhere nearby, and the only sport was taking place outside this seedy semi.

'What's going on? Is someone hiding inside . . . ?' I spoke to a stocky woman muttering to herself as her wide-eyed daughter stared up at me. But my voice was drowned in the crowd's roar. The villa's door had opened, and a bearded man in turban and black robe stood on the step, beckoning to the anxious faces in the hall behind him. Above the door was a small ceramic plaque bearing an Arabic inscription, and I realized that this modest suburban house was a mosque. I was present at an outbreak of religious cleansing.

Instructed by the policewoman, the imam urged his followers into the garden. Three Asian youths in jeans and white shirts emerged into the light, followed by an elderly Pakistani man and a woman in a jellaba carrying a suitcase. Heads lowered, they moved through the now silent crowd, guarded by the firemen and police. As she passed me, the woman stumbled on the kerb, and I caught the stale, sweat-stained odour from her robe, the reek of fear.

I raised my hands to help her, but a strong shoulder knocked me off balance. Two of the hardware store assistants in St George's shirts blocked my path, narrowed eyes staring over my head. I tripped onto one knee beside the Volvo, my hands pressed against a charred rag of plastic seating. Legs stepped over me, shopping bags swinging past my face. Without comment, the policewoman lifted me onto my feet, then walked me through the crowd to her car, where the imam sat alone in the back seat. His small congregation had vanished into the smoky air.

'You're with him?' The policewoman opened the passenger door for me. 'You can sit up front . . . ?'

'No, no. I'm passing through. I'm a tourist.'

'A tourist? We don't get many of those.' She slammed the door and turned away from me. 'Next time try Brooklands Metro-Centre. Or Heathrow . . . everybody's welcome there.'

I walked back to the car park, no longer surprised that the policewoman thought of a shopping mall and an airport as tourist attractions. I had witnessed a very suburban form of race riot, which had barely disturbed the peaceful commerce of the town. The shoppers grazed contentedly, like docile cattle. No voice had been raised, no stone thrown, and no violence displayed, except to the old Volvo and myself.

I drove out of the car park, following a sign that pointed to Shepperton and Weybridge, glad to be leaving this strange little town. I accepted that a new kind of hate had emerged, silent and disciplined, a racism tempered by loyalty cards and PIN numbers. Shopping was now the model for all human behaviour, drained of emotion and anger. The decision by the estate-dwellers to reject the imam was an exercise of consumer choice.

Everywhere St George's flags were flying, from suburban gardens and filling stations and branch post offices, as this nameless town celebrated its latest victory.

2

The Homecoming

JOURNEYS SELDOM END when I think they do. Too often a piece of forgotten baggage goes on ahead and lies in wait for me when I least expect it, circling an empty carousel like evidence being assembled before a trial.

Airports, arrivals and the departure of one old pilot filled my mind as I entered Brooklands an hour later. Around me was a prosperous Thames Valley town, a pleasant terrain of comfortable houses, stylish office buildings and retail parks, every advertising man's image of Britain in the twenty-first century. I passed a bright new sports stadium like an open-air nightclub, display screens showing a road-safety commercial that merged seamlessly into an elegant pitch for a platinum credit card. Brooklands basked. Prosperity glowed from every roof shingle and gravel drive, every golden Labrador and teenage girl riding her well-trained nag.

But I was still thinking of the frightened Muslim woman being escorted from the tiny mosque, the acid stench of her robe and the smell of terror that no perfume could mask. Something had gone seriously wrong in the Thames Valley, and already I identified her with my father, another victim of a malaise even deeper than shopping.

Three weeks earlier my father – Captain Stuart Pearson, formerly of British Airways and Middle East Airlines – set off on one of his regular Saturday afternoon outings to the Brooklands Metro-Centre. Still vigorous at seventy-five, he walked the eight hundred yards to the retail complex that was the west of London's answer to the Bluewater mall near Dartford. Joining the crowd of shoppers, he crossed the central atrium on his way to the tobacconist that stocked his favourite Dunhill leaf.

Soon after two o'clock, a deranged gunman opened fire on the crowd, killing three shoppers and wounding fifteen more. The gunman escaped in the confusion that followed, but the police soon arrested a young man, Duncan Christie, a day-release patient with a criminal record and a long history of public disturbance. He had carried out an eccentric campaign against the huge mall, and a number of witnesses saw him flee the scene.

My father was hit in the head by a single bullet, and lost consciousness as fellow shoppers tried to revive him. With the other wounded he was taken to Brooklands Hospital, then transferred by helicopter to the specialist neurology unit at the Royal Free Hospital, where he died the next day.

I had not seen my father for several years, and in the hospital mortuary failed to recognize the tiny, aged face that clung to the bony points of his skull. Given the fifteen years he had spent in Dubai, I expected almost no one to attend the funeral service at the north London crematorium. A group of elderly BA pilots saw him off, grey but stalwart figures with a million miles in their ever-steady eyes. There were no local friends from Brooklands, but his solicitor's deputy, a sympathetic woman in her forties named Susan Dearing, arrived as the service began and handed me the keys to my father's flat.

Surprisingly, there was a representative from the Metro-Centre, a keen young manager from the public relations office who introduced himself to everyone as Tom Carradine, and seemed to see even this morbid event as a marketing opportunity. Masking his professional smile with an effort, he invited me to visit the mall on my next trip to Brooklands, as if something good might still come from the tragedy. I guessed that attendance at the funerals of shoppers who had died on the premises was part of the mall's after-sales service, but I was too distracted to brush him off.

Two young women slipped into a rear pew as the recorded voluntary groaned from a concealed vent, a music that only the dead could appreciate, the sound of coffins straining like the timbers of storm-tossed galleons. One of the women laughed as the chaplain launched into his homily. Knowing nothing of my father, he was forced to recite the endless scheduled routes that Captain Pearson had flown. 'The next year Stuart found himself flying to Sydney . . .' Even I let out a giggle at this.

The women left as soon as the service ended, but I caught one of them watching me from the car park as the friend hunted for her keys. Dark-haired, with the kind of dishevelled prettiness that unsettles men, she was too young to be one of my father's girlfriends, but I knew nothing about the old sky-dog's last days. She waited irritably when her friend fumbled with the door lock, and tried to hide in the passenger seat. As their car passed she looked at me and nodded to herself, clearly wondering if I was too louche or too frivolous to match up to my father. For some reason I was sure that we would see each other again.

The traffic into Brooklands had slowed, filling the six-lane highway built to draw the population of south-east England towards the Metro-Centre. Dominating the landscape around it, the immense aluminium dome housed the largest shopping mall in Greater London, a cathedral of consumerism whose congregations far exceeded those of the Christian churches. Its silver roof rose above the surrounding office blocks and hotels like the hull of a vast airship. With its visual echoes of the Millennium Dome in Greenwich, it fully justified its name, lying at the heart of a new metropolis that encircled London, a perimeter city that followed the path of the great motorways. Consumerism dominated the lives of its people, who looked as if they were shopping whatever they were doing.

Yet there were signs that a few serpents had made their home in this retail paradise. Brooklands was an old county town, but in the poorer outskirts I passed Asian shops that had been vandalized, newsagents boarded up and plastered with St George's stickers. There were too many slogans and graffiti for comfort, too many BNP and KKK signs scrawled on cracked windows, too many St George's flags flying from suburban bungalows. Never far from the defensive walls of the motorways, there was more than a hint of paranoia, as if these people of the retail city were waiting for something violent to happen.

Unable to breathe inside the low-slung Jensen, I opened the window, preferring the roadside microclimate of petrol and diesel fumes. The traffic unpacked itself, and I turned left at the sign 'Brooklands Motor Museum', moving down an avenue of detached houses behind high walls. My father had made his last home in a residential complex of three-storey apartment buildings in a landscaped park, reached by a narrow lane off the main avenue. As I drove between the privet walls I was still trying to prepare a few pat answers for the 'interview' that would decide my fitness for the post of his son, an application that had been turned down nearly forty years earlier.

Unconsciously I reapplied for the post whenever I met him – he was always affectionate but distant, as if he had run into a junior member of an old cabin crew. My mother sent him details of my school reports, and later my LSE graduation photograph, but only to irritate him. Luckily, I lost interest in him during my teens, and last saw him at the funeral of my stepmother, when he was too distressed to speak.

I had always wanted him to like me, but I thought of the single piece of baggage on the deserted carousel. How would I react if I found a framed photograph of myself on his mantelpiece, and an album lovingly filled with cuttings from *Campaign* about my then successful career?

Holding the door keys in my hand, I stepped from the car and walked across the deep gravel to the entrance, half expecting the neighbours to emerge from their flats and greet me. Surprisingly, not a window or curtain stirred, and I climbed the stairs to the top-floor landing. After a count of five, I turned the key and let myself into the hallway.

The curtains were partly drawn, and the faint light seemed to illuminate what was unmistakably a stage set. This was an old man's flat, with its leather armchair and reading lamp, pipe rack and humidor. I almost expected my father to appear on cue, walk to the rosewood drinks cabinet and pour himself a Scotch and soda, take a favourite volume from the bookshelf and peruse its pages. It needed only the telephone to ring, and the drama would begin.

Sadly, the play had ended, and the telephone would never ring, or not for my father. I tried to wave the scene away, annoyed with my own flippancy, a professional habit of trivializing the whole of life into the clichés of a TV commercial. The unopened mail on the hall table struck a more sombre note. Curiously, several envelopes carried black bands and were addressed to my father, as if he himself would read them.

I walked across the sitting room and drew the curtains. The bright garden light flooded through the scent of stale tobacco and staler memories. In front of me, looming across the houses and office buildings, was the silver dome of the Metro-Centre, dominating the landscape to the west of London. For the first time I realized that its presence was almost reassuring.

For the next hour I moved around the flat, opening desk drawers and kitchen cupboards, like a burglar trying to strike up a relationship with a householder whose home he was ransacking. I was introducing myself to my father, even though I was paying him a rather late visit. I shook my head a little sadly over his spartan bedroom with its narrow mattress, part of a widower's self-denial. Here an old man had dreamed his last dreams of flight, a reverie of wings that overflew deserts and tropical estuaries. I opened the wardrobe and counted his six uniform suits, hanging together like an entire flight crew of senior captains. On the dressing table was a set of silver-backed hairbrushes that I assumed he had given to my stepmother, memories that would greet him each morning of this gaunt but still glamorous woman. Another memory of married years was an ancient bottle of Chanel, contents long evaporated. Pressing the cap, I picked out a faint scent, echoes of a much-loved skin.

In the bathroom I opened the medicine cabinet, expecting to find a small warehouse of vitamin supplements. But the shelves were bare apart from a denture wash and a packet of senna pods. The old man had kept himself fit, using the rowing machine and exercise cycle in the spare bedroom. In the utility room beyond the kitchen was an ironing board and a table with the maid's electric kettle and biscuit tin. Behind the piles of ironing and a row of heavily starched shirts was a workspace with a computer and printer, a few books stacked beside it.

I went back to the sitting room and scanned the shelves, with their rows of popular novels, cricket almanacs and restaurant guides to airline destinations: Hong Kong, Geneva, Miami. At some point I would go through his desk, hunting out share certificates, bank statements, tax returns, and assemble a financial picture of the estate he had left, money more than useful now that I was unemployed and likely to remain so.

But I left the drawers closed. I had learned enough to grasp that I scarcely knew this old man, and probably never would. I was looking for myself, but clearly I had played no part in his life.

In the centre of the mantelpiece was a framed photograph of a youthful airline captain standing with his crew beside a BOAC Comet, presumably my father's first command. Gallant and confident, he looked ten years younger than his crew, and might have been my junior brother.

On either side of the photograph was a set of smaller frames, each containing a woman's holiday snapshot. One showed a cheerful blonde legging her way out of a sports car. A second blonde posed in tennis whites beside a Cairo hotel, while a third grinned happily in front of the Taj Mahal. Others smiled across nightclub tables and lounged by swimming pools. All the women in this trophy corridor were happy and carefree; even the rather intense thirty-year-old in a fur coat whom I recognized as my mother seemed briefly to revive in front of my father's camera lens. The display was oddly endearing, and already I liked the old pilot and decided I would get to know him better.

I drew the sitting-room curtains, ready to leave for my appointment with Sergeant Falconer at Brooklands police station, who would bring me up to date with the investigation into the tragic shooting. Trying not to think of the deranged youth who had fired into the crowd of shoppers, I looked out at the Brooklands racing track half a mile away. A section of the embankment had been preserved as a monument to the 1930s, the heroic age of speed, the era of the Schneider Trophy seaplane race and record-breaking flights, when glamorous women pilots in white overalls lit their Craven A cigarettes as they leaned against their aircraft. The public had been seized by a dream of speed no advertising agency could rival.

A faint smell had entered the room, the tang of an expensive but unpleasant cologne. Standing in the shadows beside the drawn curtains, I saw a thickset man in a black suit pause in the doorway, right hand feeling for the light switch on the wall. In his left hand he carried what seemed to be a stout metal truncheon, which he raised to test the darkness.

Willing myself to keep my nerve, I breathed steadily and edged away from the window, hidden from the intruder by the sitting-room door. In the light reflected from the framed photographs on the mantelpiece I could see the heavily built visitor still hovering in the hall, unsure whether to enter the room. Then I tripped over a pair of my father's golf shoes, stumbled and knocked the shade from the standard lamp beside the desk. The intruder flinched back, the truncheon above his head, searching for a target. I threw myself at the door, shoulder-charging it like a rugby prop forward, and heard the man's hand hit the wall, shattering the face of his wristwatch. He turned in a flurry of huge arms, sweat and hair oil, but I pinned the door against his hand, forcing his pudgy fingers to drop the truncheon.

I lost my balance and fell across the leather armchair. When I stood up and pulled back the door, gasping at the scented air, the man had gone. Feet sounded unevenly down the stairs, the limping gait of someone with a fractured kneecap. Another door slammed, but when I went to the sitting-room window the car park and gardens were silent.

I drew the curtains and opened the windows, then sat in the armchair and waited for the intruder's scent to disperse. I assumed that I had been so awed by my father's flat that I had forgotten to close the front door after me when I arrived. The visitor with the truncheon had behaved more like a housebreaker or a private detective than a neighbour calling to offer his sympathies.

When I left for my appointment with Sergeant Falconer, I found the 'truncheon' on the floor beside the door. I picked it up, unrolling a heavy magazine, a copy of the *Journal of Paediatric Surgery*.

3

The Riot

'I'VE THOUGHT OF IT,' I said to Sergeant Mary Falconer. 'Cyclops . . .'

'Is that his name?' She spoke slowly, as if trying to calm one of her dimmer prisoners. 'The man in your father's flat?'

'No.' I pointed through the canteen window at the roof of the Metro-Centre. 'I meant the shopping mall. It's a monster – it makes us seem so small.'

Without looking up from her notes, she said: 'That's probably the idea.'

'Really? Why, Sergeant?'

'So we buy things to make us grow again.'

'That's interesting. It's almost a slogan. You should be working for the Metro-Centre.'

'I hope not.'

'I take it you don't do your shopping there?'

'Not if I can help it.' Sergeant Falconer glanced into her pocket mirror, permanently to hand beside her files, and threaded a loose blonde hair into its tight braid. 'I'd keep away from the place, Mr Pearson.'

'I will. I wish my father had taken your advice.'

'We all do. That was a terrible tragedy. Superintendent Leighton asked me to convey his . . .'

I waited for the sergeant to complete her sentence, but her mind had drifted away. She turned to the window, her eyes avoiding the Metro-Centre. A fast-tracked graduate entry, she was clearly destined

21

for higher things than consoling bereaved relatives, not an ideal role for a steely but oddly vulnerable woman. She seemed unsure of me, and nervous of herself, forever glancing at her fingernails and checking her make-up, as if pieces of an elaborate disguise were in danger of falling apart. Much of her appearance was an obvious fake – the immaculate beauty-salon make-up, the breakfast TV accent, but was this part of a double bluff? In the interview room I explained that I had hardly known my father, and she listened sympathetically, though keen to get off the subject of his death. In an effort to reduce the tension, she opened her mouth and smiled at me in a surprisingly full-lipped way, almost a come-on, then retreated behind her most formal manner.

She tapped her notebook with a well-chewed pencil. 'This man you say attacked you . . . ?'

'No. He didn't attack me. I attacked him. In fact, I probably injured him. He may be a doctor. You could check the local hospital.'

'What exactly happened?'

'I was drawing the curtains, looked round, and he was there, holding a kind of club.' I rolled up the paediatric journal and raised it across the table, as if about to strike Sergeant Falconer on the head, then let her take it from me. 'I probably overreacted. It's a fault of mine.'

'Why is that?' The sergeant stared at me for a few seconds. 'Do you know?'

'I can guess.' Something about this attractive but quirky policewoman made me want to talk. 'My mother never remarried. I always felt I had to stick up for her. If the doctor complains, say I've been under a lot of stress.'

'That's true. Sadly, it won't end for some time. Prepare yourself, Mr Pearson.' In a matter-of-fact tone, as if reciting a bus timetable, she said: 'This afternoon the accused will be brought back to Brooklands from Richmond police station. He'll be held here overnight and appear before the magistrates tomorrow.'

'Full marks to the police. Who is he?'

'Duncan Christie. Aged twenty-five, white, a Brooklands resident.

He's already been charged with the murder of your father and two other victims. We expect he will be sent for trial at Guildford Crown Court.' Sergeant Falconer pointed sternly to my bruised hands. 'It's important that nothing prejudices the hearing, Mr Pearson. You'll attend court tomorrow?'

'I'm not sure. I don't know whether I can trust myself.'

'I understand. The trial may not be for six months. By then . . .'

'I'll have calmed down? Guildford Crown Court . . . I take it he'll be found guilty?'

'We can't say. I interviewed three witnesses who are certain they saw Christie with the weapon.'

'All the same, he got away. No one stopped him.'

'There was chaos, a complete stampede. The paramedics had to fight their way into the Metro-Centre. Four thousand people fled to the exits. Hundreds were injured trying to get out. There's a moral there, Mr Pearson.'

'And my father paid the price.' Without thinking, I took her hand, surprised by its hot palm. 'Why shoot an old man?'

'Your father wasn't the target, Mr Pearson.' Quietly, she withdrew her hand, and let it lie limply on the table like an exhibit. 'The sniper fired at random into the crowd.'

'Insane . . . This Christie fellow, some sort of mental patient. Why was he allowed onto the streets?'

'He was on day release from Northfield Hospital. The doctors felt he was ready to see his wife and child. It was a judgement call.'

'You sound doubtful.'

'We're not psychiatrists, Mr Pearson. Christie was well known in Brooklands. He was always campaigning against the Metro-Centre.'

'Quite a target to pick.'

Sergeant Falconer closed her files. I expected a display of passion from her, a denunciation of this psychopathic misfit, but her tone was as neutral as ice. 'His daughter was injured by a contractor's lorry. Some steel rails rolled off during one of his demos. The company offered compensation but he refused. He kept breaking the terms of his probation and was sectioned.'

'Good. They got something right.'

'It was a way of keeping him out of prison. At the time he had a lot of support.'

'Support?' I digested this slowly, trying not to look Sergeant Falconer in the eyes. Despite the neutral tone, I felt that she was trying to tell me something, and had invited me for coffee in the canteen so that she could address the real purpose behind our meeting. I said, calmly: 'Sergeant? Go on.'

'Not everyone likes the Metro-Centre. I can't give you any names, but they think it encourages people in the wrong way. Everyone wants more and more, and if they don't get it they're ready to be . . .'

'Violent? Here, in leafy Surrey? The consumer paradise? It's hard to believe. Still, you can't miss the banners and flags, the men in St George's shirts.'

'Team leaders. They help us control the crowds. Or that's what Superintendent Leighton likes to think.' The sergeant gazed warily at the ceiling. 'Be careful if you go out at night, Mr Pearson.'

She sat back, turning her face in profile. The mask of the police-woman had slipped, revealing the emotional flatness of a strong-willed but insecure graduate. In her left-handed way she wanted my help. I remembered that not once had she criticized Duncan Christie, despite the pain and tragedy he had wrought.

I said: 'Right . . . You hate the Metro-Centre, Sergeant?'

'Not really. In a last-Thursday-of-the-month kind of way. Not hate, exactly.'

'And the Brooklands area?'

Her shoulders eased, and she put away her pocket mirror, as if she realized that self-vigilance would never be enough. 'I've applied for a transfer.'

'Too much violence?'

'The threat of it.'

I wanted to take her hand again, but she seemed to be blushing. As the afternoon ended, a reddish glow lit the deep mirror of the Metro-Centre dome, an inner sun.

I said: 'It looks like it's waking up.'

'It never sleeps. Believe me, it's wide awake. It has its own cable channel. Lifestyle guide, household hints, especially for households that know when to take a hint.'

'Racist incitement?'

'Along those lines. There are people who think it's preparing us for a new world.'

'And who's behind it all?'

'No one. That's the beauty of it . . .'

She stood up, gathering her files. I could see that she was closing herself away. To begin with she had talked to me as if I were a child, and I assumed that her role was to defuse my anger and send me back to London. But she had used our meeting to get across a message of her own. In a way, she herself was the message, a bundle of unease and disquiet wrapped inside an elegant blonde package. She had slipped a few ribbons and then quickly retied them.

As we moved through the tables, I asked: 'Did you find the weapon this Christie fellow used? What was it? Some mail-order Kalashnikov?'

'It's not turned up yet. A Heckler & Koch semi-automatic.'

'Heckler & Koch? That's a police-issue machine gun. It might have been stolen from a police station.'

'It was.' Sergeant Falconer surveyed the empty canteen as if seeing it for the first time. 'An inquiry is under way. You'll be kept informed, Mr Pearson.'

'I'm glad to hear it. Tell me, which station was it stolen from?'

'Brooklands Central.' She spoke with deliberate casualness. 'Where we are now.'

'This station? It's hard to believe . . .'

But Sergeant Falconer was no longer listening to me. She stepped to the window and peered down into the avenue beside the entrance to the station car park. A crowd was forming, well-dressed Brooklands residents in smart trenchcoats, many carrying Metro-Centre shopping bags. They filled the pavement outside the station, held back by half a dozen constables.

Several burly men in St George's shirts acted as stewards, steering people away from a young black woman who stood in the centre of the road, holding the hand of a small child. The mother was clearly exhausted, trying to cover her swollen upper lip and cheek. But she ignored the hostile crowd and stared over the glaring faces at the police station windows.

'Mrs Christie, and their bairn. Did she have to bring her along?' Sergeant Falconer frowned at her watch. 'I'm sorry, Mr Pearson. I didn't want you exposed to all this . . .'

'Don't worry.' I stood next to her at the window, inhaling her scent, a heady mix of Calèche and oestrogen. I stared at the young black woman, standing alone with her anger and fierce intelligence. 'She's got guts of a kind.'

'Don't feel sorry for her. I'll get you out into a side street.'

Flashbulbs flickered near the gates to the car park. People in the crowd were hurling bouquets of torn flowers at Mrs Christie. As she brushed away the blood-red petals a set of TV lights lit her tired face.

'Sergeant . . . the crowd's working itself up. You're going to have a riot.'

'A riot?' She beckoned me to the staircase outside the canteen. 'Mr Pearson, people don't riot in Surrey. They're far more polite, and far more dangerous . . .'

We passed the empty CID offices, where computer screens glimmered at each other across untidy desks. The staircase windows looked out over the station car park, where the crowd pressed against the cordon of constables. Uniformed officers filled the hallway below us, ready to receive the prisoner.

Already spectators were running across the car park. A police car forced its way through, siren keening, followed by a white van with a wire-mesh windscreen guard lowered like a visor. A bottle of mineral water burst against it, sending a spume of frothing Perrier across the glass.

There was a roar from the spectators already inside the gates, the visceral baying of a mob who had scented a nearby guillotine. The police officers in the reception area moved into the yard, forming a cordon around the van as its rear doors opened.

Swept into the centre of the mêlée was the young black woman, daughter clasped in her arms. I waited for someone to rescue her, but my eyes were fixed on the man who was stepping from the van. A constable threw a grey blanket over him, but for a few seconds I saw his sallow, unshaved face, scarred chin pockmarked by acne, forehead flushed by recent punches. He was unaware of the crowd and the policemen jostling him, and stared at the radio aerials above the station, as if expecting a message from a distant star to be relayed to him. His head swayed drunkenly, a vacancy of mind coupled with a deep inner hunger that was almost messianic. I could see years of poor nutrition, self-neglect and arrogance, the face of assassins through the ages, of rootless metropolitan men from an earlier era who had survived into the twenty-first century, as out of place among the four-wheel drives and school runs of prosperous suburbia as Neanderthal Man discovered in a sun lounger beside a Costa Blanca swimming pool. Somehow this misfit and dement had evaded the juvenile courts and social-service inspectors, and had taught himself to hate a shopping mall so intensely that he could steal a weapon and fire at random into a lunch-hour crowd, killing a retired airline pilot about to buy his favourite tobacco.

A scrum of police surrounded him, arms locked together as they propelled the prisoner towards the station. On the outer edge of the scrum was Sergeant Falconer, arms outstretched to calm the shouting spectators. She was watching me as I stood in the staircase window, and I was certain that she had left me on the stairs so that I could see clearly the man who had killed my father.

The reception area was empty now, except for two civilian typists who had left their desks. I stepped past them, and stood by the open doorway as the police readied themselves to rush Christie into the station. I searched my pockets for a weapon, and came up with my car keys. I gripped them inside my fist, the largest key between my index and middle fingers. One lucky blow to Christie's temple would rid the world of this mental degenerate.

Holding the key, I readied myself as Christie approached, bruised head emerging from the blanket. Seeing him beyond their grasp, the crowd surged forward, hands drumming on the sides of the van. In the crush of hatless officers trying to dodge the swinging carrier bags I saw Christie's wife scream abuse at a woman constable trying to reunite her with her daughter.

I raised my fist to aim a blow at Christie, who swayed towards me in an idiot's trance. But a powerful hand gripped my arm and forced it behind me. Strong fingers expertly stripped me of the ignition keys. I turned to find a large, military-looking man with an untrimmed ginger moustache, his deep chest and shoulders squeezed into a tweed jacket too small for him.

'Mr Pearson?' He shook the keys in my face, and steadied me as a policewoman lurched past with an arrested demonstrator. 'Geoffrey Fairfax, your father's solicitor. We've spoken on the phone. If I'm right, we have an appointment in ten minutes' time. I must say you look as if you'd rather like to get out of here . . .'

4

The Resistance Movement

'As you can see, Mr Pearson, the bulk of your father's estate goes to the pilots' benevolent fund. Unfair to you, perhaps, and rather too final for my taste.' With a resigned gesture, Geoffrey Fairfax let the cover of the antique wooden box-file fall like a coffin lid. 'But in a good cause – the widows of pilots who died in aircraft accidents. After forty years he must have known a good many. Whatever consolation that is to you.'

'A lot. He did the right thing.' I finished my whisky and carefully centred the empty glass on its coaster. To myself I thought: a first rebuff from the old man, a warning from beyond the grave. 'I won't contest the will.'

'Good. I was sure of that when I first saw you. The flat is yours, of course.' Fairfax treated me to a sly smile. 'People can be surprisingly high-minded when it comes to making their wills. Doctors bequeath their bodies to anatomy schools, even though they know they'll be cut into tripes. Wives forgive philandering husbands. I'm glad your father didn't change his will.'

'Did he say he might?'

'No. Your father was never impulsive. Except towards the end, perhaps . . . I really can't say.'

I waited for Fairfax to continue, aware that I was watching a well-rehearsed performance by one of the last actor-managers in Brooklands. Grieving but avaricious relatives were his main audience, and he clearly relished every moment. Looking around his oak-panelled office, I wondered how his cavalier ways fitted into the new Brooklands. Conveyancing office blocks in a fast-food economy of automated cash tills and shopping malls was not Geoffrey Fairfax's thing. He belonged to a world before the coming of the M25.

Framed photographs on a side table showed him as a half-colonel in the Territorial Army, and on horseback at an outing of the local hunt, before the foxes of west Surrey abandoned their ancestral farmland and took off for a better world of filling-station forecourts and executive housing patios. Like a lot of directors of old-style companies I had known, Fairfax was arrogant, vaguely threatening, and inefficient. One of the papers from my father's box-file had floated to the floor at his feet, but he ignored it, trusting that the cleaner would return it to his desk. And if she stuffed it into the waste-paper basket, who would know or care? His pink-faced intelligence had a malicious edge. He sat behind his desk in his clubman's armchair, head barely visible so that his clients were forced to strain to see him.

For a large man in his fifties he had shown quick reflexes when he rescued me from the riot at the police station, propelling me with a firm hand to the rear entrance of the car park, where a roofed pathway led to the section house and a side street off the main road. He sat me in the passenger seat of his Range Rover, and watched the crowd disperse through his wing mirror. He drove pugnaciously, almost running down two elderly women who were slow to get out of his way. Geoffrey Fairfax was an example of a rare species, the middle-class thug. There was a strain of brutality that had little to do with punch-ups on the rugby field and much more to do with teaching the natives a lesson.

'My father . . . ?' I reminded him. 'You were about to say?'

'A remarkable man. To tell the truth, we hadn't seen him at the club for a few months. Sadly, he seemed to have changed. He made some new friends, rather unusual company . . .'

'Who, exactly?'

'Hard to say. I wouldn't have thought they were really his type, but there you are. He used to be keen on bridge, liked amusing the ladies, played a wristy game of squash.' Fairfax pressed his hands against the lid of the box-file, as if concerned that my father's ghost might escape from its casket. 'Terrible business, I hope they find whoever was responsible.'

'I thought they had.' I sat forward, picking up an odd note in the solicitor's voice. 'This fellow the police brought in, the local misfit or mental case . . . ?'

'Duncan Christie? Misfit, yes. Mental case, no. Two hours in a police van can be quite an assault course. He goes before the magistrate tomorrow.'

'He looked deranged to me: I take it he's guilty?'

'It does seem like it. But let's wait and see. Calm yourself, Mr Pearson. I assume Christie will be sent for trial and almost certainly convicted. Curiously enough, we used to represent him.'

'Isn't that a little odd? A firm like yours, dealing with mental cases?'

'Not at all. We couldn't survive without them. Christie kept us busy for years. Public mischief cases, antisocial behaviour orders, attempts by various busybodies to have him sectioned. One of my junior partners acted for him when he sued the Metro-Centre.'

'Christie hated it.'

'Who doesn't? It's a monstrosity.' Fairfax's voice had deepened, as if he was berating a parade ground of slacking troopers. 'The day they broke the first sod any number of people feared what it might do. We were right. This used to be a rather pleasant corner of Surrey. Everything has changed, we might as well be living inside that ghastly dome. Sometimes I think we already are, without realizing it.'

'Even so.' I searched for some way of calming him. 'It's only a shopping mall.'

'Only? For God's sake, man. There's nothing worse on this planet!'

His temper up, Fairfax propelled himself from his chair, heavy thighs rocking the desk. His strong hands drew back the brocaded curtains. Beyond the leafy square and a modest town hall was the illuminated shell of the Metro-Centre. I was impressed that a suburban solicitor should give in to such a display of anger. I realized now why the curtains had been drawn when we arrived, and guessed that they remained drawn throughout the day. The interior of the dome glowed like a reactor core, an inverted bowl of light shining through the glass panels of the roof. A ten-storey office building stood between the mall and Fairfax's burly figure, but the lights of the Metro-Centre seemed to shine through the structure, as if its intense luminance could penetrate solid matter in its search for this hostile lawyer squaring his shoulders.

Undaunted, Fairfax turned to me, stubby forefinger raised in warning. Eyeing me shrewdly, he nodded at my scuffed shoes.

'You may not know that the place is open twenty-four hours a day. That's an extraordinary thought, Mr Pearson. A structural engineer at the club tells me that the design life is at least a hundred years. Can I ask what business you're in? Your father did tell me.'

'Advertising. I'm thinking of a career change.'

'Thank God for that. Still, you're probably sympathetic to these so-called super-malls. But you enjoy the luxury of not living here.'

'You make it sound like hell.'

'It is hell . . .' Fairfax hunched over the whisky decanter and replaced the stopper, a signal that our appointment was over. When I stood up, he turned aggressively to face me, as if about to knock me to the floor. A confused pride made him struggle with his words. 'You're from London, Mr Pearson. It's a huge flea market and always has been. Cheap goods and cheaper dreams. Here in Brooklands we had a real community, not just a population of cash tills. Now it's gone, vanished overnight when that money-factory opened. We're swamped by outsiders, thousands of them with nothing larger on their minds than the next bargain sale. For them, Brooklands is little more than a car park. Our schools are plagued by truancy, hundreds of children haunting the Metro-Centre every day. The one hospital which should be caring for local residents is overwhelmed by driving accidents caused by visitors. Never fall ill near the M25. Evening classes were popular here – conversational French, local history, contract bridge. They've all closed. People prefer to stroll around the mall. No one attends church. Why bother? They find spiritual fulfilment at the New Age centre, first left after the burger bar. We had a dozen societies and clubs – music, amateur dramatics, archaeology. They shut down long ago. Charities, political parties? No one turns up. At Christmas the Metro-Centre hires a fleet of motorized Santas. They cruise the streets, blaring out tapes of Disney carols. Checkout girls dressed up as Tinkerbell flashing their thighs. A Panzer army putting on its cutest show . . .'

'It all sounds terrible.' I was thinking about the quickest route back to London. 'Rather like the rest of England. Does it matter?'

'It matters!' Fairfax stepped around his desk, opened a glass cabinet behind the curtains and drew out a shotgun. Expertly, he snapped the breech, checking whether it was loaded. His face was flushed with more than rage, a deep tribal loathing of the people of the plain who had settled around him. 'It matters . . .'

'Mr Fairfax . . .' I felt sorry for him, still holding his red flag in front of the first motor vehicle, but I needed to leave. 'Can we call a taxi – I have to get back to my car.'

'Your car?' Fairfax waved this aside. He lowered his voice, as if the shadows in the deserted square might hear him. 'Look around you, Mr Pearson. We're facing a new kind of man and woman – narrow-eyed, passive, clutching their store cards. They believe anything that people like you care to tell them. They want to be tricked, they want to be deluded into buying the latest rubbish. They've been educated by TV commercials. They know that the only things with any value are those they can put in a carrier bag. This is a plague area, Mr Pearson. A plague called consumerism.'

Still carrying the shotgun, he remembered that I was waiting by the door. He paused, mentally ticking off the last bead in his rosary, then led me into the corridor. The offices were empty, but voices came from a conference room across the hall.

'A plague area,' I repeated. 'Can I ask what the cure is? I take it you plan to fight back?'

'Believe me, yes. We'll fight back. I can assure you we've already started . . .'

Fairfax lowered his voice, but as we passed the conference room the door opened and his deputy, Susan Dearing, looked out at us. I had last talked to her at the funeral, and she seemed embarrassed to see me. She was about to speak to Fairfax, but he waved her away with the shotgun.

Through the open door I saw half a dozen people sitting around the conference table, chairs pushed back as if they were unsure of each other. I recognized none of them, though something about the unruly hair of a young woman with her back to the door seemed familiar. She wore a doctor's white coat, like a medical attendant supervising a patients' meeting, but her right foot tapped restlessly on the floor.

We walked through to the reception area. The desk was unattended, and a young black woman sat on a bench, her daughter asleep across her lap. Mrs Christie was scarcely aware of the child, her eyes above bruised cheeks staring at the hunting scenes on the walls. One lapel of her jacket had been torn from its seams, and her hand fretted over the loose fabric, trying to hold it in place. Her face had a beaten but still determined set. She had been punched and spat upon by the crowd, but some inner conviction kept her going. Watching her, it occurred to me that she believed her husband was innocent.

Behind the reception desk a narrow passage led to a pantry. Sergeant Mary Falconer stood by a gas element, pouring warm milk from a saucepan into two cups.

'Mr Pearson . . .' Fairfax beckoned me to the door, impatient for me to leave. 'You'll drive back to London tonight?'

'If I can find the way. Brooklands seems to be off all the maps . . .' I looked back at Sergeant Falconer, who was wiping spilled milk from the gas ring, trying to fit her into the larger events that had brought me to this curious town, and this even stranger firm of solicitors. I hailed an approaching taxi, and as it stopped I shook Fairfax's hand. Before he could turn away, I said: 'Mrs Christie – she's sitting in there . . . ?'

'Who?'

'Mrs Christie. The wife of the man who killed my father. You're not representing her?'

'No, no.' Fairfax signalled to the taxi driver. 'Someone needs to look after her. She and the child are as much victims of all this as you are.'

'Right.' I walked down the steps and then turned to look up at Fairfax. 'One last question. Did Duncan Christie shoot my father?'

Fairfax avoided my eyes and stared hard at the dome. 'I'm afraid so. It certainly looks like it . . .'

It was the only thing that Geoffrey Fairfax had said that I was ready to take at face value.

The Metro-Centre withdrew behind me as I moved through the darkened streets, searching for a signpost to guide me back to London. But here by the M25, in the heartland of the motorway people, all signs pointed inwards, referring the traveller back to his starting point. 'Metro-Centre South Gate . . . West Surrey Retail Park . . . Brooklands Convention Centre . . . Metro-Centre North Gate . . .'

I was lost, and the AA guide I scanned at a deserted crossroads made sure that I was completely adrift. I passed tracts of middle-income housing, all-night superstores surrounded by acres of brightly lit parking. I thought of my confused day at Brooklands, a catalogue of missed arrivals. A father I had hardly known was dead, and the place of his last days was covering its tracks and rearranging itself into a maze.

I crossed the perimeter of the old Brooklands racing circuit. Giant floes of black concrete emerged from the darkness, a geometry of shadows and memories, a stone dream that would never awake. I could almost smell the exhaust drifting on the mist, and hear the roar of deep-chested engines, a vision of speed that long predated the shotgun and jodhpur fantasies of Geoffrey Fairfax and his squadrons of heavy hunters.

I opened the window to catch the sounds in my head, the rumble and burble of exhaust. But another noise drummed across the night air, coming from a football stadium half a mile away. Lighting arrays rose into the night sky, blurred by the heat and breathy vapour of the crowd.

I left the racetrack at the next turning, and joined the traffic moving past the stadium. The match had ended, and the crowd was spilling into the nearby streets. Men and women in St George's shirts emerged from the exits and searched for their parked cars. High above the stadium, the electronic display screens faced each other at opposite ends of the ground, as the giant image of the match commentator addressed himself across the empty stands. Fragments of his voice boomed above the traffic and the cheers of rival supporters. He was a handsome, fleshy man with a salesman's easy manner, a type I knew well from a hundred product launches, with an easy patter, a smile and a promise in every polished phrase.

A fist struck the roof above my head. The supporters crossing the road drummed on the cars, pounding out a tribal tattoo. Three men in St George's shirts stepped in front of the Jensen, forcing me to halt as they slapped the bonnet. Two women followed them, wearing the same red and white shirts, arms linked in the friendliest way. They were good-humoured but oddly threatening, as if celebrating soccer as society's last hope of violence. They walked along the line of parked cars, then stepped into a large BMW. Flashing their headlights in time to the jungle tattoo, they forced their way through the passing traffic and drove off at speed.

The commentator on the screens floated above the night, voice booming at the empty stands. Clips of muscular football action were crosscut with showroom displays of bathroom suites and microwave ovens. He was still at it when I set off northwards, his smile dying in the blur of arc lights, authentic in his insincerity.

5

The Metro-Centre

LIKE ALL GREAT shopping malls, the Metro-Centre smothered unease, defused its own threat and offered balm to the weary. I stood in the sunshine fifty yards from the South Gate entrance, watching the shoppers cross the wide apron that surrounded the mall, a vast annular plaza in its own right. In a few moments they would be bathed in a light more healing than anything on offer from the sun. As we entered these huge temples we became young again, like children visiting the home of a new schoolfriend, a house that at first seemed forbidding. Then a strange but smiling mother would appear and put the most nervous child at ease with a promise that small treats would appear throughout the visit.

All malls subtly infantilized us, but the Metro-Centre showed signs of urging us to grow up a little. Uniformed stewards stood by the entrance, checking bags and purses, a response to the tragedy in which my father had died. An elderly Asian couple approached the entrance, and were quickly surrounded by volunteers in St George's shirts. No one spoke to the couple, but they were stared at and shouldered about until a Metro-Centre security man intervened.

Tom Carradine, the public relations manager who turned up so cheerfully at the funeral, had arranged to meet me by the information desk. He was now leading the unit that offered assistance to the injured and bereaved. A printed plan that resembled a new share-issue prospectus had arrived by special messenger, outlining the many discounts and concessionary terms available at Metro-Centre stores, all on a sliding scale that strongly suggested one's death in a terrorist attack hit the maximum pay-off.

After returning to London I had slept uneasily in my Chelsea flat, and was woken by an early phone call from David Carradine. He was helpful and concerned, eager to tell me everything he knew about the circumstances of my father's death. If anything, he was rather too keen, talking about angles of fire and bullet velocities as if describing a computer game that had malfunctioned. He told me that the magistrates' hearing had been postponed to the next day, given the extent of Christie's arrest injuries and security fears after the police station riot.

I spent the day pacing the flat, irritated by its silent rooms. By now I had decided I would be present at the court. David Carradine would take me on a tour of the Metro-Centre, and I would then see Christie committed for trial. Already I was unsure about everything — the sight of Mrs Christie in my solicitor's reception area, Sergeant Falconer warming milk for her child, Fairfax's aggressive behaviour, virtually accusing me of being responsible for the giant mall on his doorstep. At the least, Christie's committal would draw a firm line under all this suburban unreality.

Turning my back on the sun, I stepped through the doors at the South Gate entrance. In front of me was a terraced city, tiers of overhead streets reached by escalators and elevator pods. A stream of aerated water marked the edge of the entrance hall, bubbling under small bridges that led to miniature landscaped gardens, each an Eden promising an experience more meaningful than self-knowledge or eternal life. Stewards patrolled the area, and desk staff recruited volunteers into the Metro-Centre security force.

As I passed the desk, a steward offered me a leaflet urging every customer to become one of the eyes and ears of the shopping mall. Two middle-aged men, a trio of off-duty secretaries and several youths in baseball caps signed their forms and were given badges to pin to their lapels. Consumer announcements broke through the background music, emphasizing that airport security ruled.

Surprisingly, no one was embarrassed by the uniformed guards and their volunteer auxiliaries. As the martial music blared, they straightened their backs and walked more briskly, like Londoners during the Blitz. In front of me was a married couple with a child in a pushchair, and without thinking I found myself in step with them.

Breaking my stride, I paused by one of the bridges, and noticed that the white paint on the rail had begun to flake. The stream splashing among the artificial rocks had lost its direction. Eddies of scum circled aimlessly, exhausted by the attempt to return to the main channel. Even the floor of the entrance hall, worn down by a hundred thousand heels, revealed a few cracks.

Despite these portents, Tom Carradine was unfailingly optimistic. Barely out of his teens, he was smiling, friendly and crushingly earnest, with the pale skin and overly clear eyes of a cult recruiter. As he sprang from the crowd and took my hand I guessed that I was the first bereaved relative to visit the Metro-Centre, and that he had already decided how to make my visit a success.

'We're delighted to have you with us, Mr Pearson.' He shook my hand warmly, appreciating that I had crossed a desert to reach this air-conditioned oasis. 'We hope you'll visit us again. Here in the Metro-Centre we're great believers in the future.'

'As I am, Tom . . .'

He guided me towards a nearby travelator, and nodded approvingly when I mounted the walkway without stumbling. He waved genially to the shoppers, his hands beating time to the music. At exactly fifteen-second intervals he turned a huge smile on me, like a safety light illuminating an underground garage.

'I like the music,' I commented. 'Though maybe it's a little too martial. Somewhere in there I can hear the Horst Wessel song.'

'It's good for morale,' Carradine explained. 'We like to keep people cheerful. You know . . . ?'

'I know. Has business fallen off at all . . . since the shooting?'

Carradine frowned, unable to grasp the concept of a trade down-turn, from whatever cause. 'At first, just a little. Out of respect, of course. But our customers are giving us wonderful support.'

'They've rallied round?'

'Absolutely. If anything, I think it's brought us all together. I know you'll be pleased to hear that, Mr Pearson.'

He spoke forcefully, unblinking eyes fixed on mine. I took for granted that he distrusted me, above all for having a father who had allowed himself to be killed, like the member of a congregation with the bad manners to drop dead beside the high altar in the middle of evensong. Death had no place in the Metro-Centre, which had abolished time and the seasons, past and future. He probably knew that I was hostile to the mall, another middle-class snob who hated glitter, confidence and opportunity when they were taken up too literally by the lower orders.

In an almost combative way, he launched into a tour guide's patter, describing the huge dimensions of the Metro-Centre, the millions of square feet of retail space, the three hotels, six cineplexes and forty cafés. 'Did you know,' he concluded, 'that we have more retail space than the whole of Luton?'

'I'm impressed. Still . . .' I pointed to the shops on either side of the travelator, filled with familiar brands of jewellery, cameras and electrical goods. '. . . You're selling the same things.'

'But they feel different.' Carradine's eyes seemed to glow. 'That's why our customers come here. The Metro-Centre creates a new climate, Mr Pearson. We succeeded where the Greenwich dome failed. This isn't just a shopping mall. It's more like a . . .'

'Religious experience?'

'Exactly! It's like going to church. And here you can go every day and you get something to take home.'

I watched his eyes tilt upwards as he listened to his words echo inside his head. He was barely an adult, but already a middle-aged fanatic in the making. I assumed he had no life outside the Metro-Centre. All his emotional needs, his sense of self, were satisfied by this huge retail space. He was naive and enthusiastic, serving a novitiate that would never end. And I had helped to create him.

The travelator reached the end of its journey, carrying us into the heart of the Metro-Centre. We were now in the central atrium, a circular concourse where shoppers strolled to the escalators that would carry them to the upper retail decks. A diffused aura filled the scented space, but now and then the beam of a concealed spotlight caught my eye. I felt that I was on the stage of a vast opera house, surrounded by a circle and upper circle packed with spectators. Everything seemed dramatized, every gesture and thought. The enclosed geometry of the Metro-Centre focused an intense self-awareness on every shopper, as if we were extras in a music drama that had become the world.

'Tom? What is it?'

Carradine had turned from me. He was staring at one of the glass elevators that climbed the floors nearest to us. On the third level, between the elevator and the railings of the pedestrian walkway, was the open hatch of a fire-control station, the brass nozzle of a high-pressure hose pointing towards us. Uncomfortable to be with me, Carradine buttoned and unbuttoned his jacket. I assumed that it was from this sniper position that my father and his fellow victims had been shot, among the sock and cosmetic counters, the vintage wine stores and laptop clinics.

Surprisingly, now that I was here, in the centre of the killing ground, I felt completely calm. Surrounded by this cave of transient treasures, guided by this nervous public relations man, death lost its power to threaten, measured in nothing more fearful than bust sizes and kilobyte capacities. The human race sleepwalked to oblivion, thinking only about the corporate logos on its shroud.

'Mr Pearson? I'm sorry, I wasn't thinking . . .'

'It's all right, Tom. No need to worry.' Trying to calm the young manager, I placed a hand on his shoulder. 'The hatchway on the third floor. I take it the shots came from there?'

'That's correct.' Carradine steadied himself with a visible effort of will. He stiffened his neck and breathed deeply to a count of six. Nothing in his training had prepared him for this reconstruction. He spoke rapidly, as if reading from a press handout. 'Two bursts of fire, at 2.17 p.m., before anyone realized what had happened. Witnesses say everyone stopped and listened to the echoes, thinking they were more shots.'

'And then?'

'Then? Total panic. All the down escalators were full, people on the upper floors were fighting to get into the lifts. It took us three days to identify all the shopping bags left behind. You can imagine the scene, Mr Pearson.'

'Sadly, I can.'

'Two people died instantly – Mrs Holden, a local pensioner, and a Mr Mickiewicz, a Polish visitor. Your father and fifteen others were wounded.' Carradine clenched his fists, ignoring the shoppers who paused to listen to him, under the impression that he was leading a conducted tour. 'It was so crowded, Mr Pearson. You have to understand the gunman couldn't miss.'

'That must have been his idea. The lunchtime surge.' I gazed around the concourse, and imagined a gunman opening fire at random. 'It's surprising more people weren't hit.'

'Well . . .' Carradine nodded ruefully as a middle-aged woman with two heavy shopping bags strained forward to whisper to him. 'The bears were hit.'

'The bears?'

'The Three Bears . . . the Metro-Centre mascots. People were very affected . . .'

Carradine pointed to the centre of the concourse. On a circular plinth stood three giant teddy bears. The father bear was at least fifteen feet tall, his plump torso and limbs covered with a lustrous brown fur. Mother and baby bear stood beside him, paws raised to the shoppers, as if ready to make a consumer affairs announcement about the porridge supply.

'Impressive,' I said. 'Completely bear-like. They look as if they can speak.'

'They can't speak, but they can move. They dance to the music. "Rudolf the Red-nosed Reindeer" was their favourite.' Soberly, Carradine added: 'We switched off the motors. Out of consideration . . .'

'Sensitive of you. And the bears were hit? I'm glad they weren't seriously injured.'

'It was a close thing.' Carradine pointed to the rounded abdomen of the mother bear, and to the left ear of the father bear. Darker squares of fur had been stitched over the original fabric, giving both creatures a rather rumpled look, as if they had been scuffling over the breakfast table. 'Our customers were very upset. They sent in hundreds of letters, get-well cards . . .'

Without thinking, we had walked over to the bears. I noticed the cards decorating the plinth, many carrying messages in adult hand-writing. There were flowers, a row of miniature teddy bears, one wearing a tiny St George's shirt, and a dozen jars of honey and treacle.

Listening to myself, I said: 'It's almost a shrine.'

'Definitely.'

'Let's move on.' I beckoned Carradine away from the stuffed trio, though I was aware that my sympathy for the bears had brought us closer together. 'It's a pity about the bears, but they seem to be well cared for. Now, which of these escalators did my father take?'

'He didn't take an escalator, Mr Pearson.'

'Sergeant Falconer said he was going up to the third floor. He bought his tobacco from a shop . . .'

'Dunhill's. But not that morning. He took the staircase to the exhibition area.'

A mezzanine deck jutted over the concourse between the ground and first floors, reached by a staircase with white rails. There was an observation platform where shoppers could rest and look down on the crowds below. A section of the mezzanine was a public gallery, hung with dioramas of new housing estates and science parks.

'We donate the space to local businesses,' Carradine explained. 'It's part of our public education programme.'

'Enlightened of you.' I waited for Carradine to inhale deeply. 'Now, where was my father shot?'

Without speaking, Carradine pointed to the observation platform. He had begun to sweat copiously, and buttoned his jacket, trying to hide the damp stain under his tie. He watched me stiffly when I climbed the dozen steps to the platform, then turned and fixed his gaze on the giant bears.

I stood on the platform, almost expecting to see my father's blood staining the metal floor. He had spent his last moments resting against the rail, tired by his walk to the Metro-Centre. The fire-control hatch was little more than twenty feet away, and I tried to imagine a bullet passing through my head. Following its possible track, I noticed a shallow groove in the railing. The staircase had been repainted, but I placed my index finger in the groove, taking the last pulse of my father's life, a final contact with a man I never knew.

'Mr Pearson – everything all right?' Carradine was relieved that the tour was over, an ordeal he had clearly never anticipated. 'If we go to my office . . .'

'I'm fine. You've earned yourself a stiff drink. First, though, I need to take a look at the fire-control point.'

'Mr Pearson? That's not a good idea. You might find it . . .'

I held his elbow and turned him to face the bears. A technician was working on the instrument panel inside the plinth, and the mother bear gave a skittish twitch, as if ducking another bullet. I said: 'I need to see the whole picture. My father died in your store, Tom. You owe it to me and the bears.'

We stood in the narrow chamber behind the fire hose, the high-pressure pump and gas cylinders next to us. The hose would project a stream of foam at the pedestrian decks and smother any burning debris that fell from the roof. Leaning through the open hatch, I could see the observation platform, the mezzanine deck and the entire concourse.

'Good. Tell me, Tom, how did Christie get in here?'

Carradine straightened his tortured body. The sweat from his hands left damp prints on the metal wall. 'The fire crews have key cards. Christie must have stolen one from their locker room.'

'It's a miracle he made it here.' We had emerged from a maze of service corridors, tunnels and freight elevators. 'It's not easy to find. Did Christie have a friend on the inside?'

'Unthinkable, Mr Pearson.' Carradine stared at me, shocked by the thought. 'Christie is very devious. He was always hanging around.'

'All the same, no one actually saw him fire the weapon. How did he smuggle it in here?'

'Sergeant Falconer told me he hid it behind the gas cylinders.'

'Sergeant Falconer? For someone so uptight she gets around . . .'

'Two women leaving the staff toilet saw Christie run to the emergency exit. Several people recognized him in the car park.'

'They all knew him?'

'He's a local troublemaker, a very nasty type.'

'That's the problem.' I moved the foam gun in its gimbals, training the brass barrel on the bears. 'All that screaming and panic – anyone running away would look like an assassin. Especially the local misfit.'

'He's guilty, Mr Pearson.' Carradine nodded vigorously, his confidence returning. 'They'll convict him.'

I gazed down at the mezzanine, wondering what had drawn my father to a property developer's pitch. Beyond the exhibition space, separated by chromium rails and a security gate, was a small television studio. There was a hospitality area of black leather sofas, and a circle of cameras and lighting arrays grouped around a commentator's desk and the guest banquettes.

'Consumer affairs programme,' Carradine explained. 'It's very popular. Customers come on, talk about their shopping experiences. The Metro-Centre has its own cable channel. In the evenings we have higher ratings than BBC2.'

'People go home and watch programmes about shopping?'

'More than shopping, Mr Pearson. Health and lifestyle issues, sports, current affairs, key local concerns like asylum seekers . . .'

A monitor in the control room had come on, and a familiar face appeared, with the same deep tan and sympathetic smile that I had seen on the giant screens at the football stadium.

★　　★　　★

The face followed us around the dome, its sunbed charm glowing from the television screen in Carradine's office, a windowless space deep in the dome's administration area. As I sipped a double espresso, glad to sink my nose in its reassuring vapour, Carradine sorted through the photographs he had pulled from his filing cabinet.

He and his assistants had spent endless hours editing out any blood-stains or panic-filled faces. The surveillance-camera stills he passed to me showed a retreat as calm and heroic as Dunkirk, younger customers helping the elderly, uniformed staff guiding children towards their grateful parents. Spilled shopping bags, scattered groceries, a screaming three-year-old with a blood-smeared face were all cropped and consigned to that vast amnesia that the consumer world reserved for the past. At the sales counter, the human race's greatest confron-tation with existence, there were no yesterdays, no history to be relived, only an intense transactional present.

I dropped the photos on Carradine's desk and turned to the tele-vision screen where the suntanned presenter was interviewing house-wives about their experiences with a new reusable cat litter. I guessed that the recorded clip would not be appearing on air.

'I've seen him before,' I told Carradine. 'Years ago. *EastEnders*, *The Bill*. He tended to play paedophiles and widowers who'd murdered their wives . . . it's that faint shiftiness.'

'David Cruise.' At the sound of the name Carradine straightened his shoulders. 'He runs the Metro-Centre cable channel. He's very popular, our customers like him.'

'I bet. He fronted a few product launches for us. I remember a cinema ad for a new micro-car. He was too big to get into it and we had to drop him. The television screen is small enough for him.'

'He's good. We're all glad he's here. The local constituency chairman thinks he'd make a great Member of Parliament.'

'He would. Today's politics is tailor-made for him. Smiles leaking everywhere, mood music, the sales campaign that gets rid of the need for a product. Even the shiftiness. People like to be conned. It reminds them that everything is a game. No disrespect –'

There was a rapid knock on the door and Carradine's secretary burst in. Close to tears, she spoke urgently to Carradine, then paused by the door as he picked up his telephone.

'Christie? What do you mean?' As he listened he struck his mouth with the palm of his hand. 'When? The court? Mr Pearson is here. How do I explain that?'

He held the receiver in one hand and carefully depressed the cradle with the other, staring at the photographs on his desk.

'Tom? What's the problem?' I walked around the desk. 'Family news?'

'Your family.' Carradine pointed the receiver at me. 'Duncan Christie.'

'What about him? Is he dead? Don't tell me he hanged himself in his cell?'

'He's alive.' Carradine stepped back, trying to leave as much space as possible between us. He stared in a level way at me, unsure whether I would be able to cope with his news. For the first time he no longer looked like a teenager. 'Very much alive. There was a special court hearing this morning. It just ended. The magistrate discharged him. He ruled there was no case to answer.'

'How? I don't believe it.' I seized the telephone receiver from Carradine and pressed it hard into its cradle, trying to silence this absurd oracle. 'It's a hoax. Or a cock-up, some legal blunder. They're talking about a different case.'

'No. It's Duncan Christie. The Crown Prosecution Service offered no evidence. The police withdrew their charges. Three witnesses have come forward, saying they saw Christie in the South Gate entrance hall when the shots were fired. They picked him out in a line-up. Christie was nowhere near the mezzanine. I'm sorry, Mr Pearson . . .'

I turned away, and stared at the presenter still smiling and teasing his housewives. I felt dazed, but I noticed that David Cruise preferred his left profile, which concealed the receding hairline above his right temple. In an almost reassuring way, his soft and ingratiating presence offered the only reality in the absurd world that my father's death and the Metro-Centre had created between them.

6

Going Home

I EXPECTED TO FIND a noisy crowd outside the magistrates' court, but the police outnumbered the few spectators. Passers-by paused on the pavement opposite the court, but the last of the photographers were packing away their equipment, deprived of their target.

Tuning to the local radio bulletin as I drove from the Metro-Centre, I heard the news confirmed. I drummed my fists on the steering wheel, certain that the law had tripped over itself. I had seen Christie close enough to punch him, and his lolling head and wandering eyes, a visible attempt to escape from himself, convinced me that he was guilty. Somehow I had to overturn this misguided and ludicrous decision. The large vacuum left in my life by my father's murder had now been invaded by another vacuum.

I left the Jensen on a double yellow line, waving to the policeman who studiously said nothing when I walked past him. I was climbing the courthouse steps when I saw Sergeant Falconer emerging through the doors. She recognized me and began to turn away, pretending to adjust her hair. Unable to escape, she rallied herself and took my arm in a firm grip.

'Mr Pearson . . . ?' Her mind seemed miles away, but she steered me into the lobby, past three uniformed constables rocking on their heels. 'You've heard? It's quieter in here. The public . . .'

'Don't worry, they've all gone shopping. No one seems upset, or surprised.'

'Believe me, it's a complete surprise.' Sergeant Falconer studied my face, relieved to find me on the edge of anger, an emotion with which her training had taught her to cope. She led me to a bench. 'Let's sit here. I'll do my best to give you any details.'

'Can't we go in? Civic awareness, and all that. Everyone should observe a miscarriage of justice.'

'The court is closed.' She smiled in a sisterly way and touched my arm. 'Mr Christie may be coming out soon. Is that all right . . . ?'

'Fine. He's innocent, isn't he?' I watched the constables sauntering about the steps, truncheons reluctantly sheathed, like salesmen deprived of their customers. Without thinking, I said: 'The police sell violence.'

'What?'

'The idea of violence.' I laughed to myself. 'Sorry, Sergeant.'

'You're upset. It's understandable.'

'Well . . .' I calmed myself, touched by her close interest. 'Half an hour ago I was sure who had killed my father, and why. A mental patient with a grudge against a shopping mall. Now, suddenly, it's a mystery again. Brooklands, the M25, these motorway towns. They're damned strange places. Nothing is what it seems.'

'That's why people move here. The suburbs are the last great mystery.'

'Is that the reason you're leaving?' I took her hand, surprised by its almost feverish warmth. There was an operation scar on the knuckle of her ring finger, the trace of an old tendon injury left by some hooligan with a beer bottle. Or had a tenacious engagement ring been surgically removed, her body holding on to a passion that her quirky mind repressed? Sergeant Falconer was wary and defensive, and not only about the confused police investigation into my father's death. I knew that she wanted me out, safely back in central London, but I sensed that she wanted herself out, free from whatever web was spinning itself around her.

'Mr Pearson? You fell asleep for a moment.'

'Right. I'm sorry. These witnesses who came forward – who are they? Greens, hunt saboteurs, pot-smoking hippies? I take it they're friends of Christie's. How reliable are they?'

'Totally. No greens or hippies. They're all people of good standing. Respectable local professionals – a doctor at Brooklands Hospital, a head teacher, the psychiatrist at the secure unit who treated Christie.'

'His own psychiatrist?'

'All of them saw him in the South Gate entrance hall when they heard the shooting. He was only a few feet away.'

'They recognized Christie? What about the earlier witnesses?'

'Unreliable. One or two people saw him running across the car park, but by then everybody was running away.'

'So . . .' I leaned back in sheer fatigue and stared at the heavy ceiling. 'If Christie didn't kill my father . . . ?'

'Someone else did. Brooklands CID are working twenty-four hours a day. We'll find him. Go back to London, Mr Pearson. You didn't really know your father. It's too late to start creating a whole lifetime's memories of him.'

'That's a little callous, Sergeant. There's always been a space in my life, and now I'm trying to fill it. One last thing. I saw you in Geoffrey Fairfax's office after the riot at the police station. He read my father's will and took me through his estate. When I left, you were heating milk for Mrs Christie's daughter.'

'So?' Sergeant Falconer watched me in the coolest way. 'I was part of the child protection unit assigned to Christie's next of kin.'

'In Fairfax's office?' I raised my hands to the air. 'He claimed that he no longer represented Christie. But he's still giving shelter to a murderer's wife.'

'Mr Fairfax had helped her before. With pocket money, hotel charges. He paid for her to take her baby on holiday. It's called charity, Mr Pearson. The better-off people in Brooklands still try to help the less fortunate.'

'Decent of them. Though Geoffrey Fairfax doesn't strike me as the charitable type. Territorial Army, riding to hounds, shotgun next to his desk. From what I saw, he's a bit of a fascist bully-boy. How on earth did he represent someone like Duncan Christie?'

'Solicitors represent the strangest people, Mr Pearson. There's no conflict of interest.'

'Exactly. Fairfax knew that Christie wouldn't be charged.'

'What are you suggesting?' The sergeant lowered her voice. 'A stitch-up involving the court?'

'Not a stitch-up. But Fairfax was confident that the case against Christie would be dropped. Otherwise he would have passed my father's estate to another firm of solicitors.'

'So how did he know?' Sergeant Falconer spoke in an offhand way, but with careful emphasis. 'Mr Pearson?'

'I can't say. But something about all this strikes me as more than a little odd . . .'

Sergeant Falconer stood up as her mobile rang. She answered it briefly, then spoke to the constables by the door. Returning to me, she smiled and briskly beckoned me to my feet.

'Go back to London, Mr Pearson. See your travel agent. I'm sorry about your father, but if you stir things up enough you'll create a hundred plots and conspiracies. Mr Pearson . . . ?'

I watched her as she waited for me to reply. She was almost trembling with impatience for me to leave. Somehow I had unsettled the ramshackle construction that she had built around herself in Brooklands, a card castle of compromises and half-truths that threatened to collapse onto her. Already I sensed that she was as much a pawn as I was. Geoffrey Fairfax had wanted me to see her in his office pantry, just as he had wanted me to see Mrs Christie sitting in the reception area.

Snapping her fingers, Sergeant Falconer turned away from me as an unmarked blue van halted outside the courthouse. The driver signalled to the constables on the steps. Doors slammed in a nearby corridor, and a group of short-sleeved ushers moved swiftly down the hall, sheltering a man whom they propelled towards the entrance.

I recognized Duncan Christie, face still bruised and unshaved, tieless white shirt buttoned to the throat, arms gripped by the ushers. For all the urgency, Christie seemed relaxed, smiling around him with the good-humoured arrogance of a millionaire footballer acquitted of a shoplifting charge. Behind him was his wife, still in her red serge jacket, torn lapel held back by a safety pin. Sergeant

Falconer dived into the scrum, held Mrs Christie and steered her down the steps.

But at least Christie had noticed me. As he approached the van he shook himself free from the ushers about to bundle him through the side door. Ignoring his wife, he seized Sergeant Falconer's arm and pointed to me as I stood alone outside the courthouse.

I walked back to my car, waving away the traffic warden who had placed a penalty ticket under the windscreen wiper and was waiting to see how I would react. For once, I was thinking about matters even more urgent than parking fines. As I started the engine I had already made my decision. Rather than return to London, I would become a temporary resident of Brooklands. These suburban streets beside the Metro-Centre and the M25 were the gaming board that my father's killer was still moving across. I was suspicious of the police, who would soon lose interest in the case. They had arrested the wrong man, and could easily do so again. Sergeant Falconer had done her best to confuse me, but the Metro-Centre seemed to disorient everyone in its shadow.

I might have been alone on the steps of the courthouse, but I had one important ally: my father. By drawing closer to him I would begin to see Brooklands through his eyes. I would live in his flat, cook in his kitchen, and even perhaps sleep in his bed. He and I were together now, and he would help me to find his murderer.

I was going home.

I moved away from the kerb, my eyes on the rear-view mirror. Thirty yards behind me, also parked on a double yellow line but free from the attentions of the traffic warden, was a familiar Range Rover, bull bars and hubcaps splashed with the best of Surrey mud. Out of curiosity, I made a sharp U-turn, and drove back past the courthouse.

Geoffrey Fairfax sat behind his steering wheel, head partly hidden inside a copy of *Country Life*, a solicitor keeping careful watch over his client.

7

Snakes and Ladders

THE SNAKES ON THE Brooklands board were only pretending to be asleep, and the ladders led anywhere.

I unlocked the front door and stepped into the darkened flat, lowering my suitcase to the floor. Around me were the few rooms, the now silent spaces of my father's life, even more unfamiliar than they had been four days earlier. I felt like a student returning after a year at a foreign university, unsettled by the strange shapes of the rooms in the family home.

No one was here to greet me, uncork a bottle of champagne or hand me the keys of my first sports car. But there was a welcome of another kind. I recognized my father's scent on the air, an old man's soft breath, the sweet tang of tobacco steeped into the curtains and carpets.

A presence I scarcely knew was already arraying itself around me. Should I sleep in my father's bed? I hesitated before entering his bedroom. Sleeping on his mattress, my head on his pillow as I dreamed of him, was too close for comfort. I left my suitcase in the hall and drew the curtains, aware that too much daylight would unnerve the ghosts.

In the bookcase beside the bed was a shelf of logbooks tracking his transits of the globe. There were biographies of test pilots of the 1960s, privately published by long-ago aircraft companies – Fairey, De Havilland, Avro – signed and dedicated to my father: 'For Stuart, who always kept flying speed . . .'

Amazingly, there was a copy of Saint-Exupéry's *Wind, Sand and Stars*, signed by my mother, sent to him two years after their divorce, a desperate attempt to reach out to him. As she lived with me in our large but sparsely furnished house, with the second-hand Mercedes and the need at all costs to keep up appearances, my father's life must have seemed effortlessly glamorous, exotic horizons coming up like an unending series of travel films.

I poured myself a small whisky before exploring his chest of drawers. Everyone had a sex life, and their own little habits, not all endearing. But there was nothing on the shelf of the bedside table, apart from a bottle of eye drops and a sachet of beta-blockers, with its line of foil punctures ending on the morning of his death. There were no sleeping pills or tranquillizers. The old pilot slept easily, and sleep was something to be dealt with quickly. My father had been a man who wanted to stay awake.

I carried my suitcase into the second bedroom, and opened the windows with their view of the Metro-Centre. Its presence was curiously inviting, filled with those treasures I had spent my childhood coveting. Despite our large house and Mercedes, the home my mother made for us was bleak. Very rarely did anything new enter our lives. We made do with an elderly TV set, an electric clock that tried bravely to guess the time, and a central heating system that whined ceaselessly to itself. Shops and department stores were places of magic. I was forever showing my mother advertisements for new toasters and washing machines, hoping that they would ease the strain of existence for her. Even my presents were rationed. A proportion of birthday gifts sent to me by her sister and friends was carefully set aside, locked away for future use, so that I was always outgrowing my gifts.

Surprisingly, I turned out to be rather spartan as an adult, living in large apartments that I kept almost unfurnished. I worked all day devising ways of selling people a host of consumer goods, but rarely bought anything unless I needed to. Childhood had inoculated me against the consumer world I longed for so eagerly.

Searching for sheets and pillowcases in the utility room, I noticed the workstation in the corner with its computer. My father's emails were still stacking up, messages and fixture lists from local sports clubs that he supported. I scrolled through the details of ice-hockey matches, archery and basketball contests. My father supported a huge number of teams, and must have exhausted himself trailing around from ice rink to football stadium to athletics ground.

But the books on the nearby shelf were even more of a surprise. Next to the yearbook of a small-arms manufacturer were biographies of Perón, Goering and Mussolini, and a history of Oswald Mosley and the British Union of Fascists. I pulled down an illustrated guide to Nazi regalia and the ceremonial uniforms of the Third Reich. The heavy, laminated paper was soft from frequent handling, and I could almost feel my father sitting at this desk and turning the pages as he scanned the illustrations of Reichsmarschalls' batons and leather SS overcoats.

A darker scent had crept into the flat. I sat back from the desk and pulled open the metal drawer. There was a clutter of Metro-Centre knick-knacks, loyalty gold cards and season passes, invitations to consumer clubs and sports events. A bulldog clip held a dozen issues of a Metro-Centre newsletter, filled with photographs of sporting club dinners, everyone in their St George's shirts. The teams looked as smart and disciplined as paramilitary units.

Present in several of the group portraits was David Cruise, the Metro-Centre cable-channel presenter, with his actor's handsome but empty face, a suntan like an advertising campaign and a smile that owed nothing to humour. His fleshy jaw made me think of Wernher von Braun posing beside a Redstone rocket in Arizona, Nazi past behind him and the future on hold.

Was my father a National Front supporter? Sleep would be less easy in the flat than I hoped. I opened the window, trying to let out the unpleasant aura, and noticed a banner hanging from the wall behind the door. This bore the emblem of a local football club, the Brookland Eagles. Embroidered in gold thread, two raptors with grotesquely hooked talons grimaced from the scarlet field.

My father's interests had taken him into some threatening arenas. The modest workstation was almost a neo-fascist altar. I paused by the neatly pressed laundry on the ironing board. Lifting one of the shirts, I unfolded the familiar St George's Cross, armorial eagles stitched to its left shoulder. I held the shirt to my chest, and imagined my elderly father wearing this threatening costume with its screaming eagles, the oldest football hooligan in Brooklands.

I stared at myself in the half-length mirror above the maid's kettle and biscuit tin. The tasselled banner hung behind me, as if I were on a podium that faced a chanting crowd. I seemed more aggressive, not in the bully-boy way of the street thugs who had driven the imam from his suburban mosque, but in the more cerebral style of the lawyers, doctors and architects who had enlisted in Hitler's elite corps. For them, the black uniforms and death's-head emblems represented a violence of the mind, where aggression and cruelty were part of a radical code that denied good and evil in favour of an embraced pathology. Morality gave way to will, and will deferred to madness.

I tried to smile, but a different self stood behind the shirt. My cautious take on the world, imposed on me by my neurotic mother, had given way to something far less introverted. The focus of my face moved from my eyes and high forehead to my mouth and jaw. The muscles in my face were more visible, the strings of a harder appetite, a more knowing hunger . . .

I threw the shirt into the empty laundry basket.

What dangerous game had my father been playing? Years of mismanaged third world airports brought out a nasty strain of racism in senior pilots. Or was there something fascist about flight itself? Death, far from closing his life, had opened the door to a dozen possible futures. Already he was a different man from the wise and sympathetic figure I had imagined. What sort of father would he have made? I sensed my free and easy childhood, scarcely controlled by my distracted mother, giving way to a more disciplined regime. Discipline as a means of instilling love . . . ?

The flat was airless, and I needed to pace a car park somewhere to clear my head. I closed the door behind me and left the apartment house, listening to my feet on the gravel, a horizontal slide area where nothing was firmly bedded.

I was sitting in the driving seat of the Jensen, waiting for my mental compass to reset itself, when a grey Audi turned into the car park beside me. A tall, middle-aged Asian in a creased business suit stepped out. As his large shoes ploughed their way to the entrance doors, I noticed that he was carrying a rolled-up newspaper in his right hand, tapping the air like a bandmaster beating time. His bulky chest and shoulders reminded me of the intruder I had pinned briefly to the wall.

'Excuse me . . . ! Sir, can you wait . . . ?'

I caught up with him in the lobby, as he searched for his keys to the ground-floor flat. Startled when I burst through the doors, he dropped the keys onto the tiled floor. None of my neighbours had called on me to express their sympathies, but this Asian resident would have seen me coming and going, and must have guessed who I was.

Trying to calm him, I introduced myself. 'Richard Pearson – I'm Captain Pearson's son. He died in the Metro-Centre shooting. You remember . . . ?'

'Of course. My deepest sympathies.' His eyes moved quickly over my grey suit and tie and then turned to the lobby doors, as if he suspected that an accomplice might be lurking outside. 'A shocking affair, even for Brooklands.'

'For Brooklands . . . ?' I bent down and retrieved his keys, then handed them to him, conscious of the rolled-up newspaper and the bandage around his right wrist. 'Tell me, Mr –?'

'Kumar. Nihal Kumar. I'm resident here for many years.'

'Good. It's a pleasant little backwater. We've met before, Mr Kumar. No . . . ?'

'It's not likely.' Kumar pumped his doorbell, too confused to use his keys. 'Perhaps when your father . . . ?'

'A few days ago. I left the door of the flat open. You probably thought a burglar had broken in. I still have your medical journal. You are a doctor?'

'Definitely not.' He gestured wearily. 'My professional background is in engineering. I'm the manager of Motorola's research laboratory in Brooklands. My wife is a doctor.'

'A paediatrician? That makes sense.' I was still puzzled by his extreme unease with me, and tried to shake his hand. 'I should have been more careful. My father's death, I was on edge.'

'It's to be expected.' Kumar seemed to relax a little, reassured that I was not about to harm him. 'It's best to keep your door locked. At all times.'

'Thanks for the tip. There's a lot of crime here?'

'Crime, certainly. And violence.'

'I've noticed that. These towns along the M25. There's something in the air. I take it there are right-wing groups here?'

'Many. They create real fear.' Kumar pressed his bell again, impatient to enter his flat. 'The Asian community is deeply concerned. In the old days there were organized attacks, but they were predictable. Now we see violence for its own sake.'

'These so-called sports clubs?'

'Sports? Just one sport. Beating people up.'

'Asians, mostly?'

'Asians, Kosovans, Bosnians. Far too many sports clubs. The police should stop them.'

'I think my father belonged to one.' When Kumar made no reply, I said: 'You knew my father?'

'Lately, not so well. When we first came to Brooklands he was very charming to my wife. He made us feel at home. Later . . .'

'He changed?'

'His new friends . . . sometimes they were here. They frightened my wife.'

'My father wasn't violent?'

'Your father was a gentleman. But the atmosphere was different . . . everywhere the red crosses, not to help people but to hurt them.'

'I'm sorry. Tell me, Mr Kumar, all this violence – where do you think it's coming from?'

'The Metro-Centre? It's possible.'

'How? It's just a large shop.'

'It's more than a shop, Mr Pearson. It's an incubator. People go in there and they wake up, they see their lives are empty. So they look for a new dream . . .'

He reached for the bell, but his front door opened quietly. An elegant Asian woman in her fifties with a high forehead and severe face stared out at us. I assumed that Dr Kumar had been listening to everything we said. Her eyes followed me up the stairs, waiting until I was safely out of sight before she stepped aside to admit her husband.

8

Accidents and Emergencies

THE WAITING ROOM in the Accident & Emergency department at
Brooklands Hospital was almost empty when I sat down. A
teenager with a bruised cheek fiddled with a broken mobile phone.
A mildly hysterical woman argued endlessly about a traffic inter-
section with her passive husband. An elderly man with a damp
tissue to his eyes waited for news of his wife. Lastly, there was
myself, more uncertain about my father than I had been when I
first arrived. Together we were a collection of the ill-equipped
and unsaved – a playground brawl, a wrong right turn, a heart
too weary to embark on its next beat, and an assassin's bullet had
brought us together.

Dr Julia Goodwin, who had treated my father when he was driven
from the Metro-Centre, would see me shortly, according to one of
the nurses. But the clock on the wall disagreed, and as usual over-
ruled her. I tried to read the local newspaper, smiled as comfortingly
as I could at the elderly man, and watched the TV set.

It was tuned to the Metro-Centre cable channel, and showed
an afternoon discussion programme transmitted from the mezzanine studio. The suntanned face of David Cruise dominated everything, and covered the proceedings like a cheap but over-bright
lacquer. He was smiling and affable, but faintly hostile, like a
bullying valet. Perhaps people in the motorway towns liked to be
shouted at.

'Mr Pearson?' The nurse positioned her broad hips in front of the set. 'Dr Goodwin will see you. For a few minutes . . . she's very busy.'

'Fine. How lucky to be busy . . .'

Dr Julia Goodwin was standing with her back to me in the small office, slamming the metal drawers of a filing cabinet as if playing an arcade pin-table. When she glanced at me through her defensive fringe I recognized the young woman at the Golders Green crematorium, watching me in a morose way as her friend fiddled with the ignition keys. There was the same evasive gaze, and I sensed that she was aware of something about me that I had yet to learn. She was attractive, but had been tired for too long, still trying to scrape a little compassion for her patients from the bottom of a long-exhausted barrel.

After introducing myself, I said: 'It's kind of you to see me. You were one of the last people to be with my father. It helps to keep him alive.'

'Good . . . I'm glad.' She placed her worn hands on the desk, like a blackjack dealer laying out the last two cards. 'I'm sorry I couldn't do more. Sometimes you try to pull off a miracle and end up making a complete balls of things, but I did my best for him. A horrible business. That awful mall . . .'

'The Metro-Centre?'

'Don't tell me you haven't noticed it?' She unbuttoned her white coat, revealing a cashmere sweater of stylish cut. 'That huge atrium, all those people shopping themselves out of their little minds. If you ask me, a standing temptation to any madman with a grudge. Sadly, your father got in the way.'

'Was he conscious at all? When you saw him?'

'No. The bullet . . .' She touched the mass of dark hair above her left ear and traced a line to the back of her neck, an almost erotic transit that exposed the silky whiteness of her scalp. 'He felt nothing. Getting him to the Royal Free was his only hope. But . . .'

'You tried, and I'm grateful. You'd met him before?'

She stared at me, then tilted her hands so that she could read her palms. 'Not as far as I know.'

'You came to the funeral. I remember seeing you there.'

She sat back, ready to end our chat, and her gaze drifted over my shoulder. She was uncomfortable with my presence, but wanted to keep me in her office. I had the sense that she had been briefed about me, and knew more of my background than might have been expected of a busy casualty doctor.

'Yes. I drove up to Golders Green with a friend. A hell of a long way, and a lousy service. Who on earth writes those ghastly scripts? You can see why death isn't exactly popular. They ought to play a little Cole Porter and pass around the canapés.' She smiled boldly, waving away her little duplicity. 'He seemed a decent old boy, so I thought I'd go. After all, Brooklands killed him.'

'You felt guilty?'

'In a way. No. What tripe! Do I really believe that? It's amazing the nonsense that can pop out of your mouth if you aren't careful.'

'When he was brought in, was he wearing his clothes?'

'As far as I know. You sound like a detective.'

'Brooklands does that to you. Can you remember what he had on?'

'Haven't a clue.' She turned and slammed a metal drawer sticking into her back. 'Is that important?'

'It might be. Was he wearing a St George's shirt? You know, the red cross –'

'Of course I know!' She grimaced and turned to the pedal bin, ready to spit into it. 'I hate those bloody shirts. I'm sure he wasn't wearing one. Does it matter? Death doesn't have a dress code.'

'Easy to say. Those shirts are the signifier for a new kind of . . .'

'Fascism? Hard word to get out, isn't it? I don't suppose you hear it that often in the King's Road. They're worn by most of our local storm troopers.' Dr Goodwin spoke firmly, addressing a thoughtless child about to burn himself on a hot stove. 'Keep away from all that vicious nonsense. Your father would have agreed with me.'

'That's what I thought. This morning I found a whole pile of them in his flat. Freshly ironed by the Filipina maid. A neighbour told me that sports-club members sometimes came to see him.'

'Hard to believe. He was seventy-five. A bit late to be beating up asylum seekers.'

'It might have made him a target. If he was wearing one when he was shot.'

I waited for Dr Goodwin to respond, but she was staring through the window at two ten-year-old boys roaming around the consultants' car park. When one of them prised the triton from a Mercedes bonnet she smiled in an almost girlish way, happy to share their freedom and irresponsibility.

'Mr Pearson?' She looked at me with an odd blend of hostility and raunchiness. 'You live in London?'

'Chelsea Harbour. Millionaire's toytown. My flat's on the market.'

'I might buy it. Anything to get away from this terrible place.'

'You don't like it? Prosperous Surrey, clean air, leafy lanes to walk the Labrador?'

'All that crap. It frightens me.' She lowered her voice. 'There are things going on here . . . you've been to the Metro-Centre?'

'It's very impressive. Pure purchasing power vibrating through the ether.'

'Ugh. It's a pressure cooker. With the lid screwed down and the hob on high.'

'And what is it cooking?'

'Something nasty, believe me. So, where are you staying?'

'At my father's flat.'

'Good for you.' She smiled unaffectedly. 'That's pretty brave.'

She stood up and I assumed our appointment was at an end, but she hovered by the door. Some kind of plan was being hatched by this attractive but edgy woman, so clearly in conflict with herself.

'I go off duty at six.' Her palm rested on the door handle. 'I think I need cheering up. You could buy me a drink.'

'Of course.' Surprised, I said: 'My pleasure.'

'Maybe. Don't bet on it. I'm in a bit of a mood. I'll meet you by the Holiday Inn. There's a bar near the open-air pool. After a couple of gins you can imagine you're in Acapulco . . .'

*   *   *

I sat in the cafeteria next to the hospital's retail centre, thinking over my meeting with the troubled Julia Goodwin. She saw herself as setting me up, and I was happy to play along. I was sure that she knew more about my father's death than she admitted. Busy doctors did not travel across the whole of London to attend the funerals of strangers. I remembered the sly way she had watched me from the crematorium car park. But she was attractive, and at least she was coming towards me. Everyone else I had met – Sergeant Mary Falconer, Geoffrey Fairfax, and my neighbour Mr Kumar – had been retreating behind elaborate screens of their own.

I opened the local newspaper, which Julia Goodwin had handed to me as I left her office. Its pages were crammed with advertisements for a huge range of consumer goods. Every citizen of Brooklands, every resident within sight of the M25, was constantly trading the contents of house and home, replacing the same cars and cameras, the same ceramic hobs and fitted bathrooms. Nothing was being swapped for nothing. Behind this frantic turnover, a gigantic boredom prevailed.

Sharing that boredom, I broke an advertising man's habit of a lifetime and began to read the editorial columns. On page three, the only space in the paper devoted to real news, was an account of the magistrates' hearing at which Duncan Christie had been discharged. 'Metro-Centre Shooting . . . Man Released . . . Police Renew Inquiries.'

I scanned the brief report, and the summaries of witness statements. The three 'prominent' witnesses were named, local worthies who testified that they had seen Christie in the South Gate entrance at the moment of the shooting.

They were named as: Dr Tony Maxted, consultant psychiatrist at the Northfield mental hospital, and William Sangster, head teacher at Brooklands High School. The third was Julia Goodwin.

9

The Beach at the Holiday Inn

THE HOLIDAY INN was a seven-storey tower, its terraced bar over-looking a circular swimming pool whose waters lapped a crescent of sandy beach. Umbrellas and sun loungers furnished the beach, and an even-tempered and ultraviolet-free light played over the scene. All this was deep inside the Metro-Centre, in a district dominated by its hotels, cafés and emporia filled with sporting goods. A visitor to the Holiday Inn, or to the nearby Novotel and Ramada Inn, could imagine that this was part of a leisure complex in a suburb of Tokyo or Shanghai.

I ordered a glass of wine from a waitress dressed like a tennis instructor and gazed over the deserted beach with its immaculate sand and rows of waiting sun loungers. The wave machine had been turned to its lowest setting, and a vaguely gastric swell, like a suppressed vomit reflex, flowed across the colourized water.

Already I wondered why Julia Goodwin had chosen this rendezvous in the mall where my father had met his death. I watched her approach the terrace, half an hour late, throwing her gum into the sluggish surf. Her hospital identification tag hung from the lapel of her jacket, and she had loosened her hair, a thick black cloud like the smokescreen of a nervous destroyer. She spoke to the waitress as if addressing a subnormal patient, and ordered a tonic water with two dashes of Angostura.

'Comfortable?' I asked when she sat herself at the terrace table. 'Why are we meeting here?'

'I'm sorry . . . ?'

'This is kitsch with a strychnine chaser. It's where my father was shot.'

Surprised by my sharp tone, she sat forward and lifted the hair from her eyes. 'Look, I thought we ought to see it together. In a way, it explains why your father died. I didn't mean to upset you. What do you think of the beach?'

'Better than Acapulco. I'm getting a tan already.'

'As good as the real thing?'

'It's not meant to be the real thing.' I decided to calm her, and shaped my mouth into the kind of easy smile favoured by David Cruise. 'It's all part of a good-natured joke. Everyone knows that.'

'Do they? I hope you're right. These days even reality has to look artificial.'

'Maybe. My father was real, hit by a very real bullet. Why do you say the Metro-Centre can explain his death?'

She sipped her tonic and Angostura, letting the points of effervescence bead on her eyelashes. She was still wary, unsure of me and my motives for seeing her. 'Richard, think about it for a moment. People come in here looking for something worthwhile. What do they find? Everything is invented, all the emotions, all the reasons for living. It's an imaginary world, created by people like you. A madman walks in with a gun and thinks he's in a shooting gallery. Perhaps he is, inside his head.'

'So . . . ?'

'Why not start shooting? There are plenty of targets, and no one looks as if they'd mind all that much.' She stopped suddenly and sat back. 'Christ . . . what bullshit. Do you believe a word of that?'

'No.' Won over, I ordered another round from the waitress. 'But you hate the Metro-Centre.'

'It's not just this ghastly place. All these retail parks are the same. Rootless people drifting about. The only time they touch reality is when they fall ill and come to see me. Educated, well nourished, kind to their children . . .'

'But savages?'

'Not all, no.' She reached up with both hands and gathered her hair together. She pinned it inside a rubber band that had probably secured a patient's medical file, and then moved my wineglass out of the way so that she could speak more forcefully. 'There's a new kind of human being who's appeared on the scene. These are people who behave in strange ways and should know better.'

'Casualty doctors?'

'Doctors, lawyers, police officers, bank managers . . . they get funny ideas in their heads. Some of them start thinking logically.'

'Is that bad?'

'Thinking logically? Out here it's dangerous. Very dangerous. It can lead intelligent people to do things they shouldn't, like acting rationally and for the public good. Take it from me. Anywhere near the M25 is dangerous.'

'Why don't you leave?'

'I will. First, there are things that need sorting out. I got myself involved in something rather foolish that I wasn't really bargaining for . . .'

She stared at a wave advancing towards us. Exposed to the light, her face was pale but surprisingly strong, marked by tremors of doubt like those of an actress unable to understand her lines. When she saw me watching her she reached up to loosen her hair, but I held her wrists and pressed them to the table until she controlled herself.

'Julia . . . take it easy.'

'Right. I'll join Médecins Sans Frontières. Go to somewhere in the third world where the beaches still smell of dead fish. I might even do some good.'

'You're doing good here,' I told her. 'Try believing in yourself.'

'Impossible. Besides, the A&E thing is self-inflicted. Drunks, car crashes, brawling, fist fights. There's a huge amount of street violence. People don't know it, but they're bored out of their minds. Sport is the big giveaway. Wherever sport plays a big part in people's lives you can be sure they're bored witless and just waiting to break up the furniture.'

'You'll have to move. Just one problem: wherever you go you'll find nothing except a new kind of boredom.'

'That sounds fun. We could go together. You invent the reality and afterwards I'll put on the band-aids.'

I liked her, and was glad that she seemed to enjoy the banter. But she withdrew from me as soon as I tried to hold her eyes, watching the waves rather than face up to whatever she was concealing.

The terrace around us had filled with evening drinkers. Groups of middle-aged men and women, almost all wearing St George's shirts, stood, glasses in hand, smoking and patting their midriffs. They spilled onto the pedestrian piazza outside the hotel entrance. The embroidered badges on their shirts showed that they were members of a Metro-Centre supporters' club. They were loud but self-controlled, hailing new arrivals with friendly cheers.

'Football supporters?' I said to Julia Goodwin. 'They seem amiable enough.'

'Are you sure? I dare say I'll be seeing some of them at A&E tonight.'

'The match started at seven – they've missed the first half.'

'These are not the sort of supporters who go to matches. They're here for the punch-up.'

'Hooligans?'

'Definitely not. They're well organized, practically local militias. Take a good look, and then keep out of their way.'

The drinkers downed their beers and left the terrace, forming into paunchy platoons each led by a marshal. They moved off to a chorus of ironic cheers, a woman member breaking ranks to dart into a nearby deli. But their marching was brisk and in step, and I guessed that Julia had arranged to meet me at the Holiday Inn so that I would get a glimpse of a darker side of Brooklands.

She pretended to fiddle with her handbag as smoke drifted across us from a dozen ashtrays. She knew what my next question would be, since she had made a point of giving me the local newspaper. A slow confession was emerging, as sluggish as the simulated wave.

'Julia . . . before I forget. You testified at the magistrates' court.'

'I did, yes. So?'

'Why, exactly?'

'It was the public-spirited thing to do. Wouldn't you?'

'Probably. Did you really see Duncan Christie there? At the time you heard the shots?'

'Absolutely.'

'How far away was he?'

'God knows. Ten or fifteen feet. I saw him clearly.'

'In all that crush of people?' I looked round, hoping that someone would switch off the wave machine. 'You remembered this one face in the crowd?'

'Yes!' Julia leaned across the table, angry with me for being so obtuse. 'I've often treated him. He's always being attacked and beaten up.'

'What was he doing in the Metro-Centre? He hates the place.'

'I haven't a bloody idea. He likes to keep an eye on it.'

'Hard to believe. For that matter, what were you doing there? You hate the place as much as he does.'

'I can't remember. I happened to be passing.'

'Like the other witnesses – his own psychiatrist who arranged to have him released that day from his mental hospital. And the head teacher who taught him at the local high school. And you. Three people who just happened to be there and thought of some shopping they needed to do. And you all arrive at the same time . . .'

'Jesus Christ . . . !' Julia drummed her fists on the table, bouncing my wineglass onto the tiled floor. 'A lot of people in Brooklands know Duncan Christie. He's the local character, almost the village idiot.'

'Right. He used to be represented by Geoffrey Fairfax's office. I saw you there the evening Christie was brought back to Brooklands.'

'Geoffrey Fairfax? Sounds unlikely. You've been listening to too many garbled stories.'

'Julia . . . for God's sake.' Impatient with her mock innocence, I raised my voice, hoping that I could jolt the truth from this likeable young doctor with her almost desperate denials. 'You were sitting with your back to me in the conference room, hiding behind that wonderful hair. I take it the people you were with were the other witnesses?'

'Yes . . .' Julia stared at the broken wineglass at her feet. 'They probably were.'

'Don't you think that's odd? Christie had only just been arrested, but already the key witnesses were lined up, synchronizing their watches. The really strange thing is that I was supposed to see you – the witnesses in the conference room, Mrs Christie in reception, Sergeant Falconer heating the milk. It was laid on like the reconstruction of a crime. Why, Julia? What was it meant to tell me?'

'Ask Geoffrey Fairfax.' She straightened her jacket, ready to leave. 'He might tell you.'

'I doubt it. He's mad, but he's sly. On the outside, a very pukka, old-fashioned solicitor. On the inside, a raving, right-wing nutter. I wouldn't expect either to pull out all the stops for this "shabby misfit".'

A little weakly, Julia said: 'People sympathize with Christie.'

'For standing against the mall? Who exactly? Small shopkeepers, Thames Valley Poujadists?'

'Not just the mall. All these retail parks look peaceful to you, but behind them something very nasty is going on. Christie and Geoffrey Fairfax saw this a long time ago.'

'Did Christie kill my father?'

'No!' Julia stood up, driving the table into my elbows. She stared wildly at the approaching wave as if it were a tsunami about to climb the beach and overwhelm her. 'I know Duncan Christie. I've stitched his scalp, I've set his fractures. He couldn't . . .'

She was shaking, unable to control herself. I leapt up and held her shoulders, surprised by how frail she seemed.

'Julia, you're right. Someone else shot my father. I want you to help me find him. Forget about Duncan Christie and Fairfax . . .'

She let me steer her into her chair. For a few seconds she held tightly to my arms, then pushed me away with a grimace of irritation at her own weakness. She spoke calmly to the wave.

'I'm sure I saw Christie near the entrance. At least, I think I saw him . . .'

10

Street People

'THIS PLACE COULD drive anyone completely sane.' Julia Goodwin scraped a fragment of glass from her shoe. 'Don't tell me there aren't any exits.'

'I'll give you a lift home. What happened to your car?'

'It's . . . being serviced.'

She strode on ahead as I paid the bill. Her confidence, of a gimcrack kind, had been restored. Her patients rarely spoke back to her, and she had been unnerved by my questions, aware that even if Duncan Christie was innocent she had in some way been lying to herself. But an unusual cover-up was taking place, parts of which I was being allowed to see.

We crossed the central atrium, skirting the giant bears with their patched fur and get-well offerings of treacle and honey. Customers wandered by, like tourists in a foreign city. There were no clocks in the Metro-Centre, no past or future. The only clue to the time was the football match on the overhead monitor screens. Arrays of flood-lights shone through the black haze, and the screens at either end of the ground carried the familiar face of David Cruise, a retail messiah for the age of cable TV.

We left the Metro-Centre by one of the exit-only doors, and walked towards the car park. Groups of sports supporters were leaving the dome, bearing the banners of local ice-hockey and athletics teams. They formed up among their four-wheel drives, and marched away in step to the evening's venues.

Following Julia's directions, we set off through the empty office quarter of the town, moving past entrances sealed with steel grilles.

'They're waiting for something,' I commented. 'Where are we going?'

'South Brooklands. I know a short cut. You're happy with one-way streets?'

'One-way? Why not?'

'The wrong way? It saves time. Risk nothing, lose everything.'

We passed the magistrates' court, then turned into an area of discount furniture stores, warehousing and car-rental firms. The football stadium seemed to remain for ever on our left, as if we were circling it at a safe distance, uneager to be drawn into its huge magnetic field.

'Okay.' Julia leaned into the windscreen. 'Turn left. No, right.'

'Here?' I hesitated before passing a no-entry sign guarding a street of shabby houses. 'Where are we?'

'I told you. It's a short cut.'

'To the nearest police pound? Doctor, always wear your seat belt. Is this some sort of courtship ritual?'

'I bloody hope not. Anyway, seat belts are sexual restraints.'

I looked out at the modest houses, with their deco doors and windows, a fossil of the 1930s now occupied by immigrant families. A terrace of small semis stood by untended front gardens, battered vans parked on the worn grass. Everything was bathed in the intense glare of the stadium lights, as if the area was being interrogated over its failure to join the consumer society. Whenever they glanced from their windows, the east European and Asian tenants would see the giant face of David Cruise smiling on his silver screens.

'Let's get out of here.' I braked to avoid a cavernous pothole. 'What a place to live.'

'You're talking about my patients.' Julia shielded her eyes from the glare. 'Mostly Bangladeshis. They're very ambitious.'

'Thank God. They need to be.'

'They are. Their biggest dream is to be cleaners and janitors at the Metro-Centre. Remember that when you next have a pee . . .'

We moved to the fringes of the residential area, and passed an ice-hockey arena for the second time, forced to slow down when a group of banner-waving supporters blocked the road. Three hundred yards from the football stadium, among the slip roads that led to the motorway, was an athletics ground laid with a lurid artificial track, bathed in the same intense glare of lighting arrays. Groups of supporters stood in the street, awaiting the result of a long-distance race.

'Why don't they go in?' I asked Julia. 'The stands are almost empty.'

'Maybe they're not that interested.'

'Hard to believe. What are they doing here?'

'They're enforcers.'

'Enforcing what?'

We reached a crossroads, and turned left into another residential district. The football match had ended, and spectators were spilling out into the streets surrounding the stadium. David Cruise was alone again, talking to his double at the far end of the ground about a range of men's colognes and grooming aids. Fragments of the sales pitch boomed through the night air, drumming like fists against the windows of the cowed little houses.

'Julia, we keep heading back to the stadium. What exactly is going on?'

'The Brooklands story. Look out for an old cinema . . . don't worry, we're not going to hold hands in the movies.'

The first spectators passed us, men and their wives in St George's shirts, good-humouredly banging the roofs of the parked cars. Part of the crowd had broken away from the main body, and was moving down a street of small Asian food wholesalers. The men were burly but disciplined, led by marshals in red baseball caps, shouting into their mobile phones. The crowd marched behind them, jeering at the silent shops. A group of younger supporters hurled coins at the upstairs windows. The sound of breaking glass cut the night like an animal cry.

'Julia! Seat belt! Where the hell are the police?'

'These are the police . . .' Julia fumbled with the catch, losing the buckle in the dark. She was shocked but excited, like a rugby girl-friend at her first brutal match.

Cars were coming towards us, driving three abreast, headlights full on. Behind them came a pack of supporters in full cry, brawling with the young Asians who emerged to defend their shops. Someone was kicked to the ground, and there was a flurry of white trainers like snowballs in a blizzard.

I swung the wheel, throwing Julia against the passenger door, and slewed the Jensen into a parking space as the cars swept past, slamming my wing mirror with a sound like a gunshot. Somewhere a plate-glass window fell to the pavement, and a torrent of razor ice scattered under the running feet.

The crowd surged past us, fists beating on the car roof. An overweight and thuggish man bellowed into his mobile while launching kicks at an elderly Asian trying to guard the doorway of his hardware shop. The supporters strode in step, chanting and disciplined, but seemed to have no idea where their marshals were leading them, happy to shout at the dark and trash whatever street they were marching down.

'Julia! Don't leave the car.'

Julia was hiding her face from the men calling to her through the passenger window, urging her to join them. I opened my door and stepped into the street. On the opposite pavement a middle-aged Asian was down on his knees, trying to steady himself against a vandalized parking meter. A thin-faced youth in a St George's shirt danced around him, feinting and kicking as if he was taking a series of penalties, cheering and raising his hands each time he scored.

'Mr Kumar . . . !'

I seized the young man by the arm and pushed him away. He shouted good-humouredly, happy to let me have a go at the next penalty. He danced off, feet scattering the broken glass. I helped Mr Kumar to stand, then steered the bulky man towards the service alley beside a small cash-and-carry.

'Please . . . my car.'

'Where are you parked? Mr Kumar . . . !'

He was dazed and dishevelled, gazing over my shoulder at the crowd as if trying to grasp who exactly they were. Then he glanced into my face, recognizing me with an appalled stare.

'No . . . no . . . never . . .'

He broke away from me before I could reassure him, heavy arms thrusting me aside, and stumbled into the darkness of the alley.

Trying to catch my breath, I followed him into the next street. The marchers were returning to the stadium, and car doors slammed as they sounded their horns and drove away. Mr Kumar had vanished, perhaps taking refuge with local friends he had been visiting. Young Asian men were sweeping glass from the pavement into the gutters, smoking their cigarettes as they listened to the night.

I walked along the deserted street, lost in the glare of the stadium floodlights. Across the road was a disused cinema, a 1930s white-tile Odeon like a shabby iceberg, for years a bingo hall and now a carpet warehouse.

A police car approached, cruising the silent streets as if nothing had happened. I climbed the steps to the shuttered box office. The ancient Odeon was no longer even a ghost of itself, and violence had long since migrated from the screen to the surrounding streets. But its tiled alcoves, like the corners of a huge public lavatory, offered a moment's shelter.

From the shadows I watched the police car pause outside the Odeon, then dip and flash its lights. I recognized the senior police officer in the passenger seat, Superintendent Leighton of the Brooklands force, whose photograph had been printed in the local newspaper that I read in the hospital cafeteria. Beside him, at the wheel, sat Sergeant Falconer, uniform cap over her immaculate Rhine-maiden hair. They waited outside the cinema, like a courting couple deciding whether to see a double feature, then flashed their lights at the empty street and continued their patrol.

Next to the Odeon was the cinema car park, empty except for a mud-spattered Range Rover. The driver was watching the street, speaking into his mobile phone. He wore a heavy Barbour jacket, trilby over his eyes, still unmistakably Geoffrey Fairfax. Beside him was a crop-haired man with a large Roman head, wearing a sheep-skin jacket. Together they resembled hunt supporters following the hounds, happy to watch the chase from the comfort of their car, fortified by a thermos of warm brandy.

But were they leading the hunt, rather than following it? In the seat behind them were two men in St George's shirts, muscled arms pressed against the windows. Both spoke freely to Fairfax and his passenger, pointing to the nearby road junctions as if describing an order of battle and reporting on the morale and enthusiasm of the troops.

A map was passed between the men, and Fairfax switched on the ceiling light. After consulting the map he started the engine, but I had seen clearly that there was a fifth person in the Range Rover.

Sitting in the rear between the two men in St George's shirts, hair loose around her shoulders, was Dr Julia Goodwin.

I walked back to my car, stepping through shadows and avoiding the Asian men trying to clear up their shopfronts. Drowned by the glare of stadium lights, flames rose from a burning house.

11

A Hard Night

LIKE ENGLISH LIFE as a whole, nothing in Brooklands could be taken at face value. I passed the next three days in my father's flat, trying to make sense of this outwardly civilized Home Counties town – a town whose civic leaders, prominent solicitors and police chief were taking part in a pocket revolution. Had I stumbled into a conspiracy that was now shaping itself around me? And had my father been one of its instigators?

The stadium riot, orchestrated by Geoffrey Fairfax under the eyes of the police superintendent, had shaken me badly. Sipping rather too much of the old man's malt, I watched the car park outside the flats, hoping to see Mr Kumar and convince him that I had not joined the attack on him. During the mêlée someone had punched my forehead, and the imprint of a signet ring starred the skin over my left eye. Staring at myself in the hall mirror, I could almost see Duncan Christie's bruised face emerging through my own.

All in all, my first taste of street politics left me feeling like an out-of-condition rugby forward in a collapsed scrum. How, at the age of seventy-five, had my father coped with the violence and thuggery? In the evening, watching television with the sound down and the curtains drawn, I listened to the stadium crowds cheering on the Metro-Centre teams. Ambulance sirens wailed through the streets, and fire engines clanged their way to the shabby districts between Brooklands and the M25.

A hard night lay over the motorway towns, far harder than central

London's pink haze. Under the cover of a packed programme of sporting events, an exercise in ethnic cleansing was taking place, with the apparent connivance of the local police. I remembered Sergeant Falconer flashing her headlights at Fairfax's Range Rover. Using the supporters' clubs in their patriotic livery, they were moving against the immigrant population, harassing them out of their run-down streets to make room for new retail parks, marinas and executive estates.

But more than a land grab was going on. Every evening there were soccer, rugby and athletics matches, where Metro-Centre teams competed with rivals from the motorway towns. Illuminated arrays glowed through the night like the perimeter lights of a colony of prison camps, a new gulag of penal settlements where the forced labour was shopping and spending.

The matches ended, but then came the drumming of fists on car roofs, a tribal call to violence. The Audis, Nissans and Renaults were the new tom-toms. Every day the local newspaper reported attacks on an asylum hostel, the torching of a Bangladeshi takeaway, injuries to a Kosovan youth thrown over the fence into an industrial estate. Metro-Centre stewards, the reports usually ended, had 'headed off further violence'.

On his afternoon cable channel, David Cruise smirked knowingly to his guests. I watched this third-rate actor, on the surface so handsome and likeable, putting his well-polished gloss on the ugly violence.

'. . . I don't want to blow the Metro-Centre's trumpet, but consumerism is about a lot more than buying things. You agree, Doreen? Good. It's our main way of expressing our tribal values, of engaging with each other's hopes and ambitions. What you see here is a conflict of recreational cultures, a clash of very different lifestyles. On the one side are people like us – we enjoy the facilities offered by the Metro-Centre, and depend on the high values and ideals maintained by the mall and its suppliers. Together they probably do a better job of representing your real interests than your Member of Parliament. No disrespect, and no emails, please. On the other side are the low-value expectations of the immigrant communities. Their suppressed womenfolk are internal exiles who never share the dignity and freedom to choose that we see in the consumer ideal. Right, Sheila?'

As always, his guests nodded their firm agreement, sitting in their black leather sofas in the mezzanine studio, the giant bears behind them. But that night brought attacks on Asian businesses by gangs of rugby and ice-hockey supporters, and a warehouse of cheap knitwear burned to the ground. And, as always, the police arrived ten minutes after the fire engines. Almost nothing appeared in the national press, where the incidents were lumped in with accounts of sporting violence and binge drinking in provincial towns.

What role had my father played in all this? I thought of the old pilot sitting at his workstation in the cluttered utility room, with the ironing board and its stack of St George's shirts, surrounded by his sinister library, a shrine to the extremist gods. Was he a casualty of an ultra-right coup, an elderly foot soldier who had lost his balance on the slippery grass of a political turf war? Conceivably, he was not an innocent bystander but the real target of the assassin.

Had the shooting at the mall been an attempt to damage the Metro-Centre? In a special feature on mega-malls the *Financial Times* reported that turnover at the Metro-Centre had failed to grow for the past year, as its novelty wore off and its customers were drawn to more downmarket retail parks in the area.

The shooting, with its dead and injured customers, had cost sales, whatever Tom Carradine claimed. But no well-run conspiracy would have hired a misfit like Duncan Christie. At the same time I found it hard to believe the witnesses who came forward to clear him. I thought of Julia Goodwin, sitting between the beefy marshals in the rear of Fairfax's Range Rover, while Fairfax consulted his war map.

I wanted to meet her again, but everything about her was almost too elusive. At the Holiday Inn, beside the placid waters of the artificial lake, she had been nervous and aggressive, a little too devious about her reasons for attending my father's funeral. At the same time I was sure that she wanted to tell me something about his death, perhaps more than I cared to know.

The entire evening had been an elaborate ruse, a clumsily handled tour of Brooklands and its accident black spots. She had known that the race riot would take place, and wanted me to witness it. But was she trying to warn me away, or recruit me into her suburban conspiracy? Dissembling was so large a part of middle-class life that honesty and frankness seemed the most devious stratagem of all. The most outright lie was the closest one came to truth.

Thinking about this moody young doctor, I carried my whisky into the utility room. I was slightly drunk as I gazed at the silent computer and the biographies of fascist leaders. I rested my glass on the ironing board and touched one of the St George's shirts. Almost without thinking, I picked up the shirt, shook it loose from its geometric folds and pulled it over my head.

I stood in front of the mirror, aware that the street brawl had made my skin glow. My father's shoulders had shrunk in his last years, as I had seen from photographs of him, and the shirt gripped my chest like the embrace of an approving parent.

12

Neon Palaces

I SAT IN MY CAR outside Brooklands High School, waiting until the last of the pupils had left. Swarming past me, they filled the nearby streets with their noise and anarchy, a teenage rabble that would soon take over the world. I liked them all, the cruel and scruffy lads with their surrealist humour, and the cruel and queenly girls.

When the teachers had driven away I left the car and walked down the drive littered with sweet wrappers, cigarette papers and cola cans, the debris of an amiable plague. I entered the main hall, still echoing with the shouts and catcalls, filled with the reek of testosterone and unlaundered sports gear.

The head teacher's secretary confirmed my appointment. Assuming that I was a would-be parent, certain to be disappointed at this over-subscribed school, she was cheerful and sympathetic. She told me that Mr Sangster was in the library but would join me shortly.

I waited outside his office for fifteen minutes, then set off in search of the head teacher. I guessed that William Sangster, one of Duncan Christie's three witnesses, was none too keen to meet me, having done his bit to set free the man about to be charged with my father's murder. Even a lifetime's coping with disagreeable parents and education committees would be little help in dealing with a son desperate for revenge.

The library was a warren of dog-eared books, billets-doux and cigarette butts stubbed out in alcoves. Sangster had left a few seconds before me, and I listened to the sound of retreating feet in a corridor.

I walked past the empty classrooms, nodded to a teacher marking exercise books beside her blackboard, and saw a tall man in a black overcoat turn quickly towards the gymnasium.

We crossed the sprung wooden floor together, separated by fifteen yards of polished surface but in step, taking part in a form of remote dancing. Sangster moved briskly, but I caught up with him as we entered a block of sixth-form classrooms.

He gave up with a resigned flourish and waited for me to join him, brushing the dandruff from his overcoat. He was an unnecessarily large man, with heavy arms and shoulders and a plump, babyish face, far younger than I expected. He avoided my offered hand, and I wondered if he was an impostor, a thirty-five-year-old actor who had somehow taken charge of a sink school and was already looking for a way out. He noticed my feet avoiding three condom sachets on the floor.

'We've . . .' He affected a mild stutter, pointing to the sachets, and smiled bleakly. 'We've . . . taught them something. Mr —?'

'Pearson. I have an appointment. Richard Pearson.'

He stared at my raised hand, as if I were trying to sell him a sex aid, and moved a deeply bitten forefinger from his babyish lips. 'Right. Your father . . . ?'

'. . . died after the Metro-Centre shooting. You were there.'

'I remember.' Sangster stared at the condom sachets. 'Tragic, absolutely. You have my sympathies.'

He beckoned me into an empty classroom and led me on a tour of the form, then indicated a desk in the front row. When I sat down he prowled along the blackboard, pausing to erase a numeral in a maths equation, clearly one of those large men who never seem to know what to do with parts of their bodies. He looked down at his left arm, as if discovering it for the first time, unsure how to fit the limb into his mental picture of himself.

Impatient to get to the point, and tired of humouring this rather odd man, I said: 'Mr Sangster, you're obviously busy. Could we . . . ?'

'Of course.' He sat in the form master's chair, and gave me his full attention, smiling in a genuinely friendly way. 'Two of our parents were injured that day, Mr Pearson. You desperately want to find who killed your father. But I'm not sure there's anything I can do.'

'Well . . . in a sense, you've already done it.'

'Is that so? How?'

'You helped to clear Duncan Christie.'

Sangster sat back, head resting against the maths equation, tolerating my rudeness. 'I testified that I saw Christie in the entrance hall when the shots were fired. I didn't help to clear him. It's not in my gift. It was an eye-witness statement.'

'You were actually in the Metro-Centre?'

'Naturally. There were two other witnesses who testified.'

'I know. For some reason, that bothers me.' Trying not to unsettle this highly strung head teacher, I put on my friendliest account-executive smile, a grimace I had hoped to abandon for ever. 'You all knew him. Isn't that odd?'

'Why?' Chair tilted back, Sangster watched me across the form master's desk, blowing out his plump cheeks like a puffer fish estimating the size of its prey. 'We wouldn't have recognized him otherwise. Why would we pretend we'd seen him?'

'That's the nub of the problem. It's difficult to think of a common motive . . .'

'Mr Pearson, are you suggesting we conspired to free Christie?' Sangster touched the blackboard behind his head, pretending to half-listen to me. 'Three respectable witnesses?'

'You are respectable. Almost too respectable. It's possible you saw someone like Christie. You might think you saw him, and naturally you feel he's innocent.'

'He is innocent. Mr Pearson, I taught him. For three years I was his maths teacher, in this very classroom. In fact, he sat at that desk where you're sitting now. Someone fired those shots, but not Duncan Christie. He's too unreliable, too erratic. He does odd jobs for me, mending the fence or mowing the lawn. He works hard for five minutes and then his mind sails off, he drops his tools and disappears for a week. His brain is a kind of theatre, where he plays games with his own sanity. He did not shoot your father.'

'Right.' I eased myself out of the ink-stained desk. 'As it happens, I agree with you.'

'You agree? Good.' Sangster stood up and brushed the blackboard chalk from his coat, reversed equations falling into dust at his large feet. He gestured me to the door. 'But why . . . ?'

'I saw him outside the magistrates' court. He was acting the killer, just to wind everyone up. He only stopped when he recognized me and knew it wasn't a game. The real assassin wouldn't have done that.'

'Well put.' Sangster nodded sagely. 'You've been through a lot, Richard, and you've kept your focus. It may look like a conspiracy, but many of us knew Duncan Christie and we didn't want to see him framed . . .'

We set off along the corridor, Sangster's huge bulk almost filling the narrow space. He had visibly relaxed, patting my shoulder as if I were a pupil who had displayed a sudden flair for differential calculus. He closed the door of his office, shutting out his intrigued secretary, collected two glasses and a bottle of sherry from a side table, and sat down at his desk. Still wearing his overcoat, he watched me sip the sweet fluid, his baby lips mimicking my own.

'Parents' sherry,' he told me. 'Makes a long day shorter. Think of it as a business aid.'

'Why not? I feel for you. Trying to educate six hundred teenagers in the middle of a circus.' I pointed to the dome visible through his windows. 'So many Aladdin's caves, a hundred neon palaces filled with treasure.'

'The only real things are the mirages. We can cope with that. Still, I know how you feel, Richard. An old man is shot down for no reason. The one common factor is the Metro-Centre. Somehow it explains everything.'

'My father and the whole consumer nightmare? I think there's a connection. Most of the people here are going mad, without realizing it.'

'All these retail parks, the airport and motorway culture. It's a new kind of hell . . .' Sangster stood up and pressed his huge hands to his cheeks, as if trying to deflate himself. 'That's the Hampstead perspective, the view from the Tavistock Clinic. The shadow of Freud's statue lies across the land, the Agent Orange of the soul. Believe me, things are different here. We have to prepare our kids for a new kind of society. There's no point in telling them about parliamentary democracy, the church or the monarchy. The old ideas of citizenship you and I were brought up with are really rather selfish. All that emphasis on individual rights, habeas corpus, freedom of the one against the many . . .'

'Free speech, privacy?'

'What's the point of free speech if you have nothing to say? Let's face it, most people haven't anything to say, and they know it. What's the point of privacy if it's just a personalized prison? Consumerism is a collective enterprise. People here want to share and celebrate, they want to come together. When we go shopping we take part in a collective ritual of affirmation.'

'So being modern today means being passive?'

Sangster slapped his desk, knocking over his pen stand. He leaned towards me, huge overcoat bulking around him.

'Forget being modern. Accept it, Richard, the whole modernist enterprise was intensely divisive. Modernism taught us to distrust and dislike ourselves. All that individual conscience, the solitary ache. Modernism was driven by neurosis and alienation. Look at its art and architecture. There's something deeply cold about them.'

'And consumerism?'

'It celebrates coming together. Shared dreams and values, shared hopes and pleasures. Consumerism is optimistic and forward-looking. Naturally, it asks us to accept the will of the majority. Consumerism is a new form of mass politics. It's very theatrical, but we like that. It's driven by emotion, but its promises are attainable, not just windy rhetoric. A new car, a new power tool, a new CD player.'

'And reason? No place for that, I take it?'

'Reason, well . . .' Sangster paced behind his desk, nail-bitten fingers to his lips. 'It's too close to maths, and most of us are not good at arithmetic. In general I advise people to steer clear of reason. Consumerism celebrates the positive side of the equation. When we buy something we unconsciously believe we've been given a present.'

'And politics demands a constant stream of presents? A new hospital, a new school, a new motorway . . . ?'

'Exactly. And we know what happens to children who are never given any toys. We're all children today. Like it or not, only consumerism can hold a modern society together. It presses the right emotional buttons.'

'So . . . liberalism, liberty, reason?'

'They failed! People don't want to be appealed to by reason any more.' Sangster bent down and rolled his sherry glass across the desk, as if waiting for it to stand up on its own. 'Liberalism and humanism are a huge brake on society. They trade on guilt and fear. Societies are happier when people spend, not save. What we need now is a kind of delirious consumerism, the sort you see at motor shows. People long for authority, and only consumerism can provide it.'

'Buy a new perfume, a new pair of shoes, and you're a happier and better person? And you can get all this across to your teenagers?'

'I don't need to. It comes with the air they breathe. Remember, Richard, consumerism is a redemptive ideology. At its best, it tries to aestheticize violence, though sadly it doesn't always succeed . . .'

Sangster stood up, smiling to himself in an almost serene way. He gazed at his huge hands, glad to accept them as hard-working outposts of himself.

We left each other on the steps outside the entrance. I liked Sangster, but I had the distinct sense that he had already forgotten me before he waved and turned back to the school. I walked away, strolling through the sweet wrappers drifting across the path, through the cola cans and cigarette packets and condom sachets.

13

Duncan Christie

A BRASS BAND struck up a spirited Souza medley, fireworks threw umbrellas of gaudy pink and turquoise light over the layabed town, car horns sounded and voices booed and cheered, greeting the Metro-Centre blimp as it sailed across the dome, more dreamlike than anything that had filled our heads during the night. The weekend was an extended sports festival, sponsored by the Metro-Centre and packed with more promises than even William Sangster could have imagined.

As I made a late breakfast I listened to the buses and coaches bringing teams and their supporters from the motorway towns. Under the evening arc lights there would be a 'Thames Valley Olympics', featuring football and rugby matches, athletics meetings, ice-hockey elimination rounds and a series of marathons and road races. Sport and shopping would celebrate a two-day marriage, to be solemnized by David Cruise. The sky would be the wedding marquee, and south-east England was invited. On the Metro-Centre cable channel the announcers worked up their audiences, playing up the mano-a-mano rivalries of the contact sports, the 'hate' matches between hockey teams from the Heathrow area.

By two o'clock, when I finally reached the Metro-Centre, the largest crowd I had seen in Brooklands filled the plaza beside the South Gate entrance, a congregation of worshippers that would have filled a dozen cathedrals. Shoppers chatted to each other, vendors in official livery carried placards listing the day's discounts in menswear, minced beef and Botox treatments. Security men murmured into their lapel radios, stewards in Metro-Centre track-suits struggled to keep clear a railed passage from the perimeter road to the entrance.

Sports-club supporters were out in force, a suburban crusader army in their St George's shirts. I parked my car in the basement garage, using the complimentary VIP pass supplied by Tom Carradine. Emerging from the lift, I found myself co-opted into a football squad running and skipping on the spot. The scent of their sweat and good cheer, the pain-blessed grunts and shouts, rose into the air towards the circling blimp. Nearby, a women's athletics club were exercising gracefully, moving like a dance class through a repertory of cheer-leader motions. Nowhere was there a single policeman.

The only sign of tension came from the perimeter road, where a battered pick-up truck had broken down by the kerb. But this was not a day for parking violations, the cardinal sin of suburbia in which everyone happily indulged, along with bouncing cheques and credit card overruns. Double-parking, like adultery and alcoholism, was a vital part of the social glue that kept the suburbs healthy.

I walked towards the stranded truck, where the crowd seemed thinner. Radios began to buzz and fret around me, the group hive coming to life in the presence of an intruder. A young man stood by the tailgate, unloading a refrigerator onto the pavement. Already a small crowd had gathered around him, mothers holding back their pointing children. A black woman sat in the driving cab as her daughter played beside her, reading a magazine and ignoring the crowd and her husband.

I had last seen the young man outside the magistrates' court, and now for the first time I had a good chance of speaking to Duncan Christie.

The largest of Christie's deliveries was still to be unloaded, a double-cabinet refrigerator with chromium doors and an ice-cube dispenser big enough for a hotel bar. Exhausted by the effort of moving his cargo, Christie leaned against the tailgate and smiled at the Metro-Centre blimp lazing above him. He had recovered from his rough treatment at the hands of the police, but his face was bruised and sallow, as if the violent storms seething within him had left their shadows on his skin.

His scarred mouth, self-cropped hair – no doubt sheared with a power tool during a building-site tea break – and general air of neglect made him look erratic and unfocused, a methadone addict forever emerging from rehab. Everything about him, from his large feet in a pair of unmatched trainers to the tic that pulled at an infected ear piercing, fixed him firmly as an urban scarecrow designed to frighten away any circling security cameras.

But his eyes were calm, and he seemed to have made his peace with the lazy blimp five hundred feet above him, as if hoping that the cameramen in the gondola would photograph the modest display of goods he had unloaded from his pick-up.

Lined up along the kerb was a selection of kitchen appliances – a spin-dryer, two refrigerators, a trio of washing machines and a microwave oven. None was new, and rust leaked from their hoses. They were the familiar furniture of every kitchen in Brooklands, but there was something surrealist about their presence that unsettled the small crowd. A middle-aged woman next to me pulled at the leash of her docile spaniel, prompting the beast to look up at me and growl menacingly.

'Right, little beauty . . .' Christie roused himself from his communion with the blimp and spat on his scarred hands. 'Time to mount you, girlie . . .'

He seized the refrigerator around its waist, rocked it from side to side and walked it towards the lowered tailgate. He was stronger than I thought, with a stevedore's hard arms, but the refrigerator was too heavy for him. When it tilted forward one of its doors fell open and trapped his right hand.

'. . . Jesus!' Unable to move, the refrigerator pressing against his chest, he glared at the unmoving spectators. 'Is none of you a fucking Christian? Maya!'

His wife watched all this through the rear-view mirror, assessed the situation and went back to playing with her daughter. I stepped forward and closed the refrigerator door, releasing Christie's numbed fingers, then helped him lower the bulky machine to the ground. He leaned against it, a winded Samson clinging to his temple.

'Thank you, sir. Thank you. A good deed these days takes courage.'

An elderly woman in a serge coat and pillbox hat peered at Christie, irritated by his apparent euphoria.

'Can you hear me?' she bellowed as he rolled his head. 'You're in the wrong place. Do you want a refund?'

'Refund?' Christie roused himself and surveyed the woman. 'I don't want a refund, madam. I want retribution.'

'Retribution? You can't get that here.' The woman turned to her husband, who was nodding at the microwave as if recognizing a friend fallen on hard times. 'Harry, what department is that?'

'You're not asking me?'

'I am asking you.'

Still bickering, they wandered off towards a troupe of drum-majorettes snap-marching beside their pipe band.

Christie took up his position near the display of kitchenware. His manner was affable, but his eyes darkened as a squall blew through his mind. He was a Petri dish of mental infections, a smear-culture of grimaces and tics. He leaned behind the refrigerator and spat on the ground, then deployed himself like a salesman, turning a wild smile onto his customers.

'Well, what am I offered?' He caressed the microwave, and addressed a young woman with a daughter pushing a small pram. 'One careful owner, perfect working order, a few chicken kievs, throw in a cheese-burger. Fully reconditioned.'

'How much?' The woman ran a finger over the greasy enamel. 'There's a written guarantee?'

'Written?' Christie rolled his eyes and confided to me: 'A sudden trust in literacy. Written, madam?'

'You know, a printed form.'

'A form . . .' Christie raised his voice to a shout above the pipe band. 'Madam, nothing is true, nothing is untrue! Say nothing, admit nothing, believe everything . . .'

The woman and her daughter moved away, taking the small crowd with them. Seeing that I was the last of his audience, Christie turned to me.

'Sir, I've been watching you. Am I right? You have your eye on that refrigerator. The big fellow . . . ?'

I waited as Christie sized me up. I was the enemy, in my dove-grey summer suit, a creature of the Metro-Centre and the retail parks. I was fairly sure that he no longer remembered me. His arrest, the violent police, his appearance at the magistrates' court, had disappeared into some garbage chute at the back of his mind.

'Yes, the big fellow.' I touched the huge wreck of the refrigerator. 'Can I assume it works?'

'Absolutely. Enough ice cubes to freeze the Thames.'

'How much?'

'Well . . .' Enjoying himself, Christie closed his eyes. 'Seriously, you couldn't afford it.'

'Try me.'

'No point. Believe me, the price is beyond your grasp.'

'Twenty pounds? Fifty pounds?'

'Please . . . the price is unimaginable.'

'Go on.'

'It's *free*!' An almost maniacal grin distorted Christie's face. 'Free!'

'You mean . . . ?'

'Gratis. Not a penny, not a euro, zilch.' Christie patted me cheerfully on the shoulder. 'Free. An inconceivable concept. Look at you. It's outside your entire experience. You can't cope with it.'

'I can cope.'

'I doubt it.' Confidentially, Christie lowered his voice. 'I come every Saturday, sooner or later someone asks, "How much?" "Free," I say. They're stunned, they react as if I'm trying to steal from them. That's capitalism for you. Nothing can be free. The idea makes them sick, they want to call the police, leave messages for their accountants. They feel unworthy, convinced they've sinned.

They have to rush off and buy something just to get their breath back . . .'

'Very good.' I waited as he lit a roll-up. 'I thought it might be a piece of street theatre. But in fact you're making a serious point.'

'Absolutely. Maya, hear the man.'

'This is your stand against the Metro-Centre, and all the other super-malls. Why not just burn them down?'

'It could be done.' Christie sucked the sweet smoke from the spliff. 'If I lit the fuse, would you hold the torch?'

'I might. As it happens, I have my own problems with the Metro-Centre. My father died in the shooting there.'

Christie puffed his spliff, and turned to look at me without surprise. For a few seconds all expression drained from his face, but he was devoid of emotion. Pain, sympathy and regret had moved to another floor of his mind. Whether or not he recognized me as the man who had watched him outside the magistrates' court was now irrelevant. I realized that even if he had been responsible for the shooting he would have long since repressed all memory of it.

'Your father? That's a hard buy.' He stepped away from me, drumming his fists on the washing machines. As his wife climbed from the driving cab he called out: 'Maya . . . a close shave. I nearly had a customer.'

'Christie, we need to go.'

She was quiet but determined, watching over her husband like a tired mental nurse. Her eyes met mine, then looked away, as if used to dealing with the human strays that Christie's aimless garrulity drew to him.

A large American car had stopped by the kerb fifty feet away, a silver Lincoln with a cable-company logo emblazoned on its doors. A chauffeur in Metro-Centre livery stepped out, and strode around the car to the rear passenger door. A waiting television unit approached the car, guided through the watching crowd by three uniformed stewards. The Steadicam operator crouched inside his harness, filming the rear-seat passenger, a familiar handsome figure who was inspecting his deep tan in a vanity mirror.

David Cruise was wearing studio make-up, ready for the tracking shot that opened his Saturday show. The camera would film him stepping from the silver Lincoln, saluting the cheering customers and drum majorettes, and then entering the consumer palace over which he presided.

A band struck up 'Hail to the Chief', and a smile touched Cruise's upper lip, a faint tremor that spread outwards to annex the muscles of his face. Energized by this grimace, he leapt nimbly from the passenger seat. He greeted the spectators like a practised politician, pinching the cheek of a delighted old lady, exchanging quips with two workmen in overalls, picking out people in the crowd and treating them to their own personal smile. I noticed his lack of aggression, and the softness of his hands, which were everywhere, fluttering around him like well-trained birds, squeezing, patting, waving and saluting.

With his lipstick, blusher and pancake make-up, Cruise seemed even more real than he did on television. He reminded me of all the minor actors I had coached while filming their commercials. The TV ad jumped the gap between reality and illusion, creating a world where the false became real and the real false. The crowd watching Cruise as he made his regal progress to the South Gate entrance expected him to wear make-up, and took for granted that he made exaggerated claims for the products they were so easily persuaded to buy. David Cruise, supporting actor in television serials that he always joined as their ratings slumped, was a complete fiction, from his corseted waist to his boyish smile. But he was a fake they could believe in.

'You're right,' I said to Christie. 'Nothing is true, and nothing is untrue. What was it? Say nothing, believe everything . . . ?'

Christie stood beside me, so close that I could hear his laboured breathing. His lungs moved in sudden starts, as if his body was trying desperately to uncouple itself from his brain. In a deep fugue, he stared at the retreating figure of David Cruise, parting the crowd like a cut-price messiah. I assumed that Christie was on the edge of an epileptic fit, surrounded by the warning aura that preceded an attack. I put my hands on his sweating shoulders, ready to catch him when he fell. But he pushed me away, straightened his back and gazed at the drifting blimp above our heads. He had willed himself into the fugue, expressing all his hatred of the fleshy actor who incarnated everything he loathed about the mall.

'Christie – it's time to go.' His wife took his arm, and whispered loudly enough for me to hear, 'Baby's getting tired.'

'Baby not tired. Baby waking up . . .'

I turned, glad to leave them to their marital games, and found myself facing a thuggish group of stewards in St George's shirts. They pushed through the crowd, grappling with each other like wrestlers in a ruck. A child screamed, setting off a deranged Airedale that started barking and biting. Trying to escape, husbands collided into their wives, and a scuffle broke out as the cabinet refrigerator toppled to the ground. Stewards shouted above the pipe band.

'Right! Let's have you! Off with this rubbish!'

Fists pounded on the side panels of the pick-up. Clutching her daughter, Mrs Christie flailed with her free hand at the brawling stewards. Fully awake now, her husband wrestled with their leader, a blond-haired bruiser with ice-hockey armour under his shirt.

I stepped back, and lost my balance when I was shoulder-charged by a heavily built woman wearing a biker's crash helmet. Through the mêlée of legs, knees and fists I saw an open-topped car draw up behind the pick-up. The driver sprang from his seat, fastening a leather jacket around his midriff, apparently eager to join the brawl.

He searched the crowd, forcefully pushing aside anyone who approached him. He was well into his fifties, with an almost jocular scowl, a boxer's rolling shoulders and the shaven scalp of a nightclub bouncer. He often appeared on television, but the last time I had seen him he was sitting beside Geoffrey Fairfax in the front of the lawyer's Range Rover. This was Christie's psychiatrist, Dr Tony Maxted, and the third of his helpful witnesses.

He saw me kneeling by the rear wheel of the pick-up and came straight towards me. He gripped my shoulders, like a well-muscled orderly with a mental patient, and laughed good-humouredly when I tried to wrench his hands away. He lifted me to my feet, and propelled me towards his car.

'Richard Pearson? We ought to leave before you beat anyone up. I think the Christies can look after themselves . . .'

14

Towards a Willed Madness

THE THIRD WITNESS.

Biding my time, I crouched in the bucket seat of the frisky Mazda as Dr Maxted steered us erratically through the streets of east Brooklands. We passed a young offenders' prison, then veered through a business park where the research laboratories of Siemens, Motorola and Astra Computers tried to outstare each other across untrodden lawns and beds of subdued daffodils that had given up waiting for their Wordsworth. Emerging into a street of glass and metal ware-housing, we joined a dual carriageway that led past a marina and water-skiing club built beside a reclaimed gravel lake.

I assumed that Maxted was trying to confuse me, constructing a maze around my head from a jumbled atlas of back streets and slip roads. When we passed the young offenders' prison for the second time I tapped Maxted's shoulder, but he pointed to the road ahead, as if the car needed my full attention.

I decided to humour him, and studied the heavy muscles of his neck, and the close-cropped hair over his broad skull. He drove the powerful car with a surprising lack of grace, his fingers barely touching the wheel, bruising the gearbox as he stamped the clutch pedal with a heavy foot. Like many psychiatrists, he needed to play games with anyone who entered his professional space, performing the private rituals of the modern-day shaman.

At last we approached Northfield Hospital, the mental asylum where Duncan Christie had been held. We paused by the gate, and

Maxted punched the horn to rouse the security guard dozing over his evening paper. We moved past a gym and sports centre, blocks of staff apartments and an inter-denominational chapel that resembled an avant-garde pissoir. We parked outside the main admin building, and walked to a side entrance behind a screen of rhododendrons. Using his swipe card, Maxted led us into a coffin-like lift.

As we climbed towards the roof he looked me up and down, nodding without comment.

'Thanks for the mystery tour,' I said. 'Quite a car, especially the way you drive it.'

'Is that a compliment?' Maxted loosened his tie. 'I wasn't trying to confuse you. Driving straight here would have done that. I'm impressed you ever found your way to Brooklands in the first place.'

'I'm not sure I did . . .'

We stepped from the lift into a windowless lobby. After dialling an entry code, Maxted beckoned me into the hallway of an airy penthouse, apparently built as an afterthought from sections of glass and aluminium panelling. Deep balconies looked out over the hospital buildings below. A mile away, across a terrain of dual carriageways and industrial estates, rose the dome of the Metro-Centre, its blimp lazing above it like a tethered soul.

Maxted gestured at the expensive but anonymous furniture, the black leather sofas and chromium lamps lighting remote areas of carpet that no one had ever visited. It reminded me of the mezzanine television studio where David Cruise held court. In a sense the cable presenter and the psychiatrist were in the same business, redefining the world as a minimalist structure in which human beings were an untidy intrusion. Fittingly, the bookshelves were empty, and in the deserted dining room the table was set for guests who would never arrive.

'It's a kind of glamorous shack . . .' Maxted gestured at the low-ceilinged rooms with a dismissive wave, but he seemed relaxed and confident, springing on his feet as if the penthouse reflected his secret view of himself. 'The new research wing was financed by DuPont. I helped to raise a lot of the cash. This is one of the perks, like having your own lift. It takes away the pain.'

'Is there any pain?'

'Believe me. Still, you're used to this kind of thing. A big London agency, seven-figure salary, share options, duplexes . . . Am I right?'

'Wrong. As it happens, I've just been sacked.' There had been a hint of longing in Maxted's voice, untouched by envy, as if he was happy to live vicariously the elegant life that the penthouse only hinted at. I pointed to the Metro-Centre, unsure why he had brought me to the hospital. 'It doesn't look quite so large from here. The best view in Brooklands.'

'Even though I'm living above a madhouse?' Maxted laughed generously, walked to the drinks cabinet and came back with a decanter and two tumblers. 'Laphroaig – private patients only.'

'Am I a patient?'

'I haven't decided yet.' Maxted steered me into the armchair facing him. His eyes ran over me, lingering on my scuffed but expensive shoes, though I decided not to tell him that I would never be able to afford another pair. He sipped noisily at the whisky, relying on his rough-edged charm to win me over. He was physically strong but insecure, glad to find shelter in the tumbler of malt. I assumed that he knew everything about me, and that Geoffrey Fairfax had told him about my enquiries.

'So . . .' Maxted put down his tumbler. 'Tell me, do you like violence?'

'Violence? What man doesn't?' I decided to let the whisky speak for me. 'Yes, probably. When I was younger.'

'Good. Sounds like an honest answer. Rugger brawls, nightclub aggro – that sort of thing?'

'That sort of thing.'

'Did you box at school?'

'Until they banned it. We formed a martial arts society to get around the ban. We called it self-defence.'

'Kick and grunt? Slapping mattresses?' Maxted smiled nostal-gically. 'What's the appeal?'

'In a word?' I looked away from his slightly prurient eyes. 'Danger.'

'Go on.'

'Fear, pain, anything to break the rules. Most people never realize how violent they really are. Or how brave, when your back's against the wall.'

'Exactly.' Maxted sat forward, fists clenched, Laphroaig forgotten. 'That's when you rally yourself, even when someone's beating the blood out of your brains.'

'Don't tell me you box?'

'A long time ago. Half-blue. But I remember how it feels. After three rounds you're alive again.' Maxted pulled the stopper from the decanter. 'That's the trouble with the video conference. Primal aggression tamped down, no straight lefts, no uppercuts to the chin. We're a primate species with an unbelievable need for violence. White-water rafting doesn't quite fit the bill. There must be something else.'

'There is. You know that, Dr Maxted.'

'I'd like to hear it from you.'

I stared hard at the dome, trying to guess at the mindset of this maverick psychiatrist, almost as odd as any of his patients. The afternoon had begun to fade, and the interior lights turned the Metro-Centre into an illuminated pumpkin. I said: 'Danger, yes. Pain, the fear of death. And outright insanity.'

'Insanity . . . of course.' Savouring the word, Maxted lay back in the sofa, resting his thick neck against the black leather. 'That's the real appeal, isn't it? The freedom deliberately to lose control.'

'Doctor, can we . . . ?'

'Right.' Having drawn the answer he wanted from me, Maxted clapped his hands. He pushed the decanter away, clearing the table between us. 'Let's get down to business. I brought you here, Richard, because there are things we ought to talk over. You've been in Brooklands a few weeks, and frankly you're cutting it a little fine. Every street brawl, every supporters' punch-up, that daft business this afternoon with the Christies . . . you're a magnet tuned to violence.'

'I'm trying to find who killed my father. The police have drifted away.'

'They haven't.' Maxted waved me down. 'Listen to me. I'm sorry about the old man. A cruel way for him to go. Sometimes the wheel spins and you see nothing but zeroes. A terrible accident.'

'Accident?' I rapped the table with my glass. 'Someone fired a machine gun at him. Perhaps Duncan Christie or –'

'Forget Christie. You're barking up the wrong tree.'

'The police didn't think so, until you and the other "witnesses" came forward. He was their chief suspect.'

'The police always jump to conclusions. It's part of their job, builds confidence with the public. You saw Christie today. He can't concentrate long enough to mend a fuse, let alone carry through an assassination.'

'Assassination?' I turned to stare at the dome, which seemed to grow in size as it glowed in the fading light. 'That implies someone very important. Who exactly?'

'The target? Impossible to say. David Cruise?'

'A cable-channel presenter? I once worked with him. The man's a nonentity. Why would anyone want to murder David Cruise?'

Maxted simpered into his whisky. 'There are folk here who'd give you a hundred reasons. He has a big power base. Sales are flat at the Metro-Centre, and without David Cruise they'd be in trouble. There's even talk of him starting a political party.'

'The kind that goose-steps? The Oswald Mosley of the suburbs? I don't think he'd be convincing.'

'He wouldn't need to be. His appeal functions on a different level. It's more your world than mine. Politics for the age of cable TV. Fleeting impressions, an illusion of meaning floating over a sea of undefined emotions. We're talking about a virtual politics unconnected to any reality, one which redefines reality as itself. The public willingly colludes in its own deception. Is Cruise up to that? I doubt it.'

'Then who was the target? And who killed my father?'

'Difficult questions, and obviously you want an answer . . .'

Maxted gestured at the air, as if trying to conjure a genie from the decanter, and I remembered him sitting in the front of Geoffrey Fairfax's Range Rover, and the headlight signals outside the shabby Odeon. But I decided to say nothing, hoping that he would lead himself into a useful indiscretion. For all his bull-necked toughness, he was uneasy about something, and more vulnerable than I probably realized. I waited as he stood up and paced the carpet, retracing a half-remembered dance step.

Impatient for an answer, I said: 'We could push the police a little harder. Find out who their main suspects are. Dr Maxted?'

'The police? They'd be touched by your faith in them. They haven't realized how much everything has changed out here. They're not alone in that. People in London can't grasp that this is the real England. Parliament, the West End, Bloomsbury, Notting Hill, Hampstead – they're heritage London, held together by a dinner-party culture. Here, around the M25, is where it's really happening. This is today's England. Consumerism rules, but people are bored. They're out on the edge, waiting for something big and strange to come along.'

'That sounds as if they're going to be frightened.'

'They want to be frightened. They want to know fear. And maybe they want to go a little mad. Look around you, Richard. What do you see?'

'Air-cargo warehouses. Shopping malls. Executive estates.' As Maxted listened to me, nodding gloomily, I asked: 'Why don't people leave? Why don't you leave?'

'Because we like it here.' Maxted raised his hands to stop me interrupting him. 'This isn't a suburb of London, it's a suburb of Heathrow and the M25. People in Hampstead and Holland Park look down from the motorway as they speed home from their West Country cottages. They see faceless inter-urban sprawl, a nightmare terrain of police cameras and security dogs, an uncentred realm devoid of civic tradition and human values.'

'It is. I've been there. It's a zoo fit for psychopaths.'

'Exactly. That's what we like about it. We like dual carriageways and parking lots. We like control-tower architecture and friendships that last an afternoon. There's no civil authority telling us what to do. This isn't Islington or South Ken. There are no town halls or assembly rooms. We like prosperity filtered through car and appliance sales. We like roads that lead past airports, we like air-freight offices and rent-a-van forecourts, we like impulse-buy holidays to anywhere that takes our fancy. We're the citizens of the shopping mall and the marina, the internet and cable TV. We like it here, and we're in no hurry for you to join us.'

'I don't want to. Take it from me, I'll leave as soon as I can.'

'Good.' Maxted nodded vigorously. 'Brooklands is dangerous. You're going to get hurt. The motorway towns are violent places. We're not talking about a few individuals who go off the rails. We're talking about collective psychology. The whole area is waiting for trouble. All these sports-club supporters, they're just street gangs in St George's shirts.'

'My father might have been wearing one when he was shot. A retired airline pilot in his seventies? The Asian family in the next flat were frightened of him. They look at me as if I were National Front.'

'Maybe you are, without realizing it.' Maxted spoke without irony. 'You have to think about England as a whole, not just Brooklands and the Thames Valley. The churches are empty, and the monarchy shipwrecked itself on its own vanity. Politics is a racket, and democracy is just another utility, like gas and electricity. Almost no one has any civic feeling. Consumerism is the one thing that gives us our sense of values. Consumerism is honest, and teaches us that everything good has a barcode. The great dream of the Enlightenment, that reason and rational self-interest would one day triumph, led directly to today's consumerism.'

I tried to reach the decanter. 'In that case, why worry? Look around you here at Brooklands. You've found the earthly paradise.'

'It's not a paradise.' Maxted tried to mask his scorn. 'Brooklands is a dangerous and disturbed place. Nasty things are brewing here. All this racism and violence. Burning down Asian businesses. Naked intolerance for its own sake. And this is only the beginning. Something far worse is waiting to crawl out of its den.'

'But if reason and light have triumphed?'

'They haven't. Because we're not reasonable and rational creatures. Far from it. We resort to reason when it suits us. For most people life is comfortable today, and we have the spare time to be unreasonable if we choose to be. We're like bored children. We've been on holiday for too long, and we've been given too many presents. Anyone who's had children knows that the greatest danger is boredom. Boredom, and a secret pleasure in one's own malice. Together they can spur a remarkable ingenuity.'

'Let's stuff baby's mouth with sweets and see if he stops breathing?'

'Exactly.' Maxted watched me smiling into my drink. 'I hope you were an only child. You've seen the people around here. Their lives are empty. Install a new kitchen, buy another car, take a trip to some beach hotel. All these sports clubs financed by the Metro-Centre are an attempt to boost sales. It hasn't worked. People are bored, even though they don't realize it.'

'So a lot of babies are going to turn blue in the face?'

'Not just babies. What's happening here involves entire communities. All these satellite towns around Heathrow and along the motorways. There's one thing left that can put some energy into their lives, give them a sense of direction. You've run advertising campaigns – any ideas?'

'None. Narcotics? A complete drug culture?'

'Too destructive. Think of . . .'

'War? It makes for good television.'

'Difficult to organize. The Thames Valley can't make territorial demands and invade Belgium. What I have in mind comes free, and is readily to hand.'

'Sex?'

'They've tried sex. Sooner or later, sex becomes hard work. Wife swapping is fun, but you meet too many people you look down on. Decadence demands a certain degree of innocence.'

'So that leaves . . . ?'

'Madness.' Maxted lowered his voice and spoke more clearly, leaving behind his usual rush of words. 'A voluntary insanity, whatever you want to call it. As a psychiatrist I'd use the term elective psychopathy. Not the kind of madness we deal with here. I'm talking about a willed insanity, the sort that we higher primates thrive on. Watch a troupe of chimpanzees. They're bored with chewing twigs and picking the fleas out of each other's armpits. They want meat, the bloodier the better, they want to taste their enemies' fear in the flesh they grind. So they start beating their chests and shrieking at the sky. They work themselves into a frenzy, then set off in a hunting party. They come across a tribe of colobus monkeys and literally tear them limb from limb. Very nasty, but voluntary madness brought them a tasty supper. They sleep it off, and go back to chewing twigs and picking fleas.'

'And then the cycle repeats itself.' I lay back, aware of Maxted's hot breath on the air. 'More race riots and arson attacks, more immigrant hostels put to the torch. So the people of the motorway towns are tired of chewing twigs. One question, though. Who organizes these attacks of madness?'

'No one. That's the beauty of it. Elective insanity is waiting inside us, ready to come out when we need it. We're talking primate behaviour at its most extreme. Witch-hunts, auto-da-fés, heretic burnings, the hot poker shoved up the enemy's rear, gibbets along the skyline. Willed madness can infect a housing estate or a whole nation.'

'Thirties Germany?'

'A good example. People still think the Nazi leaders led the German people into the horrors of race war. Not true. The Germans were desperate to break out of their prison. Defeat, inflation, grotesque war reparations, the threat of barbarians advancing from the east. Going mad would set them free, and they chose Hitler to lead the hunting party. That's why they stayed together till the end. They needed a psychopathic god to worship, so they recruited a nobody and stood him on the high altar. The great religions have been at it for millennia.'

'States of willed madness? Christianity? Islam?'

'Vast systems of psychopathic delusion that murdered millions, launched crusades and founded empires. A great religion spells danger. Today people are desperate to believe, but they can only reach God through psychopathology. Look at the most religious areas of the world at present – the Middle East and the United States. These are sick societies, and they're going to get sicker. People are never more dangerous than when they have nothing left to believe in except God.'

'But what else *is* there to believe in?' I waited for Maxted to reply, but the psychiatrist was staring through the picture window at the dome of the Metro-Centre, fists gripping the air as if trying to steady the world around him. 'Dr Maxted . . . ?'

'Nothing. Except madness.' Maxted rallied himself and turned back to me. 'People feel they can rely on the irrational. It offers the only guarantee of freedom from all the cant and bullshit and sales commercials fed to us by politicians, bishops and academics. People are deliberately re-primitivizing themselves. They yearn for magic and unreason, which served them well in the past, and might help them again. They're keen to enter a new Dark Age. The lights are on, but they're retreating into the inner darkness, into superstition and unreason. The future is going to be a struggle between vast systems of competing psychopathies, all of them willed and deliberate, part of a desperate attempt to escape from a rational world and the boredom of consumerism.'

'Consumerism leads to social pathology? Hard to believe.'

'It paves the way. Half the goods we buy these days are not much more than adult toys. The danger is that consumerism will need something close to fascism in order to keep growing. Take the Metro-Centre and its flat sales. Close your eyes a little and it already looks like a Nuremberg rally. The ranks of sales counters, the long straight aisles, the signs and banners, the whole theatrical aspect.'

'No jackboots, though,' I pointed out. 'No ranting führers.'

'Not yet. Anyway, they belong to the politics of the street. Our "streets" are the cable TV consumer channels. Our party insignia are the gold and platinum loyalty cards. Faintly risible? Yes, but people thought the Nazis were a bit of a joke. The consumer society is a kind of soft police state. We think we have choice, but everything is compulsory. We have to keep buying or we fail as citizens. Consumerism creates huge unconscious needs that only fascism can satisfy. If anything, fascism is the form that consumerism takes when it opts for elective madness. You can see it here already.'

'In bosky Surrey? I don't think so.'

'It's coming, Richard.' Maxted pursed his lips, as if to shut out all possibility of a smile. 'Here and in the towns around Heathrow. You can feel it in the air.'

'And the führer figure?'

'He hasn't arrived yet. He'll appear, though, walking out of some shopping mall or retail park. Messiahs always emerge from the desert. Everybody will be waiting for him, and he'll seize his chance.'

'Parliament, the civil service, the police? They'll stop him.'

'Unlikely. They aren't directly challenged, so they'll look the other way. This is a new kind of totalitarianism that operates at the checkout and the cash counter. What happens in the suburbs has never bothered the people in Whitehall.'

'A new Dark Age . . . What do we do?'

'We try to control it. Steer it onto the beach. A monster is stirring in the deep, and we need to get it onto the shore while it's still drowsy. Now is the time to act, Richard.'

'Right.' I finished the last of my whisky, trying not to meet Maxted's eyes. He was an impressive figure, with his huge head and powerful hands, but I too was being steered into the shallow water. He had begun to look at his watch, and I half expected the doors to burst open and admit a resistance unit led by Geoffrey Fairfax. In an offhand way, I said: 'I take it you're not alone? There are others who think like you?'

'A few of us. We can see what's coming and we're concerned.'

'Geoffrey Fairfax, William Sangster? Superintendent Leighton?'

'As it happens, yes.' Maxted seemed unsurprised. 'There are others.'

'Dr Goodwin?'

'In her left-handed way. Julia is less nervy as a doctor than she is as a young woman. Why do you ask?'

'It's interesting that you're the same group who happened to be in the Metro-Centre.'

'And saw Duncan Christie in the South Gate entrance? That's right.'

'Lucky for him. His doctor, his psychiatrist, his head teacher . . .'

'We met in the car park, and strolled in together.'

'Fair enough. And your plans now?'

'To nip this thing in the bud. If we wait much longer we'll be overwhelmed.'

'Willed madness . . .' I repeated the phrase, already a slogan in a teaser campaign. 'You think my father was killed by someone so bored he decided to choose insanity?'

'For a few seconds. Long enough to pull the trigger.' Maxted took off his leather jacket to free his arms, then reached out and gripped my shoulders in a sudden show of confidence. I could smell the sweat on his shirt, a blend of stale deodorant and sheer unease. He had been perspiring freely since we arrived at the penthouse, but the careful exposition of his fears had been more than a public health warning. He had been hiding his discomfort at having to expose his private guilt to someone who was watching him a little too closely. The bull-headed swagger was a screen carried by a thoughtful and unsure man. I remembered him sitting in the Range Rover outside the Odeon cinema, within earshot of a vicious riot that he and Fairfax had been orchestrating. Yet he had done nothing to stop it.

He released his grip on my shoulders, and did his best to straighten my suit. 'Think about it, Richard. You could help us in all kinds of ways. While you're thinking, I need to make a phone call. Help yourself to whisky and take in the view. It's going to be a hot night . . .'

'Dr Maxted, tell me.' I waited until he reached the door. 'Do you know who killed my father?'

'I think so.' Maxted studied me as if I were a dejected patient for whom the truth would be the ultimate lethal dose. 'Yes, I do.'

'But . . . ?'

'I'll be with you in five minutes. There's a lot you don't know.'

15

The Prisoner in the Tower

I LAY BACK on the sofa, watching the lights come on over the motorway flatlands, the desert wastes of retail England. It was a night of important sports matches: the arrays of arc lights above the football and athletics stadiums blazed through a hazy glare that caught every insect in the Thames Valley. Already thousands of spectators in St George's shirts would be taking their seats, ready to work themselves into a frenzy before they seized the placid town.

I sat with my whisky, in this penthouse correctly sited above a lunatic asylum. Maxted had impressed me, but I discounted his claim that he knew who had shot my father. His motives were ambiguous even for a suburban psychiatrist who appeared too often on television. There he played the same role, the tough-but-tender physician moonlighting as a nightclub bouncer, but even the television audience had failed to be taken in. He was trying to recruit me into his 'resistance' group, but I could hear the communal singing from the stadiums, great war hymns that seemed to lift the night, and I knew that Maxted and his posse of eccentric professionals were doomed.

I stepped onto the balcony and gazed at the silver back of the Metro-Centre, a self-supporting structure far more impressive than the Millennium Dome at Greenwich, a glorified tent filled with patronizing tat. The Metro-Centre was a house of treasure that enriched the lives of its visitors. Like an unimportant but hard-working merchant in a souk, I had given my entire career to the task of displaying that treasure at its best.

I returned to the living room and listened to the silence. It was easy to imagine Maxted with a prostate the size of a cricket ball, legs astride the lavatory pan, discussing a difficult patient on his mobile as he conjured the sluggish urine from his bladder.

I opened the door to the hallway. A corridor ran to the bathroom and bedroom, but there was no sound of Maxted's voice on a telephone. The flat was silent, light flaring against the windows from the display screens at the football stadium. I was alone in the penthouse, and assumed that Maxted had hurried away to deal with an emergency call, too distracted to warn me.

I pressed the lift button and watched the indicator panel, then pressed again and waited. There was no response, and the red warning light glowed steadily in the swipe unit. Without a pass card the lift was closed to me, part of the elaborate security that guarded the research laboratories and their drug stores from escaped patients.

'Maxted . . . for God's sake!'

Irritated by the endless series of charades that seemed to unfold within each other, I pounded the lift doors and pressed my ears to the metal panels. Annoyed with myself for letting Maxted play his devious games, I walked back to the kitchen. A plate-glass door led to a narrow balcony, where a short stairway joined the main fire escape.

Cautiously, giving the security system time to think, I turned the handle on the door, but it failed to open. Somewhere in the penthouse lay the fuse box and the switching unit that controlled the security locks, but my temper was up. Holding the kitchen chair by its legs, I raised it above my head and drove the steel frame into the plate-glass door. The violent blows echoed like gunfire through the empty rooms, but left the barest marks on the toughened glass. Then, after the third blow, I heard an alarm shrill far below me.

★   ★   ★

Thirty minutes later I was sitting in Maxted's black armchair, finishing the last of the whisky in the decanter and mulling over the almost deliberate way in which everyone I visited in Brooklands had plied me with alcohol. Even my father had left a substantial supply of gin and whisky, as if keen to ease the culture shock awaiting me. Fairfax, Sangster and Dr Maxted had been as quick with a bottle as an over-attentive sommelier in an unpopular restaurant.

I was staring gloomily at the decanter when the lift doors at last opened. Two security men emerged, carrying a leather restraining harness. They approached me without speaking, feinting around the furniture like dog handlers cornering an alcoholic pit bull, but I was sure that they knew who I was. After checking the flat they beckoned me to the lift.

'Mr Pearson, we'll have to see you out.'

'Good. I'll come quietly. I take it you're the Rapid Response Unit?'

'Dr Maxted said —'

'Don't tell me. I couldn't cope . . .'

I assumed that Maxted had slipped away on some errand of his own, knowing that I would set off the alarm, and had told the security men to release me half an hour later. I entered the lift, the guards behind me with their harness, ready to throw it over me at the first sign of dementia.

The doors closed. In the pause before the lift moved there was the distant sound of a powerful explosion, a loud percussive boom that entered the shaft above our heads and rocked the lift.

I stepped into the night air, and searched the sky for the burning debris of this huge firework. A police car was parked beside the rhododendron screen. The headlights were on full beam, and the distracted woman constable at the wheel was trying to speak through a blizzard of radio chatter. She saw me walk to the security barrier and signalled me to stop.

As I approached the police car a blonde-haired woman in a blue tracksuit and trainers emerged from the admin offices. She strode past me, and caught the tang of whisky on the dark air.

'Mr Pearson?' Sergeant Mary Falconer seemed surprised to find me. She pointed to the security men still watching me from the elevator. 'What are you doing here? Did you break in?'

'Break in?' I raised my hands to seize her shoulders, and then let her step back. 'This place really is a madhouse. For the last hour I've been trying to break out.'

'Break out?' She fussed with a stray hair. 'Why? How did you get in?'

'Forget it. No wonder the crime rate is soaring. Dr Maxted brought me here.'

'Dr Maxted? Are you a patient of his?'

'At this rate I soon will be. Now, I need to find a taxi.'

'Hold on a moment. Just wait there . . .'

Sergeant Falconer listened to the radio chatter and rubbed the dial of her watch. She was dressed for the athletics field, or at least a run around the neighbourhood, though scarcely a hair or eyelash was out of place. At the same time she seemed ill at ease, like a supporting actor assigned the wrong role. Once again she reminded me of a strait-laced but vulnerable teacher aware that her class had seen her in a piece of questionable behaviour.

A second police car turned off the main road and approached the security barrier, but Sergeant Falconer was too distracted to notice it. She listened to the ambulance sirens in the distance and drew a mobile phone from her tracksuit top. She stared at the text message, then crossed the road to the second police car. She took the radio earpiece from the driver, listened briefly and ran back to me. For the first time she was alert and focused, as if the script she had been following now synchronized with reality.

'Sergeant Falconer . . . ?' I held her arm. 'Something's going on. What are you people playing at?'

'Get into the car.' Avoiding my breath, she pushed me through the rear door. 'We'll give you a lift.'

'What is it?' I watched the second police car reverse and speed away. 'Have they caught the gunman?'

'Who? Which gunman?'

'The man who killed my father. They've arrested him?'

'No.' She fastened her seat belt, beckoning the woman driver to climb the grass embankment around the security barrier. 'It's the Metro-Centre. There's been a bomb attack. Heavy damage, but no casualties. So far . . .'

16

The Bomb Attack

THE TEMPLE WAS under threat, and the congregation was rallying to defend it. Crowds of football supporters filled the streets, running past our police car as it sat in the stalled traffic near the town hall. Urged on by Sergeant Falconer, the woman constable tried to force our way through the throngs of fans and evening shoppers. All the matches in the Thames Valley Olympics had been abandoned as the news broke of the bomb attack at the Metro-Centre. Supporters turned their backs on ice-hockey grudge matches and penalty shoot-outs, and set off through the streets to give succour to the stricken dome.

Six hundred yards from the Metro-Centre we could clearly see the smoke lifting from the roof, dark billows lit by cascades of sparks swept aloft in the updraughts. Still intact, the dome loomed in front of us when we reached the central plaza, as always so huge that I failed to notice the police vehicles, ambulances and fire engines drawn up around the entrance to the underground car park.

A small section of the roof was dark, a narrow triangle the size and shape of a schooner's jib sail. The huge bomb detonated in the upper level of the basement car park had torn through the floor of the Metro-Centre, the explosive pressure blowing out the glass and aluminium panels two hundred feet above the atrium. The shopping mall, according to the police radio reports, was largely untouched, and the smoke rose from the burning vehicles ignited by the bomb. Opening the passenger window, I gazed at the dark triangle near the apex of the dome. It would soon be repaired, but for the moment a section of space-time had been erased, exposing a deep flaw in our collective dream.

Sergeant Falconer showed her warrant card to the policemen keeping a lane open for emergency vehicles. Above the din of ambulance sirens an officer in a yellow jacket directed us towards the underground garage.

'Looks like a car bomb,' Sergeant Falconer told me. 'Three pounds of Semtex. There's another maniac on the loose.'

'Anyone killed or injured?'

'No one. Let's thank God for that . . .'

But her relief at the news scarcely left the sergeant any less agitated. Threads of blonde hair were springing loose from their braids. For some reason, the slightest shift from the immaculate left Sergeant Falconer looking frayed and insecure. Impatient to get into the car park, she reached across the driver and gripped the steering wheel, trying to change lanes. The car stalled, and the flustered constable flooded the engine as Sergeant Falconer drummed her fists on the instrument panel.

When we approached the entrance ramp I looked back at the plaza around the Metro-Centre, now occupied by a huge crowd, drawn to the St Peter's Square of the retail world. Everyone was staring upwards at the billows of smoke that lifted into the night. In the front row was Tom Carradine, the young manager who had first welcomed me to the dome. He darted to and fro, desperate to find a better view, too distraught to express himself in any other way, like a tennis player leaping around a court as he tried to ward off defeat by an invisible opponent with an invisible ball. The notion that anyone might dislike the Metro-Centre and wish to damage it had clearly never occurred to him.

We entered the basement car park, and followed the police guide rails into one of the delivery bays, finding a place between two articulated trucks. The night shift were being questioned by a team of investigators, and the freight carousels were stationary, stopped in mid-track at the moment of the explosion. Three-piece suites sealed in plastic sheeting, video-game consoles and coffee machines leaned against each other in a huge jumble. Over everything hung a stench of petrol and scorched rubber, and the acid dust of pulverized cement.

Police emergency lights shone through the haze, and crime-scene tapes marked out the empty parking bays being searched by forensics officers. A wedge-shaped section of the concrete ceiling had vanished, driven into the changing rooms of a health club near the atrium.

'All the customers had gone to the sports matches,' Sergeant Falconer explained. 'So they'd closed for the night. It's a miracle no one was hurt.'

I watched the forensics teams picking their way through the rubble. 'Not much to find. What are they looking for?'

'Timer fragments. A clock mechanism. Human tissues . . .' Sergeant Falconer stared at me with concern. 'This isn't the place for you, Mr Pearson. It'd be best if you went home.'

'You're right.'

My presence unsettled her, and she was eager to get away from me. Why she had brought me to the Metro-Centre in the first place seemed unclear, like Dr Maxted's motives for driving me all the way to his mental hospital.

I tried to remember where I had parked that morning, but the perspectives of everything in the basement garage seemed to have changed. I had driven around for a few minutes, searching for a place, then lost the numbered ticket during my scuffle with the thugs who attacked Duncan Christie.

A dozen cars caught fire when their petrol tanks exploded, burning fiercely before the sprinkler system came into play. Smothered in foam, the blackened vehicles sat in the wreckage of themselves, windows and doors missing, shreds of tyres peeling from their rims.

At the centre was the car that had carried the bomb, an agony of splayed body panels, exposed seating springs, engine block and drive shaft. The entire roof had vanished, and the forensics officers in white overalls were leaning into the debris, searching the carbonized remains of the instrument panel.

I assumed that the bomber had stolen the car before driving it to the Metro-Centre, and had left the bomb in the boot, directly above the fuel tank. Both the front and rear number plates had vaporized in the fireball, but the large engine had blunted the blast damage to the front of the car. A metal Guards Polo Club badge was still bolted to the front bumper.

A similar badge had been attached to my Jensen when I bought it from the young widow of a Grenadier lieutenant a few months after his death in the Iraq war. As a nod to the dead soldier, I left the badge where it was, hoping that it might catch the eye of his former comrades.

I looked away, shielding my face from the harsh emergency lights. Of all the vehicles to choose from in the Metro-Centre car park, the bomber had left his vicious surprise in my old but still sleek and handsome Jensen . . .

I took out my ignition keys and stared at the ancient fob, all that was left of the stylish tourer from a vanished age of motoring. It occurred to me that the driver, not the car, was the real target, and I had barely escaped being blown through the Jensen's roof. My hour trapped in Maxted's penthouse had probably saved me. Had I left Northfield Hospital with Maxted, and taken a taxi back to the Metro-Centre, I would have been driving the Jensen to my father's flat when the bomb detonated.

I walked towards the forensics officer picking pieces of ragged upholstery from the car's floor-pan. Within a few days, if not hours, the engine and chassis numbers would lead the police to the Grenadier's widow, and then to me.

Would they assume that I was the bomber? My father had died in the Metro-Centre, and leaving a bomb in the garage would strike the police as a likely act of revenge. The forensics officer had turned to watch me, and I noticed that I was waving the Jensen's keys in my hand, a nervous tic that had come from nowhere.

I calmed myself, and searched for Sergeant Falconer. She was standing with a group of journalists who were questioning a uniformed inspector. In a transparent plastic bag he carried a trilby hat with a ragged hole through its crown. He removed the hat from the bag and showed it to the journalists. As he spoke, his fingers flicked at a fishing fly sewn into the hatband.

The journalists scribbled into their notebooks, clearly impressed by the hat. But I was watching Sergeant Falconer. Even in the harsh glare of the emergency lights her face was unnaturally blanched. The blood had drained from her cheeks, revealing the bones beneath her skin patiently waiting for their day. She turned and swayed, then stumbled against the inspector. Still talking to the journalists, he beckoned to two policewomen behind him and they quickly helped Sergeant Falconer towards the driving cab of a forensics van parked inside the crime-scene area.

Concerned for her, I tried to cross the nearest tape, but an officer ordered me away. As I backed off, trying to clear the stench and grit from my throat, I brushed past the young constable who had driven us from the hospital.

'Is she all right?' I held her arm. 'Sergeant Falconer? She fainted . . .'

'She'll be fine. There's bad news. We've found the first victim. Or what's left of him.'

'Dear God . . . where is he?'

'In a nasty little jigsaw puzzle.' She took my hand from her arm and stared at me shrewdly, still unsure whether I was a patient at the mental hospital. 'Don't breathe in too much or look at the soles of your shoes . . .'

'I won't.' I pointed to the inspector dismissing the troop of journalists. 'The hat? Was the dead man a local fisherman?'

'A Brooklands solicitor. His name's inside it. Geoffrey Fairfax.' She raised the brim of her cap, debating whether to detain me as a possible suspect. 'Did you know him, Mr Pearson . . . ?'

I thanked the constable and climbed the steps beside the freight entrance, trying not to breathe until I reached the open air, and an even deeper darkness than the night.

17

The Geometry of the Crowd

THE POLICE WERE withdrawing from Brooklands, climbing into their patrol cars parked in the perimeter road and driving away from the mall. I walked through the huge crowd in the Metro-Centre plaza and filled my lungs with the sooty air, trying to expel the tang of dust and burnt rubber. The night hung heavily over the sullen faces, the darkness stained with the sweat of athletes' bodies, the scent of chewing gum, bottled beer and anger.

Deep in the crowd, I stood on the running board of an unattended Land Cruiser and raised my head to a brief eddy of cooler air. Tom Carradine had gone, ending his frantic tennis game with himself, no doubt working on a flurry of cheerful press releases. The citadel had been breached, but the police were going, leaving the defence to a scratch brigade of PR executives, floor managers and secretaries.

Two officers in the last patrol car watched as a group of ice-hockey supporters surrounded a forgotten Volvo and drummed their fists on the roof, the familiar tribal tattoo. The windscreen shattered, but the policemen ignored the incident and drove away.

Only the forensics team remained in the basement garage of the Metro-Centre, picking through the debris of my car. Already I missed the classic Jensen, with its elegant body and huge American engine. I found it hard to believe that Geoffrey Fairfax had set out to kill me. Conceivably the solicitor had seen the bomber planting the device in my car, and tried to defuse it before I returned.

Or was I being framed by Fairfax and his shadowy group, set up as the likely bomber, obsessed by my hatred of the Metro-Centre? These were cold questions with even colder answers. The half decanter of Laphroaig I had downed in the penthouse had evaporated from my bloodstream the moment I recognized the shattered Jensen.

I watched the perimeter road, waiting for police reinforcements to arrive. A restless crowd several thousand strong surrounded the Metro-Centre, moving in vast currents within itself. Sports groups circled the mall, football and ice-hockey fans pushing past each other as they roamed the darkness. There was no hostility between the groups, but I could almost smell the anger, the coarse breath of a disturbed beast searching for an enemy.

An ice-hockey cheerleader, the blond thug who had attacked Duncan Christie, strode through the press of people, his fists punching the air. He was moving at random, gathering more and more spectators into his train. Then he lost them when they peeled away and followed a pair of huge weightlifters whose rolling gait cleared their way through the throng.

Family groups, fathers with teenage sons and wives keeping watch on their daughters, still gazed at the Metro-Centre as the last smoke rose through the fissure in the roof. But most of the spectators had turned their backs to the dome. The crowd was watching itself, a congregation of the night waiting for the service to begin.

The Land Cruiser heaved sharply, and a window pillar struck my cheek. I gripped the roof rack as the vehicle rocked from side to side. A group of athletics fans, middle-aged men in team shirts, surrounded the Land Cruiser and tore off the aerials and wing mirrors. People turned to watch them, with the detached stares of office workers viewing the excavation of a building site.

I stepped down from the running board and joined the crowd. A cheer went up as the Land Cruiser tilted on its offside tyres, received a final push and fell heavily to the ground like a stricken rhino. Its alarm lights came on, blinking in panic. Expert hands reached behind the petrol tank, and a clasp knife severed the fuel line. Petrol pooled around the rear tyre, a stench that made me gag.

A cigarette lighter flared in the darkness. There was a flash of light, and miniature flames glowed on the ground, racing around each other. The spectators moved back, hundreds of faces lit in a camp-fire circle. Then a single flame ten feet high lifted from the vehicle, and within an instant the Land Cruiser was an inferno of seared paintwork and exploding glass.

When I reached the perimeter road, still waiting for the police to arrive, three more cars were burning. Smoke drifted over the heads of the crowd, and a few people followed me, shadowing my foot-steps and changing direction as I did. Three ice-hockey supporters strode on my right, while an elderly couple in St George's shirts kept in step on my left. Behind them came a large group of supporters, silently drinking from their beer cans. When I turned to avoid a traffic sign the entire column swung after me. I stopped to pick a strip of burnt rubber from my shoe, and they marked time without thinking, then resumed their strolling pace when I set off again.

None of them looked at me, or seemed aware that I was leading them. They followed me like commuters in a crowded railway terminal, trailing anyone who had found a gap through the press of travellers. The unique internal geometry of the crowd had come into play, picking first one leader and then another. Apparently passive, they regrouped and changed direction according to no obvious logic, a slime mould impelled by gradients of boredom and aimlessness.

Trying to lose them, I crossed the perimeter road. Ahead lay the Brooklands main thoroughfare, a high street of office buildings, shops and small department stores that led to the town hall. At least five hundred people were following my lead, though a few had over-taken me like pilot fish. Together we had drawn off other sections of the crowd in the Metro-Centre car parks. Groups of several hundred supporters crossed the perimeter road and set off through the side streets. Gangs of young men in St George's shirts playfully rough-housed with each other. The Metro-Centre was forgotten, the last smoke rising from its dome, a mournful Thames Valley Vesuvius.

I walked on, keeping as close as I could to the office entrances. Within fifty yards I realized that the crowd had forgotten me. Forced together by the narrow street, everyone moved shoulder to shoulder. I had served my role, and the logic of the crowd had dispensed with me.

I rested in the entrance to an insurance company and watched the people passing by, cigarettes glowing in the darkness, spray confetti arcing across the shop windows. A sound system blared out bursts of rock music. I was breathing rapidly, and felt strangely excited, as if about to make love to an unfamiliar woman, in charge of myself for the first time since my arrival in Brooklands.

And still there were no police. I passed a small car forced to stop on the pavement, roof dented by heavy fists. The grey-haired driver clutched his steering wheel, too shocked to step from his vehicle. Gangs of youths hurled beer bottles at the upstairs windows of a local newspaper, and the sound of falling glass cut through the jeers. A trio of eastern European men emerged from the doorway of an agency recruiting night cleaners for Brooklands Hospital. They were quickly set upon. Noses bloody, arms shielding their faces, they fought their way into a side street through a gauntlet of kicks and punches.

Fifty yards ahead was the main square, spotlights playing on the balcony of the town hall. A celebratory dinner for the winning sports teams was being held by the mayor and his councillors, and a film crew waited on the balcony, lights in place.

Within minutes a huge crowd of supporters filled the square, whistling and shouting at the town hall, overrunning the municipal gardens and trampling the flowerbeds. A modest cordon of uniformed constables guarded the steps of the town hall, but no other police had been drafted in, as if the near-riot moving through the streets, the burning cars and vandalized shops, were part of the evening's festivities.

New arrivals pressed into the square, athletics teams carrying their banners, ice-hockey claques wearing their helmets and elbow guards. I edged around the fringes of the crowd, and climbed the steps of Geoffrey Fairfax's law offices. The premises were dark, with steel grilles bolted across the doors and windows, as if the staff had been aware that a riot was scheduled for that evening.

A cheer went up from the crowd, followed by a din of hoots and whistles. Brooklands' mayor, a prominent local businessman who was wearing his insignia and chain, came onto the balcony with the captains of two football clubs. Confused by the restless crowd, and the sight of a car burning in a nearby side street, the mayor made an effort to call for quiet, but his amplified voice was drowned by the boos. Beer bottles flew over the heads of the nervous police and shattered on the civic steps.

Then the boos ended, and the square fell silent. People around me were clapping and whistling their approval. A huge cheer went up, followed by a medley of hunting horns, good-humoured hoots and shouts.

Two men stood on the balcony behind the mayor. One was David Cruise, dressed like a bandleader in white tuxedo and red silk cummerbund, grinning broadly and raising his arms to embrace the crowd. He bowed his head, a show of modesty that struck me as odd, given that his giant face with its unrelenting smile presided over Brooklands from the display screens at the football ground. In reality, his face seemed small and vulnerable, as if the effort of shrinking himself to human size had exhausted him.

The mayor offered him the microphone, clearly hoping that Cruise would calm the crowd and defuse its anger after the attack on the Metro-Centre. The cable announcer ducked his head and tried to leave the balcony, but found his way blocked by Tony Maxted. Thuggish in his dinner jacket, shaven head gleaming in the camera lights, the psychiatrist held Cruise's arms and turned him to face the crowd, like the senior aide of a president with the first signs of Alzheimer's and unsure what audience he was meant to be addressing.

Scarcely loosening his grip, Maxted prompted Cruise with a few lines of dialogue, shouting them into his ear as the crowd began to jeer. Behind the two men was William Sangster, a leather bowling jacket over his evening wear. He was strained but smiling, puckering his plump cheeks as if trying to disguise himself from those in the crowd who might recognize their former head teacher. He and Maxted pushed Cruise to the balcony, each raising one of the announcer's hands like seconds rallying a boxer who had stepped uneasily into the ring. They seemed to be urging Cruise to assume the leadership of the crowd and challenge the powers of the night who had defiled the Metro-Centre.

Cruise, however, refused to give in. He waved to the crowd, but he had switched off his smile, a gesture that seemed to say he was switching off his audience. He turned his back on the noisy square, forced his way between Maxted and Sangster, and left the balcony.

There were catcalls as the mayor took the microphone. Football rattles whirled, unheard in any stadium for years, their grating clatter like the chitter of monkeys. The crowd was restless and on the edge of its patience. Beside me, a woman and her teenage daughter, both in ice-hockey shirts, began to whistle in disgust. They needed action, without any idea what form this might take. They had waited for David Cruise to tell them and lead them forward. They would follow him, but they were just as ready to jeer and deride him. They needed violence, and realized that David Cruise was too unreal, too much an electronic illusion, a confection of afternoon television at its blandest and sweetest. They hungered for reality, a rare event in their lives, a product that Cruise could never endorse or supply.

Hoots and cheers rose around the square as Tony Maxted spoke into the microphone. But he was too thuggish, with his Roman head and mask-like face that revealed everything. The crowd wanted to be used, but in their own way. An ironic Mexican wave moved around the square in a blizzard of whistles trained by years of practice at the decisions of blind referees. A group of youths set fire to a park bench, tearing branches from the municipal shrubbery to feed the flames.

A blow struck the side of my head, almost knocking me from my feet. A huge explosion sounded from a nearby street. Everyone ducked as the flash lit the trembling windows around the square. The aftershock thrashed the trees, sucking at the air in my lungs and straining my ribs. A vacuum engulfed the night, then hurtled back into itself.

18

A Failed Revolution

EVERYONE WAS RUNNING, as if trying to chase down their fears. Panic and anger raced in a hundred directions. Within a minute the square was empty, though the town hall and nearby law offices were unharmed. The explosion jarred clouds of dust from the elderly pointing, and wraiths of vapour floated like the palest smoke, the bestirred ghosts of these antique piles.

The bomb had exploded in a narrow side street of lock-up garages, but no one was hurt, as if Brooklands was a stage set, an adventure playground haunted by malicious and incendiary children. I listened to the ambulance sirens swerving through the streets, the seesaw wail of police klaxons. Beyond them rose a louder and deeper sound, the baying of a crowd around an enemy goalmouth.

Riot stalked the streets of Brooklands for the next hour. It wore two costumes, farce and cruelty. Gangs of football supporters broke into every Asian supermarket and looted the alcohol counters, making off with crates of beer that they stacked in the streets and turned into free bars for the roaming crowd. The riot soon began to drink itself into befuddlement, but bands of more determined ice-hockey followers joined forces with track-and-field supporters and marched on an industrial estate in run-down east Brooklands, a night-time wilderness of video cameras and security patrols. Frantic attack dogs hurled themselves at the chain-link fencing, driven to a frenzy by the banner-waving marchers who tossed their looted burgers over the wire.

Waiting for the police to arrive, I followed this barely disciplined private army to a gypsy hostel beside a bus depot. The aggressive whistles and chanting terrified the exhausted Roma women trying to restrain their husbands. I left them to it, and walked back to the town hall. An overturned car burned outside the ballet school as a breakaway group of boxing supporters tried to provoke the students, whom they saw as a pampered and idle breed of dubious sexuality.

Beyond the football stadium a hard core of violent demonstrators invaded a Bangladeshi housing estate. They burned a football banner in the garden of a shabby bungalow, a fiery cross doused in petrol siphoned from the old Mercedes in the drive. When the bungalow's owner, an Asian dentist I had seen in the hospital, opened his door to protest, he met a hail of beer cans.

Through all this pointless mayhem moved Dr Tony Maxted in his Mazda sports car, still wearing his dinner jacket like a playboy revolutionary. Whenever the riot seemed to slacken he left his car and roamed through the crowd, sharing a can of beer and leading the singsongs, filming the scene on his mobile phone. As I expected, few police appeared through the smoke and noise. They remained on the perimeter of Brooklands, keeping out any curious visitors. On the roof of the town hall I saw Sangster standing beside Superintendent Leighton, surveying the riot with the calm gaze of landowners observing their tenants at play, as if burning cars and racial brawls were boisterous recreations that suited the brutal peasantry of the motorway towns.

But the outside world had begun to take notice. Behind the town hall two police motorcyclists intercepted a BBC news team setting up their camera. They ordered the crew back into their van, told the driver to reverse and escorted the vehicle back to the M25.

A small crowd watched them go, disappointed that the Brooklands riot, the town's only claim to fame since the 1930s, would not be on the breakfast news. In the brief silence before they found something else to attack I listened to the latest bulletin on a radio shared by two teenage girls in St George's shirts. Street fights between rival sports fans were taking place, the reporter noted, an outbreak of England's traditional pastime, football hooliganism. The town's police force, he added, was on alert but was being kept in reserve.

Disappointed by their enemies, the rioters began to turn on themselves, and the night wound down into a series of drunken brawls and bored attacks on already looted premises. Turning my back on all this, I set off through the quieter side streets. I was lost, and I wanted to be. I hated the riot and the racist violence, but I knew that the crowd was disappointed by the failure of the evening to ignite and set the motorway towns ablaze. Already I guessed that the bomb placed in my Jensen had been an attempt to light a fuse. But a vital element was missing from the minds of the bored consumers who made up the Brooklands population. Marooned in their retail paradise, they lacked the courage to bring about their own destruction. The crowd outside the town hall had wanted David Cruise to lead them, but the cable presenter was too unsure of himself. The riot had ended with the frustrated mob glaring at itself in the mirror and breaking its bloodied forehead against the glass.

I knew now that we had all been manipulated by a small set of inept puppeteers. A group of prominent local citizens who felt threatened by the Metro-Centre had mounted an amateurish putsch, an attempt to turn back the clock and reclaim their ancient county from a plague of retailers. Geoffrey Fairfax, Dr Maxted, William Sangster among others, probably with the connivance of Superintendent Leighton and senior police officers, had seized the chance given them by the Metro-Centre shooting that led to my father's death. Only a direct attack on the great shopping mall would rouse a deeply sedated population. No vandalized church or library, no ransacked school or heritage site, would touch a nerve. A violent revolt, the cordite of civil strife in suburban Surrey, would force the county council and the Home Office to react. The retail parks would close, the fox would return to his haunts, and the hunt would gallop again over abandoned dual carriageways and through the forecourts of forgotten filling stations.

Meanwhile, my martyred Jensen was on its way to the police forensics lab, and I might find myself arraigned as the instigator of a failed revolution . . .

19

The Need to Understand

A LINE OF AMBULANCES appeared through the smoke and haze, waiting outside the Accident & Emergency entrance of Brooklands Hospital. The rioters had moved down the street facing the hospital, wrecking several of the shops. The broken windows of a travel agency lay on the pavement in front of me, a glass snare ready to bite the ankles of any incautious stroller.

I picked my way through the ugly needles, and noticed a woman in a white coat who stood beside a parked car, gesturing in a vague way at the drifting smoke. Recognizing Dr Julia Goodwin, I felt a rush of pleasure in seeing her, and for a moment the whole disastrous evening fell behind me.

'Julia? What's happened? You look . . .'

'Mr . . . Pearson? God, everything's happened.' She seemed confused, fists drumming on the car as if haranguing an obstinate patient. 'What are you doing here?'

'I've been taking part in a riot.' I tried to calm her, holding her wrists in my hands, a pair of pulses that seemed to throb to a different beat. 'Are you . . . ?'

'All right? What the hell do you think?' She wrenched her hands away from me, and noticed an ambulance driver stepping from his cab. She waved to him rather giddily, and lowered her voice, eyes swerving across the haze. 'Richard, you're pretty sane, some of the time. What exactly is going on?'

'Don't you know?'

'I haven't the least idea.' She stared at the car, and said matter-of-factly, as if not wholly believing herself: 'Geoffrey Fairfax is dead.'

'The bomb at the Metro-Centre. Tragic . . . I'm sorry for him.'

'He was a bit of a thug, actually.' Saying this seemed to revive her. 'He tried to defuse the bomb.'

'Who told you that?'

'Sergeant Falconer. An odd little fish; I wouldn't like her interrogating me. Geoffrey must have seen the device in the bomber's car. She says they'll trace the owner. Who drives around with a bloody bomb in the back seat?' She turned to me and without thinking brushed the soot from my shoulder, as if grooming a neighbour's cat. 'Richard, this whole place is going mad.'

'I think that's the idea. It didn't really work, though.'

'What are you talking about? Have you seen Tony Maxted and Sangster?'

'All over the place. They're everywhere. Practically cheerleaders.'

'They're trying to lower the temperature. Calm people down, and head off anything really ugly. The police are backing them.'

'Is that what Sergeant Falconer said?'

'More or less. She was a bit shaky, as you'd expect. I don't know what Geoffrey Fairfax saw in her . . .'

I held Julia's shoulders, trying to steady her when she stumbled against the car. I pointed to the hospital, as an ambulance driver switched off his engine. 'Shouldn't you be in –?'

'A&E? My shift ended ten minutes ago.' Reminded of her professional role, she eased me away and straightened her gown. 'Thanks for the help. You're very sweet. It's amazing there aren't more casualties. Kicking in windows, setting fire to cars – people in Brooklands seem to have the knack. I want to get home, but look at this . . .'

She pointed to the shattered windscreen, a spider's web of fractured glass left by a baseball bat. Raising her head, she began to wail softly to herself.

'Julia, we'll call a taxi.' I tried to take one of her hands. 'Listen, I'll walk you back to the hospital. Perhaps you should see someone?'

'Who?' My inept question stopped her in mid-breath. 'One of the medics? Holy Jesus!' She blew the hair out of her eyes, genuinely amazed by me. 'Richard, I work with them all day. There isn't one of the little shits I'd trust myself with . . .'

'Fair enough.' I leaned over the windscreen and used my elbow to force in the glass. 'You can still drive the car. Just keep the speed down.'

'Good.' Brightening, she said: 'I'll give you a lift. Where's your car?'

'It . . . the engine blew up. They've taken the car away to have a look at it.'

'Too bad. I know the feeling.' She opened the door and swept the beads of glass from her seat. Settling herself behind the wheel, she said: 'In the end, the street is all you can trust.'

We drove through the empty town, fragments of windscreen glass blowing onto our laps. The Metro-Centre was quiet, the last smoke rising from the overturned Land Cruiser. A fire-engine crew were hosing down another gutted vehicle in the deserted plaza. The riot had ended, as if full time had been called by a referee. A few supporters walked home, St George's shirts tied around their waists, bare-chested husbands arm in arm with their wives. A police car cruised past them, quietly retaking the night.

Driving calmed Julia. She peered through the hole in the windscreen, and whistled at the burnt-out cars.

'Richard, what happened here? Something new and very dangerous is going on.'

'You're right. The bomb at the Metro-Centre was the signal. The damage to the dome was supposed to trigger a general uprising.'

'It did.'

'No. Tonight was just another football riot. Maxted and Sangster are being used. I don't know about Geoffrey Fairfax. The real people behind the bomb want street revolution, something violent and ugly, spreading to all the motorway towns. With David Cruise as the Wat

Tyler of cable TV, leading a new peasants' revolt. Then the police and Home Office will move in. Close down the dome, wheel on the cucumber sandwiches and relaunch the kingdom of Surrey.'

'It nearly happened.'

'Not quite. David Cruise wouldn't take the bait. He hasn't spent all these years in television for nothing. He could see it was a set-up.'

'But why? I hate the damned dome, but I don't want to kill anyone.'

'You've still got your job. There are people who were doing very nicely and feel left out. Power has moved to the Metro-Centre and the retail parks along the M25. It's a new kind of consumerism – sponsored football teams, supporters' clubs, marching bands, stadium lights blazing all night, cable TV. A lot of people don't like it. The police, the local council, old-style businessmen who can't get their noses in the trough. They want to discredit the Metro-Centre, and they'll do anything to harm it.'

'Tony Maxted? And Bill Sangster?'

'They're too amateurish. For Maxted the whole thing is a case study. One day he'll write a book and get it adapted on BBC2. Sangster is different, how and why I don't know.'

'I do. Listen, he's drawn to the madness of it all. Every day he has to hold his school together, a huge effort of will. Why bother? Secretly, he's tired. He wouldn't mind if the whole bloody place was flushed down the loo . . .' She reached out to grip my hand. 'Richard, I'm sorry about Brooklands, it's been a nightmare for you . . .'

I sat back, glad to be with this spirited and chaotic young woman, even in this shambles of a night, which had left me more confused than ever. Part of me wanted to confront Julia Goodwin about my father's fatal injury and the mysterious role played by Duncan Christie. She wore her unease over the old man's death like a badly tailored shroud. Emotions crowded her face, competing for space among its frowns and grimaces. Like a child, her guilty feelings played around her mouth and bared teeth, fretting her tired eyes and the muscles of her cheeks. At times, her entire personality was a courtroom sitting in judgement on herself.

When we reached my father's flat she turned carefully into the drive, then lost her bearings in the darkness. A privet hedge thrashed what was left of the windscreen, sending a shower of sharp beads across us. I took the wheel, forced the gear lever into neutral and let the car freewheel across the gravel. Julia peered into the driving mirror, wincing at a tiny nick on her forehead.

'You ought to look at that.' I helped her from the car. 'There's an old airline first-aid kit. Have a drink while I call a taxi . . .'

I hesitated before opening the front door of the flat, unsure how Julia would respond to my father's presence in every leather armchair and ashtray. At first she was stiff and awkward, as if expecting him to appear and challenge her. But she seemed at home when she emerged from the bathroom, a plaster over her eyebrow. She circled the living room, warming her hands around the tumbler of brandy, smiling at the pipe stands and the chorus line of framed photographs. Had she been the last of my father's lovers? I could imagine her in the kitchen, reminding him about his next flu jab as he cooked an omelette for her.

Surprisingly, she was at ease with me, and sat on the arm of my chair, a hand on my shoulder.

'Richard? Are you holding on?'

'Just about. That was one very bizarre day. I'm glad you're here.'

'I wanted to see it.' She winced at the tireless seesaw of a distant alarm. 'Richard, I warned you strange things are going on.'

'I'm not sure what is going on. After lunch I met the local wild man of the desert – your friend Duncan Christie. Completely mad and completely sane at the same time. Then Maxted locked me up in his loony bin. I got out thanks to his blonde stooge, Sergeant Falconer, and the next thing I knew I was leading a riot. For ten minutes this huge crowd was actually following me.'

'We have to follow someone. Poor devils, there's nothing else in our lives.'

'Not much, anyway. That's why I made a very good living – everything we believe comes from advertising. Tonight was different, though. The Metro-Centre bomb was supposed to light a fuse, but it didn't work.'

'Maybe it wasn't advertising anything?'

'You're right. There needs to be a message. Next time I'll remember.'

'Another wild man from the desert. Dear Jesus . . .' She took her drink and sat on the coffee table facing me. 'Listen, Richard. You're waking up into the nightmare you helped to script. Go back to London. The suburbs are far too weird for you. Why did you leave your job?'

'It left me. To tell the truth, I was sacked. Pushed out by a rival who knew all my weaknesses.'

'How come?'

'She was my wife. In fact, I'd reached the end of the road.'

'With her?'

'And with the advertising business. The economy is rolling along an endless plateau, and consumers are bored with the view. Something strange is needed to get them to sit up.'

'How strange?'

'Strange, and more than a little mad. That was my big idea. We even had a slogan – "Mad is bad. Bad is good." We tried it out once, with a new micro-car, but people got killed. No one liked it after that.'

'Terribly dull of them.'

'That's what I thought. Another of the great advertising break-throughs that got nowhere.'

'Its time will come.' She brushed her hair back from her face, as if exposing herself to me, the removal of yet another of the veils that hung between us. 'How well did you know your father?'

'Hardly at all. My mother never got over his leaving her. For years she told me he had died in an air crash. Cheques would arrive on my birthday and she'd claim they came from the other side. I always thought high-street banks were outposts of heaven. The curious thing is that I've got to know him better since he died.'

'I'm sure he was a fine man.'

'He was. With one or two odd ideas.'

'Interesting . . .' She moved around the living room, and peered into the corridor that led to the bedrooms. 'Can I snoop around? These days, you don't see where your patients live.'

I followed her into the kitchen, and watched as she glanced at the modest array of herbs and spices. She patted the basil plant I had bought, tore off a leaf and raised it to a nostril. She was tired but stylish, clearly moved by the memories of the old man she had tried to keep alive for a few last hours. I trailed after her, already roused by her scent, a perfume of her own distilled from beauty, bloody-mindedness and chronic fatigue.

'So this is where he slept?' She stood in the doorway of my father's bedroom, nose quickening at the dark, picking up the spoor of an old man's body. She stepped forward and switched on the bedside lamp, then sat on the bedspread, smoothing the stress lines from the silk fabric.

'Julia . . . ?'

'Here . . .' She beckoned me to sit beside her. As if without thinking, she loosened the top button of her shirt. 'So . . . his head lay on that pillow. An old pilot's dreams. Think of them, Richard. All those endless runways . . .'

'Julia . . .' I sat beside her and held her shoulders. I realized that she was shaking, a faint trembling as if she had caught a sudden chill, a cold draught from a door onto the dark that had come ajar. A desperate woman was sitting on my father's bed, about to make love to his son for reasons that had everything and nothing to do with sex, the kind of clutching and violent love that only the bereaved ever experience.

She took my hand and slipped it inside her shirt, then placed it over her breast. 'You don't have to like me.'

'Julia . . .' I tried to calm her. 'Not here. Let's go into my bedroom. Julia . . . ?'

'No.' She spoke flatly, in an almost coarse voice. 'Here.'

'Dear, try to —'

'Here! It's got to be here!' She turned a fierce gaze on me. 'Can't you understand?'

20

The Racing Circuit

I LEFT HER sleeping in my father's bed. It was still dark when I woke at four, uneasy with the odd contours of the mattress, the narrow hollows of an old man's hips and shoulders, and the more unsettling imprint of his mind. Julia lay beside me when I sat up, then turned and nestled easily into the aged pilot's mould. A strange night passage had exhausted her. Restless dreams followed a fierce act of love. She had seized me as if I were a demon to be pinioned, a delegate from my father's grave. Sex with me was part atonement and part restitution, an act of penance.

I sat on the bed, stroking the cloud of dark hair, and gripped her free hand, hoping to force something of my affection into her. There was a faint answering pulse, like a thank-you note slipped under the emotional door, and she sank into a shallow morning sleep that would last for hours.

I needed to get out and run the streets before anyone else was up. As I pulled on my tracksuit I carried out a quick inventory of myself. A bleak list: I missed my car, my job, my friends in London. I missed my father, whom I had never known, and I missed the quirky but likeable young doctor I had met at the hospital, with whom I had shared a bed but scarcely knew any better. Some kind of guilt and unease separated us, despite all the warmth I clearly felt for her. Had she failed my father in some way during his last hours in the intensive care unit? Sitting astride me, she made love as if trying to resuscitate a corpse. I listened to her breathing, a child's small burps and swallows, sounds shaped like bliss, and thought of the daughter that Julia and I might have one day.

But I needed to leave the flat and visit the Brooklands circuit, and hear the ghosts of engines rumbling in the dark.

A carton of orange juice in my hand, I jogged out of the estate and set off for the racetrack half a mile to the south. Around me the residential streets were still silent, the suburbs of nowhere, immaculate pavilions that reminded me of the stylish tombs on the mortuary island in the Venice lagoon.

A section of the Brooklands embankment rose through the darkness, thirty feet high at its peak, its ridge line cut by an access road. I ran through this narrow corridor, and then stopped at the beach of ancient concrete. I thought of my father visiting the track in the 1930s, a small boy stunned by the reek of fuel oil and expensive perfume, the scent of glamour and danger. Spectacular crashes filled the newsreels of the day, heroic deaths that were England's answer to the dictators across the Channel, and expressed the kingdom's unconscious need for war.

'Hello . . . ? You down there . . . come up and join me. You get a better view of the race . . .'

Above me, on the upper slope of the embankment, a man was strolling through the darkness. He wore a white tuxedo, as if he had strayed from an all-night party. He beckoned to me with an actorish gesture, but moved cautiously along the pitted concrete, as if a lifetime of treacherous floors had taught him to be wary of any surface. Seeing that I was too out of breath to climb up to him, he made his way down the slope.

I waited for him to reach me, and noticed an American car parked on the road below. A chauffeur in a peaked cap leaned against a door, smoking a cigarette and drawing small sketches on the dark air with its red tip.

'Right . . .' David Cruise took my hand, smilingly easy and avuncular, as if greeting a new contestant onto his cable show. 'It's worth going up there, you can still feel the slipstream. Listen – did you hear that?'

'Hold on. A Bugatti, I think. Four carburettors, or maybe a Napier-Railton.'

'That's it!' Pleased that I had played my role in his little routine, Cruise shook my hand. 'Mr –?'

I introduced myself, but Cruise waved my name into the misty dawn air, taking for granted that he was too famous to identify himself. Without being aware of it, he was playing to the camera, which I sensed was somewhere beyond his favourite left profile.

'Good, good . . .' He savoured the air, as if relishing the tang of burnt rubber. 'Wonderful . . . unlimited horsepower, twenty-litre engines. Nothing like it today. We have the technology, but we can't build a dream.'

'Formula One? No?'

'Come on . . . millionaires in asbestos suits plastered with logos. This was the real thing.'

'More than the Metro-Centre?'

Cruise stopped to glance at me as we made our way down to the Lincoln. 'The Metro-Centre? I wish I could see it lasting seven years, let alone seventy.'

He gazed over the dark rooftops of the town, where the last haze of smoke from a few smouldering cars merged into the morning mist. At the football stadium the giant screens were still lit, showing an intermission commercial to the deserted stands. His screen self spoke to an elderly team supporter about her new bedroom suite, his hand bouncing the mattress as if inviting her for a romp.

Cruise silenced me with a raised fist, and stopped to watch himself. His mouth mimed in response to his signature repertory of engaging smiles, the shy grimaces that expressed a deep interest in his studio guests.

Despite the dim light, I could see him clearly in the pale aura of suburban fame that surrounded him. The dark was his medium, the deep blackness disguised as the interior of a TV studio. I was struck by how small he seemed, though he was almost six feet tall, with the kind of muscled physique found among gym users. He was bantering and easy-listening, but never ironic about himself. A minor deity should never express doubt over his own existence. In every way he was a creature of afternoon television, with a head of silver hair sculpted to show off the lower half of his face and hide his high forehead and the inner coldness of his eyes. Long ago he had convinced himself that he liked and felt at ease with ordinary people, and the illusion had sustained him.

A brief cascade of sparks flared beyond the north stand of the stadium, a warehouse put to the torch, an insurance scam taking advantage of the night's fires.

Cruise winced and turned towards his car. 'Madhouse – looting, arson, broken windows . . . there was a bomb at the Metro-Centre. As if we haven't got enough problems.'

'I saw the damage. The police took me into the basement.'

'You were there? Brave man. They planted the bomb in someone's car.'

Cruise had reached the Lincoln, where the driver stood by the open passenger door. I decided to take a chance, and said: 'My car, as it happens.'

'Your car?' Cruise paused before getting into his rear seat. He noticed me for the first time, a face in a studio crowd that the director had pinpointed through his earpiece. 'They blew up your car? Poor man. You must have been shocked.'

'I was. An old Jensen. Beautiful car: nothing worked, including the rear lock.'

'Obliterated? Thank God the bomber was killed.' Cruise pointed to the silent embankment. 'And that's why you came here, to the racing circuit. You wanted to hear those engines again. The authentic thing, like your Jensen.'

'You might be right.'

'I am right!' Cruise held my shoulders in a pair of powerful hands, as if comforting a bereaved contestant. 'I know – that's why I came. It's a ruin, but it's the only part of Brooklands that's real.'

'The Metro-Centre is real.'

'Please . . .' He took my arm. Deep in thought, he walked me away from the Lincoln. 'Listen, I've seen you before?'

'Yesterday. Outside the Metro-Centre. You arrived for your afternoon show.'

'No. Somewhere else. Years ago.' He stared into my face with the cold eye of a pathologist recognizing a cadaver. 'You were younger, tougher, more ambitious. Your voice was higher, you ordered me around. God, I needed that job. What business are you in?'

'Advertising.'

'That's it! The crazy Skoda commercial. I played the dangerous driver. Everyone thought it was mad.'

'It was mad. That was the idea.'

'My agent warned me not to do it. Too weird, he said. I'd be type-cast. Fat chance, I hadn't worked for a year. It turned out I was too big for the car, they couldn't see my eyes. But after that I never looked back. My agent was fighting them off. In a way, thanks to you . . . ?'

'Richard Pearson. You were very good.'

'No, I was still trying to act. A big mistake in this business. You have to be yourself. That takes a lot of working at. Every one of us is a cast of characters. I told myself I was a director putting on a new play. All these people turn up at the audition, and they're all me. Some are more interesting than others, some are more real, some can reach your heart. This happens every morning when I wake up. I have to choose, and I have to be ruthless. You understand that.'

'Absolutely. It's a matter of finding the right roles. The kind of roles where you don't need to act.'

'That's it. I remember, last year you won an industry award. At the Savoy, I saw you collect it . . .'

Cruise straightened up, leaving his thoughts to float away across the embankment. I assumed that I would soon be forgotten, the creator of his career left here like the Ben Gunn of this concrete beach.

Then I noticed that the driver had walked around the Lincoln to the offside. Both passenger doors were now open.

'Richard . . .' Cruise's sunburnt hand took my elbow, steering me towards the car as if moving a lucky contestant to his prize. 'Let's have some breakfast at my house. There are one or two things we need to talk over. You can give me your advice. Already I feel we can work together . . .'

21

A New Politics

'BROOKLANDS? THE WHOLE place is off its rocker. I just don't get it.' David Cruise screwed up his paper tissue and threw it at the camera mounted on a tripod beside the swimming pool. 'What on earth was happening last night?'

'I think you know.' I watched the surface of the water, as calm and eventless as plate glass. 'An attempted putsch.'

'Putsch?'

'A palace revolution.'

Cruise grimaced into his make-up mirror. 'Where's the palace?'

'We live in it. The Metro-Centre and all the retail parks between here and Heathrow. You and me and the people who watch your TV shows.'

'Not enough of them – that's the problem. Who was meant to lead this revolution?'

'You know that as well. You were.'

'Me? I'll remember, the next time I need a dressing room and a courtesy car. Some revolution, some palace . . .'

We were sitting by the indoor pool attached to Cruise's house on the Seven Hills estate, an exclusive Weybridge community once home to the Beatles, Tom Jones and other pop celebrities. The domed glass roof – a deliberate echo, I assumed, of the Metro-Centre – resembled an observatory open to the heavens, but the only star ever watched by David Cruise was himself.

The house was a substantial Tudorbethan pile, its rooms large enough to serve as squash courts, furnished like an out-of-season hotel. In an office next to the cloakrooms the day staff negotiated the fees for Cruise's charity engagements and dealt with his fan mail. As soon as we arrived, Cruise scanned his faxes and emails, then led me through the empty rooms to the swimming pool, where we lay back in sun loungers beside the bar. Two docile Filipina girls served us breakfast – pawpaw, coffee and lamb cutlets – but Cruise was more interested in his large vodka.

I watched him settle his fleshy body in the lounger, white tuxedo and ruffed shirt well displayed. As we walked through the rooms of this mansion he had seemed bored by it, and vaguely suspicious of what was supposed to be his own home, aware that it was little more than a stage set.

Despite myself, I rather liked him. He discounted his own success, and was searching for some kind of certainty in his life, though his entire career was built on illusion and a set of emotional three-card tricks. His manner was overbearing, but he was deeply insecure and forever manipulating me into flattering him.

Meanwhile I decided to carry out an experiment, my last attempt to spring loose from the web of conspiracies that was responsible for killing my father. So far I had achieved almost nothing, playing the amateur detective who blundered into danger, perpetually dazed by the doors slammed in his face.

But in one area I was a complete professional, in that electric realm where advertising and popular taste met and fused. Brooklands and the motorway towns were the ultimate consumer test panel, and here I could put into practice the subversive ideas that had cost me my career. At Brooklands there were no ethics committees to keep an eye on me, no strategy meetings forever urging caution, and no ambitious wife waiting for me to make a mistake. If I could change the mental ecology of this uneasy Surrey town, and release the wayward energies of its people, I might penetrate the polite conspiracies that held them down, and find why my father had died so pointlessly.

For the moment, at least, I had made my first valuable ally. David Cruise was the most important person I had met in Brooklands, and one of the few who was ready to talk. He seemed vulnerable, eyeing me cannily over his vodka, as if he felt that the Metro-Centre bomb was aimed at him. This cable presenter, housewives' pin-up and local ombudsman probably lacked a single friend.

I remembered leaving the Brooklands circuit with him. As we sat in the rear seat of the Lincoln, I had told him that my father had visited the racetrack as a boy. Almost without thinking, Cruise reached out and gripped my hand, sealing a comradeship fused in the fire of terrorism. And for all his blandness, a personality as soft and depthless as a TV commercial, he had stood up to Tony Maxted and Sangster, refusing to play their game.

'I admire you for turning them down,' I told him as the Filipina girls drifted silently between us, taking away the breakfast trays. 'They were offering you the keys to the kingdom.'

'Or Guildford Prison.' Cruise lightly touched the tiny bottom of the older Filipina. 'They had everything set up, the crowd going wild, the follow-up bomb, a complete circus. They wanted me screaming from a balcony. A suburban dictator based at the Metro-Centre – can you imagine it?'

'I can. Every shopping mall and retail park turning into a local soviet. A popular uprising that starts at the nearest Tesco. It's possible. There's a hunger for violence, that's why sport obsesses the whole country. Everyone's suffocating – too many barcode readers, too many CCTV cameras and double yellow lines. That second bomb really got them going.'

'That was the idea.' Cruise studied his empty glass, as if in mourning for the first drink of the day. 'Kill a few people and everyone thinks they've had a good time. Not for me – it's always safer to stick to what you know nothing about. In my case, sport and home improvements. Forget about right-wing cliques hiding behind their family crests.'

'I have. But the groundswell was still there. I could feel it in the crowd. They wanted you to lead them. You're the figurehead who stands in everyone's mind for the Metro-Centre. You keep the supporters' clubs on their toes, you can say what everyone secretly feels about immigrants and asylum seekers. You're the star in every housewife's dreams . . .'

'Too much me . . . that's the problem. I have to carry the whole Metro-Centre.' Cruise lay back, eyes lowered, lips forming and re-forming a series of half-smiles, the signal that he was about to be sincere. 'Listen, Richard – you have to understand. I'm a fake.'

'Come on . . .'

'No. I play a role. I'm still an actor, I act being a sports commentator. Do I know anything about sports? Between you and me, almost nothing. I've never sliced a tee shot, never potted a black, never scored a try or missed a penalty.'

'Does that matter?'

'No. In fact, it's a help. The best commentators know nothing about sport. Their commentaries are the kind that viewers would give. "He's playing a straight bat, she's concentrating on winning . . ." Bloody silly. I'm in the looking-glass business, I give the public the kind of face they want to see in the bathroom mirror when they get up. Someone who shares their boredom and tells them a visit to the Metro-Centre is the answer to all their problems.'

'You do a great job. I was outside the town hall last night. They like you.'

'Who knows? They cheer, then they boo.' Cruise leaned forward, lowering his voice. 'You may not believe it, Richard, but when I was young most people disliked me. Instinctively. They disliked the friendly smile, the bonhomie. They thought I was acting all the time. Even my parents avoided me. My father was a working-class GP. He specialized in hypochondria, it was the easiest to cure. My mother was a full-time case study. They scrimped and saved to send me to a private school; now I have to hide the accent and pretend I come from some Heathrow suburb. Every time we meet I know they think I've failed.'

'You haven't. People here believe in you.'

'Don't say that. If enough people believe in you, it's a sure sign you'll end up nailed to a cross. It's a job, an assignment. Sometimes I feel I'm not up to it any more.'

'You are up to it, and it's not just a job.'

I waited, as Cruise seemed to sink into a trough of introspection and self-pity. He lay back in the sun lounger, his body stirring like a snake trying to shed its skin, a sleek carapace that lost its lustre as he watched. Then he sat up, shaking himself free of any self-doubt, and threw his empty vodka glass into the swimming pool. The flat surface dissolved into a rush of fleeing waves, which Cruise watched like a crystal-gazer stirring the future.

'Richard?' He beckoned to me. 'Go on. I think you have a few ideas for me.'

'Right. I'd like to lay something out. A different approach.'

'That's good – the Metro-Centre could use some help.'

'And you've got exactly what it needs. A new kind of politics is emerging at the Metro-Centre, and you're in the perfect place to lead it.'

'Once, maybe . . .'

'Now. I see you as tomorrow's man. Consumerism is the door to the future, and you're helping to open it. People accumulate emotional capital, as well as cash in the bank, and they need to invest those emotions in a leader figure. They don't want a jackbooted fanatic ranting on a balcony. They want a TV host sitting with a studio panel, talking quietly about what matters in their lives. It's a new kind of democracy, where we vote at the cash counter, not the ballot box. Consumerism is the greatest device anyone has invented for controlling people. New fantasies, new dreams and dislikes, new souls to heal. For some peculiar reason, they call it shopping. But it's really the purest kind of politics. And you're at the leading edge. In fact, you could practically run the country.'

'The country? Now I am worried . . .' Cruise gripped the arms

145

of his lounger, overcoming the temptation to stand and pace up and down. He looked at me with the intense gaze he turned upon the guests on his daytime show, and I could see that everything I said had already crossed his mind. 'You're right – I can lead them. I know it's there, inside me.'

'It's there, all right. Believe me, David.'

'I do a lot of charity work, opening retail parks, big hypermarkets out on the M25 – it helps viewers get cabled up to the Metro-Centre. There are millions of people out there, in all those towns around Heathrow. They're bored, they want to be tested. They've got the two-car garage, the extra bathroom, the timeshare in the Algarve. But they want more. I can reach them, Richard. One problem, though – what's the message?'

'Message?' I stood up, raising my hands so that Cruise stayed in his seat. 'There is no message. Messages belong to the old politics. You're not some führer shouting at his storm troops. That's the old politics. The new politics is about people's dreams and needs, their hopes and fears. Your role is to empower them. You don't tell your audiences what to think. You draw them out, urge them to open up and say what they feel.'

'Avoid slogans, avoid messages?'

'No slogans, no messages. New politics. No manifestos, no commitments. No easy answers. They decide what they want. Your job is to set the stage and create the climate. You steer them by sensing their mood. Think of a herd of wildebeest on the African plain. They decide where they want to go.'

'How big is this herd? A million? Five million?'

'Maybe fifty million. Think of the future as a cable TV programme going on for ever.'

'Sounds like hell . . .' Cruise chuckled in a guilty way to himself. 'But five million, now that's a very big afternoon audience. How do I control them, impose some kind of focus? The whole thing could start to go mad.'

'Mad? Good. Madness is the key to everything. Small doses, applied when no one is really looking. You say turnover is going down at the Metro-Centre?'

'Not down. It's a sales plateau. A sure sign there's a steep cliff nearby. We've done everything.'

'Everything? You've tried the classic friendly approach, giving the customers what they want. Or what you think they want. You need to try the unfriendly approach.'

'Tell them what they ought to want?' Cruise waved this away. 'It doesn't work.'

'No. It's too authoritarian, too nanny state. It's not new politics.'

'And what is that?'

'The unpredictable. Be nice most of the time, but now and then be nasty, when they least expect it. Like a bored husband, affectionate but with a cruel streak. People will gasp, but the audience figures will soar. Now and then slip in a hint of madness, a little raw psychopathology. Remember, sensation and psychopathy are the only way people make contact with each other today. It won't take your viewers long to get a taste for real madness, whether it's a product or a political movement. Encourage people to go a little mad – it makes shopping and love affairs more interesting. Every so often people want to be disciplined by someone. They want to be ordered about.'

'Exactly.' Cruise slapped the arm of his chair, and listened to the echo move around the pool. 'They want to be punished.'

'Punished, and loved. But not like a fair-minded parent. More like a moody jailer, watching them through the bars. There's a sharp slap waiting for people who don't head straight for the furniture sales, or pay up for the new loyalty card.'

'They'll walk away.'

'They won't. People need a little bit of abuse in their lives. Masochism is the new black, and always has been. It's the mood music of the future. People want discipline, and they want violence. Most of all they want structured violence.'

'Ice hockey, pro rugby, stock-car racing . . .'

'That's it. The new politics is going to be a little like pro rugby. Try it out on your next consumer show. Don't change your style, but now and then surprise them. Show an authoritarian edge, be openly critical of them. Make a sudden emotional appeal. Show your flaws, then demand loyalty. Insist on faith and emotional commitment, without exactly telling them what they're supposed to believe in. That's new politics. Remember, people today unconsciously accept that violence is redemptive. And in their hearts they're convinced that psychopathy is close to sainthood.'

'Are they right?'

'Yes. They know that madness is the only freedom left to them.' I sat down in my sun lounger and waited for Cruise to reply. 'David . . . ?'

Cruise was staring at the pool, once again as smooth as a dance floor. He turned and pointed both forefingers at me, a trademark gesture he employed when a guest uttered an unexpected insight.

'It has possibilities. Richard, I like it . . .'

PART II

22

The Trenchcoat Hero

THE HEATHROW TOWNS had cleared the runway, lifted their wheels and were learning to fly, borne aloft on the bosomy thermals of the bright August sun. As I left the motorway and approached the outskirts of Ashford I could see the tasselled pennants flying from an out-of-town hypermarket, transforming this ugly metal shed into a caravel laden with treasure. St George's flags flew from passing cars, and floated from shops and houses. The livery of the local football and athletics teams decked the town hall and the multi-storey car park, giving a festival kick to the noisy air.

A sports parade headed down the high street, led by a pipe band and a troupe of majorettes, bare-thighed schoolgirls dolled up in Ruritanian tunics and shakos emblazoned with the logo of the sponsoring superstore. They strutted past, forcing the traffic to stop for them, followed by teams waving to their supporters who crowded the pavements and office balconies.

Behind them came the marshals and stewards in St George's shirts, marching smartly in time to the brass band that brought up the rear. Everywhere classrooms and workstations were abandoned as the hot pulse of civic pride and enthusiasm swept through this nondescript town. Any drop in output, any shortfall at the cash registers, would be more than made up by a surge in productivity and a few hours of overtime.

I sat in the stalled traffic and waved to a group of supporters who had spontaneously formed up behind the marshals, joining the parade as it marched to the coach park near the railway station. From there they would be bussed to Brooklands, spend the afternoon shopping in the Metro-Centre and then cheer on their teams in the local league.

Feet stamped past me, arms grazing my rented Mercedes. But I liked these people, and felt close to them. Many were middle-aged, white knees rising and falling, vigorous and unrushed. Their crusader shirts were covered with stitched medallions, in effect scout badges for adults, another of the schemes I had devised. Each bore the name of a local retailer, and gave their wearers the look of Grand Prix drivers. David Cruise and I expected a certain resistance, but the medallions were hugely popular, reinforcing the sense that people's lives were only complete when they advertised the consumer world.

A vast social experiment was under way, and I had helped to design it. The neglected people of the motorway towns, so despised by inner Londoners, had found a new pride and solidarity, a social cohesion that boosted prosperity and reduced crime. Whenever I left the motorway near Heathrow I was aware of entering a social laboratory that stretched along the M25, involving every sports arena and housing estate, every playground and retail park. A deep, convulsive chemistry was at work, waking these docile suburbs to a new and fiercer light. The orbital cities of the plain, as remote as Atlantis and Samarkand to the inhabitants of Chelsea and Holland Park, were learning to breathe and dream.

As the brass band moved away I waited for the traffic to clear, for once in no hurry to escape from London. Three months after first meeting David Cruise, I had sold my Chelsea Harbour flat to a young brain surgeon. Our solicitors had finally exchanged contracts, after cliff-hanging weeks bedevilled by the surgeon's sharp-eyed wife. She had spotted me pacing around an empty bedroom as she poked and pried, and misread my last doubts about moving permanently to Brooklands. 'Where?' she asked, when I explained my reasons for selling up. 'Does it really exist?'

She suspected a secret flaw, perhaps a zeppelin mooring mast on the floor above or a sewage outfall ten feet below. She endlessly circled the dining room, visualizing the eternity of dinner parties that constituted her dream of the good life. The future for her was an escalator of metropolitan chatter so lofty that it generated its own clouds. When she left I squeezed her hand suggestively, trying to elicit a microsecond's passion, a hint of sexual mischief, a saving flash of amorality. Go mad, I wanted to say, go bad. Sadly, she walked off without any response. But that was inner London, a congestion zone of the soul.

All the same, I had certain doubts over moving to Brooklands. I was leaving behind my baffled friends, my bridge and squash evenings, a former lover I was still close to, and even my ex-wife, with whom I had a spiky but intriguing bi-monthly lunch. Then there were all the pleasures and discontinuities of metropolitan life, from the cast room at the V&A to the shit in the letter box. To my friends I was apparently giving up all this in return for an obsessive quest to find my father's killer.

I was still determined to track down the gunman who had shot my father, but for the time being his death was no longer centre stage. The Brooklands police claimed that they had failed to trace the Jensen's owner. I assumed they were well aware that the car belonged to me, but had their own reasons for not questioning me about the bomb. Perhaps they feared that I would embarrass them by referring to the unsolved mystery of the Metro-Centre shooting. As long as I could, I preferred to keep out of their way and think about my father. In a sense I knew him far better than at any time in the past, but had I redeemed myself in his eyes? I doubted it. Meanwhile, I had stumbled on a far more important means of restoring my faith in myself. A new future waited to greet me: forgiving, full of surprises, and ready to redeem all my failures.

The traffic was still stationary in the high street, though the parade had gone and the police were reduced to playing some obscure game of their own. I rested my head against the window pillar, and looked up at the billboard above a TV rental store, advertising the Metro-Centre and its cable channels. There were now three channels, mixing sport, consumer information and social affairs, and they were popular viewing in the motorway towns.

The advertisement showed a grainy close-up of David Cruise, no longer the primped and rouged anchorman of afternoon television, but the fugitive and haunted hero of a *noir* film. He sat at the wheel of his car, staring at the open road and whatever nemesis lay in wait for him. An eerie glare lit the grimy windscreen and exposed every pore in his unshaved face. The chocolate tan had long faded. This David Cruise, though clearly the cable channels' chief presenter, was closer to the desperate loners of trenchcoat movies, doomed men sleepwalking towards their tragic end.

How this gloomy scenario tied in with the infinite consumer promise of the Metro-Centre was unclear, and when I sketched out the scene for Tom Carradine and his public relations staff they had objected vigorously. But the director, set designer and even Cruise himself all instantly saw the point and carried the day for me.

Another Metro-Centre poster, almost the size of a tennis court, filled the side of a town-centre office block. It showed Cruise in a nightmare replay of a Strindberg drama, threatening and confused as he stared across a display floor of showroom kitchens, a husband who had woken into the innermost circle of hell.

The series of posters were stills from thirty-second commercials on the cable channels. They presented Cruise as a trapped creature of strange and wayward moods – grimacing, frowning, angry, morose, hallucinating and obsessed. He would stare almost ecstatically at a battered dustbin, as if some revelation was at hand, or ring a doorbell at random and scowl at a startled housewife, ready to slap her or beg for sanctuary. In others he haunted the Brooklands racing circuit, the squeal of tyres like torture in his head, or followed a group of schoolgirls across a Heathrow concourse like a would-be child-abductor.

A surprisingly good sport, Cruise played the roles in a skilful and sensitive way, moving through a baleful consumer landscape of car showrooms, call centres and gated estates. The storylines were meaningless, but audiences liked them. Together they made sense at the deepest level, scenes from the collective dream forever playing in the back alleys of their minds.

As Cruise's media adviser, I had taken a gamble, but I was ready to spin the wheel and risk everything. Audience figures surged, and all over the motorway towns the first copycat posters soon appeared, playing on a suppressed need for the bizarre and the unpredictable. At the junction of Ashford High Street and the dual carriageway was a billboard advertising a local insurance company's endowment policies. It showed a deranged young woman dragging a blood-spattered child across a deserted car park, watched by a smiling couple who picnicked beside a Volvo with a damaged wing.

I laughed generously at the clever in-joke. Like all the posters, it was advertising nothing except its own quirky waywardness. Yet the concept worked. Everywhere sales boomed, and the Metro-Centre activated two dormant cable channels. People from the Home Counties, and even from inner London, drove like tourists through the motorway towns, aware that these invisible suburbs were lit by a new fever. They cheered on the massed sports teams that strutted and wheeled around the Metro-Centre car parks, they straightened their shoulders as the marshals bellowed and stamped. They watched the disciplined files of marching athletes, the ceremonial hoisting of banners, the loyalty-card supporters chanting 'Metro . . . Metro . . .'

Unknown to its busy executives and sales staff, the Metro-Centre had become the headquarters of a virtual political party, financed by its supporters' clubs and gold-card memberships. It issued no manifesto, made no promises and outlined no programme. It represented nothing. But several St George's candidates, standing on no platform other than their loyalty to a shopping mall and its sports teams, had won seats on local councils. Their chosen party political broadcasts were the thirty-second commercials I had devised for David Cruise.

To his credit, Cruise had done a superb job, justifying all my hopes for him. He agreed to every suggestion I put forward, eager to give everything to these tense if meaningless psychodramas. He coped manfully with the flood of valentines and marriage proposals, and never forgot that he was a talk-show presenter. His modest range was a large part of his appeal, and allowed every male viewer to think of himself in these haunted roles, and every female admirer to imagine herself as the heroine playing Jane to this neurasthenic Tarzan of the suburban jungle.

'Years of failure,' he often told me, 'are the worst preparation for overnight triumph.' And the best preparation? 'Years of success.'

He was still affable and engaging, despite his sly pleasure in his new-found aggression. He would bully and abuse the self-immersed wives and dull husbands who appeared on his consumer programmes, yet without causing offence. His impatience with the dimmer guests, his clenched fists and evident stress, merged easily into the desperate characters he played in the noir commercials.

He remained the voice of the Metro-Centre, the ambassador from the kingdom of the washing machine and the microwave oven, but he was also the leader of a virtual political party whose influence was spreading through the motorway towns. Like other demagogues, he traded on the psychopathic traits in his personality. Yet he had emerged, not from the bitter streets and working men's taverns of depression-era Munich, but from the hospitality rooms of afternoon TV, a man without a message who had found his desert.

The last of the coaches sped down the dual carriageway, carrying teams and supporters to Brooklands, police outriders with their head-lights flashing. The waiting traffic moved forward, impatient to set off in pursuit.

I squeezed through the amber, saluted by a beaming constable who waved me on. Despite my role at the Metro-Centre, I was thinking of Julia Goodwin. We would meet later that afternoon, when she finished her shift at the hospital, and already I envied the patients she would be touching with her worn and tired hands.

A vague sense of unresolved guilt hovered between us, as if she had aborted our child without telling me. But at least this edginess showed her fierce honesty. I guessed that she had been involved with Geoffrey Fairfax, Dr Maxted and Sangster in an attempt to exploit the Metro-Centre shooting for their own ends. The three men tried again on the night of the bomb attack, hoping to seize power with their puppet Bonaparte, the reluctant David Cruise. They had singed their eyebrows and now kept their heads down, but Fairfax had destroyed himself, either setting the bomb in my car or trying to defuse it.

The coroner, perhaps prompted by Superintendent Leighton, brought in a verdict of death by misadventure, but Fairfax was quickly abandoned by his legal colleagues. I was one of the few mourners at his funeral, mourning my Jensen as much as this eccentric solicitor, part-time soldier and full-time fanatic. Geoffrey Fairfax belonged to the past and a Brooklands that had vanished, while I had committed myself to the Metro-Centre and the memory of my father, to Julia Goodwin and the new Brooklands of the future.

23

The Women's Refuge

THE TRAFFIC INTO Brooklands was slowing again, delayed by police setting up steel railings and no-entry signs, part of the lavish preparations for the weekend sports rally and parade. Several key football matches would take place that evening, and there were hard-fought finals in the rugby, basketball and ice-hockey competitions.

Cricket, as I noted whenever Julia asked me for the test-match scores, was not played in Brooklands or the motorway towns. Contact sports ruled the field of play, the more brutal the better. Blood and aggression were the qualities most admired. The hard tackle was the essence of sport, the kind of violence that flourished in the margins of the rule book. Cricket was too amateurish, its long-pondered intricacies trapped in a cat's cradle of incomprehensible laws. Above all, it was too middle-class, and unconnected to the kind of impulse buying favoured by Metro-Centre supporters. Julia told me that she had captained the cricket team at her girls' school, but her interest in the game was a whimsical stand against the far harder stadium values that now dominated Brooklands.

We were meeting at three, when her shift ended at the hospital. She hated the sports rallies, the unending din of marching bands that drummed at the windows above the wail of ambulances and fire engines. Usually she would be on duty, dealing with the human wreckage stretchered into the A&E triage rooms. Thinking of herself for once, she manipulated the rosters to give us a rare free weekend.

I hoped that I would share at least part of it with her, but she had recently kept me at arm's length. We had yet to make love again after the uneasy night together in my father's bed. Sex with me had been an act of penance, expiating some unadmitted guilt. Whenever we met she watched me warily, hair over her eyes as if to veil any tell-tale signs. But I was always glad to be with her. I loved her moods and bolshieness, the cigarette stubbed out in a slushy sorbet, the adversarial relationship with her car, the handsome black cat who slept beside her like a demon husband. Everything between us inverted the usual rules. We had begun with sex of a fraught and desperate kind, followed by a long period of wooing. As far as I knew, I had never let her down, and I hoped that one day she would finally forgive me for whatever she had done to my father in the past.

Waiting in the traffic that approached the Metro-Centre, I watched the columns of supporters marching to their assembly points in the residential side streets. Lines of coaches were parked under the sycamores and beeches, decked with St George's flags. Supporters now came from as far as Bristol and Birmingham, attracted by the martial mood that gripped the town, ready to stamp through the streets, cheer their lungs out and spend their savings in the retail parks that sponsored the events.

Twenty thousand visitors occupied Brooklands every weekend. In the comfortable driver's seat of the Mercedes, I marvelled at how disciplined they were, obeying the brusque commands of the stewards steering them to the Metro-Centre, thousands of suburban crusaders emblazoned with logos and moving as one. At synchronized intervals, in an effort to keep the middle-aged blood flowing, phalanxes of ice-hockey or basketball supporters would snap to attention and mark time on the spot, arms swinging like blades in a human wind farm.

Impatient to get home, I checked my text messages, hoping that David Cruise had survived for forty-eight hours without me. There was a brief message from Julia, saying that she would now be working until six at the Asian women's refuge. Brooklands High School had broken up for the summer, and Sangster had lent part of the school to Asian women and children so intimidated by sporting revellers that they refused to go home.

Impatient to see Julia, I turned into the empty bus lane and drove to the nearest side street, then set off through the residential avenues crowded with coaches. Marshals were controlling the traffic, forcing private cars to give way to the lumbering behemoths. Most of the middle-class residents detested the sports weekends, so I picked a St George's pennant from the rear seat and clipped it to the windscreen pillar, then put on my St George's baseball cap. At the next check-point I was waved through by the marshals, and exchanged vigorous salutes with them.

The cap and pennant were a disguise, but one that worked. I hated the self-importance of these pocket gauleiters, but the sense of an enemy sharpened the reflexes and lifted everyone's spirits. Visiting league teams and their supporters were seen as friendly citizens of the new federation of motorway towns, the conference of the Heathrow tribes. Everyone in Brooklands was a friend, but out there some-where was the 'enemy', constantly referred to by David Cruise on his cable programmes but never defined.

At the same time, everyone knew who the real enemy was – subver-sive elements in local government offices, the county establishment, the church and the old middle classes, with their jodhpurs and dinner parties, their private schools and anal-retentive snobberies. I sym-pathized with the marching supporters, and was ready to back them in any confrontation. They had seized the initiative and were defining a new political order based on energy and emotion. They had re-dramatized their lives, marching proudly and in step with the military enthusiasm of a people going to war, while staying faithful to the pacific dream of their patios and barbecues. All this might be part of a huge marketing strategy, but I felt revived by the strutting swagger, the disci-pline and rude health. There was a hint of arrogance that could be dangerous after dark, but a dash of Tabasco spiced up the dullest dish.

My father would have approved.

Avoiding the Metro-Centre and its gridlocked streets, I entered down-town Brooklands. Many of the shops were boarded up for the weekend, but I noticed a trio of sports-club stewards outside a Polish-run camera shop. They carried leaflets and recruiting literature, along with a selection of flags and bunting, but these were forgotten in their heated altercation with the young Polish owner. A pale young man with receding hair, he was frightened by the stewards but standing up to them, while his nervous wife tried to draw him back into the shop. Two of the stewards pushed the Pole in the chest, trying to manoeuvre him into provoking them.

I hesitated as the lights changed, tempted to get out and intercede, and sounded my horn. The stewards turned on me aggressively, then saw the Metro-Centre flash on the windscreen with its picture of David Cruise. They saluted, waved the Pole back to his wife and swaggered off down the street, kicking the steel shutters.

I drove on, embarrassed and a little guilty. Sports-club stewards were a plague in the motorway towns, intimidating Asian and east European shopkeepers, harassing small businesses until 'voluntary' contributions were paid. Those who refused were visited by drunken supporters who roamed the streets after dark. But these protection rackets were tolerated by the police, since the marshals and stewards did their job for them by keeping order in the towns.

I closed my mind to all this, thinking of the confident marchers on their way to the Metro-Centre. In time the thugs and racists would fade away. Besides, English sports fans were famous for their pugnacity. My conscience slept uneasily, but it slept.

Ten minutes later I drove into the staff car park at Brooklands High School, tossed the St George's pennant into the back seat and stopped beside Sangster's unwashed Citroën. Vandals haunted the school, and had broken several windows in the admin building. But the authority of a head teacher, even one as moodily eccentric as Sangster, offered some protection. Generously, he had offered the gymnasium and a block of empty classrooms to the frightened Asian women. Their husbands stayed behind, defending their burnt-out houses, trying to run their threatened shops and businesses.

As I arrived two Asian men were unloading suitcases from a paint-splashed car. Sangster and a group of students from the art college were strengthening the fence behind the gymnasium, blocking a side entrance with wooden stakes and barbed wire.

Sangster gave me a limp wave, then touched his forehead, doffing an imaginary hat in an almost feudal salute. I remembered his large figure in the rioting crowd on the night of the Metro-Centre bomb attack, and his odd behaviour, restraining the rioters but encouraging them at the same time. He knew that I was suspicious of him and tried to be patronizing. But he had failed, and I had succeeded.

Three times a week an antenatal clinic was held in the gymnasium for the Asian women, run by Dr Kumar, my elusive downstairs neighbour. The last patient was gathering her bundles together. Her children sat on a bench by the parallel bars, watching me with their large, unblinking eyes. They ignored my friendly smile, as if good humour might signal a new kind of aggression.

Julia and Dr Kumar sat in the kitchen, sharing a cup of tea from a thermos. Seeing me, Dr Kumar stared angrily into my eyes, frowned and left without a word.

I held Julia's shoulders and kissed her forehead. I waved to Dr Kumar, but she put on her coat and walked briskly away.

'Fierce lady. Have I offended her?'

'Of course. You never let her down.'

'A shame. I'm on her side. She always avoids me.'

'I can't think why.' Julia found a clean cup and poured the last of the tea, then sat back and smiled as I winced at the sharp tannin. 'I keep telling her you're decent, responsible and rather likeable.'

'That doesn't sound much fun. What a thing to say.' I poured the tea into the sink and ran the tap. 'Tell her to watch my commercials for David Cruise.'

'I did. She says there's a new one. Something about a man laughing in an abattoir.'

'What did she think of it?'

'She said you're beyond psychiatric help.'

'Good. That shows she's warming to me. Why was she so hostile?'

'Look in the mirror.' Julia pointed to the nightwatchman's shaving mirror above the sink. 'Go on. Risk it.'

'Oh, my God . . . no wonder the children were frightened.'

I was still wearing the St George's cap. I placed it on the table and slapped my forehead. Julia snatched it away and tossed it into the nearby pedal bin.

'Julia, I'm sorry . . .'

'Never mind.' Julia reached across the table and took my hands. I realized how tired she was, and wanted to embrace her, conjure away the dry skin and the unfamiliar bones pushing through her face. I tried to touch her cheeks but she held my wrists, as if calming a fractious patient. 'Richard, are you listening?'

'Dear . . . I haven't seen you for days. Relax a little.'

'I can't. Things here are desperate. The school was attacked last night. Sangster drove them away but they broke a lot of windows. The Asian children were terrifed. One of the mothers had a miscarriage.'

'I'm sorry. At least you weren't involved.'

'I should have been. I spent four hours at the hospital, stitching up a lot of drunken yobs. Why do they do it?'

'Attack a school? All those years of boredom. A mysterious head teacher who frightened the wits out of them.'

'It's nothing to do with that. Attacks are going on everywhere – Hillingdon, Southall, Ashford. They want these people out.'

'"People"?'

Julia struck the table with her fist. 'I'll call them what I bloody like! Bangladeshis, Kosovans, Poles, Turks. They want them moved to a huge ghetto somewhere in east London. Then they can deal with them when they're ready.'

'Julia, please . . .' I knew that she was bored with me for trying to raise her spirits. 'Isn't that a little . . . ?'

'Apocalyptic?'

William Sangster stepped into the kitchen, his large bulk blocking the windows and throwing the small space into shadow. He took off his canvas gloves and dropped them onto the draining board, then slumped into a chair, counting his huge limbs as an afterthought. He seemed tired but at ease, as if events taking place around him confirmed everything he had expected. There was a growth of beard on his plump and babyish cheeks, like a faulty disguise.

'Apocalyptic . . .' I repeated. 'A few stones? Just a little.'

'I hope you're right.' Sangster tilted back his head and addressed the ceiling, as if preferring not to be reminded of his dim pupils. 'In my experience, one stone through a window is a fairly accurate predictor that another stone will soon follow. Then two more. Hard stones make for hard data. Add a few frightened Muslim families into the equation and you can extrapolate in a straight line – all the way to a cluster of gateway towns on the Thames flood plain.'

'Close to the container port at Rotherhithe.' Julia glared at me meaningfully. 'And that strange airport they want to build on the Isle of Dogs.'

'So . . .' Sangster shook the empty thermos, and laid a large hand gently on Julia's shoulder. After a night of turmoil he was exhausted beyond mere tiredness, moving into a zone where any wild-eyed fantasy was probably true. 'Do you think Julia is being apocalyptic? Richard?'

'As it happens, I don't. It's ugly, very ugly. I'll do what I can, talk to the marshals and find out which supporters came down here.'

'Good.' Sangster nodded sagely. 'Julia, he'll talk to the marshals. Maybe they'll tell us when the next attack is. Richard, you could issue a bulletin. Like those old war films – target for tonight. Hillingdon, Ashford, alternate target Brooklands. What do you think, Richard? See it as a marketing campaign.'

'Isn't everything these days?' Aware that they were both light-headed with fatigue, I said: 'Listen, I'll talk to the police.'

'The police?' Sangster looked owlishly serious. 'We didn't think of that. Julia, the police . . .'

I let this pass. 'Look, I hate the violence. I hate the racist attacks. I hate the protection rackets and the bully-boy tactics. But these people are a fringe.'

'Only a fringe?'

'A vicious fringe, admittedly. But very few people are involved. Wherever you find sport you find hooligans. Contact sports appeal to any riffraff looking for violence. Don't judge what's happening by what you see at night.'

'Fair point,' Sangster conceded. 'Go on.'

'Move around during the day. Disciplined crowds, everyone on best behaviour. I watched them an hour ago. Whole families out together – healthy, fresh, optimistic, keen to cheer on their teams. Friendly rivalry, heads held high.'

'And the banners?' Julia leaned across the table and gripped my wrist. 'Have you seen them? Like Roman legions. It's incredible.'

'Right. Banners flying. There's a new pride in the air, all along the motorway towns. People are more confident, more positive. The M25 was a backwater left over from Heathrow, a joke no one wanted to share. Dual carriageways and used-car lots. Nothing to look forward to except new patio doors and a trip to Homebase. All the promise of life delivered door to door in a flat pack.'

Sangster nodded, inspecting his deeply bitten nails. 'And now?'

'Revival! There's a spring in everyone's step. People know their lives have a point. They know it's good for the whole community.'

'And good for the Metro-Centre?'

'Naturally. We provide the focus and fund the new stadiums and the supporters' clubs. We use the cable channels to keep up the pressure.'

'Pressure?' Julia tried to unclench her fists, irritated by everything I said. 'To sell your washing machines and microwaves . . .'

'They're part of people's lives. Consumerism is the air we've given them to breathe.'

*   *   *

Julia had turned away, refusing to listen to me as she hunted through her handbag for her mobile phone. She stood up and patted me on the head. 'There's a call I need to make. I'll be back in a moment.'

'Don't forget we're having dinner tonight. Julia?'

'I hope so.' She paused at the door and stared hard at me. 'The air they breathe? Richard, people breathe out as well as breathe in . . .'

24

A Fascist State

'RICHARD . . .' SANGSTER TAPPED the table with his heavy knuckle, recalling me to his inquisition. 'I hope you realize what you're doing.'

'Not exactly.' We sat at opposite ends of the table, undistracted by Julia's presence. 'You're going to tell me.'

'I am.' Sangster examined his swollen hands, and picked a splinter from his thumb. 'In a way it's quite an achievement. Back in the nineteen-thirties it needed a lot of twisted minds working together, but you've done it by yourself.'

'Is my mind twisted?'

'Definitely not. That's the disturbing thing. You're sane, kindly, with all the genuine sincerity of an advertising man.'

'So what have I done?'

'You've created a fascist state.'

'Fascist?' I let the word hover overhead, then dissipate like an empty cloud. 'In the . . . dinner party sense?'

'No. It's the real thing. There's no doubt about it. I've been watching it grow for the past year. It's been stirring in its mother's belly, but you knelt down in the straw and delivered the beast.'

'Fascist? It's like "new" or "improved". It can mean anything. Where are the jackboots, the goose-stepping Brownshirts, the ranting führer? I don't see them around.'

'They don't need to be.' Sangster watched me with a quirky smile that never completely formed, as if I were a destructive pupil he disliked but was unaccountably drawn to. 'This is a soft fascism, like the consumer landscape. No goose-stepping, no jackboots, but the same emotions and the same aggression. As you say, there's a strong sense of community, but it isn't based on civic rights. Forget reason. Emotion drives everything. You see it every weekend outside the Metro-Centre.'

'Sports supporters, cheering on their rival teams.'

'Like Goering's "gliders"? Anyway, these teams aren't really rivals. They're all marching to the same brass band. As for a true sense of community, people get that in traffic jams and airport concourses.'

'Or the Metro-Centre?' I suggested. 'The People's Palace?'

'And a hundred other shopping malls. Who needs liberty and human rights and civic responsibility? What we want is an aesthetics of violence. We believe in the triumph of feelings over reason. Pure materialism isn't enough, all those Asian shopkeepers with their cash-register minds. We need drama, we need our emotions manipulated, we want to be conned and cajoled. Consumerism fits the bill exactly. It's drawn the blueprint for the fascist states of the future. If anything, consumerism creates an appetite that can only be satisfied by fascism. Some kind of insanity is the last way forward. All the dictators in history soon grasped that – Hitler and the Nazi leaders made sure no one ever thought they were completely sane.'

'And the people in the Metro-Centre?'

'They know that, too. Look how they react to your new cable ads.' Sangster pointed a grimy finger at me, grudgingly forced into a compliment. 'A bad actor howls from the roof of a multi-storey car park and we think he's a seer.'

'So David Cruise is the führer? He's fairly benign.'

'He's a nothing. He's a "virtual" man without a real thought in his head. Consumer fascism provides its own ideology, no one needs to sit down and dictate *Mein Kampf*. Evil and psychopathy have been reconfigured into lifestyle statements. It's a fearful prospect, but consumer fascism may be the only way to hold a society together. To control all that aggression, and channel all those fears and hates.'

'As long as the bands play and everyone marches in step?'

'Right!' Sangster sat forward, jarring the table against my elbows. 'So beat the drums, sound the bugles, lead them to an empty stadium where they can shout their lungs out. Give them violent hamster wheels like football and ice hockey. If they still need to let off steam, burn down a few newsagents.'

Raising his arms as if to surrender, Sangster stood up and turned his back to me. As he read the messages on his phone I stared through the window. A taxi had pulled into the main entrance of the school, and stopped in front of the admin building.

'Your taxi?' I asked Sangster when he put away his phone.

'No. There's work I have to do here.' He gestured at the fence, where the students were threading a strand of razor wire between the posts. 'Meanwhile, we're organizing a deputation to the Home Office – Julia, Dr Maxted, myself, a few others. I'd like you to join us.'

'A deputation . . . ? Whitehall . . . ?'

'The seat of power, so they say. We may not see the Home Secretary, but Maxted knows a junior minister he met on a television programme. Something has to be done – this thing is spreading along the M25, sooner or later the noose will tighten around London and choke it to death.'

'What about the police?'

'Useless. Whole streets are torched and they claim it's football hooliganism. Secretly, they want the Asians and immigrants out. Likewise the local council. Fewer corner shops, more retail parks, a higher tax yield. Money rules, more housing, more infrastructure contracts. They like the bands playing and the stamping feet – they hide the sound of the cash tills.'

'That's today's England. Whitehall?' I looked away. 'I'm not sure there's a lot of point. What's happening in the motorway towns may be the first signs of a national revival. Who knows, the end of late-stage capitalism and the start of something new . . . ?'

'It's possible.' Sangster stood over me, and I could smell his stale, threatening clothes. 'Will you join us?'

'I'll think about it.'

Sangster held my shoulders in his huge hands, a bear's grip. 'Don't think.'

We left the kitchen and stepped into the gymnasium. A line of Asian women and their children sat against the parallel bars, suitcases in front of them, new arrivals being processed by Dr Kumar.

'Sad. Very wrong.' I said to Sangster: 'Their houses have been torched?'

'No. But they're fearful of what may happen tonight. Let me know about the Home Office delegation.'

'I'll get Julia to call you.' I glanced into the women's changing room. The antenatal clinic had ended, and the lockers holding the medical supplies were sealed. 'Julia . . . Where is she?'

'She's gone home.' Sangster was watching me with a faint hint of smugness. 'A taxi came for her.'

'I could have given her a lift. We're having dinner tonight.'

'Perhaps not . . .'

Sangster walked away, smiling to himself as he strode across the polished wooden floor. I nodded to Dr Kumar, who ignored me, and searched the side corridors for Julia. I was sorry she had left for home, irritated and distracted by Sangster's talk of fascism. I suspected that he had deliberately provoked her into leaving. At the same time he had spoken with such force that he seemed to be making the case against which he was arguing. I intrigued Sangster because I was part of the fierce new world he was drawn to. Mathematics might be his subject, but emotion was the ungelded horse he rode so brutally. Not all the would-be gauleiters in Brooklands were manning traffic checkpoints.

In the playground an Asian woman passed me, swathed in dark shawls, a billeting docket in one hand, small son manfully trying to help her with the suitcase. Two Asian men approached, but neither offered any aid, so I stopped the woman and took the suitcase from her. Helped by the boy, I carried it to the classroom block and left it inside the entrance, where an older Asian woman halted me with a raised hand.

Catching my breath, I looked out at the dome of the Metro-Centre, its silver surface lit by a trio of swerving spotlights. On the M25 drivers were slowing to watch the parades, as they listened to David Cruise's commentary on their car radios. The suburbs were coming alive again. A malignant fringe had done its damage, terrifying a blameless minority of Asians and east Europeans.

But a corpse had revived and sat up, and was demanding breakfast. The moribund motorway towns, the people of the Heathrow plain, were positioning themselves on the runway, ready to take flight.

25

Lonely, Lost, Angry

As usual, Tom Carradine was waiting at the kerb when I stopped near the South Gate entrance of the Metro-Centre. Before I could release the seat belt he had opened the door and switched off the ignition. Confident and enthusiastic, he was dressed in the new uniform of the public relations department, a braided powder-blue confection that might have been worn by one of Mussolini's air marshals.

'Thanks, Tom.' I waited as he helped me from the car and locked the doors. 'This gives a new dimension to valet parking. In my next life I'll come back as a Merc or BMW . . .'

'The VIP car park for you, Mr Pearson. The Jensen still being repaired?'

'Well . . . I think it's come to the end of its natural life.'

Carradine nodded promptly, but there was a sharp-eyed caution about him that had become more pronounced since the bomb in the basement garage. The Metro-Centre had been attacked, and every customer was now a potential enemy, forcing a revolution in his world view. For Tom Carradine the Metro-Centre was never a commercial enterprise, but a temple of the true faith that he would defend to the last yard of Axminster and the last discount holiday. He gazed at the great concourse in front of the dome, filled with crowds of shoppers, marching supporters in their team livery, wide-eyed tourists, pipe bands and majorettes. A TV camera on a crane circled the scene, ever vigilant for any fanatic with an explosive waistcoat. Narrowing his eyes, Carradine beckoned me forward. Two marshals preceded us, affably clearing a way through the press of people.

'You're wearing your new uniform,' I said to him. 'I'm impressed. I feel I ought to salute you.'

'I salute you, Mr Pearson. You've done everything here. I'll never forget you brought the Metro-Centre back to life. You and Mr Cruise. Everybody really loves the latest cable ad.'

'The abattoir? Not too gloomy?'

'Never. Existential choice. Isn't that what the Metro-Centre is about?'

'I think it is.'

'Dr Maxted explained everything on his programme yesterday. By the way, Mr Pearson, the Metro-Centre tailor is calling this afternoon. He'll be happy to measure you up for your uniform.'

'Well, thanks, Tom.' In an unguarded moment I had tried on one of the new jackets. 'I'm not sure, though . . .'

'Three rings, lots of scrambled egg on the cap peak.'

'I know. I'm just a writer, Tom. I dream up slogans.'

'You're more than a writer, Mr Pearson. You've given us all heart again.'

'Even so. It's a little too military . . .'

'We have to defend the Metro-Centre.'

'I'm with you there. But is it in danger?'

'It's always in danger. We have to be ready, whatever happens.'

I watched the muscles flexing in his cheeks. For all his flattery, the offer of a uniform was a clever power play of his own. Everyone in the uniform would be under Tom Carradine's command, myself included. The threat to the Metro-Centre had sharpened his reflexes, but he remained the fanatical youth leader, eager to sacrifice himself for his principles.

We approached the South Gate entrance. Above the cantilevered marquee were a pair of loudspeakers used for crowd control, operated from a kiosk outside the doors. Through the din of pipe bands and marching feet I heard a succession of amplified clicks and stutters as someone adjusted the controls.

Then a harsh voice boomed over our heads:

'NOTHING IS TRUE! NOTHING IS UNTRUE...!'

Carradine stopped and held my arm, as if the sky was about to fall onto the dome and slide down the roof towards us.

'...UNTRUE! NOTHING IS...HEAR YE...NOTHING IS TRUE...!'

Carradine broke away from me, racing through the startled shoppers staring into the air. The two marshals followed him, manhandling young mothers and old ladies out of their way. They rushed towards the control kiosk and seized a tall youth in a string vest and frayed denims who was waving the microphone like a club, trying to fend them off.

When I reached the kiosk he was lying on the ground and being viciously kicked by the marshals. Blood poured from his nose and left ear. I recognized Duncan Christie, striking the marble floor with his chin as if in an epileptic fit. Carradine was stamping on Christie's hands, and pointing frantically at the microphone that swung from its cord, almost mesmerized by this threat to the Metro-Centre. He had lost his peaked cap, but a small boy in a sailor suit found it among the swirl of feet and handed it back to him. Carradine placed it defiantly on his head, momentarily disoriented.

'Tom, take it easy...' I held his shoulders, trying to calm the confused manager, then waved the marshals away from Christie. 'It's a prank – no one's hurt.'

The marching bands filled the air, and the crowd pressed through the doors, Christie's slogan already forgotten. Winded and bruised, the blood from his nose pooling on the marble floor, Christie lifted himself onto his knees. He looked up at me and nodded warningly, as if willing me to turn back from the Metro-Centre.

One of the marshals leaned down and bellowed into his face. Christie raised a hand to quieten him, then twisted away and lunged towards me, arms outstretched to seize my shoulders.

Carradine and the marshals threw themselves on him, struggling to control his long, violent body, skin and ragged clothes slippery with dirt and grease. They kicked his feet from under him, but as fists jarred his forehead an arm reached out to me. He seized my left hand and pressed a hot stone into my palm.

As Christie was dragged through the crowd I opened my hand, shielding it from any curious gaze.

Lying in my palm was a live round of ammunition.

Weighing the round in my hand, I moved through the entrance hall and mounted the travelator to the central atrium. After the moments of ugly violence, the air in the Metro-Centre was pleasantly cool and scented. The ambient sound system played a pleasant melody of marching songs, a sweetened reworking in the Mantovani idiom of the Horst Wessel song and the Chorus of the Hebrew Slaves. The music was distant and unobtrusive, but almost everyone was in step.

Still shaken by the brutal attack on Christie, I held the bullet up to the light. I tried to read the symbols stamped on the base of the cartridge. Christie had fought to press the round into my hand, but his message was of the rather oblique kind that he favoured. I doubted if he was threatening me. At the same time this gift of a bullet, probably of the same type that had killed my father, carried a clear signal from Christie, and not one that I wanted to hear . . .

In the centre of the atrium the three giant bears stood on their podium, paws beating time to the music, an amiable trio whose button eyes saw nothing and everything. In their toylike way they displayed a touching serenity. At their feet were more offerings of honey and treacle, and several 'diaries' penned by admirers which detailed their imaginary lives. In a light-hearted moment David Cruise had suggested a commercial in which he attacked the bears and chopped off their heads, but I had vetoed this. For one thing, the bears reminded me of all the toys never given to me during my childhood.

I climbed the stairs to the mezzanine studio where Cruise was conducting his afternoon discussion programme. The open deck was filled with visitors, as close to Cruise as the tighter security allowed. I found a chair in the exhibition area and watched a monitor screen relaying the last exchanges of the programme.

Cruise was tieless, dressed in the shabby black suit and tired white shirt that was now his trademark, an ensemble I had based on the costume worn by the doomed heroes of gangster films, desperate men on the verge of madness. Cruise had lost weight, and his signature tan was whitened down by the make-up department, giving him a hungry and martyred gaze, the fugitive messiah of the shopping malls.

Cruise was holding forth to his circle of docile and obedient housewives.

'... "community", Angela? That's a word I *hate*. It's the kind of word used by snobby, upper-class folk who want to put ordinary people in their place. Community means living in a little box, driving a little car, going on little holidays. It means obeying the rules that "they" tell you to obey. Sheila, you don't agree? Frankly, the hell with you. Go back to your little box and polish your little dinette. Community? I know what an Asian community is. I know what a Muslim community is. We all know, don't we? Yes . . . I hate community. For me, the only real community is the one we've built here at the Metro-Centre. That's what I believe in. The sports teams, the supporters' clubs, the gold-card loyalty nights. Sheila? Just shut up. I want to say something that's going to shock you. Ready? When I leave here and go home, how do I feel? Betty, I'll tell you. I feel lonely. Maybe I drink too much and feel too sorry for myself. I miss you girls. Sheila, Angela, Doreen, and everyone watching. I miss your mad questions and your crazy, beautiful dreams. I have these odd ideas – yes, Sheila, those too – I want to tear down the old world and build a new order, something like the one we're building together inside the Metro-Centre. I know I'm right, I know we can bring a new world to life. It's started here inside the Metro-Centre, but it's spreading all over the real England. If you can smell the motorway you're in the real England. You can feel it, can't you, Cathy? Deep inside you. No, not there, Sheila. Come and see me later and we'll find it. Yes, I'm lonely, I don't sleep well, part of me, frankly, is a little bit bonkers. But I'm right, I've seen the future and I *believe*. I want to do things even I can't mention. I need you all, and I need you here . . .'

The peroration wound to its climax, as the key camera closed in on Cruise's haggardly handsome face. The producer made his wind-up signal, the housewives sank back, looking stunned, and Cruise disconnected his microphone and dashed for his dressing room.

Within seconds, phone calls, emails and text messages would arrive from viewers desperate to help Cruise assuage his demons. There would be invitations to barbecues, honorary memberships of sports clubs, heartfelt 'please, please' calls. More recruits would pour in, drawn towards the Metro-Centre. This was a political movement, but one without any supporting bureaucracy of placemen and jobsworths. The will to power came from the bottom up, from a thousand check-outs and consumer aisles. The promises were visible and within arm's reach in the displays of merchandise. Cruise's obsessions and sexual hang-ups were the compass-dance of a demented king bee, guiding the hive to a destination it had already chosen. His chat-show act, based on scripts I tailored around him, might be a performance, but it validated the hunger and restlessness of his audience. The house-wives mailing their photographs to him were performing rituals of assent, expressing their longing for a faith beyond politics.

I walked between the cameras as the crew shut down their equip-ment, complimented the producer and his assistant on another superb effort, then let myself into Cruise's dressing room.

He lay back in front of the picture window that overlooked the central atrium, generously saluting any concourse visitors who waved to him.

'Richard! Did you see the show?'

'You were great. Lonely, lost, angry. More than a hint of the mentally deranged. I almost believed you.'

'It's all true. I wasn't acting.' He sat up and grasped my hands. 'I'm finding myself out there. I'm laying myself bare, tearing shreds off my flesh, letting the blood trickle over the mike. Things I didn't know about myself. God, the stuff waiting to come out. All the psychic shit backed up for years.'

'Don't hold it in. People need that stuff. It's pure gold.'

'You think so? Really?' He waited until I nodded vigorously. 'I'm going mad so they can stay sane.'

'The show's over. Try to take it easy.'

'I'm fine.' He lay back and raised his hand, waiting for me to pass him his glass of vodka and tonic. 'It takes me a while to land. I have to fly so high, there's some strange weather up there. I spent years humiliating my guests and got nowhere. Now I humiliate myself and I'm a huge success. What do you make of that?'

'It's the air we breathe.'

'You're right.' He pointed to a reproduction on his dressing table of one of Francis Bacon's screaming popes, as if recognizing himself in this demented pontiff who had glimpsed the void hidden within the concept of God. On a bizarre impulse I had given the reproduction to Cruise, and he had taken a keen interest in it. 'Richard, tell me again – what exactly is he screaming at?'

'Existence. He's realized there is no God and mankind is free. Whatever free means. Are you all right?'

'Fine. I know the feeling. Sometimes . . .'

Still holding the glass of vodka, ready to place it in Cruise's limply hanging paw, I sat in the armchair next to the sofa, the position of an analyst listening to a disturbed patient. These chat-show performances were changing Cruise. He had begun to resemble the distraught heroes he played in the commercials. His face was thinner and more angular, and he had the ashy pallor of a hostage released after years of captivity.

'So, Richard. Sold your flat? Goodbye Chelsea, goodbye all those nancy dinner parties. You're part of Brooklands now, you're committed to the Metro-Centre. We'll put you on salary.'

'Well, not a good idea.'

'I won't order you around. Anyway, you've earned it. Sales and viewing figures are up, and that's not just the Metro-Centre. It's all along the M25. There's something new out there, and I'm giving it to them.'

'Something violent. That frightens me a little.'

'I feel for you, Richard. Sitting for years behind a big desk in Berkeley Square, you still believe in the human race. People like violence. It stirs the blood, speeds the pulse. Violence is the best way of controlling them, making sure that things don't get really out of hand.'

'They have already. These attacks on Asians and asylum seekers, the fiery crosses in front gardens. You didn't want all that, David. Some of these supporters are using the sports rallies as a cover for racist attacks. Setting fire to streets of houses. It's ethnic cleansing.'

'Street theatre, Richard. Just street theatre. Maybe I wind them up a little, but the crowds want blood. They believe in the Metro-Centre, and the Asians don't come here. They have a parallel economy. They've excluded themselves, and they're paying the price.'

'Even so. Can you talk to the chief marshals? Try to calm things down?'

'Right. I'll see what I can do.' Bored by this talk and my wheedling voice, Cruise sat up and waved away the glass of vodka. 'Think of them as skid marks, Richard. Roadkill. But we have to keep driving. Remember – "Mad is bad. Bad is good"?'

'I meant it. I still do.'

'Good. Maybe we need to go further, engine up the product a little. I could talk more about my alcoholism and drug use.'

'You're not an alcoholic. You're not a drug user.'

'That's not the point.' Cruise watched me patiently. 'Alcoholism, drug addiction. They're today's equivalent of military service. They give you a kind of . . .'

'Man-to-man authenticity?'

'Exactly.' Cruise raised a forefinger, calling me to attention. 'Take sex compulsion. I've been looking at that book you gave me.'

'Krafft-Ebing?'

'That's the one. It's full of ideas. We could slip one or two into the programme, see how the sofa ladies react.'

'They'd have a heart attack.' Trying to reassert my control, I stood up and turned my back to the picture window and the shoppers waving from the floor of the atrium. 'Be careful people don't start to pity you. It's far better if they fear you. Don't give too much away. Be more punitive, more demanding.'

'The stick, not the carrot?'

'Be more mysterious. Get rid of the Lincoln. It's too American, too show business.'

'Hey! I love that car.'

'Swap it for a black Mercedes. A black stretch Merc with tinted windows. Aggressive but paranoid. At the same time make it clear you're manipulating their emotions. Make shopping an emotionally insecure experience. Forget value for money, good buys, all that liberal middle-class rubbish. We want bad buys. Try to touch their unease, their dislike of all those people who look down on consumerism.'

'The old-style county set? I like that.'

'Another point.' I circled the sofa, apparently deep in thought. 'You need your audience, but now and then deride them. You despise them, but you need them. Play the unpredictable parent. Invent some new enemies. Tell people to join a consumer club at the Metro-Centre if they want to be part of their real family. Defend the mall is the message.'

'Defend the mall.' Cruise nodded solemnly. 'That's it.'

'Tell people to join the gold-card evenings, the discount shopping nights when they can go on TV. Keep them on their toes with the threat of withholding affection. Treat them like children – it's what they really want.'

'They are children!' Cruise threw his hands in the air, then gave a middle-finger salute to the picture window. 'I love it, Richard. I'm glad we talked this through. You can feel it happening – MPs are phoning up to help, they say they want to be part of the organiz-ation. I tell them there is no organization! Even the BBC offered me a show.'

'You declined?'

'Of course. People here would cut off my balls.'

'We don't want that . . . What would Cory and Imelda think?'

Laughing at this reference to his Filipina maids, Cruise stood up and patted me on the back. A red star pulsed on his control panel, and he saluted smartly. 'Right. Rehearsal for the evening show. Stay to watch?'

'I'll get home and catch it there. I'm still settling in.'

'Take your time.' Cruise followed me to the door, an arm around my shoulders. 'Someone told me you were off to London again.'

'News to me. When?'

'This Home Office delegation. Julia Goodwin, Maxted, Sangster. They want more police involved in our lives.'

'That's the middle-class way.'

'You're not going?'

'Definitely not.'

'Good. The Metro-Centre is your real home, Richard. Your father would have understood that.'

I left the dome by one of the side exits and joined the late-afternoon crowd that filled the plaza outside the Metro-Centre. Three separate rallies were taking place. Marching bands stamped and wheeled, supporters' clubs cheered the high-stepping majorettes. The motorway towns were out for the day, small children on their fathers' shoulders, teenage girls in saucy gangs. Families glowed with health and optimism, cheering and clapping in rhythm. I still assumed that I was part of a merchandising operation that was ringing all the tills in the Thames Valley, but something far larger was under way, a new kind of England that was disciplined, proud and content. The burning Asian houses belonged to another country.

26

A Bullet in the Hand

I DROVE BACK TO my father's flat, ready to shower and wash away the cloying scent of the dome's sterilized atmosphere. A fire engine blocked the access lane, reversing slowly towards the avenue. I shouted to one of the firemen, but he was intent on manoeuvring the huge vehicle. A tang of seared paint and charred plastic filled the air, seeping into the privet hedges and touched by a third ingredient that reminded me of a butcher's shop.

I waited until the fire engine reached the avenue, and drove down the exhaust-filled lane, followed by an ambulance with its lights flashing in my rear-view mirror. Two police cars and a breakdown truck were parked in front of the flats. The building was intact, residents watching from their windows as a group of my neighbours were questioned by a woman police officer.

I parked by the refuse bins, letting the ambulance drive up to the entrance. Crime-scene tapes surrounded a small Fiat, which sat on flattened tyres, retardant foam deliquescing on the gravel like crab spawn on a beach. Police engineers shackled a steel cable to the car, ready to winch it onto the loader.

I walked towards the entrance, waving to my neighbours, who as usual failed to respond. The glass door was starred by a bullet hole, and a pool of blood covered the tiles. Above my head a window closed sharply, and an elderly couple speaking to the police officer fell silent when I approached. Frowning at me, they stepped back, as if I were returning a little too early to the scene of my crime.

'Keep back. Mr Pearson, can you hear me?'

I turned to find Sergeant Mary Falconer warning me away from the blood-soaked tiles. She stood so close to me that I could smell the powder on her face. She scrutinized me warily, as if searching for a pointer to the violent crime that had reached the doors of this once peaceful enclave.

'Sergeant? I didn't see you. This car . . . ?'

'It's all over. There's no danger of fire. Can I ask what you're doing here?'

Her chin was raised, eyes narrowed as she looked down her nose at me. I could tell that she had changed sides since the Metro-Centre bomb. I remembered how she had almost fainted after hearing that Geoffrey Fairfax had been killed. She had been closely involved with Fairfax and Tony Maxted, but her crisp manner made it clear that this belonged to the past. The faction in the Brooklands police who had allied themselves to this odd clique had gone to ground, and I assumed that Superintendent Leighton was climbing a different corner of the cat's cradle of local politics, and had taken Sergeant Falconer with him. Had she once had an affair with Geoffrey Fairfax? I doubted it, though this rather frozen woman with her always immaculate make-up probably needed to feel subservient to a powerful man.

'Mr Pearson!'

'What am I doing here? This is where I live. I've moved into my father's flat.'

'I know that.' She was more aggressive than I recalled, shoulders squared and head canted to one side as if ready to push me into the flowerbed. 'Why are you here now?'

'I've just come home.' I stepped past her, as the residents in the porch moved away. 'What exactly is going on?'

Sergeant Falconer waited until the burnt-out Fiat was tied down to the loader. Lowering her voice, she confided: 'Your neighbours don't like you much, do they?'

'What have they been saying? This is nothing to do with me.'

'Nothing? Where were you an hour ago?'

'At the Metro-Centre. In David Cruise's dressing room. Hundreds of people must have seen me.'

'Did you use a phone? Contact anyone?'

'You mean send a signal? What happened here?'

Almost casually, she said: 'There was an attack on the Kumars just after five o'clock. Mr Kumar was driving home in his wife's car. A group of ice-hockey supporters followed him from the street and assaulted him as he tried to leave the car. Your neighbours saw them spray petrol over him and set him alight.'

'Good God . . . poor man. Is he . . . ?'

'Somehow he got out through the passenger door and reached the hall. The gang were jeering and singing while Dr Kumar tried to revive him. She went to speak to them, but one of the supporters took out a handgun and shot her through the chest.'

'Why . . . ? God almighty . . . Are they all right?'

'We'll know when we get them to hospital. If you have any information, Mr Pearson, it's important that you give it to me.'

'Information . . . ?'

The paramedics emerged from the Kumars' flat, pushing a wheeled stretcher. Somewhere under the oxygen mask and the silver foil was Mr Kumar, bulky figure deflated by the restraining straps. Sergeant Falconer drew me away when I tried to approach him. The paramedics slid Kumar into the ambulance and ran back for his wife. Numbed by the sight of this elegant woman reduced to a parcel of barely human wreckage, I stared at the ambulance until it drove away, siren wailing as if bringing the news.

The driver of the breakdown truck reversed across the drive, and the passenger door of the Fiat swung open above our heads. Clinging to the frosted window like scorched parchment was a patch of what resembled human skin.

Without thinking, I gripped Sergeant Falconer's arm. 'This gang – who were they?'

'Who?' The sergeant stared at me, as if I was being tiresomely facetious. 'Don't you know?'

'Why on earth should I? Sergeant?'

'Some people think you had a motive. You wanted the Kumars out of your block.'

'That's absolute rubbish. I don't approve of these attacks.'

'Maybe not. But you're doing a lot to encourage them.'

'With a few TV commercials? We're trying to sell refrigerators.'

'You're selling a lot more than that.' She moved me away from the reversing truck. 'If David Cruise is king of the castle, you're his grand vizier.'

'Writing advertising slogans?'

'Oh yes . . . the kind of slogans that convince people that black is white, that it's all right to go a little mad. You think you're selling refrigerators, but what you're really selling is civil war, nicely wrapped up as sport.'

'Then why aren't the police doing more? You've let things get out of control.'

For the first time Sergeant Falconer was evasive. She turned away from me, composing her expression and arranging her full lips squarely across her teeth. 'We're in control, Mr Pearson. But our resources are stretched. The chief constable feels we might provoke even more violence if we ban the marches and rallies.'

'You agree with him?'

'It's hard to say. The Home Office sees this as a matter of community discipline. There are outbreaks of soccer hooliganism every four or five years. Containment is the official policy, not confrontation . . .'

'Gobbledegook. Families are being driven out of their homes, shot on their own doorsteps. Dr Maxted is leading a delegation to the Home Office, demanding more action. I might join them.'

'Don't.' The sergeant took my arm. Lowering her voice, she stepped closer to me. 'Be careful, Mr Pearson. Go back to London and get on with your life. I'm afraid Dr Maxted is wasting his time.'

'Really? You've changed sides, Sergeant. Not so long ago you were running errands for Geoffrey Fairfax and his little clique, and heating milk for a murderer's baby.'

'Duncan Christie was discharged. The police offered no evidence.'

'Quite right. He'd served his role, shifting attention from the real killer. Fairfax and Superintendent Leighton kept him dangling long enough to stir up trouble for the Metro-Centre. By the way, what happened to the superintendent? I haven't seen you driving him around.'

'He's on indefinite sick leave.' Sergeant Falconer tried to step away from me, but I had backed her against the flowerbed. She waved to the two constables interviewing my neighbours, but neither responded. 'The bomb attack was a huge strain on the Brooklands force.'

'I bet it was. At least the superintendent missed getting his brains blown out. I hope he didn't supply the bomb to Geoffrey Fairfax.'

'Mr Pearson? Is that an accusation?'

'No. Just a passing thought.' I took the round of ammunition from my pocket and held it up to her. 'Recognize it, Sergeant? Police-issue Heckler & Koch, I'm ready to bet. Someone gave it to me outside the Metro-Centre this afternoon. Not so much a friendly warning, more of a get-well card, telling me to keep looking.'

Sergeant Falconer reached out to take the round, but I closed my hands around her fingers, pressing the warm bullet into her soft palm. I was surprised that she made no attempt to free her hand. She watched my eyes in her level way, undisturbed by my overtly sexual play, and waiting to see what I would do. If it was true that she liked to attach herself to powerful men, then there was a vacancy in her life now that Fairfax and Superintendent Leighton had moved from the scene. As David Cruise's vizier, I was certainly powerful, and might fill that vacancy. The Heckler & Koch bullet, identical to the one that had killed my father, was my valentine to her. By getting close to this attractive but conflicted woman, watching her heat the coffee milk in my father's kitchen, I might learn the truth about his death.

'Mr Pearson?' She freed her hand, but made no attempt to take the round from me. 'More passing thoughts?'

'In a way. A lot more interesting, though.'

'Good.' Her poise had never deserted her, whatever the cost in later humiliation. 'I see you're driving a different car.'

'It's leased. My Jensen was in an accident.'

'Nothing too serious?'

'Hard to say. Somehow I don't think it's going to get through its MOT.'

'That's a shame. Dr Goodwin thought it suited you.' She raised her chin, and managed a faraway smile. 'You know – a little past its prime, but handsome enough for a spin. Erratic steering and hopeless brakes. A tendency to veer off into dead ends . . .'

'Not exactly roadworthy?'

'It doesn't look like it. Try being a pedestrian, Mr Pearson. But watch your feet . . .'

She walked away from me, her smile fading into a smirk, and joined the two constables completing their interviews. I had unsettled her, and any concern she had once felt for me had gone. But emotions in the conventional sense probably mattered little to Sergeant Falconer. She attached herself to powerful men, fully expecting to be humiliated, and almost welcoming any rebuffs that came her way. She had played her part in the interlocking conspiracies that had flourished after my father's death, probably without ever realizing that other lives would be at stake.

Yet my own role was even more compromised. I saw myself as taking part in a merchandising scheme in a suburban shopping mall, using a 'bad is good' come-on that was meant to be the ultimate in ironic soft sells. I had recruited a third-rate cable presenter and sometime actor to play the licensed jester, the dwarf at the court of the Spanish kings. But the irony had evaporated, and the slogan had become a political movement, while the cable presenter had expanded a hundredfold and was ready to burst out of his bottle. The ad man was faced with the final humiliation of being taken literally.

For the first time I regretted that I had sold my Chelsea Harbour flat. I turned to the bullet-starred door, more than ready for a cold shower and a colder drink, but my foot seemed to stick to the entrance tiles. I looked down at my shoe, and realized that I had stepped into the pool of Dr Kumar's blood. Sergeant Falconer waved to me as I took off my shoe and limped into the hall.

27

An Anxious Intermission

VIOLENCE AND HATE were coming out to play.

The Kumars survived, the doctor with a deep puncture wound to her left lung, and her husband with severe burns to his chest and arms. I tried to visit them at Brooklands Hospital, but the relatives who arrived from Southall turned me away. One of the nephews who kept guard over Dr Kumar manhandled me to the lift and threatened to kill me if I appeared again. Julia Goodwin, sadly, avoided me and refused to take my calls. My neighbours were equally hostile, staring through me on the stairways and declining to park anywhere near my Mercedes.

The delegation to the Home Office led by Sangster and Dr Maxted came to nothing. The junior minister offered them the usual assurances, but he represented a marginal Birmingham constituency with high unemployment and was only too keen to import the magic formula of sport, discipline and consumerism.

For the next week I remained at the flat, alone with my father, thrown back on my memories of the old pilot or, more exactly, on my reconstruction of him from the few clues he had left me. From the start I had separated myself from his right-wing views, his St George's shirts and Hitler biographies, and the obsession with Nazi regalia. I loathed all that, as I loathed the attacks on the Asian communities near the M25. Nevertheless, my neighbours saw me as a sinister manipulator helping to sell, not refrigerators and microwave ovens, but a flat-pack führer and an ugly suburban fascism. Consumerism and a new totalitarianism had met by chance in a suburban shopping mall and celebrated a nightmare marriage.

Meanwhile, the sporting weekends seemed to last for ever, moving without a break through the working week. A packed list of fixtures filled every venue from Brooklands to Heathrow. Mini-leagues and knockout championships brought coachloads of supporters to the Metro-Centre, where they marched and countermarched behind their drum majors. There were so many fixtures, so many local finals mutating into league quarter-finals and area semi-finals, that supporters were light-headed from the endless cheering. They needed to stamp and shout and wave their banners, to believe passionately in something or, failing that, in nothing.

At night, grimly, they preferred nothing. National radio and TV bulletins made clear that violence rose as sports fever mounted. Attacks on Muslim shops and community centres were now as routine as a post-match pint. After the evening football games any Chinese and Indian takeaways near the stadium were attacked by gangs of supporters looking for violence. On his cable show David Cruise commented slyly that the easiest way to find a curry house was to look for black eyes and broken windows.

Around the Metro-Centre the sports-club marshals, dubbed honour guards by Tom Carradine, had merged into paramilitary units, protecting hypermarkets and retail parks from 'thieves and outsiders', who were blamed for the drunken damage. David Cruise casually referred to the 'enemy', a term kept deliberately vague that embraced Asians and east Europeans, blacks, Turks, non-consumers and anyone not interested in sport.

New enemies were always needed, and one in particular was soon found. The traditional middle class, with their private schools and disdain for the Metro-Centre, became a popular target. Bored after trashing another halal butcher's and another Sikh grocer's, gangs of supporters took to roaming the more prosperous residential areas, jeering at any half-timbered house with a rose pergola and a tennis court. A Harrods or Peter Jones van caught in the motorway towns was promptly spray-painted and had its tyres let down. Teenage girls clip-clopping their docile nags under the beech trees of comfortable avenues were followed by hooting cars emblazoned with St George's insignia. Bizarrely, the aerosolled Star of David began to appear on the garage doors of the most snootily gentile barristers and architects.

I urged Cruise to call for restraint, but he was too busy showing off his new Mercedes, a black stretch limousine that he christened 'Heinrich'. With the Filipina girls bouncing on the jump seats behind the chauffeur, he swept from stadium to ice-hockey rink to athletics ground. Standing in the directors' box, Cory and Imelda simpering beside him, he boomed at the crowd, his amplified voice drumming through the night sky. As 'Heinrich' made its threatening progress through the streets, he gave a continuous commentary to an on-board camera, reminding his viewers of gold-card and select-entry evenings at the Metro-Centre. For all his suggestive by-play with the Filipinas, and the strong hint that more than slap and tickle went on in their shared jacuzzi, he urged his viewers to defend their 'republic' against the corrupt alliance of the snobbish middle class and the snootier London boroughs who had always despised the motorway suburbs.

But Cruise's worries were for show only. The reign of the bully had begun. Led by Cruise and the Metro-Centre, the new movement was sweeping through the Home Counties. Supporters in St George's shirts swaggered down high streets from Dagenham to Uxbridge, hunted in packs through middle-class estates and terrorized every golden retriever in sight.

Three days after the attack on the Kumars, a gang of sports supporters invaded the Brooklands magistrates' court where two marshals charged by the police with attempted murder were being sent for trial. The supporters jeered the police officers and shouted down the elderly neighbours testifying that they had seen the attack. The hearing broke up, and the shocked magistrates adjourned the case, releasing the accused men on a nominal bail.

The next day supporters' groups invaded social security offices in Brooklands, Ashford and Hillingdon, demanding an immediate increase in supplementary benefit for those who left their jobs to become marshals at the local retail parks.

Despite the growing climate of fear, what was left of the county establishment firmly supported David Cruise and his brand of ideological consumerism. Mayors, MPs and even church leaders saw Cruise and the Metro-Centre as calming influences. They admired the new discipline, especially as it drove up property values and brought a surge in activity to every cash counter within ten miles of Heathrow. Crime continued to fall throughout the Thames Valley, and police chiefs dismissed the attacks on Asian and immigrant communities as the exuberance of a few sports fans.

Reassuringly, there was no obvious centre to the new movement. There were no cold-eyed strategists plotting to seize power. If all this had faint echoes of fascism, it was fascism lite, a mild and non-toxic strain.

I was far less sure, and stayed by the television set, amazed by the optimistic bulletins sent in by BBC reporters in the Metro-Centre car parks. Admiring the self-confident crowds and marching bands, they reminded the viewers that no one was organizing these displays of local pride.

But violence and hate, as always, were organizing themselves.

28

The Old Man's Quest

THINKING OF THE Kumars, both fortunately on the mend, I switched off the BBC news. I listened to the passing sirens of police cars and ambulances, by now an integral part of the Brooklands festival. I paced around the lounge, staring at my father's framed photographs and logbooks. Years in the Middle East had turned him into a right-wing fanatic with his ugly library and Roman banners. But his grip on me still held, and I half believed that he would have supported everything I had done at the Metro-Centre.

Unsettled by so many doubts, I left the lounge and walked past the kitchen to the utility room. I kept the door locked, avoiding even a glimpse of the neatly ironed shirts and Hitler biographies. But now I needed to call again on his support, and the key was in the lock.

I sat at the desk, a workstation disguised as a shrine, and began with his computer. My father's estate was still moving through probate, a process delayed by Geoffrey Fairfax's death and passed to another of the senior partners, and most of his records were filed away in various computer folders.

I scanned the list of folders: income-tax returns, share holdings, BUPA subscriptions, nursing homes in the Brooklands area, under-takers and their fees, golf courses near Marbella and Sotogrande, light airfields in the Algarve. The last folder was labelled 'Sports Diary'.

Expecting to find a list of veteran car rallies, I opened the folder, ready to read his account of the London-to-Brighton run.

But the diary recorded meetings of a rather different kind. The image of my father in a raccoon coat, sitting high among the brass and leather of an antique Renault or Hispano-Suiza, faded quickly. Turning my eyes from the screen, I could scent the well-thumbed pages of the Hitler biographies, and the peculiar chemical reek of the coated paper that publishers seemed to reserve for atrocity photographs.

The sports diary covered the last three months of my father's life, and recorded a number of racist incidents he had witnessed, attacks on Asian shops and asylum seekers' hostels. Each entry described the sporting event that provided cover for the post-match incident, the number of supporters present, the damage inflicted and my father's general thoughts on the supporters' esprit de corps, background and professions.

The first entry had been logged on February 3.

Byfield Lane sports ground. Spartan League quarter-final. Brooklands Wanderers 2 Motorola FC 5. Thirty Brooklands supporters met at the Feathers, a regular rendezvous. At least ten had been to the match. Wore a St George's shirt and was warmly welcomed. At 9.15 we formed up and marched down to the industrial estate. A Bangladeshi newsagent's was attacked, windows broken, soft drinks and chocolate bars taken. Good-humoured, and no racist shouts. Seen as a prank by everyone. Members: supermarket junior manager, a call-centre worker, two delivery drivers, hospital clerk. Few knew each other, but they stayed together when police car cruised past, and waited for me to catch up with them. Decent types, mostly married, sport brings them together. No interest in Hitler and the Nazis. National Front they see as a joke.

A fortnight later my father was at the ice-hockey stadium.

Brooklands Bears 37 Addlestone Retail Park 3. The wide margin set everyone going. Hard contact sport acts like adrenalin. Inner group of a dozen met at the Crown and Duck. Elbow and shoulder pads under St George's shirts. They kept me at arm's length until I spoke loudly about 'middle-class snobs'. Picked up twenty supporters waiting in car park and moved to bus depot. Chinese takeaway attacked. Cook and wife watched patiently as spring rolls thrown at walls. Manager emptied cash till, offered them money, was kicked to the floor for his pains. Indignation at thought of taking money. Open violence and racist anger, but community pride. Feel they are defending Brooklands, though no idea against what. Draughtsman, taxi driver, dental mechanic, hotel receptionist. Have cars, own homes, wives and children. Stick together, but looking for leadership.

I read through further entries. My father had joined a variety of supporters' clubs. He seemed aware of the limitations of these saloon-bar racists, and was trying to gain entry to a more senior level of the leadership, if that existed. He was clearly worried that the unco-ordinated attacks would slip into anarchy. He listed attacks on Asian property, the assault on a hostel for Kosovan refugees and the trashing of an unofficial gypsy caravan park.

In an April 12 entry he reported:

Local derby at an out-of-town football stadium. Tin shack stands with the latest giant-screen technology, like Sopwith Camel fitted with a Rolls-Royce turbofan. Tremendous atmosphere, a real sense of a united community. Good-humoured, passionate people. A hundred or so supporters, all from Metro-Centre clubs, formed up in the car park and set off for east Brooklands. Wrecked a Bangladeshi tailor's, then broke into a large Asian supermarket. Running battles with Sikh youths armed with knives and iron bars. The St George's shirts meant something. The supporters stood their ground, bare fists against the Asian knives, holding the line as their grandfathers did at Arnhem and Alamein. Fine men, careful to protect me, though I was a damned nuisance. Best NCO material: store managers, electricians, shoe-shop salesmen.

They long for discipline and leadership. The Metro-Centre alone gives a focus to their lives.

My father described driving a seriously injured man to Brooklands Hospital.

We laid him in the back seat of the Bristol. Blood all over the leather. I put my foot down, outrunning the police Vauxhalls, earned many heartfelt handshakes. 'Anything you need, Dad.' When I asked to meet their leaders they looked blank.

He went on:

I realize there are no leaders. A Metro-Centre newsletter about a discount carpet sale is all that holds them together. They long for authority and some kind of deeper meaning in their lives. They need someone to admire and follow. The destination doesn't matter. The nearest to a leader is a presenter on the cable channel called David Cruise. He winds them up at matches, but he is inadequate, an ex-actor lost without a script. He is dangerous, because the Metro-Centre is the mainspring of their empty lives.

Growing danger of a high-speed stall. The whole town will flip over and head for the ground at 400 knots. Will the passengers mind? Everything I've read about the Nazi leaders shows that their followers didn't fear disaster but actively welcomed it.

My chief problem – there's no one I can talk to about all this. Sport dominates everything, and fringe violence is part of the culture. Police too tolerant, and anyway see immigrants as a source of trouble, even if they aren't to blame. The only person I've met is a Northfield psychiatrist, Dr Tony Maxted. An odd man, with an agenda of his own. Part of him welcomes the

violence – it confirms some academic theory. He was very
taken with my description of a high-speed stall.

Sadly, the Bristol was stolen during the night. Found torched in
a lay-by on the Weybridge road. I loved the old lady, and it's
galling that it had to pay the price. At all costs, avoid being
conspicuous. At any level, politics is a herd game . . .

On April 30:

There's a limit to the infiltration I can carry out. The demos are
getting more violent. I'm fit but no use at street fighting. Took
a punch full-face from a young Bangladeshi defending his
mother. Didn't realize I was trying to help her. The group
admire my 'guts' but tell me to go home.

It's astonishing how well my masquerade has worked. No one
suspects an old British Airways pilot. Chief regret is that I have
frightened my neighbours, especially Dr Kumar and her
husband. But I have to keep up the disguise for a few weeks
longer. These Metro-Centre sports clubs are dangerous and need
to be stopped. The supporters are turning into a freikorps,
though they don't realize it. That's the strange thing. When I saw
Fairfax about my pension he said: 'Who are the leaders?'
Obvious question everyone asks. There are no leaders. Yet.
Sooner or later some hard-eyed thug with the gift of the gab
will seize control in a bloodless coup. Already there's talk of a
new 'republic' stretching from Heathrow to Brooklands, the
whole M3/M4 corridor. A new kind of dictatorship based on
the Metro-Centre. I tried to raise this with Fairfax, but he talked
about his golf handicap. He's part of a curious little cabal, they
may have political ambitions of their own.

Then, on May 2, the last entry.

I watched the cable presenter David Cruise. Likeable in an actorish way. A highly developed feel for people's 'small' emotions. Dangerous? He's a toy, waiting to be wound up by anyone ready to make the effort. He might appeal to a certain kind of rootless person who believes in nothing and has worked out some pie-eyed theory to justify his own emptiness.

Tomorrow I will put on my St George's shirt and try to get on his programme. I'll play the old BA pilot card and stage a demo of my own. Warn people of the danger of too much sport and nothing else. Sooner or later a messiah is going to appear . . .

I closed the folder and sat back, my eyes scarcely noticing the führer moustache and forelock on the spine of a Hitler biography. I felt a vast relief, and a surge of confidence in this suburban flat and its memories. I felt close to my father again, and impressed by the bravery of this old man. He had known that something was wrong, and was determined to reach the source of the deep malaise that threatened his pacific community. His apparent membership of the St George's clubs had convinced his neighbours and convinced me. To a larger extent than I wanted to admit, I had relied on my father to justify my support for the Metro-Centre and its sporting militias.

I now knew the truth, and I could admire my father and accept myself. I no longer needed to avoid the mirrors in the apartment. At the same time, these undercover missions raised a number of questions about his death. Had he been betrayed by a friend in whom he confided? Geoffrey Fairfax would have ratted on him without a qualm. Had someone slipped into the flat and checked his computer files? I thought of the 'curious little cabal' led by Fairfax and Superintendent Leighton, which had drawn Julia Goodwin into its fraying web. Had the cabal dealt with the meddling old man, recruiting some disgraced police marksman as their assassin, who had shot my father dead as he climbed the staircase to the mezzanine studio? Out of the smoke-screen of rumour they then produced Duncan Christie, misfit and urban scarecrow, and kept him in place long enough for the killer's trail to be stamped into the dust. Even Sangster and Dr Maxted may have had no idea of Fairfax's real game. The fool's mate set out on the chessboard concealed a far more elaborate gambit . . .

To Fairfax's dismay, the murdered old man was replaced by his son, an even greater meddler. The bomb in my car, left there by the impatient solicitor, should have removed a minor nuisance from the board.

But at long last the pieces were beginning to fight back against the players.

29

The Stricken City

THERE WAS TOO little air in the flat. Even with the windows open, I felt suffocated. Schemes and conspiracies were leaping out of trap doors around me, then evaporating into mist. I needed to clear my head, and the only place in Brooklands untouched by the Metro-Centre was the racing circuit, a monument to a far saner dream of speed.

I left the flat and went down to my car. The chanting crowd at the athletics ground, the bursts of cheering and the commentator's relentless harangues, together bruised the afternoon. The din drummed against the windows of nearby houses, turning a pleasantly sunny day into a summer in Babel.

I drove through the residential avenues towards the circuit, past the wrought-iron gates and the St George's flags. Every day a few more of them flew from improvised flagpoles, or flapped weakly from brass porch lanterns, a feeble attempt to ward off the roaming supporters' clubs, ensigns of surrender that marked the capitulation of a powerful class.

Half a mile from the circuit the road was closed by a police barricade. Officers stood by their car, signalling the traffic towards a detour. Ignoring their advice, I turned into a side street, but the next approach road was sealed off by police tapes. Detour signs sent the traffic on an endless tour of half-timbered houses, and I had a momentary vision of Brooklands' entire middle class, its prosperous lawyers, doctors and senior managers, being confined to their own ghetto, with nothing to do all day except groom their ponies and swing their croquet mallets.

Glad of the chance to walk, I parked outside the entrance to a nursing home and set off on foot. Police patrolled the junctions, but there was little traffic near the racing circuit. I crossed the perimeter road, and approached the section of embankment.

As always, I could hear engines running in the distance, the deep-throated roar of unmuffled exhausts and the hacking gasps of carburettors hungry for air. Only a small section of the circuit remained, but in my mind, and in my father's mind, the great track was intact. The banked surface still carried the sports cars that raced for ever through faraway afternoons, in a happier world of speed and glamour and elegant women in white helmets and overalls.

Engines sounded, but not in my head. I followed the path alongside the access road that cut through the embankment. The car park beside the industrial estate in the centre of the circuit was filled with police and military vehicles. Dozens of camouflaged vans and canvas-topped trucks were backed onto the embankment. Buses converted to mobile diners, pantechnicons loaded with aerials and communications gear, and flat-bed trailers carrying three huge bulldozers were parked on the runway of the disused airfield within the circuit. Dozens of police and soldiers in overalls crossed the runway to a metal warehouse in the industrial estate, commandeered as a temporary barracks.

I was walking through the vehicle park of a large invasion force, and assumed that it was about to rehearse the seizure of Heathrow Airport after a terrorist attack. A soldier sat in the driving cab of a camouflaged truck, smoking a cigarette as he studied a road map.

I walked across to him, but a police car with lights flashing left the road and climbed the embankment behind me, its wing grazing my knees. A constable leaned from his window and waved me away without speaking, then watched me until I left the circuit.

I walked back to my car, surprised by the scale of this military operation. Vehicles were still arriving, stopped and checked by military police. Aldershot, the chief garrison town of the British Army, was only a few miles beyond the M25, and I guessed that a large-scale civil-defence exercise was under way.

When I reached my car I paused to look up and down the deserted avenue. The detour signs were still in place, and the St George's flags hung slackly from the garden gates. But a complete silence lay over the town. The amplified commentaries and communal singing had died away, and for the first time in days, if not weeks, no one was cheering.

A young woman ran towards me from the drive of the nursing home, propelling a pushchair with a startled child. She seemed distraught, buttons bursting from her blouse, and I raised my hands to calm her.

'Let me help you, please . . . are you all right?'

I assumed that she was a bereaved relative, and was ready to comfort her. But she pushed past me, swearing when she tripped on the kerb. She pointed wildly at the sky.

'The dome's on fire!'

'The dome? Where?'

'It's on fire!' She waved at the rooftops. 'They're burning down the Metro-Centre!'

She fled with her child, the last inhabitant of a stricken city.

30

Assassination

A SILENCE LOUDER than thunder lay over Brooklands. I could hear
the traffic moving along the M25, and pick out the engines of individual trucks and coaches. Stadiums and athletics grounds had
emptied, and all evening fixtures were postponed. Everyone was
waiting for news from the dome.

Like most people, I spent the afternoon watching my television
set. From the living-room windows I could see the narrow column
of white smoke that rose from an emergency vent in the roof of the
Metro-Centre. In the still air it climbed vertically, trembled and then
dispersed into the cloud cover.

I guessed that an electrical fault in the air-conditioning plant
was to blame. The fire would be brought under control and the
rumours of arson promptly scotched. But the ITN and BBC news
teams reporting from the South Gate entrance were uncertain of the
cause, and unable to assess the damage. The reporters both confirmed
that the dome had not been evacuated, and reassured any relatives
watching that there were no casualties. A view of the central atrium,
taken with a concealed camera, showed the strolling crowds, the three
bears swaying and jigging to the music, and no signs of panic.

By contrast, the Metro-Centre's three cable channels talked up the
threat, claiming that unknown arsonists had tried to burn down the
dome. Relays of announcers spoke of serious damage costing tens
of millions of pounds, and of sinister enemies determined to raze
the entire structure to the ground.

Live coverage showed David Cruise at the forefront of the battle, wearing a red helmet and firefighter's suit. In a series of handheld shots from the basement garage, he stepped from the cabin of an emergency vehicle, conferred urgently with a white-faced Tom Carradine and a team of Metro-Centre engineers, and pressed his healing hands to the maze of pipes and cable ducts in the generator room. Gasping into his oxygen mask, he shared bottles of a well-advertised mineral water with an exhausted fire crew. When he addressed the camera he was in no doubt about the threat to every Metro-Centre customer and every sports-club supporter. Rubbing his flushed forehead, his cheekbones stylishly marked with a dark commando stain, he said:

'All of you out there . . . this is David Cruise, somewhere in the front line. Listen to me, if I can still get through to you. We need your support, every one of you watching. Make no mistake, there are people out there who want to destroy us. They hate the Metro-Centre, they hate the sports clubs and they hate the world we've created here.' He coughed into his oxygen mask, brushing aside the attractive paramedic who tried to calm him. 'This time we'll have to fight for what we believe. The people who did this will try again. I want you all to be ready. You created this, don't let them take it away. There are enemies out there, and you know who they are. If I don't see you again, you can be sure I went down fighting for the Metro-Centre . . .'

An hour later the smoke still rose from the roof, a white plume almost invisible in the late-afternoon light. A BBC journalist had entered the basement, and reported that the source of the fire was now clear. A large hopper filled with cardboard cartons had been set ablaze, but this was under control.

David Cruise, however, was closer to the action. He climbed from an inspection hatch and wearily doffed his helmet, then whispered hoarsely about the dangers of igniting the Metro-Centre's oil stores. 'We're talking about timed devices,' he darkly informed his cable viewers. 'Be on the alert, and check your garages and basements. Every one of us is a target . . .'

At seven o'clock he would address his cable audience from the mezza-nine studio. I watched him play his role, an extra now promoted to be the star of his own towering inferno. The engineers around him looked vaguely embarrassed, but Cruise was completely sincere, the naturalized citizen of a new kingdom where nothing was true or false. Most of his audience probably knew that the fire in a rubbish hopper was a ruse designed to rally support for the Metro-Centre, for reasons not yet clear. They knew they were being lied to, but if lies were consistent enough they defined themselves as a credible alter-native to the truth. Emotion ruled almost everything, and lies were driven by emotions that were familiar and supportive, while the truth came with hard edges that cut and bruised. They preferred lies and mood music, they accepted the make-believe of David Cruise the firefighter and defender of their freedoms. Consumer capitalism had never thrived by believing the truth. Lies were preferred by the people of the shopping malls because they could be complicit with them.

Sadly, real fires burned on the outskirts of Brooklands. By the early evening a huge crowd had gathered outside the Metro-Centre, a suburban army dressed in its St George's shirts. Sports clubs formed up and marched away, heading for the outskirts of the town as if to defend the walls of a besieged city. As I feared, outbreaks of burning and looting soon struck the Asian and immigrant housing estates.

But the gangs were quick to find other targets. Bored by the punch-ups with desperate Bangladeshis and exhausted Kosovans, they attacked the further-education college near the town square with its irritating posters advertising classes in cordon bleu cooking, archae-ology and brass rubbings. The public library was another target, its shelves swept clear of the few books on display, though the huge stock of CDs, videos and DVDs was untouched.

Other gangs invaded the Brooklands Cricket Club, where they def-ecated on the pitch, and the Gymkhana Riding School, a stronghold of the would-be middle class, which was swiftly put to the torch. The TV news showed wild-eyed horses galloping through the Metro-Centre car parks, their singed manes alive with sparks. Even the police station and magistrates' court were under threat, cordoned off by a thin blue line of officers in riot gear.

Ominously, the BBC reported that fights were breaking out between the supporters' groups – unable to find any new enemies, they were turning on themselves.

I was trying to phone Julia Goodwin, and warn her that the Asian women's refuge was in danger, when David Cruise began his address to his new 'republic', transmitted live from the mezzanine studio in the Metro-Centre. He had swapped his fireman's overall for a stylish combat jacket, but the make-up girls had left untouched his ruffled hair and oily bruises on his cheeks. He was fighting off his own hysteria, aware that his sports clubs might rampage through a modest county town, but the referee was about to blow the whistle and there would be no extra time. What the television reporters still called football hooliganism was what central government termed civil insurrection. The army and police were waiting.

Cruise leaned forward into the camera, ready to rally his loyal audience, and unable to resist his familiar cheeky smile. But as he opened his mouth, displaying his strong teeth and muscular tongue, he seemed to slip from his chair. A spasm of indigestion brought a hand to his chest, and his eyes lost their focus. He swayed to one side, elbow sliding across the desk, and tore the lapel microphone from his jacket. He reached out to clutch at the air, eyes rolling under their lids. His smile seemed to drift away, an empty smirk deserted like an abandoned ship. He held himself upright, and then fell forward from his chair, head across his bloodstained script.

Five seconds later, the screen went blank. There was a brief silence, and then a deep roar rose from the Metro-Centre as the crowd watching the screens above the South Gate entrance let out a cry of anger and pain, the visceral bellow of an animal goaded at the point of death. The sound rose over Brooklands, drumming at the windows and echoing off the nearby roofs.

I turned to the Channel 4 news. The reporter stared uneasily at her autocue, ready to interrupt herself.

'We're hearing reports . . . of an assassination attempt at a Brooklands shopping mall. Eyewitnesses claim that a lone gunman . . . we don't know yet if –'

I switched off the set and stared at the darkened room. Someone had shot David Cruise, but I found it difficult to cope with the notion that he had been seriously injured. I knew him too well, and had helped to create him. He was so pervasive a figure, dominating almost every moment of my life at Brooklands, that he had long since become a fictional character. He had floated free into a parallel space and time where celebrity redefined reality as itself. His anguished slide across the table, the desperate way in which he had torn the microphone from his bursting chest, had been the latest episode in the series of noir commercials I had devised for him. In fact, I had switched off the set to avoid turning back to the cable channel and seeing the consumer product that sponsored the episode.

But already I was forgetting David Cruise. Julia Goodwin would be at her wits' end, trying to protect her Asian women from the ferocious backlash that would soon follow. Bereft of their champion and cable philosopher, the supporters' clubs would go berserk, attacking anything in their sights.

I strode into the hall and unlocked the cupboard where I stored my suitcases. My father's golf bag, clubs untouched for months, leaned against the rear wall. I pulled out the heavy leather bag, felt between the putters and drew my father's Purdey shotgun into the light.

On the shelf above was a box of twelve-bore shells, enough to see off any hooligans trying to ransack their old school. Nothing was true, and nothing was untrue. But the real was making a small stand against the unreal.

31

'Defend the Dome!'

A CAR APPROACHED, tyres raking the gravel outside the entrance to the flats. Its headlights were on full beam, flooding the car park like a film set. I leaned through the rear passenger door of the Mercedes and stowed the shotgun on the floor, wrapped in my raincoat. Its butt rested on the transmission hump within easy reach of the driving seat.

The headlights of the visitor's car still flared in my face. The driver stepped out, a burly man who left his engine running. He stared around him, bald head almost glowing in the dark, then recognized me.

'Right . . . I thought you'd be here. Leave that and come with me.'

'Who the hell . . . ? Dr Maxted?'

'I hope so – nothing's certain now. Look snappy.'

'Wait . . . where are we going?'

Maxted stared at me as I hesitated, one hand moving towards the shotgun. He was exhausted but determined, his troubled face openly hostile as he peered at me. Wearily he took my arm.

'Where? Your spiritual home – the Metro-Centre. For once you're going to do something useful.'

'Hold on . . .' I watched the fires rising into the night sky and pointed to my Mercedes. 'There's a shotgun in the back.'

'Forget it. If we need that, it's already too late. We'll take my car.'

'You heard the news flash? About David Cruise?'

'Someone put a bullet through him.' Maxted stepped into the Mazda sports car. 'On air! My God, I have to hand it to you people. Don't tell me that was something you dreamed up?'

'No . . .' I slid into the cramped passenger seat. In the light reflected from the porch I could see Maxted's swollen face, knuckle marks bruising his cheek. 'Is he alive?'

'Just about.' Maxted reversed and ran over a rose display. He winced at the hooting horns and the din of traffic in the avenue, the shouts and cheering that had returned to Brooklands. 'The bullet knocked out a lung – let's hope he lasts the night.'

'Who shot him? Do they know?'

'Not yet. Some Bangladeshi who's had his shop trashed once too often, maybe a Kosovan who's seen his wife slapped around.' Maxted accelerated down the narrow drive, then braked sharply as we reached the avenue, a free-for-all of stalled traffic, veering headlights and panic-stricken pedestrians. He shouted above the din. 'One thing David Cruise had was an unlimited supply of enemies. That was part of his strategy. You know that, Richard. You planned it that way.'

I ignored this jibe, thinking of the hours I had spent in Cruise's swimming pool, watched by the Filipina maids. 'Where is he? Brooklands Hospital?'

'The first-aid unit at the Metro-Centre. Until he stabilizes it's too risky to move him. Let's hope the unit is well equipped. I never thought I'd say it, but David Cruise is one person we need to keep alive.'

'And if he dies?'

'People here are ready to flip. Not just Brooklands, but all along the motorway towns. I don't like what's been going on, but the next chapter could be a lot nastier.'

'Elective . . . ?'

'Psychopathy? You've got it. Willed madness.' Maxted swung the sports car into the traffic stream, a motorized babel of horns and whistles. 'They don't know it, but they've been waiting for the trigger. Sooner or later some nobody would turn up with the key and put it into the lock for them.'

'And did he?'

'Turn up? Oh, yes.'

'Who?'

'You.' Maxted overtook a pick-up truck packed with banner-waving supporters. 'You wrote the script for our pocket führer. A suburban Dr Goebbels . . . what did you think you were doing? Selling washing machines?'

'Something like that. It worked.'

'It worked too well. Late capitalism is scratching its piles and trying to figure out where next to shit. All the privy doors are closed except one. Buying a washing machine is a political act – the only real kind of politics left today.'

We sat in the stalled traffic, the air dinned by a rising clamour of horns. Supporters in St George's shirts darted between the cars, drumming on the roofs. Everyone in the Thames Valley was converging on the Metro-Centre. It rose above the houses and office blocks, an immense white ghost, a mausoleum readying itself for death.

'And the fire this afternoon?' I asked Maxted, shouting over the noise. 'At the dome?'

'Don't be taken in. That was David Cruise trying to light the fuse.'

'It was a stunt?'

'Absolutely. He needed to set off an uprising, but he knew he'd left it too late. He'd heard about the army units waiting at the race-track.'

'I saw them this afternoon. They look as if they mean business.'

'They do.' Maxted laughed into the raucous horns. 'That must have sobered you up.'

'I already was sober. I checked my father's computer and read his diary. He wasn't a St George's supporter. He hated all the sports clubs and the whole Metro-Centre thing.'

'I'm glad to hear it. Now you've got someone better to look up to.'

'He tried to infiltrate the movement and find who's leading it. It's just possible that's why he was shot.'

'Maybe.' Two ice-hockey fans sat on the Mazda's bonnet, beating time with their fists, and Maxted sounded the horn until they leapt away through the confusion of headlights. He bellowed at me: 'No one is leading it. I'm sorry your old man was killed, but this is a bottom-up revolution. That's why it's so dangerous. Sangster and I were trying to damp it down. We wanted Cruise out of the studio and into the street where he could see what was going on. But reality was never his thing.'

'Why haven't the government moved in? Brooklands has been out of control for months.'

'Not just Brooklands. The Home Office want to see what happens. The suburbs are the perfect social laboratory. You can cook up any pathogen and test how virulent it is. The trouble is, they've waited too long. The whole M25 could flip and drag the rest of the country into outright psychopathy.'

'Impossible. People are too docile.'

'People are bored. Deeply, deeply bored. When people are that bored anything is possible. A new religion, a fourth reich. They'll worship a mathematical symbol or a hole in the ground. We're to blame. We've brought them up on violence and paranoia. Now, what's happening here?'

The traffic was moving around a Range Rover parked outside a Tudor-style mansion. A gang of sports supporters were breaking the car's windows with iron bars. The driver, a shocked young matron in a sheepskin jacket, tried to remonstrate with them, pushing away one of the youths who was fondling her.

'Maxted . . . we ought to help.'

'No time.' Head down, Maxted drove on, joining the main boulevard that ran to the dome. 'We need to get you to the Metro-Centre before the roof lifts off.'

'You want me to talk to David Cruise?'

'Talk? Julia Goodwin says the man's on a ventilator.'

'Julia? She's there?'

'Sangster drove her from the refuge. Julia knows we have to keep Cruise alive.'

'And what can I do?'

'Take over from David Cruise. You know the production team, they'll be glad to have you. You wrote the scripts so you should be word-perfect. Speak to the camera, urge everyone to go home and cool down. Say the whole sports-club programme is a PR exercise, a marketing experiment that failed. Cobble something together, but say you were wrong.'

'I wasn't wrong.'

We abandoned the car five hundred yards from the dome. Maxted drove onto a traffic island, and we stepped out between the lines of cars and buses bringing supporters to the Metro-Centre from all over the Thames Valley. A huge crowd packed the open plaza, staring at the dome as if waiting for a message. They watched the display screens over the South Gate entrance, as two linkmen described Cruise's battle for life in an emergency operating theatre set up in the first-aid station.

Maxted pushed through the spectators, showing his doctor's ID card and shouting at a marshal who tried to turn us back. Behind us, headlamps flared along the perimeter road, the sweeping spotlights of police and military vehicles forcing their way through the traffic. An armoured personnel carrier rammed Maxted's little Mazda and tossed it to one side. Heavy trucks with bull bars shouldered the smaller cars out of their way and shunted them brutally onto the verge. Squads of police in riot gear marched forward under a creeping barrage of megaphoned orders.

'Richard! Snap out of it!' Maxted seized my arm. 'Head for the South Gate entrance.'

The crowd moved with us, a mulish mob forced by the police against the dome. Fights broke out, fists flailing through the workmanlike rise and fall of police truncheons. A young woman dropped to the ground, knocked senseless when she tried to defend her husband. Her children began to shriek, voices soon drowned by the blades of army helicopters cuffing the night air. Searchlights swept the storm of dust stirred by the downdraught, probing the more resolute sections of the crowd. Elite supporters' clubs joined battle with the aggressive snatch squads seizing their marshals. A police horse reared, its padded legs flinching from the rain of base-ball bats. The bitter tang of CS gas mingled with the stench of vomit.

The crowd yielded, retreating to the South Gate entrance. I steadied an elderly woman listening to her mobile phone. She tried to elbow me away, then cried out: 'They want to close the dome!'

I shook her birdlike shoulder. 'Why? Who want to?'

'The police! They're closing the dome!'

All around me the cry was taken up, a fearful mantra that flashed like a spectre from mouth to mouth.

'Closing the dome . . . ! Closing the dome . . . !'

Everyone was shouting. The crowd surged towards the entrance, a frantic riptide that swept us with it, carrying us under the display screens, past the first-aid tables, through the doors and into the brightly lit haven of the entrance hall. People were stumbling, hands clutching each other, shoes lost in the stampede, consumers returning to their sanctuary, to their fortress temple and sacred asylum.

A new cry went up.

'Defend the dome . . . !'

32

The Republic of the Metro-Centre

FLEEING FROM THE tear gas and the police truncheons, the last of the crowd burst past the doors into the entrance hall. The searchlights seemed to follow us into the dome, and the iron din of the helicopters drummed at the roof over our heads, the language of pain roaring through the cheerful interior light.

I tripped over a shopping trolley and fell to my knees, bringing down a black woman and two children who clung to my jacket. Tony Maxted had vanished, swept away by the rush. People were boarding the travelator, seeking safety in the vast interior of the Metro-Centre, waving their loyalty cards at the astonished counter staff who came to the doors of their shops.

I stood up, and noticed that I had lost my left shoe. Sandals, trainers, court shoes and even a pair of carpet slippers lay scattered among the abandoned shopping bags. I found my brogue beside a broken stiletto heel, and remembered a large woman in a fur coat stepping on my foot, then screaming abuse at me.

Beyond the doors a line of soldiers with shields and batons were dispersing the hundreds of spectators who had stepped from their cars on the perimeter road. Police constables in riot gear and vizored helmets now sealed off the entrance, and ignored the television cameras recording the scene from the location vans of the main news channels.

But already a modest fightback had begun. Spurred on by the camera lights, a group of marshals and supporters in St George's shirts were bolting the outer doors. They sealed the manual locks, unwound a heavy hose from the emergency fire-control station and threaded the brass nozzle through the door handles.

The police ignored all this, taking for granted that they could break down the doors whenever they wanted. Two inspectors conferred, watching the marshals assemble a barricade of sales counters and display stands, clearly unconcerned by all this fierce determination. By neutralizing the Metro-Centre, the police had defused the threat of a civil uprising, and the ringleaders of any open rebellion had conveniently isolated themselves from their supporters outside the dome.

Sitting on a chair beside the enquiry desk, I peeled off my bloody sock and tied my handkerchief around my foot. I watched the marshals rallying their teams, admiring their doomed efforts to defend the mall. Many of the customers trapped inside the dome by the riot were now helping to build the barricade, and their commitment to the Metro-Centre was more than a set of slogans. They resented the police ambush, and the involvement of the army. The helicopters endlessly soaring over the roof were trying to intimidate them, and they had decided to stand their ground. Everyone cheered on a women's judo team who carried a hamburger kiosk across the hall, leaking a trail of hot fat. Clapped by their menfolk, they swung the kiosk to and fro and launched it onto the barricade. Even the inspectors gave an admiring salute.

I stood up, trying to clear my throat of the dust and tear gas. The public-address system played a medley of Strauss marches, and the information screens announced the opening of a new crèche. Customers still sat in a nearby coffee house with their double espressos and Danish pastries. But for all their bravery, the Metro-Centre had struck its iceberg. I needed to find Julia Goodwin, and help her to move David Cruise to Brooklands Hospital before we sank together.

Outside the dome a column of riot vehicles and military trucks had drawn up. Spotlights were trained on the doors, turning the entrance hall into a giant hallucination of swerving shadows. The police had forced three of the doors, and a squad of a dozen constables approached the barricade, but for the moment made no attempt to dismantle it. A senior officer, an assistant commissioner of the Surrey police, began to address the watching crowd, fragments of his amplified message barely audible above the blare of the helicopters.

'. . . from tonight the Metro-Centre will close for renovations . . . management in full agreement . . . concern for customers . . . for your own safety leave in an orderly way . . .'

At least five hundred people were crammed into the entrance hall and the nearby shopping aisles. Staff, sports-club supporters, customers caught in the riot, and passers-by driven by panic to seek refuge in the dome were together waiting for something to happen. Many wanted to leave, but fell silent as a militant minority shouted abuse at the assistant commissioner.

At a signal, the constables began to dismantle the barricade, first hurling aside the hamburger kiosk, slipping and sliding in the fat. Scuffles broke out in the watching crowd, and children shrieked at the grappling shadows projected by the spotlights onto the walls of the entrance hall.

'Right . . .' I shifted my weight from my injured foot, ready to join the exodus from the Metro-Centre. 'It's all over. Small revolution in Thames Valley . . .'

'Not quite.' Beside me an elderly man in a grey topcoat, briefcase in hand, smiled to himself in a resigned way. I had noticed him taking shelter behind the enquiry desk, and assumed he was leaving the dome when the riot began. He pointed to the staff entrance near the cloakrooms. 'I fear we won't see our beds tonight . . .'

Pushing aggressively through the crowd, and almost marching in step, was a group of marshals, Metro-Centre engineers in orange overalls, and some fifty supporters in St George's shirts. At their head was Tom Carradine, still in his sky-blue public relations uniform, but no longer the earnest figure whose faith in the mall I found so touching. He seemed small but poised, as watchful and unsmiling as a bullfighter faced with a stupid but dangerous bull. Behind him, forming his personal bodyguard, were the two marshals who had hurled Duncan Christie to the ground as he tried to press a bullet into my palm. Both marshals carried shotguns that I assumed they had looted from the many gun shops in the dome. Carradine's right hand was raised above his head, and he signalled to the marshals with small movements of his forefinger. He was confident and undaunted, glad to be rising at last to the supreme challenge that faced him.

Hard on the marshals' heels came William Sangster, broad shoulders swaying from side to side, massive head ducking like a boxer's before climbing into the ring. His eyes scanned the crowd, as if searching for any former pupils who were still playing truant. He smiled in a disoriented way, unsure of himself and what he was doing with these armed men.

A shot rang out, a sharp roar like the slamming of a door. The concourse fell silent. A raised shotgun pointed to the ceiling, as the faint smoke from its barrel faded on the sweating air. The assistant commissioner lowered his megaphone, and the constables dismantling the barricade stopped to wait for their orders.

Carradine handed the shotgun to the marshals. He took off his peaked cap, revealing his blond hair swept back from a surprisingly steep forehead. He listened to the silence that filled the entrance hall, and then spoke briefly into the microphone passed to him by a marshal. His magnified voice in its motorway accent boomed over the heads of the police and soldiers outside the dome.

'The Metro-Centre is secure . . . Withdraw all army units . . . Repeat, the Metro-Centre is secure . . . We have hostages . . . Repeat, we have hostages . . .'

The sounds echoed through the mall, drumming against the roof. Carradine, the marshals and engineers were staring upwards, as if expecting salvation to descend from the sky. Even Sangster had stopped ducking his head and leaned back.

'What are they doing?' I kept my voice down and spoke to the elderly man standing wearily beside me. 'They're waiting for a miracle.'

'Unlikely . . .' He tried to summon a signal on his mobile, but gave up. 'Still, you're on the right track.'

'These hostages? Who are they?'

'That I can tell you. *We* are . . .'

There was a gasp from the crowd, and a hundred hands pointed to the ceiling of the security lobby, the narrow vestibule leading to the entrance hall. A steel fire door was slowly falling from its housing, shutting out the barricade, the assistant commissioner and his officers.

A deep metallic rumble like the clenching of a giant's teeth filled the hall as the fire door settled onto the floor. The vibration moved away, a subsonic wave that seemed to take in smaller tremors from the exit doors of the dome, the answering calls from the furthest outposts of a vast vault that was sealing itself off from the world.

I stared at the heavy shield, and helped the elderly man to the chair by the enquiry desk. He thanked me and said: 'Your foot's bleeding.'

'I know. Tell me − are we sealed in?'

'It looks like it.'

'The North Gate entrance?'

'I imagine that's also closed.'

'And the side exits?'

'Everything. The car parks and freight entrance.' He raised a hand to calm me, seeing that I was agitated. 'It's the fear of fire, you see. Any draught would turn a small blaze into a furnace.'

'Right . . .' I was surprised by how calm he seemed, as if he had known what would happen and had detached himself from all the excitement long before it began. He stared in a regretful way at his useless mobile, resigned to the prospect of being unable to contact his wife. Trying to rest my foot, I asked: 'I take it you work here?'

'In Accounts. We tend to have a good idea what's going on. Mr Carradine is a very determined young man, but these shopping malls haven't learned how to cope with violence. When they do . . .'

'War will move into the world's consumer spaces? That's quite a thought. Up till now, being a washing machine has been a safe option. There was a shooting here this evening.'

'The television actor? I'm very sorry. It's probably best not to know if it really happened.' He shook my hand. 'I'll rest here for a bit. You'll need to find a bed for the night. There's a huge selection to choose from . . .'

He sat in his chair behind the enquiry desk, a grey-haired sphinx ready to answer all questions but ignored by the crowd drifting across the entrance hall and unable to find its bearing. Carradine and his entourage had set off on an inspection tour of their new domain, apparently uninterested in the fate of all those trapped inside the dome.

I walked over to the steel fire door, so massive that it muffled all sounds of police and army activity. An emergency escape panel was set into the fire door, and I was tempted to make a run for it, but its electrical locks would be too much for me.

Besides, a new and more interesting world was waiting for me inside the dome, a self-contained universe of treasure and promise. The crowd was drifting back into the mall, resigned to a future of eternal shopping. The republic of the Metro-Centre had at last established itself, a faith trapped inside its own temple.

PART III

PART III

33

The Consumer Life

IN AN HOUR I would be leaving the dome. For the last time I crossed the deserted terrace of the Holiday Inn and stepped onto the beach beside the lake. Within the lobby the latest group of hostages to be released was checking out of the hotel, ready for their transfer to the South Gate entrance. Guarded by their marshals, they shuffled through the doors, several almost too weak to walk. I waved to them, trying to remind them that in a few minutes they would breathe a different air, but none of them noticed me. There were tired mothers with restless teenage daughters, wives steering elderly husbands, a pallid McDonald's assistant whom Dr Maxted had treated for hysteria, and a young couple barely coping with a fever picked up from the polluted water.

Julia Goodwin had selected them the previous evening from the pool of five hundred remaining hostages, insisting that the disease risk they posed made them urgent candidates for release. When I presented the list of names to Tom Carradine he rejected Julia's choice out of hand. Fanatical in his defence of the Metro-Centre – and, according to Maxted, showing the first clinical signs of paranoia – he sat in his make-up chair at the mezzanine studio, tapping the sheet of paper with his eyebrow brush. He spent hours preparing himself for the camera, but had never actually appeared on the in-house channel, saving this moment for his last stand. I assumed that deep in the race memory of PR managers was the belief that when they appeared live on television a miracle would follow. The seas would part, and the sky would fall.

Carradine stared cautiously at the list, searching for any coded message to the police and journalists waiting behind the security cordon around the dome. Finally he gave in, silencing Julia when she graphically described the symptoms of typhoid and typhus. He edged away from the exhausted doctor with her feverish corneas, a model of all the diseases that the police negotiators warned would soon break out in the dome, and signed the list with one of his dozen Montblanc pens.

As he knew, Julia held the trump card, at least for the time being. Severely injured, David Cruise lay in her makeshift intensive care unit, holding on to life by an effort of will long after his body had decided to call it a day. But once this card was played, and the ventilators and transfusion pumps were disconnected, Julia Goodwin would lose her authority. She and I would join the hostages in the squalid basement of the Holiday Inn.

At that point the real game of the dome would begin, as Carradine and his henchmen stabilized their rule. The micro-republic would become a micro-monarchy, and the vast array of consumer goods would be Carradine's real subjects.

I stood on the sand, staring at the oily surface of the lake as the hostage group shuffled away. The marshals still saw me as David Cruise's media adviser, and reined in their abuse. A Zimmer frame scraped the marble floor, but the group was silent. An hour later they would step through the emergency hatch and face the world's television cameras. In return, the police would hand over a portable air-conditioning plant that would cool the intensive care unit.

At the last moment I would slip in among them, after Julia added my name to the list. I wanted to stay with her, and help with the rougher chores at the temporary clinic she had set up in the first-aid unit. But she was concerned for my ankle infection, which had resisted all the antibiotics available in the Metro-Centre's thirty pharmacies. Beyond that, she worried about the larger infection incubated within the dome that had begun to affect all of us: a deepening passivity, and a loss of will and any sense of time. The treasure house of consumer goods around us seemed to define who we were.

I hobbled along the sand to a deckchair set up on the water's edge. I rested here every evening, when the endless sports commentaries in David Cruise's recorded voice at last died away, ringside accounts of long-forgotten matches relayed through the public address system. Then the dome's ceiling lights were dimmed and a grateful silence fell over the Metro-Centre.

I sat in my tilting chair and drank enough whisky from my flask to blunt the fever in my swollen ankle. The silence was even more soothing, before the night patrols began to swear and stamp their way around the dome, torches searching the empty stores and cafés for any intruders. The artificial twilight lasted until the morning. During the long night hours, the ghost creatures of the dome, the thousands of cameras and kitchen appliances and cutlery canteens, began to emerge and glow like a watching congregation.

I reached down to an empty beer can at my feet, and tossed it into a nearby waste bin. Beyond a three-feet radius of my chair, the beach was littered with bottles and empty food cartons. The water never moved, but a scum of cigarette butts and plastic wrappers formed a tide line. At least for the moment, consumerism had beached itself on this filthy sand. Within a few hours, once the police had debriefed me and the doctors confirmed that I was free of infectious disease, I would be back in my father's flat.

After only five days, the deterioration of the dome was starting to gather pace. In the first flush of victory, Carradine and his marshals found that they had locked themselves inside the mall with almost three thousand people for company – an inner core of several hundred sports supporters and Metro-Centre employees, determined to defend the dome against all comers, and a larger group of customers caught by the riot and spectators who fled into the entrance hall to escape the police truncheons. Almost all were keen to leave once the threat of violence was lifted.

Tom Carradine rose to his hour. The engaging PR man was showing a hard steel. Cannily, he played on the presence of some two hundred small children in the dome, dishevelled and hungry, parted from their favourite computer games and too frightened to sleep in the arms of their exhausted mothers. At midnight on the first day, when an army assault team abseiled from their helicopter onto the roof of the dome, Carradine released a distraught mother who had suffered a heart attack. Her stretcher, eased through the emergency hatch in the South Gate fire door, was accompanied by two weeping toddlers clinging to Julia Goodwin's hands.

The exhausted but still attractive doctor made a powerful impact on the nation's television screens, as I saw from my set at the Holiday Inn. Julia warned the police negotiators that further casualties would follow if they tried to break into the dome, and that many children would die in the crossfire between the marshals and the army marksmen. She then selflessly stepped back into the dome and returned to her care of David Cruise, with a promise from the police that a complete intensive care unit would be provided by Brooklands Hospital. No mention was made of the fact that Carradine refused to release Cruise, who had become Hostage Number One, but no further attempts were carried out to penetrate the Metro-Centre.

Secure behind their fire doors, with their own power generators and an unlimited supply of food, drink and hostages, Carradine and the marshals soon consolidated their position. They set out their demands – that all threats to close the dome be lifted, that no charges be brought against its defenders, and that the Metro-Centre re-open for business, along with its supporters clubs and sports teams. The hapless general manager of the mall, flanked by his cowed department heads, was escorted to the mezzanine studio and declared that he was ready to throw open the doors and begin trading again.

Naturally, the Home Office refused to negotiate, but by now a huge media presence surrounded the dome. Beyond the perimeter road, where the police set up their outer cordon, dozens of TV location crews followed every move. Supporters from the motorway towns filled the streets of Brooklands in a huge show of solidarity.

Commentators described the seizure of the dome as a populist uprising, the struggle of consumer man and his consumer wife against the metropolitan elites with their deep loathing of shopping malls. The people of the retail parks were defending a more real Britain of Homebase stores, car-boot sales and garden centres, amateur sports clubs and the shirt of St George.

Carradine and his marshals took full advantage of this. Fortunately, the crowd trapped within the dome soon grasped that there was no immediate threat to their lives. The twenty supermarkets inside the Metro-Centre were stocked to capacity with fruit and vegetables, fresh meat and poultry, pizzas and cook chill meals. Its freezer cabinets held a glacier of ice cream. On shelves within easy reach was enough alcohol to float the dome into the North Sea.

Like Tony Maxted, I was amazed that there was little looting. None of the restaurants and cafés were functioning, but the crowd dispersing across the mall in the hours after the lock-down moved in an orderly way through the supermarkets. The cash tills were silent, but customers paid for their purchases, dropping their money into the honesty buckets which the marshals placed beside the tills. Everyone knew that the Metro-Centre was ready to sustain them. The aisles and concourses were their parks and neighbourhoods, and they would keep them clean and law-abiding.

Afterwards, the marshals steered us to the hotels and staff rest rooms in the dome, and to the furniture and bedding departments of the big stores. I spent the night in the Holiday Inn, sharing a double room on the third floor with Tony Maxted. We slept in our clothes, windows sealed against the unending night noises of the police and army, the searchlights sweeping across the dome's semi-transparent skin.

Maxted was a restless sleeper, haranguing me in his dreams. The room was stuffy, the water pipes in the bathroom fluting and whining as the pressure fell and airlocks interrupted the system. The next morning, when I stepped onto the balcony, the outside air was as warm as the tropics.

Both Maxted and I took for granted that the siege would end that day. But neither Carradine nor the Home Office was ready to compromise. All morning a dishevelled crowd waited in the entrance hall, arguing with the marshals who guarded the fire door. Others drifted away with their fractious children, already bored by the fourth ice cream of the day. They sat at the café tables in the central atrium, like passengers abandoned by their airlines. I strolled among them as they checked their watches, reassuring each other that they would be home in an hour.

Carradine and his marshals had other ideas. They realized that once they survived the period immediately after the dome's seizure the crisis would pass and their power would grow. The concern of both the general public and the Home Office would move from the future of the Metro-Centre to the safety of the hostages. Carradine's engineers were working hard on the Metro-Centre's power supply, ensuring the most efficient use of its oil reserves. Carradine ordered that the under-roof lighting arrays should be switched off. Many of the shops and stores seemed to recede into an inner darkness, an uncanny transformation. As people moved down the unlit aisles, searching for tin-openers and disposable wipes, the strange gloom gave the impression that an air raid was imminent. Entering one of the larger hardware stores, I felt my way past the counters, surrounded by hundreds of knives, saws and chisels, their blades forming a silver forest in the darkness. A more primitive world was biding its time.

By late afternoon of the second day everyone realized that a further night lay ahead, and that all of them were now hostages. At this point, as the police negotiators lost their patience and the lights faded into the dusk, Carradine made an astute move. He was being closely advised by Sangster, whose huge and shambling figure with its babyish face followed the young manager around like an ambitious fight promoter with a promising featherweight. Tony Maxted approved of the head teacher's involvement. 'He'll keep an eye on things, hold a tight rein on the hotheads,' he assured me, but I had heard this before. I sensed that Sangster saw the seizure of the Metro-Centre as an interesting social experiment, and was in no hurry to see it end.

When the army helicopters resumed their tiresome patrols above the dome, Carradine called a public meeting in the South Gate entrance hall. Taking up a suggestion made by Sangster, he notified the police negotiators that he would release five hundred hostages on each of the next three days, and demand no concessions in return.

Immediately the crisis eased. The police postponed any attempt to invade the dome. Skilfully finessed by Carradine and Sangster, they were forced to wait until the last of the hostages had stumbled through the emergency hatch into freedom. The mutineers, meanwhile, had rid themselves of a large part of their security problem, lessened the drain on the dome's resources, and raised the hope of further releases and a peaceful end to the siege.

At seven o'clock that evening, the first tranche of hostages stepped from the dome into a blizzard of flashbulbs. Mostly elderly customers, young mothers and their toddlers, and several dozen teenage mall rats, they were sent by bus to Brooklands Hospital and then rejoined their families. The rest of us selected our suppers from the supermarket shelves and retired to our stifling hotel rooms, exhausted enough to sleep through the helicopters and searchlights.

Forgotten in all this was the lonely figure whose attempted assassination had triggered the uprising. David Cruise still lay in his intensive care unit in a back room at the first-aid station, carefully tended by Julia Goodwin and two off-duty nurses who volunteered to help her. Barely conscious and unable to speak, he hovered in a medical nowhere zone of tubes, drips and ventilator pumps, at once forgotten and the most important person in the dome. Julia protested to Carradine, but the young manager refused to release him, claiming that he would soon recover and take over the leadership of the revolt.

The police, meanwhile, had arrested his would-be assassins, two Bosnian brothers whose motorcycle repair shop had been torched by a gang of football rioters. They walked into the Brooklands police station, confessed to the crime and surrendered the weapon, a gun-club target rifle they had smuggled onto one of the upper-level retail decks above the mezzanine studio. No one needed to question their motives, but whatever their motives were, they clearly fitted the crime.

★　　★　　★

Sitting in my chair on the beach, I finished the whisky in my flask. Part of me was drunk, but at the same time I felt queasily sober, like someone trapped on a runaway roller-coaster. I needed to leave for the South Gate entrance hall and hide myself among the hostages due to be released within the next half-hour. My foot was still badly infected, but in my mind I had detached myself from it, as if the throbbing wound was a tiresome relative who insisted on tagging after me. At the same time I felt reluctant to leave the Metro-Centre, though it was difficult to find a reason for staying. But did I need a reason . . . ?

I lay back in the chair, gathering my strength for the short walk. High above me were the upper decks of the shopping mall, railed terraces filled with fading palms and potted plants, a botanical garden running towards its death in the sky. Now that the lifts and escalators were out of action, almost no one made the long climb to the seventh floor, where the saturated air seemed to perspire into a heavy mist.

But someone was looking down from the seventh-floor railing, partly hidden behind the yellowing fronds of a large yucca. A man stared steadily at me, uninterested in the activity taking place on the floor of the dome, the hostages window-shopping or sitting at the cafés with their week-old newspapers.

I sat up and eased myself from the chair, aware that I was a conspicuous target as I sat alone on my private beach. Was the intruder a police marksman, smuggled into the dome through one of the dozens of ventilator and sewage pipes, with a hit list of prominenti to be disposed of? The man who was watching me carried a small firearm, and a black barrel emerged from his leather jacket. Unlike the police snatch squads, he wore no helmet or chin-strap.

Aware that I had noticed him, he leaned forward over the railing. I could see his face, as sharp as an axe blade, and the odd plates of his forehead, a geometry of disjointed thoughts. A pallid and undernourished skin stretched over the pointed bones, bruised by more than camouflage paste.

'Christie . . . ? What the hell are we doing . . . ?'

I stood up, speaking to myself in a slurred mutter. Bowing his head, the man stepped back. For a few seconds he vanished behind the yucca, and then reappeared with a hand raised over his shoulder.

'Christie . . . !' My voice seemed to dent the dark water that lay listlessly against the beach. 'Come down, man . . . You're a target . . . !'

As I stumbled against the chair, knocking it onto the sand, the man hurled something towards me. I lost sight of the object as it flew through the misty air, but it landed ten feet from me, a bronze node that glinted in the scruffy sand.

I tried to steady myself, and felt the strong hands of a marshal grip my arms.

'Mr Pearson?' One of the burly weightlifters detailed to keep an eye on me had been sitting in the terrace bar when he heard my shout. 'You're not hurt?'

'He missed me. It's over there.'

'I didn't hear a shot. Let's get you indoors.'

'Indoors? We're already indoors. Aren't we?' I was mulling this over as he steered me to the terrace steps. I had lost my chance of joining the hostage release from the South Gate entrance, but I needed to see the object on the beach.

In the moments before the marshal's heavy foot stamped it into the sand I managed to clear my eyes, and recognized the same bullet and cartridge case that Duncan Christie had pressed into my palm outside the Metro-Centre.

34

Work Makes You Free

VERY LITTLE HAD changed, I told myself, but nothing was quite the same. By the end of the second week we were still convinced that we would soon be released from the Metro-Centre. That morning the remaining hostages emerged from their hotels, sleepless and dishevelled, and looking as if their dreams had attacked them. They selected a breakfast of sorts from the soft drink and confectionery shelves of the nearest supermarket, washed themselves in a litre of Perrier water, and then assembled in the South Gate entrance hall, ready to play their roles in an eternal baggage handlers' strike.

By now nearly two thousand hostages had been freed, but those who remained were aware that their value to Tom Carradine and his mutineers had risen steeply. Barely a dozen were released each day, and Julia Goodwin no longer bothered to present her list in person. She had already despaired of me, and shook her head wearily whenever I appeared, asking about David Cruise's health. Ask about your own health, her tired but punitive gaze seemed to say.

Out of duty, I hobbled to the South Gate entrance and joined the hostages patiently forming themselves into a queue. Tired of waiting, a group of parents with older children tried to force their way through the marshals guarding the fire door. Cheered on, they kicked aside the security rails and demanded to be released.

The reaction was prompt and violent. The marshals drew their batons, and the parents were pushed back with a show of force that hushed everyone in the entrance hall and left two of the husbands bleeding from head wounds. Behind his screen of bully-boys, Sangster watched all this with a resigned but understanding smile.

I wanted to talk to the head teacher, but I felt uneasy with him. He had begun to sway from side to side like a fourth atrium bear, keeping time to the music inside his head. His role was too ambiguous for comfort, and he had moved from hostage to principal ringleader without taking off his overcoat.

After the brutal response by the marshals everyone stared silently at the open floor where the scuffles had taken place. Bloody skid marks covered the tiles, and Sangster stepped forward and began to scrutinize them in a strangely obsessive way, like an anthropologist examining the foot paintings of a primitive tribe. Rousing himself from his reverie, he stepped through a service door and reappeared with a mop cart and bucket. Watched by the crowd, he swabbed away at the skid marks, squeezed out the bloodstained mop and worked it up and down the floor until the marble gleamed again. The hostages stared stolidly at their reflections but remained silent.

I said nothing to Sangster or Tony Maxted about my sighting of Duncan Christie, deciding to keep this to myself. The bullet thrown onto the beach, like the one he had pressed into my hand, was his way of reminding me that the Metro-Centre had killed my father, and that the agents of his death were now with me inside the dome. I kept my eyes on the high galleries, but Christie had disappeared into the mist that separated the seventh floor from the sky.

Rumours swerved around the Metro-Centre, phantoms that flew by day. I dozed for an hour behind the enquiry desk, and woke to find the hostages discussing the news that David Cruise had begun to revive in the intensive care unit. He had removed his oxygen mask and spoken to several witnesses about his determination to defend the Metro-Centre and return it to its rightful place in the M25 community.

I dismissed this as a near-hysterical fantasy, but Tom Carradine arrived and confirmed the good news through his megaphone. He looked confident and charismatic in his freshly pressed uniform, but almost too lucid for comfort, speaking with an amphetamine fluency, eyes bright and unblinking as he surveyed the exhausted hostages. Nonetheless, he announced that he would celebrate the good news by freeing a further fifty hostages. His decision was relayed to the police negotiators at their post beyond the fire door, and dominated the lunchtime television bulletins.

Everyone lined up for the selection, trying to look their worst as Carradine and Sangster moved along them. Parents did everything to irritate their already fractious teenagers, wives urged their middle-aged husbands to mumble and drool. Most of us were too tired to think of feigning exhaustion, but Sangster pointed to an ailing widow who had been injured by police truncheons and showed the effects of mild concussion.

The hostages accepted their fate, but a group of well-to-do Pakistanis were convinced that they had been deliberately ignored. They surrounded Carradine in a rage of indignation, shouting and thrusting at his shoulder. Sangster quickly signalled to the marshals, who forced back the gesticulating group and kicked open their parcels. To a chorus of jeers, they held aloft the silkily expensive underwear, then trampled the garments underfoot. The elderly barrister who was the family patriarch worked himself into a fury of anger, shouting abuse at Carradine and by chance spitting on his shirt. Batons were being drawn as I left the ugly scene.

I disliked the violence and limped back to the first-aid post, hoping to see Julia Goodwin. The marshals guarding David Cruise had seen enough of me for the day and turned me away, so I sat on the podium beneath the bears. Half an hour later I heard the emergency hatch clang shut as the last of the returnees stepped shakily into freedom.

About three hundred hostages now remained, and the same number of mutineers. The latter formed a hard core of supporters who had forsaken everything, their homes and families, their jobs and cars and loft extensions, to defend the Metro-Centre.

Despite their efforts, conditions in the dome were steadily deteriorating. Without the powerful air-conditioning units, the temperature inside the mall continued to climb. The supermarket floors were slick with melted ice cream oozing from their cabinets, and a foul air rose from the defrosting meat freezers. The water pressure was too low to fill the lavatory cisterns, and a farmyard stench enclosed the Ramada Inn where the dome's director and senior staff were held prisoner. The Metro-Centre, once bathed in a cool and scented air, was turning into a gigantic sty.

At two o'clock that afternoon, when the hostages drifted off in search of lunch, they found all the supermarkets closed. They peered through the doors, rattling the chains and padlocks, until the public address system ordered them to assemble in the central atrium. Carradine appeared thirty minutes later, descending the staircase from the mezzanine, and informed us that lunch was off the menu until we cleaned up the supermarkets and returned them to their previously immaculate state. He called on everyone to remember their pride in the Metro-Centre, and repay the debt they owed the mall for transforming their lives. The hostages would be divided into ten work groups and each of these would be assigned a supermarket.

Carradine gazed triumphantly at the glum faces and listened to Sangster whispering in his ear. He then announced that the work groups would take part in a competition. The team that did the best job of cleaning and waste disposal during the next week would be allowed to leave the dome.

As the hostages dispersed, queuing to collect their mops and pails, I caught up with Sangster, still smiling slyly to himself.

'Richard? Good . . .' He laid a huge arm across my shoulders. 'Rather a neat wheeze, don't you think?'

'"Work Makes You Free"?'

'Who said that? It's very true. It keeps alive the sporting instinct, and gives them something to live for. At the same time it weeds out the stronger and more determined elements.'

'Those who might cause trouble?'

'We can't lose. A sick hostage is much more valuable than a robust one. And less dangerous. Don't worry, I'll see that you're excused from cleaning duties.'

'I'm very grateful. It's good to have a friend in high places. As it happens, I can barely walk.'

'Your foot?' Sangster frowned with distaste at my bloodstained bandage. 'We could find you a sedentary job. Rinsing mops, say? Is it psychosomatic?'

'I hadn't thought of that. I'll ask Tony Maxted.'

'I would.' Sangster stared at me with a straight face, then broke into a cheery grin. 'You want to stay here, Richard. You know that.'

'I don't agree.'

'Of course you do. This place is your . . . spiritual Eden. It's all you have to believe in.'

'Never. Tell me – the siege, when will it end?'

'Let's wait and see.' Sangster seemed almost gleeful at the remote prospect. 'That's what's so interesting. This isn't about the Metro-Centre: it's about England today. Now, go back to your room and rest. You're too valuable to be ill. When David Cruise wakes, you'll be there to cheer him up.'

'Will he wake?'

Sangster turned to wave. 'He'd better . . .'

I watched the hostages shuffle to their workstations, with all the enthusiasm of patients ordered to clean their own hospital. Discipline ruled, and a more martial spirit prevailed. The cartons of perished pizzas, the shoals of rotting fish fingers, the thousands of cartons of rancid milk were stripped from the shelves and carted away to the refuse hoppers in the basement. Carradine and Sangster introduced a strict rationing system, and we queued for our modest meals of corned beef, pilchards and baked beans.

Negotiations continued with the police, who were increasingly impatient as the release of hostages slowed, but the lack of violence forced them to bide their time. A full-scale assault would leave scores of hostages dead, and the Metro-Centre was a sniper's paradise. More to the point, floor-to-floor street battles would inflict millions of pounds' worth of damage on the unprotected merchandise.

A few hostages, the last of the sick and elderly, were released. On the portable radio that Maxted gave to me in an attempt to keep up my spirits, I listened to an account of their debriefing. All the freed hostages were carefully searched for any plundered jewellery, watches and cameras, but from the very start of the siege none had been found. No one had slipped a single fountain pen or gold chain into their pockets. The consultant psychologists were baffled by this, but a likely explanation struck me a few days later when I wandered through a large furniture emporium near the Holiday Inn.

Vaguely searching for a more comfortable mattress than my fever-sodden berth in the hotel, I stood in the entrance to the store as the pilot lights shone on the freshly waxed floor. A work party had moved through the ground level, and the tang of polish hung on the unmoving air, making me feel almost giddy. By sweeping out these temples to consumerism, by wiping and waxing and buffing, we made clear that we were ready to serve these unconsecrated altars. Every shop and store in the Metro-Centre was a house of totems. We accepted the discipline that these appliances and bathroom fittings imposed. We wanted to be like these consumer durables, and they in turn wanted us to emulate them. In many ways, we wanted to *be* them . . .

Water lapped at my feet, a cooling stream that drained away the fever in my bones. Half asleep in my deckchair beside the lake, I listened to the wavelets tapping at the sand. Somewhere was the rhythmic murmur of deep water, the same tides that my father had sailed as he circled the globe.

The chair legs sank into the wet sand, tipping me forward. I looked down to find the water swilling around my ankles. The lake had come alive, its surface rolling towards the shoreline.

Someone had switched on the wave machine. I stood up as dark water sluiced across my feet, covered by a slick of lubricating oil. Two engineers stood outside the Holiday Inn, working at the fuse box that controlled the lighting arrays around the roof and terrace. Bars of strip neon glowed and dimmed as the emergency generator pushed out its erratic current. Moving through the fuses, the engineers had switched on the wave machine. Roused in its watery vault, the machine stirred and woke, driving the deep water across the lake.

I stepped back onto the dry sand, as the waves washed through the debris of beer cans and cigarette packets, receding when the undertow sucked them into its deeps. A stronger wave rolled in, nudging a greasy freight of floating magazines and a soggy raft that I guessed was a waterlogged cushion from a restaurant banquette, trapped for weeks under the wave machine's paddle.

The lumpy parcel, crudely lashed with rope and duct tape, drifted towards me, and with a last heave bumped against my chair. As I stepped forward, about to kick it back into the water, the undertow turned it onto its side. A figure with human features lay trussed inside a small carpet, perhaps a piece of teak statuary that one of the hostages had tried to hide before leaving the Metro-Centre.

A wave washed over the figure, dispersing the glaze of oil and dirt. Eyes with intact pupils stared up at me, and I recognized the blanched face of the Pakistani barrister I had seen remonstrating with Carradine.

Behind me, the engineers switched off the current. A last wave rolled across the beach, its foam hissing among the beer cans. With a faint sigh, the undertow retrieved the body and drew it down towards the dark floor of the lake.

35

Normality

DAVID CRUISE WAS dying, among stuffed elephants and kangaroos, surrounded by cheerful wallpaper and plastic toys, in sight of the television studio that had created him.

The Metro-Centre's first-aid post, now housing an intensive care unit, occupied a suite of rooms below the mezzanine, usually visited by small children who had scraped their knees and pensioners with nosebleeds. For the present, the toys were corralled inside a playpen, and the reception room once manned by a kindly sister was filled with beds commandeered from a nearby store. The six patients lay on luxurious mattresses, unwashed pillows leaning against quilted boudoir headboards. Almost all were elderly hostages unable to keep up with Carradine's more dictatorial regime.

Tony Maxted was crouching on a chair beside a white-haired woman, trying to extract a broken dental plate. He waved to me and pointed to the treatment room. He seemed unsurprised to see me, though every morning he urged me to make the most of my Sangster contacts and join the few hostages still leaving the dome.

Julia Goodwin, though, seemed surprised when I walked into the treatment room. Pale and nerveless, her neck flushed by a persistent rash, she was almost asleep on her feet, trying to break the seal on a bandage pack while searching for a stray hair over her eyes. As always, I was glad to see her, and had the odd sense that as long as I was with her, emptying the pedal bins and foraging for packets of herbal tea, she would be all right. An absurd notion, which reminded me of my childhood motoring trips with my mother, when I strained forward to watch the road as she argued with herself over the traffic lights.

'Richard? What happened?'

'Nothing.' I tried to prompt a smile from her. 'Nothing's happened for days. We could be here for ever.'

'You were supposed to leave. What are you doing here?'

'Julia . . . I'll make some tea.' I pulled a packet of Assam breakfast tea from my shirt. 'I've been tracking this down for days. Leaf, please note, not tea bags . . .'

'Wonderful. That'll block the drain for good.' She held my shoulders, yellowing eyes under her uncombed hair. 'You shouldn't be here. I'll speak to Carradine.'

'No. I was held up at the hotel.' I decided not to alarm her over the dead barrister. 'There was a security problem – someone thought he saw Duncan Christie.'

'Not again. People are seeing him all the time. It must be some sort of portent, like flying saucers.' She took my hands and turned my anaemic palms to the light. 'You have to get out of here, Richard. If there's a release tomorrow . . .'

'I will. I will. I want to leave.'

'Do you? Maybe. Let's have a look at that foot.'

Julia rebandaged my foot, using a fresh strip of lint, part of a consignment supplied, reluctantly, by the police. We were sitting in the pharmacy next to the treatment room, and our chairs were close enough for me to embrace her. Her fingers fumbled at the tie, and I took over when she seemed to lose interest. Her mind was elsewhere, in one of the high galleries closer to the sun, rather than in this airless clinic with its erratic air conditioning.

'Good . . .' I patted the bandage with its clumsy bows. 'That should keep me going.'

'I'm sorry.' She leaned briefly against my shoulder, and then watched me with a faint smile. She was waiting for me to produce a 'gift' from my pockets, perhaps a foil sheet of antibiotics looted from a chemist's shop. 'It's been a hell of a night. I keep hearing helicopters. Tomorrow, go straight to the entrance hall – you'll be on the list.'

'I'll get there. Don't worry.'

'I do worry. We're short of everything. We might as well close up shop.'

'Why? The chemists here are packed with enough drugs to fit out a hospital.'

'Haven't you heard? It's all got to stay as it was. We're not allowed to touch a thing.'

'Even for emergencies? I don't get it.'

'Dear man . . .' Julia placed her worn hands around mine, for once glad of the physical warmth. 'Emergencies don't exist any more. For Carradine and his people everything is normal. He and Sangster did their ward round this morning and decided all the patients were getting better. Even the old pensioner who died in the night.'

'And David Cruise?'

'He's holding on . . .' She avoided my eyes and listened to the faint sighing of the ventilator from the empty storeroom, converted into Cruise's intensive care unit. 'I ought to take a look — I keep forgetting about him.'

I followed her into the storeroom, where Cruise lay in his makeshift oxygen tent. As always, the sight of him stretched inertly in his maze of wires and tubes made me deeply uneasy. The lithe and athletic figure with his tactile charm had vanished, as if the monitors and gauges were steadily pumping his life from him and transferring his blood and lymph to their voracious machines.

Only his hair survived, a blond mane lying across the phlegm-soaked pillow. I stood beside Julia as she adjusted the ventilator, now and then stroking the hair like the pelt of a sleeping cat. Cruise's head had shrunk, his cheeks and jaw folding into themselves, as if his face was a stage set being dismantled from within. A transfusion bag hung from its stand and dripped serum into a relay tube, but the television presenter seemed so empty of life that I wondered if Julia was trying to revive a corpse.

'Richard? He won't recognize you.' She led me back to the treatment room. 'Now, we'll find something for you to do.'

'Julia . . .' I put my arm around her shoulders, trying to steady her. 'How is Cruise?'

'Not good.' She lowered her voice to a whisper. 'I've got to get him to the hospital, but Carradine won't let him leave. Sangster says he'll be up in a couple of days.'

'How long can he last?'

'Not long. We'll have to use car batteries to run the ventilator.'

'How long? A day? Two days?'

'Something like that.' Her eyes darkened. 'If he died . . .'

'Would it matter?'

'They believe in him. If anything happened . . .' She laughed to herself, a desperate chuckle. 'It's a pity they can't see him now, all those people who marched and stamped.'

'Julia, hold on.'

'You corrupted him, you know.' She spoke matter-of-factly. 'Still, it's a kind of revenge.'

'For what? Losing my job?'

'Your job? Your father's death, for God's sake. This pays for it. In a way, I'm glad for you.'

'Why?' I took her arm, trying to hold her attention before her mind could slide away. 'David Cruise had nothing to do with my father's death.'

'Cruise? No. But . . .'

'Others did? Who? Is that why you went to the funeral?'

Her gaze, once so thoughtful and concerned, drifted away into the borders of fatigue. But her hands touched my chest, searching for refuge. The attempted murder of David Cruise had relieved her of the guilt I had sensed since our first meeting, an anger at herself that had always come between us.

'Julia? Who . . . ?'

'Quiet!' She smoothed her hair. 'The consultants are here. They're starting their ward rounds.'

Three marshals in St George's shirts had entered the first-aid post and were strolling around the ward. Ignoring Tony Maxted, they began to read the clinical notes attached to the bed frames. With heavy earnestness, they bent over the patients and tried to take their pulses.

I started to protest, but Maxted caught my arm and bundled me through the entrance.

'Right. We can take a breather.' He was ruffled but unabashed. 'They know I'm a psychiatrist – not the most popular profession in the Metro-Centre. I can't think why . . .'

We sat on the plinth below the bears in the centre of the atrium, surrounded by jars of honey and the fading get-well messages. Trying to ease my ankle, I took off my shoe and stood up. I wanted to be with Julia, and resented being frogmarched from the first-aid post. But Maxted wearily pulled me against the baby bear's massive paw.

'Maxted . . . is Julia safe?'

'Just about. Rape isn't a problem . . . yet, I'm glad to say. The Metro-Centre is more important than sex.'

'What are we doing here?'

'Keeping you out of harm's way. The bears are a tribal totem – you should be safe for a while.'

'Am I in danger? I didn't know.'

'Come on . . .' Maxted examined me wearily, taking in the sweat caked into my jacket, my hands bruised from prising the lids off corned beef tins, the tramp-like appearance that would once have barred me from the Metro-Centre. By contrast, Maxted was still wearing a shirt and tie, and maintained his professional air under the shabby lab coat. 'As long as Cruise hangs on, you'll be okay. Once he goes, all hell is going to break loose.'

'I thought it had.'

'Not yet. Take this siege – what's the strangest thing you've noticed?'

'No looting?'

'Spot on. Not a diamond stud pinched, not a Rolex trousered. Look around you. These aren't consumer goods – they're household gods. We're in the worship phase, when everyone believes and behaves.'

'And if Cruise dies?'

'When, not if. We'll move into a much more primitive and

dangerous zone. Consumerism is built on regression. Any moment now the whole thing could flip. That's why I'm still here – I need to see what happens.'

'Nothing will happen.' I tried to push away the probing paw of the baby bear. 'The siege will end any day now. Everyone's bored. It could end this afternoon.'

'It won't end. Carradine doesn't want it to end. His mind's been under siege ever since he arrived at the Metro-Centre. Sangster doesn't want it to end. All those years trapped in that terrible school, teaching those kids how to be a new kind of savage.'

'And the Home Office?'

'They don't want it to end, though they're being subtle about it. This is a huge social laboratory, and they're watching from the front row as the experiment heats up. Consumerism is running out of road, and it's trying to mutate. It's tried fascism, but even that isn't primitive enough. The only thing left is out-and-out madness . . .'

Maxted broke off as a squad of some fifty hostages trudged into the atrium, led by a marshal with a shotgun. They carried buckets and mops, brooms and aerosols of furniture polish, enough equipment to buff and shine the world. Surprisingly, they were in good spirits, as if determined to be the best cleaning squad in the dome.

Together they formed up below the mezzanine terrace, waiting as Carradine and Sangster walked down the steps where my father had met his end. An aide carried a pile of St George's shirts, neatly pressed and store-new.

'What's going on?' I asked Maxted. 'Don't tell me Carradine is going to complain about the ironing. The siege must be over.'

'Nice idea. But I don't think so . . .'

Carradine briefly addressed the cleaning squad. Sangster prowled behind him, eyes searching the upper terraces under the roof. The marshal signalled to his force, and a dozen members of the squad lowered their brooms and buckets to the floor and stepped forward. Carradine moved along the line, shaking them by the hand and handing over a St George's shirt.

'Maxted – it's some sort of sick game . . .'

'No. It's exactly what you see. They're being sworn in. They're no longer hostages and they're joining the rebellion.'

'Joining . . . ?'

Without thinking, I stood up, steadying myself against Maxted's shoulder. I watched the dozen former hostages don their shirts, then move away in an informal group, exchanging banter with Sangster. They were at ease with themselves and the vast building, with the deep rose light that lit the entrances to the stores and cafés around the atrium. They were immigrants to a new country, already naturalized, citizens of the shopping mall, the free electorate of the cash till and the loyalty card.

'Richard . . .'

Maxted spoke warningly, but I was watching the ceremony. At the last moment a thirteenth volunteer, a sturdy young woman in jeans and a biker's leather jacket, stepped forward to volunteer. All doubts satisfied, she walked up to Carradine, came smartly to attention and claimed her St George's shirt.

Holding my shoe in one hand, I began to limp forward, then felt Maxted take my arm.

'Richard, let's sit down and think . . .'

He guided me back to the bears. Carradine and Sangster moved away, and the marshal drilled off his depleted hostage squad, assigning them to a supermarket near the atrium.

Maxted took the blood-caked shoe from my hand. Smiling a little wanly, he tapped it against his free hand.

'Richard, what were you doing? Any idea?'

'Not much.' I looked up at his almost kindly face. 'I wasn't thinking.'

'That's what I mean. Now, go back to the hotel. I'll see you later and we'll find something to eat.'

'But, Julia . . . ?'

'I'll see she's all right.' He handed me the shoe. 'Dear chap, you were going to join them. The Metro-Centre finally got to you . . .'

36

Shrines and Altars

THE FIRST SHRINES had begun to appear, wayside altars for passing shoppers, places of pause and reflection for those making endless journeys within the universe of the dome.

At dawn, when the last gunfire had died down, I stepped onto the balcony of my room at the Holiday Inn. No one within the dome had slept through the night, and a thin mist filled the shopping thoroughfares, a hazy fog of insomnia that haunted the arcades and pedestrian decks, in places dense enough to conceal an army marksman.

I assumed that the police commandos had withdrawn, and that the real danger, as always, came from one's own side, from Carradine's untrained militia. After thirty seconds on the balcony, inhaling the over-ripe air with its guarantee of another tropical day, I wiped the sweat from my face onto the net curtain and found my way to the bathroom.

Two bottles of Perrier were all that remained of my stock. Standing in the shower stall, I drank one and then poured the second over myself, feeling the vivid, carbonated stream bring my skin alive.

As usual, I avoided the washbasin mirror, where I would be joined by the tramp-like figure who shared the bedroom with me. Whenever I saw him, bearded and scarily calm, he moved towards me like a sharp-eyed beggar spotting a prospect. Then he flinched away from me, repelled by my body odour and the even more rancid stench of deep and dangerous obsessions.

Still nominally playing my role as David Cruise's adviser, I was left alone by Carradine and his marshals as they rallied their three hundred supporters, kept careful watch on the few score remaining hostages and defended the Metro-Centre against the armed might of a government. Meanwhile I did my best to look after Julia Goodwin, scavenged through the abandoned supermarkets and brought her enough food to feed her four patients and herself.

I always stayed until she had forced herself through the tins of frank-furters, condensed milk and foie gras, rewarding me with a plucky smile. Her two volunteer nurses had long since left the dome and returned to their husbands and children, but Julia was still determined to stay to the end. I sensed that in caring for David Cruise, keeping him forever on the edge of death, she was performing a penance similar to the shared bed into which she had drawn me at my father's flat.

We were now into the second month of the Metro-Centre siege, and time had begun to dilate in unexpected ways. Days of sweaty boredom merged into each other, broken by the unending quest for food and water as Carradine's quartermasters opened another super-market for a few hours. Then everything would change abruptly, as Carradine released four or five of the more exhausted hostages. In exchange, the bathroom taps ran for half an hour, enough time to fill the baths and lavatory cisterns and stave off the danger of a typhoid epidemic.

But the patience of the police and Home Office had run out. Unsurprisingly, their willingness to go for the long haul, in the hope that the mutineers would lose heart or fall out among themselves, seemed to fluctuate with public interest in the siege. The television crews around the dome had been drifting away for weeks, and a Home Office junior minister blundered badly when he described the seizure of the Metro-Centre as part of an industrial dispute, a sit-in by disgruntled staff. When the siege was dropped from the main TV bulletins and exiled to late-night discussion programmes on BBC2 I knew that there would be a show of strength.

At three o'clock that morning, as I lay on the sofa beside the win-dow, trying to breathe the humid, microwave air, I heard helicopters crossing the dome. Searchlights swerved and loudspeakers blared. Stun grenades exploded against the metal panels high above the atrium, showering debris on the luckless bears. A powerful explosion blew a hole in the dome above the portico of the North Gate entrance. A joint army and police commando entered the mall, and swiftly overpowered the small group of rebels defending the entrance. Unable to raise the fire door, the commandos moved to their primary target, the eighty remaining hostages held in the banqueting hall at the Ramada Inn.

As it happened, two days earlier Sangster had moved the hostages from their squalid quarters at the Ramada Inn and marched them to the empty Novotel. When the commandos burst unopposed into their original target they found themselves stumbling through the darkness among overflowing latrine buckets. This gave Carradine and his armed defence units time to arrive on the scene and surround the Ramada Inn.

A fierce firefight followed, which the police and army were certain to win. Tragically, a group of hostages at the Novotel made the mistake of overpowering their guards. After leaving the hotel, they raced across the central atrium towards their rescuers.

As a propaganda measure, and to deceive the police spy cameras that Sangster knew would be watching their every move, he had given the hostages a fresh set of clothes, equipping them with St George's shirts. The commandos, assuming that they were faced with a suicide charge by defiant rebels, opened fire at point-blank range. Five of the hostages, including the general manager of the Metro-Centre and two of his department heads, were killed on the spot. The commandos withdrew, the helicopters ended their patrols, and the police loudspeakers faded into their own huge embarrassment.

But an even stranger phase of the Metro-Centre siege was about to begin.

At eight o'clock, when there was no sign of police or army activity, I left the Holiday Inn and made my way towards the first-aid post. I wanted to make sure that Julia was unharmed, and help her with any wounded brought in during the night assault. Limping on my shooting stick, which I had filched from the best sporting goods shop in the dome, I followed a circular route that would bypass the central atrium.

A hundred yards from the Holiday Inn, I found myself in a thoroughfare of shops that specialized in electrical goods. All were unshuttered, since none of Carradine's supporters would think of stealing from them. Their interiors were transformed by darkness into a street of caves crowded with treasure. I paused to gaze into these magical grottoes, aware that I was surrounded by all the toys I had so longed for as a child, and could take whatever I wanted.

Nearby was a store with a still intact pyramid of sample wares in its doorway. A trio of microwave ovens supported columns of computer towers, topped by a plasma television screen, the whole display decorated like a Christmas tree with a dozen digital cameras, lenses gleaming in the half-light. The structure had been lovingly designed to resemble an altarpiece. Bouquets of artificial flowers lay at its base, and a circle of candles surrounded a framed photograph of David Cruise. An almost religious aura glowed from the shrine, a votive offering to the threatened spirit of the Metro-Centre.

A few minutes later, in an alleyway behind the Novotel, I came across another of the pyramids, a modest tableau built from dozens of mobile phones and DVD players. Part sales display and part consumer shrine, it was clearly a prayer point for pilgrims on the great circuits of the Metro-Centre.

Beguiled by this votive trail, I had entered the northern sector of the mall. Little sunlight penetrated the roof, and the seven-storey galleries threw the lower levels into a twilight that even the brightest neon never fully dispelled. The rental charges were the lowest in the dome, and the shopping areas were dominated by cut-price travel agencies, bookshops and charity stores, areas of commerce where the lack of light was no disadvantage.

A spotlight flared in the North Gate entrance hall, briefly blinding me as I moved down a narrow street of car-rental offices and discount air-ticket agencies. From the doorway of a luggage store I watched the repair team at work. Metro-Centre engineers stood on a mobile scaffold, securing the roof section blown out by the police and army commandos. Sparks from a welding arc showered through the gloom, dancing among the glass and metal debris on the floor.

'Mr Pearson . . . step back.'

Behind me I heard a metal display stand being dragged across the stone floor. The spotlight swung across the ceiling of the entrance hall, and the shadows veered and swerved around me like a demented dance troupe.

'Richard . . .'

Only a few steps from me, a woman in belted blue overalls was watching from a doorway. The overalls bore no badges, but I was sure that she was wearing a police uniform favoured by crowd-control units. A blue peaked cap covered her eyes, but revealed her carefully braided blonde hair, and I recognized the strong chin and the broad mouth forever downturned in apology.

'Sergeant Falconer . . . ?' I moved towards her as she beckoned to me with a pair of night-vision goggles. 'Be careful, the marshals are armed . . .'

'Mr Pearson, come with me . . .' She spoke softly, hissing at me through the gloom. 'I'll get you out now.'

'Sergeant?'

'Listen! It's time to leave the Metro-Centre. You've been here too long.'

'Sergeant Falconer . . . I have to stay – they need me here.'

'No one needs you. Try to think for once.'

'David Cruise . . . Dr Goodwin . . .'

'They're leaving, Mr Pearson. They're all going.' Her face was briefly lit by the reflected spotlight. Baring her teeth, she whispered: 'Soon you'll be alone here, Mr Pearson. You're a little boy lost in a toy factory . . .'

'Sergeant, wait . . .'

But she had vanished into a maze of shadows and doorways.

'Mary . . . listen . . .'

I called out, and felt a pair of strong hands seize my shoulders and pull me into the light. A marshal wearing a St George's shirt stared into my face. He ran a hand over my beard, recognizing me with some effort.

'Missing your girlfriend, Mr Pearson? You look all in, mate. Mr Sangster said you might be here . . .'

He led me into the uneasy glare of the entrance hall. A golf cart had arrived, towing a luggage trailer in the livery of the Ramada Inn. Sangster was at the controls, his huge frame in its black overcoat almost squeezing out Tom Carradine. The PR manager sat beside him, eyes still resolute, hunched over his bandaged arms. He had been wounded in the previous night's action, leading his squad of marshals from the front, but his courage and determination were intact.

Laid out on the trailer were five bodies, the unlucky casualties of the commando assault.

37

Prayers and Wool-Wash Cycles

'RICHARD, YOU LOOK a mess, poor man . . .' Sangster ordered the marshal to release me. Smiling like an indulgent parent, he put a protective arm around my waist. 'Too many strange dreams. Far too many . . .'

'They are strange.' I tried to clear my head. 'Sangster, I saw Sergeant Falconer. And Duncan Christie . . .'

'There you are.' Sangster chuckled to himself, still light-headed after the excitements of the night. 'You always were a dreamer, Richard.'

'Sangster, listen –'

'Think of it like this.' He raised his huge hands to silence me, exposing his deeply bitten nails. 'The Metro-Centre is dreaming you. It's dreaming all of us, Richard.'

'Sergeant Falconer was here. If she can get in, there must be other police inside the dome.'

'Others? Of course there are. They want to join us. They can't do us any harm. We control the Metro-Centre. Now, let's get on with the transfer.'

Still holding my waist, he turned to the trailer carrying the five bodies. Armed marshals stood in a circle around the golf cart, ears tuned to the distant sounds of army helicopters. Sangster's hands gestured at the air, as if conducting an invisible choir. His tall figure dominated the entrance hall, but he still deferred to Carradine, who sat quietly in the cart's passenger seat, staring at his bandaged arms.

The former publicity manager was grey with fatigue and blood loss, but his confidence was intact, and he clenched and unclenched his jaws as if savouring the aftertaste of the night's violence.

Then he caught my eye, and stared at me for a moment too long, and I could see that he knew the game was up. Yet in a way this gave him the freedom to do anything, however deranged.

'Sangster . . .' I struggled to lower my voice. 'Is Carradine . . . ?'

'He's fine. Last night was a shock. The police betrayed us. All that shooting. I keep warning Tom that violence is the true poetry of governments. Right, then . . .'

He steered me to the trailer, as if wanting me to stare at the bodies. Already they were turning blue in the morning light. The only victim I recognized was the Metro-Centre general manager, his eyes wide open as if puzzled by his unaudited and unplanned death. A bullet had pierced his neck, but he had scarcely bled, as if deciding to surrender his life with the least fuss.

'Sangster . . .' I turned away from the grimacing mouths. 'What happens now?'

'The exchange. We can't keep them in the Metro-Centre. Carradine has a list of demands.'

'Are the press here?'

'A few agency reporters. They squat on cornices, fouling the stone. Why?'

'The police and army killed them. Make sure the reporters know that.'

'We will . . .' Sangster turned to stare at me. His huge head began to nod. 'You've given me an idea. Brilliant man . . .'

Carradine waited in his seat, painfully raising his left hand to read the list of demands. Sangster sat beside him, and began to stroke his shoulder, as if grooming an old dog.

'Tom? You're doing well. Don't be afraid to look angry. There's been a change of plan. I want you to tell the police negotiator that *we* shot the hostages. All five of them.'

'We did . . . ?' Carradine's eyes stirred in their deep sockets. 'All five?'

'We executed them in retaliation. Can you remember?'

'All five? That would be —?'

'Murder? No. It shows we're strong, Tom. Last night was an unprovoked attack. Many of our people could have died. As the occupying military power we are entitled to retaliate. Tell them, Tom — next time we will shoot ten hostages . . .'

Satisfied with the deception, Sangster boyishly rubbed his hands and led me through the armed marshals. Their eyes forever scanned the high galleries, as if waiting for a messiah to overfly the dome. We watched the trailer being uncoupled from the golf cart and wheeled to the emergency hatch of the fire door.

'Good . . .' Sangster's nostrils flicked. 'Those bodies were getting a bit ripe. Even for you, Richard . . .'

'I've let myself go. Why, I don't know. I was supposed to leave with the last hostage release.'

'What's happening here is too interesting to leave.' Sangster nodded eagerly, eyes brightening again now that the bodies were being lifted through the hatch. 'You know that, Richard. All this is the culmination of your life's work.'

'In a way. I wanted to keep an eye on Julia.'

'Good. It's time for the patients to watch the physicians — that's the twenty-first century in a nutshell.' He gestured with both hands at the tiers of retail terraces and the silent escalators. 'You created the Metro-Centre, Richard. But I created these people. Their empty, ugly minds, their failure to be fully human. We have to see how it ends.'

'It's already ended.'

'Not quite. People are capable of the most wonderful madness. The kind of madness that gives you hope for the human race.'

We were following the stationary travelator that led from the North Gate entrance to the central atrium. We passed a kitchenware store with a display pyramid outside its doors, an altar of expensive oven dishes, fruit strainers and paper flowers adorning a publicity photograph of David Cruise.

'Sangster . . .' I pointed to the shrine. 'Here's another . . .'

'I've seen them.' Sangster stopped and bowed his head in solemn show. 'They're prayer sites, Richard. Altars to the household gods who rule our lives. The lares and penates of the ceramic hob and the appliance island. The Metro-Centre is a cathedral, a place of worship. Consumerism may seem pagan, but in fact it's the last refuge of the religious instinct. Within a few days you'll see a congregation worshipping its washing machines. The baptismal font that immerses the Monday-morning housewife in the benediction of the wool-wash cycle . . .'

With a wave he turned and left me, walking back to the North Gate entrance hall, one hand tapping the travelator rail. I watched him whistling to himself, and then set off towards the central atrium, where the stronger sunlight was dispersing the warm mist.

I opened the handles of my shooting stick, and rested in front of an unlooted deli that had remained closed throughout the siege. Exquisite moulds climbed out of cheese jars and pesto bowls, turning the interior into an art-nouveau grotto.

I was almost asleep when a shot sounded from the central atrium, echoing around the upper circle of galleries. There was an erratic burst of rifle fire, followed by cries and shouts that merged into a wave of ululation, the stricken keening of a Middle Eastern bazaar. I assumed that another commando raid was taking place, but the sporting rifles were firing at random, an expression of collective grief and outrage.

As I reached the central atrium a crowd of mutineers in St George's shirts besieged the first-aid post. A group of marshals emerged from the doors, clearing a path through the throng. They propelled a hospital bed fitted with serum drips and electrical leads hanging from its head rail, and raced alongside it like tobogganists setting off on the Cresta run.

As they swept past me the crowd of supporters ran beside them, firing their shotguns into the air. Someone stumbled and I had a glimpse of the bed's occupant, a desiccated mummy with a childlike face under an oxygen mask, topped by a pelt of blond hair.

A distraught woman in a tear-stained St George's shirt approached me, muscular arms above her head, as if ringing a mortuary bell. Trying to calm her, I gripped her hand.

'What happened? Is Dr Goodwin . . . ?'

'David Cruise . . .' She pushed me away, and stared beseechingly at the impassive bears on their plinth. 'He died . . .'

38

Tell Him

'WE'RE CLOSING THE shop, Richard.' Tony Maxted paced around the cluttered treatment room, waving away the stench from the pails of soiled bandages. 'I advise you to come with us. You've been here far too long, for reasons even I don't understand.'

'We've all been here too long.' I sat on a broken-backed chair kicked aside when the marshals burst into the first-aid post. 'How exactly do we get out?'

'Hard to say yet. But things are on the turn. God knows what could happen.'

Maxted drummed his fingers on the sink. He was decisive but unsure of everything, and patted Julia Goodwin on the shoulder to settle himself.

She sat at the far end of the metal table, her back to the looted pharmacy cabinets. With her bruised forehead and torn blouse she resembled a casualty doctor who had barely fought off an assault by a deranged patient. I wanted to sit next to her and take her worn hands, but I knew that she would see the gesture as mawkish and irrelevant.

'When did David Cruise die?' I asked. 'During the night?'

Maxted glanced at Julia, who nodded briefly to him. He waited for a gunshot to echo its way around the atrium and said: 'Four days ago. We did everything we could, believe me.'

'Why did they take him?'

'Why?' Maxted stared at his palms. 'They think they can revive the poor man.'

'How?'

'I wish I knew. I'd make a fortune. Resurrection as the ultimate placebo effect.' Seeing my impatience, he added: 'They're taking the body on a tour of the Metro-Centre. All that merchandise is supposed to bring him back. It's worth a try.'

'Does it matter?' Julia spoke sharply, tired of two bickering men. 'At least they don't think we killed him.'

'Four days?' I thought of the ventilator pumping away, and Julia tiptoeing around the oxygen tent. 'How did they know he was dead?'

'They smelled it.' Maxted reached into the refrigerator and took out a bottle of mineral water. He washed his hands in a splash of the brittle fluid and then drank the last drops. 'Now it's time to go. When Cruise doesn't sit up and read out the sports results these people are going to flip. I doubt if the police understand that.'

'Sergeant Falconer is here,' I said. 'I saw her an hour ago near the North Gate.'

'Mary Falconer?' Julia sat forward, suddenly alert. 'What was she doing?'

'Keeping an eye on Sangster. He'll soon take over.'

'That's what I'm afraid of.' Maxted kicked a pedal bin out of his way. 'The magus of the shopping mall, a messiah without a message. You helped to write the script, Richard. The message is: there is no message. Nothing has any meaning, so at last we're free.'

'Falconer's on to him,' I said. 'She'll make sure he doesn't go too far.'

'I doubt it.' Maxted sat at the table and spread his hands over the surface. 'I suspect she's on a different mission.'

'Looking for Duncan Christie?'

'Something like that.' Maxted glanced sharply at me, avoiding Julia's eyes. 'Unfinished business. We need to find him, for his own safety.'

'Why?' I pressed. 'Does it matter?'

'Matter?' Maxted stared at the table, as if expecting his cards to be dealt. 'It does matter. Because Christie's in danger.'

'Good.' Taking a gamble, and almost too tired to care, I said calmly: 'He shot my father. You know that, doctor. You've always known it.'

'Well . . .' Without thinking, Maxted turned in his chair, clearly searching for an exit. 'That's not something I can discuss . . .'

'He also shot David Cruise. Not those Bosnian brothers, whoever they are. Cruise was his real target all along.'

'That's a big jump, Richard.'

'Not really.' I waited for Julia to speak, but she was staring fixedly at Maxted. 'What I can't understand is why you've all been protecting him.'

'Tell him.' Julia stood up, rapping the table with her fist. She pulled back the hair from her forehead, wincing at a bruise on her scalp. 'Maxted, tell him.'

'Julia, it's not that easy. The context . . .'

'Fuck the context! *Tell* him!'

Julia stepped around the table towards Maxted and picked a knife from the sink. She was no longer angry with herself but with the foolish men who had brought her to this makeshift clinic in a besieged shopping mall. Her shoulders squared against Maxted, willing him to back away from her. I could see the relief she felt as the truth hovered in front of us, ready to spill over in a torrent.

'Julia, sit down . . .' Maxted offered her a chair, and beckoned to me, trying to enlist my help in calming this enraged woman. 'Context is important. Richard has to understand what our intentions were . . .'

'Never mind our intentions!' Julia waited until she could control herself. 'Tell him who killed his father.'

'Christie did.' I spoke as matter-of-factly as I could. 'I know that, Julia. It was obvious from day one.'

Julia nodded, then raised the knife to quieten me. 'Yes, Christie pulled the trigger. He fired the shots. I'm sorry, Richard, desperately sorry for that. So many people killed and badly wounded. It was a blunder from the start. But Duncan Christie didn't kill your father.'

'Who did?'

'We did.' Julia pointed to herself and Maxted. 'We planned it, and we gave the order.'

'Hold on . . .' Maxted took the knife from Julia's hand. 'Julia and I were on the fringe. There were a lot of others.'

'Sangster, Geoffrey Fairfax, Sergeant Falconer . . .' I recited the names. 'Various other people who gave their support, but preferred to stay in the shadows. The mayor and one or two councillors, Superintendent Leighton and senior police officers . . .'

'The old Brooklands establishment,' Julia commented wearily. 'Terrible bores, the lot of them. Dangerous bores. There was even a clergyman, but Maxted frightened him off. All that talk about elective insanity.'

'He thought I meant the Christian Church.' Maxted added: 'They'd already had one assassination too many, and weren't looking for a second.'

'Assassination?' I pushed myself away from the table. 'You planned to kill my father. Why?'

'Not your father. He was never the target.' Maxted sank his exhausted face into his hands. 'Go back six months, Richard. Brooklands was in turmoil, along with all the other motorway towns. More than a million people were directly involved. Racist attacks, Asian families terrorized out of their homes, immigrant hostels burnt down. Football matches every weekend that were really political rallies, though no one there ever realized it. Sport was just an excuse for street violence. And it all seemed to spring from the Metro-Centre. A new kind of fascism, a cult of violence rising from this wilderness of retail parks and cable TV stations. People were so bored, they wanted drama in their lives. They wanted to strut and shout and kick the hell out of anyone with a strange face. They wanted to hero-worship a leader.'

'David Cruise? Hard to believe.'

'Right. But this was a new kind of fascism, and it needed a new kind of leader – a smiley, ingratiating, afternoon TV kind of führer. No Sieg Heils, but football anthems instead. The same hatreds, the same hunger for violence, but filtered through the chat-show studio and the hospitality suite. For most people it was just soccer hooliganism.'

'But the bodies kept arriving at the morgue.' Julia reached across the table and gripped my wrist, angry with me even for being a victim. 'I counted them, Richard.'

'Asian and Kosovan bodies.' Maxted wiped a fleck of spit from his mouth. He stared at it, as if disgusted with himself. 'Julia had to deal with the relatives. Weeping Bangladeshi wives and deranged fathers of children with third-degree burns . . .'

Thinking of the Kumars, I said: 'So you decided to do something?'

'We had to move fast, while the whole nasty business was still controllable. A soft fascism was spreading through middle England, and no one in authority was concerned. Politicians, church leaders, Whitehall turned their noses up. For them it was just a brawl in a retail park off some ghastly motorway.'

'But you knew they were wrong?'

'Absolutely. Think of Germany in the nineteen-thirties. When good men do nothing . . . We needed a target, so we picked David Cruise. He wasn't ideal, but shooting him down in the Metro-Centre, in the middle of one of his television rants, would make a powerful point. People would think hard about where they were going.'

'So you needed a triggerman. And you came up with Duncan Christie?'

'I found him.' Maxted waited as Julia raised her hands in mock wonder. 'He was sitting in a secure ward at Northfield. A misfit who'd twice been sectioned, a borderline schizophrenic with a fierce hatred of the Metro-Centre. His daughter had been injured and he wanted revenge. He was a missile primed to launch. All we had to do was point him at the target.'

'You weren't worried about the . . . ?'

'Ethics of it all? Of course, we were planning a murder! We talked it through a hundred times. I kept Julia out of it – I knew I'd never convince her.'

'I thought Christie was letting off a bomb. A smoke bomb.' Julia pressed her hand to her bruised scalp, forcing herself to wince with pain. 'So I gave my support. Madness – how did I think it would ever work?'

'It did work.' Maxted ignored her protests. 'Everything was arranged. Geoffrey Fairfax knew his stuff. Sadly, when the hour came the only thing missing was the target.'

'But my father and the bears filled in.' I rearranged the dirt on the table, and then drew my father's initials. 'How many of you were involved?'

'A small inner group. Fairfax was in the driving seat. He'd served in the army, he knew and loved the old Brooklands. He saw the Metro-Centre as a spaceship from hell. Superintendent Leighton supported us, but he had to be careful. He'd join our meetings, then slip away early. Sergeant Falconer was under Fairfax's thumb – he'd got her mother off a shoplifting charge. She supplied the weapon, a standard Heckler & Koch, apparently mislaid by the armoury. Leighton covered up for her.'

'Sangster?'

'He reconnoitred the target area. Tom Carradine was an old pupil, and very proud to take his headmaster on a tour of the Metro-Centre and show off the fire and emergency systems. He gave Sangster a security pass for his visiting "nephew". An hour before the shooting Sangster hid the weapon in the fire-control station.'

'And Julia?'

'I did nothing!' Julia tore a children's drawing from the wall and crushed it in her hands. 'I didn't think anyone would get killed, or even wounded . . .'

'You did almost nothing.' Maxted waited until she tossed the crumpled drawing among the bloody bandages in an overflowing bin. 'Julia had treated Christie's daughter after the accident. He may be schizoid but he's no fool. He wasn't sure we were serious. She gave him beta-blockers to calm him down and convinced him he was doing the right thing. Christie believed her, and that was vital.'

'I drove him to the Metro-Centre.' Julia half closed her eyes, smiling faintly to herself. 'When we parked he didn't want to get out of the car. He actually asked me if he should go ahead. I said . . .'

'You said yes.' Maxted sat back in his chair, letting the point sink in. 'He trusted you, Julia.'

'But after the shooting . . .' Puzzled, I asked: 'Weren't you afraid that Christie would talk?'

'Only if he went on trial. Hours of CID grilling, months in a remand centre away from his wife and daughter – he'd have given away everything. We knew that killing David Cruise would be easy. The cover-up was the difficult part. It was vital that Christie be arrested.'

'Why? Arrested?'

'Arrested and brought before a magistrate. If enough witnesses testified that they saw Christie at the time of the shooting and he was nowhere near the atrium the case against him would be dismissed. Especially if the witnesses knew Christie well and were worthy members of the local community.'

'His doctor, psychiatrist, head teacher. So that's why you went to the entrance hall. You were protecting Christie.'

'And ourselves. If Christie confessed to the murder no one would take his word against ours. Misfits and psychotics are confessing all the time to crimes they haven't committed.' Maxted sighed to himself. 'It was almost the perfect murder.'

'Almost?'

'The victim failed to turn up. We'd told Christie to hide the weapon and get away, but he lost his nerve. He'd come that far and he needed a target.'

'My father? He hated David Cruise and the sports clubs.'

'Not your father. That was a tragic blunder. Christie was firing at the bears. He hated them even more than he hated Cruise. Especially as his daughter liked to watch them bobbing about on a children's programme. He fired blindly, and hit your father, along with other visitors to the mall. I take responsibility, Richard. Innocent bystanders, collateral damage, they're easy phrases to say . . .'

I nodded coldly, refusing to spare Maxted any of his contrition. He had spoken truthfully, but the truth was not enough. I wanted to see him serving years of imprisonment, but I knew that Julia would be with him, her life and career destroyed. She was standing with her back to me, hands wiping her eyes, and I understood now the hostility and guilt that had stood between us since my arrival.

I said: 'So you smuggled Christie out of Brooklands? Where, exactly?'

'Sangster drove him to a disused chicken farm near Guildford that Fairfax had helped foreclose. His wife and daughter turned up in a camper van. I kept him sedated and told him we'd try again. He was definitely up for it.'

'The police found him so quickly. Someone must have tipped them off.'

'We did.' Maxted whistled through his teeth without thinking. 'We needed to get him cleared by the magistrate. The deaths were tragic, but we hoped everyone would see sense. In fact, the opposite happened. The Metro-Centre shooting stirred everything up. People felt frightened. They could cope with Asian youths defending their shops, but a deranged assassin with a machine gun . . . ? There were rallies at the sports grounds night after night, Brooklands was seriously threatening to turn into a fascist republic. But it never made that final flip.'

'You sound disappointed. Why not? Too British?'

'In a way.' Maxted listened to a volley of shots echo through the atrium. 'Sporting rifles – that about spells it out. The problem was David Cruise. He was too amiable, too second-rate. Then a minor miracle happened, someone we hadn't counted on turned up.'

'Me?'

'Right. You turned up. Your father had died, and you wanted to know why. It didn't take you long to realize that something very fishy was going on.'

'Julia came to the funeral. That started me thinking.'

'Richard . . .' Julia stood shivering behind me, her hands on my shoulders. 'I'd helped to kill a fine old man. I knew how stupid I'd been, listening to all this talk about elective madness.'

'Talk, maybe. But I was right.' Maxted quietly ignored her, addressing me directly. 'The assassination failed, but everything moved up a gear. It needed a final push. A bomb in the Metro-Centre, a huge riot that would overwhelm the police, David Cruise proclaiming an independent state.'

'He was too canny for that.'

'So we found. The riot went ahead, Sangster planted another bomb near the town hall, and we did our best to stir up the crowd. But without Cruise it was hopeless. Fairfax's death frightened off a lot of our key supporters.'

'How did he die?'

'I guess his fingers were rusty. Never liked the man. He was always a bit too impetuous. The last person to be a bomb-maker.'

'But why pick my car?'

'That was Fairfax's idea. He knew you were on to something. And he loathed you, anyway. It was a warning, a reminder of how easy it would be to frame you. Leighton and Sergeant Falconer went along with that – it's why you were never charged and the car's owner-ship was never identified. We had you where we needed you. But everything collapsed when Cruise refused to take the bait. He came from the TV world, and he needed an autocue. Then a new friend appeared with the right kind of skills and a taste for stylized violence.'

'A suburban Dr Goebbels?'

Maxted stared at me with real distaste, then managed a weak smile. 'You saw fascism as just another sales opportunity. Psychopathology was a handy marketing tool. David Cruise was your tailor's dummy, a shrink-proof shaman of the multi-storey car parks, Kafka in a tired trenchcoat, a psychopath with genuine moral integrity.'

'Still, everyone admired him.'

'Why not? We're totally degenerate. We lack spine, and any faith in ourselves. We have a tabloid world-view, but no dreams or ideals. We have to be teased with the promise of deviant sex. Our gurus tell us that coveting our neighbours' wives is good for us, and even conceivably our neighbours' asses. Don't honour your father and mother, and break free from the whole Oedipal trap. We're worth nothing, but we worship our barcodes. We're the most advanced society our planet has ever seen, but real decadence is far out of our reach. We're so desperate we have to rely on people like you to spin a new set of fairy tales, cosy little fantasies of alienation and guilt. We're worthless, Richard – to your credit, you know that.'

'And David Cruise knew it. Who shot him? Did you organize that?'

'Definitely not. That must have been Christie, finishing the job. He's somewhere here, a fugitive protected by the one place he hated.'

'And Sergeant Falconer? Is she after him?'

'I assume so. I dare say Superintendent Leighton can feel the wind changing. I wouldn't be surprised if she has other targets.'

'You and Sangster? And Julia?'

'And you, Richard. Don't forget that.'

Julia had left the room, too nervous to look me in the face. She spoke to the last of the patients, an elderly couple who had been swept into the Metro-Centre on the night of the riot. Sensibly they had taken refuge, while the elevators still worked, in a health-food restaurant on the sixth floor. They held out there for more than a month, living on dates, figs and pomegranates, like travellers in a new desert, too timid and too sensible to walk down the escalators into the hell unfolding below them.

I followed Maxted into the entrance to the first-aid post. The atrium was deserted, its floor covered with debris that had fallen from the roof.

'So what happens now?' I asked. Despite everything he had told me, I still liked him. He was restless and insecure, but trying to conduct his life according to a set of desperate principles. He would never be brought to trial for the deaths and injuries he had caused. He lived out a fantasy, as quietly deranged as any psychiatrist I had met, the only real inmate in the asylum he ruled.

'Try not to think.' Maxted clasped and unclasped his bruised hands. 'I hope the police decide to rush the place. Carradine and Sangster still have hostages locked into the Novotel, plus a couple of hundred hard-core supporters. They have nothing to lose. Meanwhile, here's a first taste of real madness . . .'

He pointed to the bears on their podium. Nearby was the bed holding the body of David Cruise, secure inside his oxygen tent. His tour of the Metro-Centre was over, and he had been left like a slain hero to the kindness of the bears. Half a dozen supporters in St George's shirts knelt on the floor, faces raised to the stuffed beasts.

'What are they doing?' I asked Maxted. 'Waiting for the music?'

'They're praying. It's your consumer dream come true, Richard. They're praying to the teddy bears . . .'

Leaving Maxted, I stepped slowly across the atrium, avoiding the spurs of glass and torn aluminium that had fallen from the roof. Somewhere above me, on the abandoned galleries, Duncan Christie would be waiting for another target to appear. He had killed David Cruise – was I, the ventriloquist, the next bull's-eye in his sights?

I passed the group of praying supporters, avoiding the stench that rose from David Cruise's bed. Several of them had jars of honey in front of them, offerings to the deities who guided their lives. One middle-aged woman in a St George's shirt, blonde hair knotted behind her neck, was rocking to and fro, humming to herself. Her husband, a hefty fellow wearing ice-hockey armour, joined her, and I heard their consoling verse.

> . . . if you go down to the woods today,
> you'd better go in disguise.
> For every bear that ever there was . . .

39

The Last Stand

ITS OWN SHADOWS stalked the Metro-Centre. Twice during the night I was woken by Carradine's marshals, firing at random into the dark. Helicopters soared tirelessly above the roof, searchlights throwing restless shadows that leapt from a hundred doorways, like the crazed remnants of a routed army.

At 5 a.m. I gave up any hope of sleep. Barely able to breathe, I sat behind the balcony curtains, thinking through Maxted's account of my father's death, and how a group of amateurish conspirators had blundered into murder. But their crime was now little more than a small annexe to what was taking place in the Metro-Centre. In the three days since the abduction of David Cruise's body, and his failure to rouse himself for a curtain call, life within the dome had severed its last links to reality.

Despite all the violence, the vast mall was an unlooted treasure house that preserved the intact dream of a thousand suburbs. In the unlit interiors of furniture stores, in carpet emporiums and demonstration kitchens, the heart of a despised way of life still beat strongly. Leaving Sangster and his self-hating motives to one side, I admired Carradine and his mutineers, and the robustly physical world they had based on their consumerist dream. The motorway towns were built on the frontier between a tired past and a future without illusions and snobberies, where the only reality was to be found in the certainties of the washing machine and the ceramic hob, as precious as the iron stove in a pioneer's shack.

At six, having destroyed the possibility of sleep, the helicopters withdrew, and dawn began its queasy descent through the dome's roof, a cumbersome special effect staged for an exhausted audience. The pearly, metallic light exposed the silent plazas of a retail city whose streets were too dangerous to walk, whose crossroads waited like targets for the unwary.

Supermarkets were open all day, for anyone hungry enough to venture between the aisles and risk blundering into a meat locker that incubated every known disease. Freezer cabinets as hot as ovens would suddenly burst from their hinges, each one a vent of hell exhaling a miasma that drifted over the display counters. After digging in the rubble of unwanted cans, I would finally find a few tins of pâté, artichoke hearts in vinegar, jars of butter beans as pale as death.

I would then make my way to Julia, climbing to the second-floor gallery that circled the atrium, take a service staircase to the mezzanine and rush the final few steps past the landing where my father had been shot. An exhausting route, but Julia depended on my modest shopping trips. Limping on my infected foot, which she ritually rebandaged, I made my twice-a-day runs like a gentleman caller in a city under siege. Julia slept in a bed next to the elderly couple, with whom she shared her rations. In the treatment room she made friendly small talk, her eyes on the supermarket bag, like an unfaithful wife determined to survive. She knew I had forgiven her, but she hated me to watch her eat, as if part of her rejected her own right to life. Like everyone, she waited for the siege to end. I urged her to join me in the Holiday Inn, but she refused to leave the first-aid post, the only refuge of sanity in the dome.

At noon, when the shadows briefly left us to ourselves, a few people crossed the atrium and began praying to the bears. Loyal supporters too weak to work, they wandered around the dome, rattling the grilles of the empty supermarkets in the hope of finding something to eat. One or two of them had marked barcodes on the backs of their hands, trying to resemble the consumer goods they most admired.

I watched them as I moved along the second-floor deck, feeling sorry for them until I discovered that my favourite deli had been looted during the night. This Polish speciality shop had been a modest haven of eastern European delicacies, spurned by the sweeter palates of Brooklands man and woman. Now it had been stripped of everything remotely edible, its doors chained and padlocked.

Unable to face Julia with an empty shopping bag, I decided to climb to the third floor. Pulling myself up the hand rail was a huge effort, but I rested on every landing, and there was safety on the upper floors. Madness lay below like the mist that covered the atrium.

I reached the third-floor gallery and sat on the top step until my head cleared. Beside me, pools of liquid evaporated in the sunlight. I watched them shrink and dissolve, unsure if I was seeing a mirage. Other drops formed a trail along the arcade, splashes from a casually carried bucket. I dipped my fingers in the nearest pool and raised them to my mouth. Immediately I thought of my Jensen, and the familiar aromatic reek of filling stations.

Petrol? Ten feet away, outside a discount furniture store, was a set of wet shoeprints, a trainer's sole clearly stamped on the stone floor. I stepped into the foyer and searched the three-piece suites, drawn up like a dozing herd.

Petrol, I was sure. I found the source in a demonstration dining room, a domestic universe of rosewood-effect tables, polished chairs and curtains swagged over glassless windows, missing only the dinner-party chatter relayed from a loudspeaker. A jerrycan stamped with the logo of the Metro-Centre motor pool sat under the dining table, its cap missing, giving off a potent stench in the overheated air.

I backed away from it, aware that the smallest spark would ignite the vapour. I left the store and moved along the deck. The arcade of furniture stores was an arsonist's paradise, retail space after retail space filled with inflammable sofas and varnished cabinets.

Was this a last-ditch threat by Carradine and his Metro-Centre supporters? Six stores along the arcade, I found a second jerrycan in a bedding store, surrounded by a harem's wealth of goose-down pillows, fluffy quilts and duvets. The aroma of a hundred filling stations, threatening but somehow enticing, drifted from the silent stores and rose into the haze below the roof.

Fifteen minutes later I reached the top floor, where a third jerrycan sat on the landing above the stairwell, petrol slopped around it. A police helicopter drifted over the dome, throwing its spidery shadows across the galleries, a flicker of rotor blades scrambling through the dead vines and yuccas.

Above the cuffing downdraught I heard the fracture-cry of plate glass falling to the floor. A display stand collapsed in the entrance to a kitchenware store, hurling saucepans and pieces of heavy ovenware onto the landing. I pressed myself against the wall, almost expecting a furnace of petroleum vapour to explode from the store.

Lying at my feet between a colander and a copper steamer was a police-issue firearm, a Heckler & Koch machine gun of the type that had killed my father. I stared down at it in a befuddled way, trying to grasp how it had become a useful kitchen aid for the busy Brooklands home-maker.

Without thinking, I picked the weapon from the floor, surprised by its weight. The firing pin was cocked, and I held the pistol grip, easing my forefinger around the trigger.

I peered into the darkened shop. A woman in a black police uniform, dishevelled blonde hair torn from her scalp, struggled among the scattered saucepans. She thrashed on the floor, kicking at a cascade of falling frying pans, a demented housewife attacking her own home. She lunged at a man who burst from the darkness, and seized him around the waist. He threw her aside and emerged into the light, feet sliding on the saucepan lids, like an enraged husband escaping for ever from suburban life.

He gasped at the air and turned to me, seeing me for the first time. His camouflage jacket stank of petrol, as if he were about to combust spontaneously in the sunlight. He calmed himself, and a scarred hand reached out for the machine gun that I pointed towards him.

Recognizing Duncan Christie, I stepped back and levelled the weapon at his chest. Christie edged forward, aware that I would probably miss him if I fired. His quirky mouth with its unhealed lips worked through a set of grimaces, some whispered message to himself. His hand tried to grip the barrel of the gun, but as he stared into my face, willing me not to fire, he recognized me through my beard.

'Mr Pearson? Remember? Duncan Christie . . .'

Sergeant Falconer leaned against the doorway, too exhausted to throw herself at Christie. She gasped something into the radio clipped to her left shoulder, then signalled to me with her free hand.

'Shoot him, Richard! Shoot him now!'

I watched Christie, well aware that I was holding the actual weapon that had killed my father. Looking at this hopeless misfit, sustained by a single obsession, I knew that his life was about to end, expiring in the sights of a police marksman waiting in the upper galleries.

'Mr Pearson . . .' Christie exposed his broken teeth. 'You know what happened. She made me kill your father . . .'

Sergeant Falconer shouted in warning as Christie lunged towards me. I moved across the arcade, raised the weapon above my head and flung it over the rail.

'Go!' I shouted at Christie. 'You know what to do! Run . . . !'

Sergeant Falconer stood unsteadily among the clutter of saucepans, one hand on an injured knee, the other trying to tether her blonde hair to her head.

'Mr Pearson? For pity's sake, you're madder than he is.'

'I forgive him.' I listened to Christie racing along the gallery below us, running through endless arcades of autumn fashions and television sets, fleeing from a universe of digital cameras and cocktail cabinets. 'He can go – if he can find somewhere.'

'Forgive him?' Sergeant Falconer switched off her radio. The bruises on her forehead were showing through her pale skin, but she seemed far more determined than the uneasy woman I had seen making tea in Fairfax's office. I guessed that she had put the murder conspiracy behind her and found a new compass bearing in her life. 'Forgive him? For your father? It doesn't matter.'

'No? It's all that does matter. For what it's worth, I forgive you. I don't think you knew what you were doing.'

'Maybe not. Anyway, it's too late. Just get out of here. Take Dr Goodwin and anyone else. You're in real danger.'

'Why? Sergeant . . . ?'

'They're coming in. It's all over, Mr Pearson. You'll have to find another playgroup.'

'And Christie?'

'I'll arrest him later.'

As she spoke there was a heavy explosion from the South Gate entrance hall. The deck swayed beneath my feet, and the roof of the Metro-Centre lifted slightly and then settled as a cascade of dust fell like talc. The smog cloud that covered the atrium seethed and swirled, billows chasing themselves around the bears.

The siege was ending.

40

Exit Strategies

AT LAST TOGETHER, our hands gripping the head rail, Julia and I propelled the bed through the doorway of the first-aid post and set off for the South Gate entrance. After twenty yards we were both exhausted. Out of control, the bed veered into an overturned golf cart. The elderly couple who were Julia's last patients lay strapped to the mattress. As we jolted through the scatter of roof debris they closed their eyes, alarmed by the erratic excursion and the panic that now gripped the dome. Bent over the head rail, I saw them trying to reassure each other that all would be well, neither believing it for an instant.

'We're almost there, Mrs Mitchell,' I told her. 'You'll be home soon, warming the teapot.'

'Home? I don't think this is the right way, Mr Pearson. We usually go to the No. 48 bus stop. Dr Julia . . . ?'

'We'll find it, Mrs Mitchell.' Julia winced as we slewed across a floor of broken glass, then clung to my shoulder when I straightened the bed's wayward front wheels. 'I'll tell the driver to wait for you.'

'Maurice . . . did you hear that?' Mrs Mitchell's sharp eyes noticed the dust clouds escaping through the fractured roof. 'It's all been such a fuss about nothing . . .'

The past, in its small but persistent ways, was returning to the Metro-Centre, though few of those left behind had Mrs Mitchell's acuity. Carradine's defenders at the South Gate entrance were falling back, many of them stunned by the controlled explosion that had blown down a section of the fire door. A few die-hard marshals were building a barricade beside the travelator, piling up café chairs and tables. Hostages ran in all directions, distraught and speechless after their forced stay in the Ramada Inn and Novotel. A few huddled in shop doorways, still clutching the carrier bags they held when the siege began. Julia shouted to them, urging them to leave. She pulled my arm and pointed helplessly to two hostages hiding among the mannequins in the window of a dress shop and trying to mimic their calm and plastic detachment.

Almost too weary to walk, she fell behind me, stumbling through the debris and dust. I stopped and took her arms, then made her sit at the foot of the bed.

'Julia, stay there – I can push on my own . . .'

'Just for a minute. Richard, where are the police?'

Blocked by a barricade, I reversed and manoeuvred the bed into a side thoroughfare that led past the Holiday Inn. The lake was black as death, a tar pit freighted with horrors, but elsewhere the lights were coming on. Neon tubes stuttered and steadied themselves, logos glimmered through the dust. Strip lighting flooded the shops and stores, revealing a hundred polished counters. Crazed patterns raced across the display screens, the brain tracings of a giant struggling to awake from its deranged sleep.

'Richard . . . all these lights.' Julia looked up in a dazed way at the arrays of gleaming bulbs. 'They're going to open for business . . .'

'Not yet. Snipers, I guess. The police need to flush them out.'

I steered us past the Holiday Inn with its familiar glowing sign. The wave machine was stirring the sluggish water into a nightmare brew, but as we approached the South Gate entrance hall an even stranger smell surrounded us, a cool flavour that I had first scented as a child.

'Richard? What is it?' Julia stepped down from the bed and nervously filled her lungs. 'It tastes of . . . trees and sky.'

'Fresh air! We're there, Julia . . .'

Ahead of us, though, were a dozen of Carradine's marshals in

St George's shirts, shotguns and rifles strapped to their shoulders with the barrels facing the floor. They were disciplined and marching in step, but their heads were bowed, like a defeated team leaving the field after a fierce but losing struggle, each player communing with himself.

At their head was Tony Maxted, wearing a crisply white surgical coat that he had secretly saved for this moment. He was tired but confident, doing his best to encourage this breakaway group whom he had persuaded to call an end to the siege. He moved up and down their ranks, smiling and talking to each man in turn as they moved towards the waiting light.

Maxted flinched when another controlled explosion burst through a nearby emergency exit. The strap muscle beneath his bald scalp seized his skull and threw his head back. He stumbled and reached out to two of the marshals, then seemed to lose his bearings in the swirl of dust.

I leaned against the head rail, too weary to push. The entrance hall was covered with debris, and a section of the fire door lay in the sun. Masked figures in dark uniforms moved through the intensely lit air.

Behind us an even brighter glow illuminated the interior of the dome, turning an immense spotlight onto the underside of the roof. Shadows wavered and swayed from every doorway, like nervous onlookers unsure whether to believe their eyes.

Flames rose from the seventh-floor galleries around the atrium, lazy blades of light that seemed to wake together and race around the high keep of the retail citadel. Soon the top three decks were burning briskly, every balcony and doorway bursting into blooms of fire. The petrol-soaked settees and carpets, the demonstration dining rooms and ideal kitchens were giving themselves to their own fiery ends.

The platoon in St George's shirts stopped to look back, tired faces revived by the fire, colour returning to their cheeks after the twilight weeks. They were roused by the sight of the Metro-Centre consuming itself, as if welcoming this last transformation.

'Right! Keep going!' Maxted strode down the ranks, clapping his hands, trying to wake them from their trance. 'Come on, lads! We're there . . .'

Debris was falling from the roof, clouds of super-heated dust that had burst into flame as air was drawn into the dome. I could feel the huge mall shifting its weight, its frame members flexing in the heat. A gale rushed past us, cooler air speeding through the vents of a furnace.

'Wake up, the lot of you!' Maxted struck one of the marshals on the shoulder, trying to rouse the man and hold his attention. 'Let's move! We'll all be incinerated . . .'

The marshal turned, aware of Maxted for the first time. He seemed to emerge from a deep rigor, and seized the psychiatrist by the collar of his white coat. Other hands gripped his arms, forcing his body into a crouch. A tremor ran through the platoon, a spasm of anger, fear and pride. Together they turned their backs to the entrance hall. They moved forward, carrying Maxted like a totem at their head, running towards the blaze, his hoarse cries lost in the fierce drumming of the inferno.

41

A Solar Cult

'WHAT HAPPENED TO Tony Maxted?' Julia asked.

We stood by the police railings and gazed across the empty plaza at what remained of the Metro-Centre. Much of the dome was intact, a curved wall like the stand of a circular stadium. But the apex had collapsed, falling into the furnace of shops, hotels and department stores. Three weeks after our escape, smoke and steam rose from the ruin, watched by a dozen fire crews drawn up within fifty yards of the structure. A small crowd appeared each day, staring at the stricken mall as if unable to grasp what had happened. The Metro-Centre had devoured itself, a furnace consumed by its own fire.

'Richard . . . poor man, are you still here?'

'I'm not sure. It feels rather strange. In a way we shouldn't be watching . . .'

'No? Where should we be? Sweet man, part of you will be forever beachcombing near the Holiday Inn . . .'

She took my arm to reassure me, but kept a wary eye on my shifting moods. For the first time her hair was reined in over her left shoulder, exposing her face. Three nights under sedation at Brooklands Hospital, and long days of sleep in her bed at home, had transformed her from the haggard refugee I had pushed to safety from the dome. That morning I had heard from her for the first time, when she left a text message suggesting that she drive me to the dome.

Parking outside my father's flat, she smiled approvingly when I crossed the gravel, stick supporting me as I swung my foot in its surgical boot. I knew there and then that she was at ease with herself and ready to be at ease with me. I had rescued her from the furnace of the Metro-Centre, and in the mysterious logic of the affections this single act erased her guilt over the part she had played in my father's death. Victims had to pay twice for the crimes committed against them.

By contrast, I was still exhausted, barely able to keep awake, watching the TV news, hobbling around the flat and cooking boiled eggs that I found waiting for me the next day. But the sight of the Metro-Centre woke me. I was glad to be with Julia, and slipped my arm around her waist.

'Richard . . . ?'

'Sorry, I was dreaming. What happened to Maxted? They found his body yesterday. Hard to identify in all that ash. One thing you can say about consumer durables, they give off a lot of heat.'

'Where was he?'

'In the atrium. I think they tied him to one of the bears.'

'What a hell of a way to go.' Julia shuddered, tempted to unrein her hair. 'He was rather devious, but I liked him. Why did the marshals turn on him? He was leading them out of the dome.'

'They "flipped". Willed madness, he called it. Remember Nazi Germany, Stalinist Russia, Pol Pot's Cambodia? It never occurred to Maxted that he could be the last victim.'

'And Sangster? I don't think he got out.'

'Most people didn't.' I held Julia's shoulder, trying to calm her. 'Sergeant Falconer, Carradine, all those marshals and engineers who helped him seize the dome. The fire . . .'

'Did Duncan Christie set it off?'

'Hard to say. He wasn't very good at anything. His wife has taken the child and disappeared. I hope he's with them.'

'If Christie didn't start the fire, who did?'

'No one. The army commander gave the order to turn on the lights. Once the police opened the doors the air flooded in. One spark somewhere was all it needed. Instead of flushing out any snipers they started a solar cult.'

Lips pursed, Julia listened to me. 'So . . . Geoffrey Fairfax, Maxted, Sangster, Sergeant Falconer, Christie – the people who killed your father are all dead. Except for one.'

'Julia . . .' I dropped my stick and embraced her. She held her head from me, exposing her chin and neck, and I could see the scars brought to the surface of her skin like a guilty rash, a last flush of self-contempt. 'You didn't kill my father. If you'd known what Fairfax and Sangster had really planned you'd have stopped them.'

'Would I?' Julia forced her eyes to look away from the dome. 'I'm still not sure.'

'Something very dangerous was happening here. You needed to act.'

'But the wrong people got hurt, as they usually do.' Julia retrieved my stick and pressed it into my hand. 'I have to get to the hospital – all these check-ups, they're a disease in their own right. I'll give you a lift home.'

'Thanks, but I'll stay here for a while. There are a few things . . .'

We walked to her car, parked on the nearby kerb. She settled herself behind the wheel, watching me through the bright new windscreen as I arranged my mind.

'Richard? You're trying to say something?'

'Right. Why don't we meet this weekend – you can stay in my father's flat?'

'Your flat, Richard.' She corrected me solemnly. 'Your flat.'

'My flat.'

'Brave chap. That took some doing. You're on – I'll take my chances with a wounded man.'

'Good. I'll have to learn how to clean the bath.'

'I'll come, if you tell me something. I've been thinking about it all week.' She pointed to the dome and the watching crowds, their impassive faces turned towards the plumes of smoke and water vapour.

'When you and David Cruise started all this, did you know where it would end?'

'I can't say. Perhaps we did . . . in a way, that was the whole idea.'

She thought over my reply, once again the serious young doctor, and drove away with a mock-fascist salute. I waved to her until she had gone, inhaling the last traces of her scent on the air. Tapping the ground before each step, I moved through the crowd and found a free place at the railings. The Metro-Centre was as much a tourist attraction as it had ever been. Visitors drove from the motorway towns to gaze at its smoking carcass, once the repository of everything they most valued. None of them, I noticed, was wearing a St George's shirt. Tom Carradine's seizure of the dome had sent a seismic jolt through the Heathrow suburbs, and the ground beneath our feet was still shifting.

The policewoman who carried out my debriefing told me that all marches and most of the sports fixtures had been cancelled. Post-match violence and racist attacks had fallen away, and many Asian families were returning to their homes. The cable channels had reverted to an anaesthetic diet of household hints and book-group discussions. Once people began to talk earnestly about the novel any hope of freedom had died. The once real possibility of a fascist republic had vanished into the air with all the vapourizing three-piece suites and discount carpeting.

I gripped the police railing in both hands, the stick crooked over one arm. In some ways the dome reminded me of a crashed airship, one of the vast inter-war zeppelins that belonged to the lost era of the Brooklands racing circuit. But in other ways it resembled the caldera of a resting volcano, still smoking and ready to revive itself. One day it would become active again, spewing over the motorway towns a shower of patio doors and appliance islands, sun loungers and en-suite bathrooms.

I remembered my last moments in the dome, looking back at the fires that raced along the high galleries from one store to the next. In my mind the fires still burned, moving through the streets of Brooklands and the motorway towns, the flames engulfing crescents of modest bungalows, devouring executive estates and community centres, football stadiums and car showrooms, the last bonfire of the consumer gods.

I watched the spectators around me, standing silently at the railing. There were no St George's shirts, but they watched a little too intently. One day there would be another Metro-Centre and another desperate and deranged dream. Marchers would drill and wheel while another cable announcer sang out the beat. In time, unless the sane woke and rallied themselves, an even fiercer republic would open the doors and spin the turnstiles of its beckoning paradise.

P.S.

Ideas,
interviews
& features ...

About the author

About the book

Read on

Biographical Sketch

James Graham Ballard was born in Shanghai, China, in 1930. After the Japanese attack on Pearl Harbor in 1941 he and his family were interned in the Lunghua Civil Assembly Centre to the south of Shanghai. They remained there for the rest of the war, an experience that Ballard would draw on for his novel *Empire of the Sun*.

In 1946 he moved to England with his mother and sister, and three years later went to King's College, Cambridge, to study medicine. At the same time he began writing short stories, originating and developing themes that he would later return to in his novels. An interest in the transforming effect of science and technology on the conditions of modern life, and his comparison of the fiction writer to the scientist ('faced with an unknown terrain or subject . . . all he can do is devise various hypotheses and test them against the facts') reflect this early training. However, in 1951 Ballard abandoned his clinical studies and enrolled at the University of London to read English. Jobs as a copywriter and encyclopaedia salesman followed, before he decided to join the RAF in 1953. It was during this period that he discovered science fiction.

Ballard left the RAF in 1954. In 1955 he married Helen Matthews and a year later their first child was born. In 1960 the family moved to Shepperton, and two years later Ballard resigned from his job as Assistant Editor of the magazine *Chemistry and Industry* to devote himself to writing full-time. At the end of the year his breakthrough novel, *The Drowned World*, was published. It was followed by two further 'global disaster' novels, *The Drought* (1965) and *The Crystal World* (1966). In the 1970s he changed tack and *The Atrocity Exhibition* (1970), *Crash* (1973), *Concrete Island* (1974) and *The Unlimited Dream Company* (1979) established his reputation as an avant-garde writer with both readers and critics.

Author photograph by Jerry Bauer

With the publication of *Empire of the Sun* in 1984, Ballard entered the mainstream, gaining wider public attention for his work. The book was awarded the James Tait Black Memorial Prize for Fiction and was shortlisted for the Booker. Although its tone and content differ from Ballard's earlier work, its desolate landscapes – abandoned cities strewn with cars and tanks – are reminiscent of earlier books.

In 1996 *Cocaine Nights*, the first in a series of four books to explore human 'psychopathology', was published, followed by the provocative *Super-Cannes* in 2000, *Millennium People* in 2003 and *Kingdom Come* in 2006.

Ballard turned down a CBE for services to literature, joking that he might have been tempted to accept it 'had I been entitled to call myself Commander Ballard'.

Papering Over the Cracks

J.G. Ballard talks to Sarah O'Reilly

Kingdom Come, with its cast of marauding hooligans and morality-free 'pillars of the community', dwells on the dark and dangerous side of human nature. Is this sensitivity to the depths our behaviour can plumb attributable to any particular experience you've endured, do you think?
Yes. I think a number of experiences, particularly during my childhood in the Far East during the Second World War, encouraged me to regard the human race as potentially quite dangerous. People brought up in the comfortable suburbs of western Europe and North America tend to think that human beings are at heart governed by a kind of enlightened self-interest; that they are thoughtful and humane above all. I'm not sure if that is true. If you look at the behaviour of, say, the warring factions in Iraq at the moment with their endless suicide bombings and terrible carnage, or the civil war in the former Yugoslavia, where the most incredible brutality and ethnic cleansing took place, or if you go back to the Second World War in Europe, when tens of millions died in the most brutal way, I'm not convinced that human beings can be *trusted* beyond a certain point. I think they are quite capable in the right, or rather the wrong, circumstances of behaving irrationally. That's certainly my experience.

People think that the events in *Kingdom Come* are a bit extreme, but they actually aren't. For example, about two years ago there were riots in an IKEA store near the North

Circular road in London. People abandoned their cars and were fighting over sofas; there was a huge riot in which people were hurt. Football hooliganism has been a terrible stain on the national character, and it could come back. Nothing I describe is all that extreme.

It's interesting that you mention the IKEA riots when discussing *Kingdom Come* because in the British media they weren't reported in a serious way at all.
I think it's because we have a sort of *Passport to Pimlico* view of social behaviour in this country. It's an Ealing-comedy, *Dad's Army* view of the world: we laugh, but forget that in the real world there is a war going on too, as it were. We like to think of England as a big brown teapot with a nice tea cosy over it but actually we should remember that there isn't always tea in the pot. Sometimes it's something a little stronger.

There's a line in *Kingdom Come* which says: 'Like English life as a whole, nothing in Brooklands can be taken at face value.' Was that your experience of English life, when you moved here in 1946?
I think the English are great actors, there's no doubt about it, and we're all performing roles whether we're aware of it or not. We don't have the sort of frankness and openness of the Australians, or Americans or Canadians. In England there's a very ▶

❝ The English are notorious for their pleases and thank yous, but what the pleases and thank yous actually do is hide an underlying aggression and unease. ❞

Papering Over the Cracks *(continued)*

◀ complex social landscape dominated by the class system, which still seems to be very strong. Here people tend not to say what they think. It's also because we're a crowded island. We behave like people on a crowded aircraft or, if you like, a crowded lifeboat: we put on a face that is designed to lower the temperature, allowing everything to carry on without too much discomfort. The trouble is that this hides the underlying truth about what we feel. Look at how the English are notorious for their pleases and thank yous: when we go into a shop we please and thank you to such an extent that visitors are amazed. After all, you're paying for the thing; you don't need to say thank you. But what the pleases and thank yous actually do is hide an underlying aggression and unease. They are all to do with our desire to paper over the cracks – and there are a *lot* of cracks.

Kingdom Come seems to have anticipated the recent resurgence of film noir. Is there something in the air at the moment?
I think it taps into the same thing. In *Kingdom Come* Pearson believes that you've got to dip a toe into the waters of psychopathology to provide the kind of high-tension excitement that people need, because everyone in the consumer world is very bored. This is the thing about suburbia: there's enormous boredom, and we've reached the stage where people need something a little frightening, a little deviant, to take notice. It's not enough these days to say this detergent washes whiter; you've got

> 6 If you believe that England is all cricket grounds and villages and cycling to evensong then you're going to find *Kingdom Come* about as soothing as a punch in the face. 9

to put a spin on it of some kind. Yes, I think there's something in the air. Compare, say, TV programmes like *Inspector Morse*, which had a gentleman detective sipping his pint and listening to Mozart as he solved a crossword puzzle, and something like *CSI*, where you're looking at a corpse on an autopsy table, and ribcages are being opened like suitcases. It's dangerous because I think violence and madness have a huge appeal, and it'll move into the area of politics sooner or later too. We've already seen it, in fact, with the rise of the Nazis.

Your own narrator in *Kingdom Come* is described as 'beyond psychiatric help'.
Yes, although that particular reference is actually a joke at my expense. When I submitted the manuscript of my novel *Crash* to Jonathan Cape in 1972 the reader was the wife of a psychiatrist and she recommended the book be rejected, saying that I was 'beyond psychiatric help'. I of course took it as the greatest compliment – total artistic success!

Does *Kingdom Come* match the dictionary definition of a 'Ballardian' novel? Is it concerned with 'dystopian modernity, bleak man-made landscapes and the psychological effects of technological, social or environmental developments'?
It's certainly not a bleak novel. It has the bright glitter of big shopping malls, and is quite upbeat in tone, so I don't think one should take that dictionary definition too literally. Having said that, if you do believe ▶

A Writing Life

Where do you write?
In my sitting room.

When do you write?
Morning and early afternoon.

Why do you write?
The great mystery.

Pen or computer?
Pen, then type myself.

Silence or music?
Silence.

How do you start a book?
I usually write a detailed synopsis.

And finish?
With a large full stop.

What objects do you always carry with you?
Latchkeys, I hope.

What single thing would improve the quality of your life?
A time machine.

What is the most important lesson life has taught you?
Risk everything for what you believe.

Which writer has had the greatest influence on your work?
Aldous Huxley.

Papering Over the Cracks (continued)

◀ that England is all cricket grounds and villages and cycling to evensong then you're going to find *Kingdom Come* about as soothing as a punch in the face.

You're noted as being a writer who's interested in the landscape and how it evolves.
I think that's true. Many people have complained that old town centres are being abandoned because huge retail parks are opening on the outskirts of towns. The whole social landscape of England is changing tremendously, and particularly, I think, around the big motorways. Not that the people who work in newspapers and television ever visit these areas. They come back from their cottages in the West Country and they look down from the M4 at places like Staines and Slough and Hounslow and they give a shudder and drive on! But it is happening.

Lastly, I have to ask about your own shopping habits.
I hate shopping! It drives me mad. I do as little of it as possible. A big retail park is my idea of hell. Every so often I need to buy a new washing machine and it leads me into a nervous breakdown.

Remaking the World
by J.G. Ballard

I think the enemy of creativity in the world today is that so much thinking is done for you. The environment is so full of television, party political broadcasts and advertising campaigns, you hardly need to do anything. We're just drowning under manufactured fiction, which satisfies our need for fiction – you scarcely need to go and read a novel.

Cyril Connolly, the Fifties critic and writer, said that the greatest enemy of creativity is the pram in the hall, but I think that was completely wrong. It was the enemy of a certain kind of dilettante life that he aspired to, the man of letters, but for the real novelist the pram in the hall is the greatest ally – it brings you up sharp and you realise what reality is all about. My children were a huge inspiration for me. Watching three young minds creating their separate worlds was a very enriching experience.

For most of my working life as a professional, which began over 40 years ago, what kick-started the day was a large Scotch and soda. After my wife died, I was bringing up my children on my own much of the time: getting them up and to school and finding their satchels, all that sort of thing, and I needed a change of climate. I used to find that a couple of large Scotches did the trick – it created a different microclimate inside my head.

I find the imaginative pressure has always been strong, thank God. I've always felt that I had this message I had to bring the reader – a deluded notion, I'm sure, but it's kept me ▶

Remaking the World *(continued)*

◄ going. I've also always been a very disciplined writer, because that's the only way you ever get anything done. Usually when I'm writing a novel I set myself 1000 words a day, and I stick to it religiously, even if I've got a hangover. I sometimes stop in the middle of a sentence, which isn't a bad idea, as the next day it's very easy to get back into it.

As for learning to be creative, I think there's a lot of basic-level storytelling skills that you need to be born with. I wrote from a pretty early age, eight or nine, and I've always had a very vivid imagination. If you've got a strong imagination it's there all the time, it's working away. You're kind of remaking the world as you walk down a street, reinventing it. I have a walk every day and a good think about things. I sometimes think maybe this town is a complete conspiracy, or maybe it's a very advanced kind of psychological experiment – all these ideas occur to me and every now and again I think: 'Hey, that's not bad. That's worth pursuing.'

❝ When I'm writing a novel I set myself 1000 words a day, and I stick to it religiously, even if I've got a hangover. ❞

Have You Read?
Other books by J.G. Ballard

Vermilion Sands
An automated desert-resort designed to fulfil
the most exotic whims of the idle rich,
Vermilion Sands now languishes in uneasy
decay, populated by forgotten movie queens,
solitary impresarios and the remittance men
of the artistic and literary world. In a
microcosm where prima donna plants are
programmed to sing operatic arias and dial-
a-poem computers have replaced poets,
Vermilion Sands anticipates a society in
which entertainment is the dominant
industry, consumption the core of the
economy and boredom the principal evil.

High-Rise
Within the concealing walls of an elegant
forty-storey tower block, the affluent tenants
are hell-bent on an orgy of destruction.
Cocktail parties degenerate into marauding
attacks on 'enemy' floors and the once-
luxurious amenities become an arena for
technological mayhem. . . In this classic
visionary tale, human society slips into
violent reverse as the inhabitants of the
high-rise, driven by primal urges, recreate a
world ruled by the laws of the jungle.

'Ballard's finest novel . . . a triumph'
The Times

Cocaine Nights
When Charles Prentice arrives in Spain
to investigate his brother's involvement in
the death of five people in a fire in the ▶

◄ upmarket coastal resort of Estrella de Mar, he gradually discovers that beneath the civilised, cultured surface of this exclusive enclave for Britain's retired rich there flourishes a secret world of crime, drugs and illicit sex.

'Britain's number one living novelist. This adds a glinting new facet to his achievement – Ballard, detective-novelist extraordinary' *Sunday Times*

Super-Cannes

A disturbing mystery awaits Paul and Jane Sinclair when they arrive in Eden-Olympia, a high-tech business park in the hills above Cannes. Jane is to work as a doctor for the executives who live in this ultra-modern workers' paradise. But what caused her apparently sane predecessor to set out one morning and murder ten people in a shooting spree that made headlines around the world? As Paul investigates his new surroundings, he begins to uncover a thriving subculture of crime that is spiralling out of control.

'Sublime . . . an elegant, elaborate trap of a novel, which reads as a companion piece to *Cocaine Nights* but takes ideas from that novel and runs further. The first essential novel of the 21st century' *Independent*

Millennium People

When a bomb goes off at Heathrow it looks like just another random act of violence to psychologist David Markham. But then he discovers that his ex-wife Laura is among the victims. Acting on police suspicions, he starts to investigate London's fringe protest movements, falling in with a shadowy group based in the comfortable Thameside estate of Chelsea Marina. Led by a charismatic doctor, the group aims to rouse the docile middle classes to anger and violence, to free them from both the self-imposed burdens of civic responsibility and the trappings of a consumer society – private schools, foreign nannies, health insurance and overpriced housing. Markham, seeking the truth behind Laura's death, is swept up in a campaign that spirals rapidly out of control. Every certainty in his life is questioned as the cornerstones of Middle England become targets and growing panic grips the capital . . .

'Terrifying and strangely haunting . . . A riveting work from a writer of rare imaginative largesse, a bearer of bad tidings, unforgettably told' *Daily Telegraph*

Find Out More

WATCH:

One of J.G. Ballard's top ten films:

Alphaville *(Jean-Luc Godard, 1965)*
Mad Max 2 *(George Miller, 1981)*
The Man Who Fell to Earth *(Nicolas Roeg, 1976)*
Dark Star *(John Carpenter, 1974)*
Barbarella *(Roger Vadim, 1967)*
Dr Strangelove *(Stanley Kubrick, 1963)*
Orphée *(Jean Cocteau, 1950)*
The Incredible Shrinking Man *(Jack Arnold, 1957)*
Close Encounters of the Third Kind *(Steven Spielberg, 1977)*
Solaris *(Andrei Tarkovsky, 1972)*

LISTEN TO:

Ballard's literary influence has been acknowledged by authors Martin Amis and Will Self, and filmmakers David Cronenberg and Steven Spielberg have turned his books into movies, but Ballard's most intriguing impact has been on the music scene.

Steinbeck may have inspired the odd Bruce Springsteen album and Mick Jagger's 'Sympathy for the Devil' may be distantly related to Bulgakov, but in terms of musical influence, few authors beat Ballard. Joy Division's lead singer Ian Curtis was an avowed devotee (the band even released a song bearing the name 'The Atrocity Exhibition') and Ultravox vocalist John Foxx once admitted 'reading way too much J.G. Ballard'. The Eighties classic 'Video Killed the

Radio Star' (the first video to be played on MTV) by The Buggles was inspired by Ballard's short story 'The Sound-Sweep'. Members of the The Human League, Siouxsie and the Banshees and Cabaret Voltaire have also name-checked the author in their music.

More recently Madonna's Drowned World tour in 2001 took its inspiration from Ballard's early novel of the same name, whilst the new punk rave band Klaxons named their debut album after Ballard's 1982 short story collection *Myths of the Near Future*. Even Thom Yorke, media-shy lead singer of the band Radiohead, is said to have discussed Ballard on his blog in recent weeks.

Not an avowed follower of music, Ballard's own favourite piece of music is 'The Teddy Bear's Picnic'. 'I could listen to it happily forever,' he has said.

Here's a list of his other *Desert Island Discs*, selected in 1992:

'**Don't Fence Me In**' (Cole Porter) performed by Bing Crosby and The Andrews Sisters (1944)

'**Put the Blame on Mame**' (Fisher/Roberts) performed by Rita Hayworth (1946)

'**Falling in Love Again**' (Hollander/Connelly) performed by Marlene Dietrich (1931)

The Marriage of Figaro (Mozart, 1786)

'**The Girl from Ipanema**' (Antonio Carlos Jobim, 1962)

The Barber of Seville (Rossini, 1816)

'**Let's Do It**' (Cole Porter/Peter Matz) performed by Noel Coward (1955)

SURF:
·······································

He doesn't use it himself, but J.G. Ballard
has described the Internet as 'the most vital
culture today', and his fans have certainly
embraced its possibilities. Here's a list of the
best Ballard websites around.

www.ballardian.com
With all the latest Ballard news, plus
interviews and features, this website is worth
keeping an eye on. It's divided into
subsections that cover everything from
Ballard's thoughts on gated communities
and invisible literature to cyberpunk and
theme parks. There's also a great
bibliography section so you can remind
yourself of Ballard's work to date.

www.jgballard.com
An excellent site for those harder-to-find
articles and features.

www.solaris-books.co.uk/Ballard/
If you want to vote on your favourite Ballard
novel, or find out what everyone else thinks,
check out this website. You can also sign up
for email alerts to keep abreast of all the
Ballard news.